David Alex Jones

FACES

The Survivor Trilogy: Book Two

Cover Art by Lianne Viau Photography

Published by:
Apparently Normal Publishing
Waterloo, Ontario, Canada

ISBN (Paperback Edition) 978-0-9948796-2-2
Version 2023.01.01

LAND ACKNOWLEDGEMENT

This book was written in Southwestern Ontario, Canada, on land located within the Haldimand Tract, land that was granted to the Haudenosaunee of the Six Nations of the Grand River, and is within the shared traditional territory of the Neutral, Anishinaabe, and Haudenosaunee peoples

TABLE OF CONTENTS

FOREWORD

"A 2012 study by Nigel Lowe and Victoria Stephens at the Cardiff Law School in the United Kingdom found that the global number of Hague Convention applications to retrieve an abducted child had risen by 45 per cent since 2003.

According to a U.S. State Department report, the number of new international parental child abduction cases in the United States alone has doubled since 2006, from 642 to 1,135, with the majority of cases involving children taken to one of the convention's 89 signatory countries.

But the child return rate is far from satisfactory. In 2009, the report said, only 436 children abducted to or wrongfully retained in other countries were returned to the U.S."

Nicholas Keung, Immigration reporter,
The Toronto Star, February 22, 2013

PROLOGUE

ANGELA BARANYI stared at the two faces that filled the TV news screen, and a chill raced down her spine. The first face displayed on her antiquated portable television was that of a smiling, respected pastor of a growing evangelical church in Victoria, British Columbia. The second face, a young boy, she recognized from the family portrait in Pastor Soren's New York office. She watched in disbelief.

Those who knew Pastor Soren gave testimonials, hoping that nothing sinister had happened to him or his son. He was a loving husband and father - a man of God whose mission in life was to spread God's word and to help others who were less fortunate. They were sure there was a suitable explanation for what had happened.

Even though the Amber Alert covered the entire western half of Canada and the United States, there was still no sign of Soren Kristiansen or his son Jonah. It wasn't possible, they all said, that Pastor Kristiansen could have kidnapped his own son. Surely the authorities must be wrong.

But Angela knew differently. The Soren Kristiansen she knew was a man of many faces. He was a chameleon. In him she saw the cunning, calculating face of somebody who was always searching for a way to get whatever he wanted from anybody who came into contact with him. In his smug, disingenuous smile, she saw a man who secretly laughed at others, even while they swooned from being in his presence. She should know. She was once one of his admirers.

She knew his face from another time and another place. It had only been two years since she had fled from New York and gone underground to escape from his grasp. But now she was weary from running and hiding - from constantly looking over her shoulder, in case Soren or his subordinates were on her trail. She knew she did it to protect her two children, but she was worn-out from the constant need to be vigilant every second of her life. She felt the chill surge through her spine again. This time she recognized it as fear. It was the feeling she'd had when she first realized how dangerous a man he was, and what he was capable of doing to those who challenged him.

Angela's thoughts were interrupted by the voice of an African-American woman, the local news anchor, who was giving the latest update on the investigation into the boy's disappearance. The young boy's photo had replaced that of his father, and was displayed prominently in the upper right corner of the screen as the newscast continued.

"Police in Victoria won't comment on reports that they were investigating irregularities in the financial operations of Pastor Kristiansen's online ministry, The World-Wide Community of Christ, at the time of the young boy's disappearance. This isn't the first controversy to tarnish Pastor Kristiansen's image. He was also implicated in the disappearance of a Cleveland woman in 2004. Although he admitted to having a sexual encounter with the woman, he has repeatedly denied having anything to do with her disappearance. Rumours have also been circulating that Pastor Kristiansen's marriage has been on the rocks over the past year."

"So, it's about time they're finally catching up with you, Soren," she said to herself. "Now it's your turn to be on the run."

This wasn't news to Angela. Her mind started to wander. Her eyes roamed around the seedy second-floor office. It wasn't that the office space was old. Nothing in Las Vegas was very old, since most of the city had sprung to life over the past forty years of glitter and opulence. But large parts of the city were run-down and tired. These were the areas of the city housing the thousands of poorly-paid drones who cleaned hotel rooms, cooked in kitchens, and served drinks to the throngs of tourists who visited the city each year. The dirty, neutral-colored walls and the stained overhead ceiling tiles made the office look as tired as Angela felt. An aging AC unit in the roof vibrated and growled as it struggled to cope with the rising late-afternoon temperature in the office.

The room was sparsely furnished. A medium-sized safe, standing about four feet in height and anchored to the wall with heavy bolts, was grey, shiny, and new. It held the documents for her two identities, Anna Benz and Grace Wagner, as well as a substantial amount of cash for emergencies, in case she had to go on the run again. The brand new safe stood in stark contrast to the well-used office and the rest of its furnishings. A small wooden table, with a microwave often sitting on top, stood against the wall on the opposite side of the room from the safe. Beside it, a small bar-fridge hummed. The small appliances allowed Angela to come out of her floodway hideout at the end of each day to have a hot meal.

Against the back wall of the dingy room, to the right of the office's entrance, a solitary wooden door, painted the same nondescript colour as the walls, marked a small bathroom. Lacking a shower, this was where she settled for sponge baths to wash away the odor and grime of the underground floodways, where she'd spent much of her time since coming to Las Vegas. On the left side of the entrance, half a dozen dresses and assorted blouses and camisoles hung on plastic hangers. The small wardrobe had been sufficient for her excursions into the world of business in Los Angeles as Anna Benz, and should continue to serve her well in Las Vegas.

The centerpiece of the room was Angela's laptop computer, which sat atop a medium-sized contemporary office table from IKEA. It was her lifeline to the world, and her connection to the intricate network of financial transactions she had woven to launder and hide the small fortune she had stolen from Soren. An aging rolling office chair sat in front of the table and computer.

Her old portable television was mounted on top of two red plastic milk crates she'd borrowed from behind the convenience store on the ground floor below.

The office, along with its mélange of furnishings, had been enough to meet Angela's needs. But she knew the time was near when she was going to have to abandon the space and leave Las Vegas. The seed of an idea was germinating in her mind.

I can't keep running and hiding like this. I might be the only one who can help track Soren and find the boy. He won't be expecting me to be coming after him. He's not your ordinary run-of-the-mill child abductor. He has almost unlimited resources. Even worse, he has connections in high places that the police can't even imagine. But I know how he thinks. I have the ability to follow his digital footprints. He's a dangerous adversary, and I'm going to have to be extremely cautious. But I'm going to have to hunt him down if I ever hope to get my life back.

The newscast continued with video of a blonde woman with short, wavy hair. Angela also recognized her face from the portrait in Soren's New York office. It was Anika Kristiansen, Soren's wife and the boy's mother, appearing in front of reporters. Beside Anika, a handsome brown-haired man stood with his arm wrapped around the woman's upper back, his hand resting on her shoulder for support. Angela was confused. She knew she'd seen the man's face before in a different context, but she couldn't make a connection at the moment.

"Jonah, honey, I love you and miss you very much," Anika said, sniffling into reporter's microphones, tears clearly welling in her bloodshot eyes. *"We'll have you home very soon, honey."*

Anika sniffled again. Tears began to stream down her face and she struggled to find words.

"Soren, for Jonah's sake, I beg you to turn yourself in so he can come home. And to the public, both in British Columbia and the Pacific Northwest, if you see the man or the boy in these pictures, please contact your local police immediately."

Anika broke down, sobbing uncontrollably, and the brown-haired man put both of his arms around her to console her. The newscast cut back to the local news anchor. New video of a construction accident at one of the huge construction sites on the Las Vegas Strip, replaced the Amber Alert story.

Angela realized that tears were filling her own eyes as she watched Anika's emotional plea. She knew too well the pain of not being able to be with her children. It had been over two years since she chose to disappear, leaving her own two children, Julia and Nicholas, in the custody of her aging parents in Cleveland. Her heart ached from not being able to contact them, or to tell them she was alive. But for their sake, her disappearance had to look suspicious. It was best for the world to assume she was dead.

Angela choked back her tears and turned her attention to the laptop in front of her to distract herself. Since her disappearance, she hadn't dared to have contact with anybody in her former life, let alone access the intricate corporate computer network of Soren's financial empire. It would be suicide to use her old access codes.

"If I'm going to find out what he's up to, I'm going to have to find a way to get back into the WWCC system," she said to herself.

She skipped back into the bathroom and slipped on a pair of sweatpants and a t-shirt, her cold nipples straining against the tight cotton shirt. She sat down in her rolling chair, leaned back and stretched, and allowed her mind to mull over potential solutions to her problem. After a moment, a smile spread across her face. Her hand started sliding a mouse around on the table, clicking buttons and typing hurriedly on the keypad.

It's simple, Angela. Just hit him the same way he hits his unsuspecting church members - with an email message that he'll never suspect. First you need to search for Domain Names...

Angela typed in the domain name for *World-Wide Community of Christ.* As expected, the domain search engine told her the name was taken, but it gave a number of useful suggestions for similar domain names. Angela tried again, this time typing *World_Wide* instead of *World-Wide*.

"Voilà!" Angela said, smiling to herself. "It's available."

She went to work setting up her bogus website and email server, hoping to catch Soren off guard. Once that was done, she set up a fake user account in her name. When she was finished, she had a mail server that looked almost identical to the WWCC mail server.

Next, she searched her laptop for the video clips she took of Soren outside the Four Seasons hotel in Beverly Hills. Once she located them, she scanned through the clips until she found the one she wanted — a shot of Soren raising his head and staring at her in her sunglasses and ball cap, as she hid her face behind the video camera. In that moment, watching the clips again, she realized how close she came to having him recognize her. She shivered again, and then she set to work, editing a few clips into a thirty-second video of her brief encounter with Soren. Thirty seconds should be long enough for her purposes, she thought. After setting up an account on a new video sharing service called *YouTube*, she uploaded her movie onto the Internet.

While the movie clip was uploading, she carefully composed her email message:

To: Soren Kristiansen
From: Angela Baranyi, IT Dept.
Subject: I'm watching you.

Hello Soren. I'm sending you this message, and a link to an interesting video, as a friendly reminder that I'm always watching you. I just want to make sure you are keeping your end of our bargain. I hope you are continuing to do everything in your power to make sure Julia, Nicholas, and my parents stay healthy and safe.

FACES

I think the attached video clip will impress upon you how easy it would be for me to harm you any time I wish.

Angela.

As the video finished uploading, she attached a hyperlink to the email message. What Soren didn't know, was that she had also planted instructions within the hyperlink to embed a Trojan virus on his computer.

At last, with one final click of her mouse, her mail message hurtled out into cyberspace. If all went well, Soren would open the link when he got a chance to read his mail. But since he was on the run, it could take days for him to get that chance. When he did, her Trojan would plant itself deep within the Windows Registry on his computer while he watched the video. Once planted, the Trojan would destroy virtually all traces of itself.

She felt a sense of satisfaction. Along with it, she felt a smile on her face. It had been far too long since she'd enjoyed those sensations of pride and self-confidence. Once the Trojan started doing its job, it would start creating a clone of Soren's hard drive on the new external hard drive that was connected to her laptop. And once the clone was complete, she would be able to reboot her computer and search every file on his computer, including his browser history. But as long as Soren was on the run, it could take days, or even weeks, for the synchronization to complete.

"All I can do now is wait and hope," she said to herself. "Game on, Pastor Kristiansen! Let's just see which one of us is best at hiding and changing our face. I dare you to find me before I find you!"

She leaned back in the flimsy office chair, her mind drifting again as she stretched. It was hard to believe that it had only been a month since she'd experienced the shock of seeing herself in the portrait on the TV news. That was the moment when she knew that her carefully constructed underground life was going to start unravelling.

Suddenly, something clicked in her mind and she jerked herself upright in the chair.

That face — the news report with Anika Kristiansen — that's where I've seen him before!

Angela's fingers went to work, quickly bringing up the news article and video of the newscast about the spectacular deaths of Philippe Morel and Michelle Whitney in Palm Springs. She searched through the video until she came to photos showing the faces of the key players in the debacle. She instantly recognized the picture of Dan Whitney as the man who was supporting Anika Kristiansen at today's news conference. The faces of Whitney and Francesca Capellini were side by side in the news article. She felt confused.

How the hell does Whitney know Anika Kristiansen? The Palm Springs deaths don't have anything to do with Jonah's kidnapping and the Amber Alert, so what's the link? How could I be so unlucky as to have Whitney involved with both the Capellini woman and Anika Kristiansen? How could I have known Capellini would take my picture? How could I have known that my face would be flashed on TV for the whole world to see?

Angela's state of confusion caused her to retreat back inside herself, feeling her inner turmoil again. On one hand, part of her wanted to be strong again—like she did when she first moved to New York, and later when she finally decided that she couldn't continue to work for Soren. It was the part of her that wanted to hunt him down and help bring him to justice. But on the other hand, there was a part of her that was very afraid—afraid of confronting Soren again, and afraid of what he might do to Nicholas and Julia. If he could kidnap his own child, what else was he capable of doing? But more than anything, she was afraid that she might fail. And it was that frightened part of her that was telling her to keep running and hiding.

She replayed the Palm Springs news clip again, freezing it so she could stare into Capellini's portrait of her, and gaze into her own eyes. In them, she saw the fear and distrust that she'd felt on that March afternoon two years ago when Capellini took the photo. The candid portrait was bringing her face to face with what she had become over the past two years and what she was feeling now.

I've become weak and afraid. I've become a completely different Angela, and I don't like what I see.

She thought back to first time in her life that she'd managed to bounce back from fear, lack of self-confidence, and depression. It was after she'd divorced David. Then a funny thought occurred to her and made her chuckle.

Maybe I have to thank Soren for one thing, after all. If it hadn't been for him, I wouldn't have rediscovered that stronger, more confident part of myself again. I wouldn't have started to feel like I could survive on my own again. I was finally starting to believe in myself when I worked for him and when I left New York. Look at the guts it took to steal his money and to meet with those bankers in Geneva. But something happened to me between the time I came back from Switzerland with all that money, and when I arrived in Los Angeles. I started out as a survivor, and I ended up cowering and hiding like a sewer rat.

Angela felt a familiar weight descending on her shoulders and chest again. She recognized it as her old friend—guilt. She found herself struggling to breathe at the same time that she was trying to choke back her tears. This time, she wasn't successful. The dam broke and tears flooded down her face. She finally gave in to all of her conflicting emotions, and she felt completely overwhelmed. She pushed her laptop away and laid her head on her arms. Sadness and loneliness washed over her like a tidal wave. She wept uncontrollably until she was exhausted and her eyelids grew heavy. The flow of tears only ceased when she finally cried herself to sleep.

PART FOUR: MISSING

CHAPTER 1

A NONDESCRIPT grey mini-van made its way down Blanshard Street towards downtown. It was ten-thirty a.m. on a sunny late April day in Victoria, the picturesque capital of British Columbia. The blond-haired man behind the wheel drove cautiously, making sure to avoid doing anything that would attract attention to the vehicle.

"Are we almost there, Daddy?" asked the five-year-old boy in the back seat. A brand-new Blue Jays baseball cap covered his freshly shaved hair and cast a shadow over his face.

"Yeah, almost there," the driver mumbled. He turned to the woman seated beside him in the passenger seat. "Can you keep him quiet? All we need is for him to open his mouth and wreck everything. Do your job, Beth!"

The van made a right turn onto Bellville Street. The harbour and the Empress Hotel came into view.

"Look, Jonah," the woman said. "There's the harbour. We're almost at the ferry. Do you remember how important it is to remember our story? We don't want the bad people to catch us, do we?"

Jonah's mouth turned down at the corners, a confused look covering his face.

"Why are the bad people chasing us? Why isn't Mommy coming?" he asked.

"Shhhh!" Beth whispered. "Remember, we're pretending that I'm your mommy right now. If the man at the ferry asks you what your name is, what do you say?"

"John… John Dailey Junior," Jonah said by memory.

"And what's your dad's name?"

"His name's John Dailey too. And your name is Elizabeth Dailey. You're my mom," Jonah said.

"Excellent," the woman said. "You're going to do a good job of fooling the bad people."

"But why isn't Mommy coming with us?" Jonah repeated.

"I've already told you!" the driver shouted. "The devil has sent some very bad people who don't like Daddy's church. They don't like us spreading God's word, so they're spreading lies about Daddy and our church. If Mommy comes with us, they'll be sure to find us all. So Mommy is going to stay at home for a while. In a few days, she's going to try to run away from the bad people so she can be with us in Seattle. Now, smile and pretend that we're a happy family. We're going to visit Grandma and Grandpa, okay?"

"Okay," Jonah pouted.

Soren Kristiansen slowed the van as they approached the ferry terminal.

"You've got the passports ready?" he grunted to Beth.

"Yes, don't worry. I've got everything. Just relax."

"Don't you worry about me," Soren snorted. "Just make sure you and John Junior don't screw things up!"

Soren made another right turn onto a short road that carried them down a ramp to the Black Ball Ferry Terminal. He pulled up to the ticket booth and rolled down his window. A cheery middle-aged woman greeted him.

"How many passengers?" she asked.

"Two adults and one child," Soren answered.

"Do you have acceptable photo ID for entry into the U.S.?" the woman asked.

"Yes, we all have passports." He turned to Beth. "Do you have those passports, honey?"

Beth smiled and handed the passports to Soren.

"You'll need to show those at U.S. Immigration Pre-Clearance, just ahead. That'll be seventy-five dollars."

Soren handed the passports back to Beth and reached for his wallet, counting out a number of bills and handing them to the ticket agent.

"Thanks, sir. Have a pleasant trip."

"Thank you, ma'am. You have a nice day too," he said, flashing his warmest smile at the agent. He turned his head and looked at Jonah in the back seat.

"Okay, Jonah. This is it. All you have to do is remember that you're John Dailey Junior, and Beth here is your mom. That's easy, right?"

"Yes, Daddy."

Soren focused ahead at the security cameras, mounted on posts as the ramp descended towards U.S. Immigration. He donned his dark glasses and ball cap, making sure not to show his newly cut, very short blond hair.

"Okay then, everybody. Put on your best smiles!" he said.

Soren let his foot off the brake, allowing the van to creep along down the ramp behind a line of other vehicles, making its way towards Customs pre-clearance.

THE M.V. COHO slowed as it neared its mooring at the ferry terminal in Port Angeles, Washington. Clearing immigration pre-clearance in Victoria had gone without a hitch. The trio's crossing of the Strait of Juan de Fuca had been smooth. The almost fifty-year-old car ferry swayed gently from side to side with the small swells that rolled from west to east through the passage.

Deep inside his body, Soren felt energized by anticipation, like an athlete preparing for an important game. He was psyched. He looked at Beth and Jonah, who both looked tense. There was only one other thing that could possibly go wrong. But Anika was still at work, and she wouldn't be picking Jonah up from kindergarten for another two hours. She wouldn't even know yet that her son was gone. Soren donned his dark glasses and removed his cap, making sure his new look was captured on security video surveillance.

"Smile and relax, you two," he said. "Just make believe you're visiting Grandma and Grandpa, Jonah. Show the officer how excited you are to be in the United States. And Beth, just pretend we're really visiting your parents. Everybody ready?"

Beth and Jonah nodded in silent acknowledgment. The van was now at the head of the Immigration line. Finally, the light turned green. Soren lowered his window, allowing the vehicle to roll up to the Immigration booth. A short female agent in full body-armour, gun on her hip, greeted them with a frown on her face.

"Citizenship?" the agent demanded, craning her neck to look through Soren's open window at Beth and Jonah. Soren took the passports from Beth and handed them to the agent.

"Canadian," he answered.

"Reason for your visit?" the agent asked. She was all business, not cracking even the faintest smile.

"We're visiting my wife's parents in Seattle," Soren answered casually.

The Immigration agent scanned each of their newly acquired, forged passports, one at a time. Soren wasn't anxious. He knew the forgeries were almost perfect and the chances of detection were slim. He smiled and waited patiently. The agent was taking her sweet time. Finally, she looked through Soren's window and looked directly at Beth; then looked at the photograph on her passport.

"Your full name, ma'am?"

"Elizabeth Dailey," Beth answered.

"Your parents' address in Seattle?"

"666 West Raye Street," Beth said.

The agent looked closely at Beth's passport one last time.

"You're a Canadian citizen now?"

"Yes. I was born in Seattle, but I got my Canadian Citizenship after I married my husband. My maiden name is Andersson."

The agent leaned into Soren's window again, this time looking at Jonah.

"And what's your name, young man?" she asked.

"John Dailey Junior," he announced with pride. "But Mommy and Daddy call me John Junior."

"Do they, now," the agent said, finally cracking a faint smile at the young boy's response. She turned her attention to Soren, first looking at his shaved head, then his passport photo, which had a full head of blond hair.

"Can you remove your sunglasses, please?"

She glanced back and forth between the passport photo and Soren's exposed face.

"Anybody ever mistake you for the golfer?" she asked.

"All the time," Soren answered, laughing. "It gets tedious after a while, but what can ya do?"

This time the agent's face broke into a smile. She handed the passports back to Soren.

"I'll bet it does. Have a nice visit, folks."

"Thanks," Soren answered. "We will. Have a good day yourself."

The agent handed the passports back to Soren, who immediately donned his sunglasses. As they drove away, he raised the van's window, smiling to himself. He just cleared his first major hurdle.

He hadn't planned on running quite so soon, but Soren sensed it wouldn't be long before the authorities started looking into the church's finances. He also sensed that Anika was ready to leave him, and he couldn't let a custody battle get in the way of having Jonah. It wouldn't be the first time that trusting his intuition had saved him.

But now, it was only a matter of hours before Anika and the police would be after him. It was time to disappear.

ANIKA KRISTIANSEN rushed from her medical office. She was late for picking up Jonah from kindergarten. Her car beeped back at her as she pressed her remote to unlock it. She flung the door open, dropped into her seat, and slammed the door behind her. She grabbed her phone from her purse and tossed the bag into the passenger seat. Flipping open the phone, she dialed the kindergarten's number.

"Hello?… This is Dr. Kristiansen… I'm terribly sorry, something came up and I had to deal with it… I'm on my way now, but I'll be about ten minutes late picking up Jonah," she said hurriedly.

The female voice on the other end hesitated before answering.

"Anika?" the woman answered, confusion in her voice. "Is that you?"

"Yes, is that you, Janice? Why? Is something wrong?"

"I thought you knew. Soren picked up Jonah at ten o'clock this morning. He told me about your parents' accident. He said he was meeting you at home so you could leave for Calgary as soon as possible. I hope they weren't hurt badly!"

Anika shivered. A chill surged through her body. A feeling of dread began to descend over her. Something was terribly amiss.

"I haven't heard any details yet, Janice. I probably missed Soren's call. Things were crazy at the office. I'll call you to let you know if Jonah's going to miss some days. Thanks," she said, as she pressed the hang-up button on her phone. She dialed Soren's mobile number. It rang repeatedly and then went to voicemail.

Hello. This is Pastor Kristiansen. I'm not able to answer the phone right now. Please leave me a message and I'll call you back as soon as possible. Have a blessed day.

Anika's heart was racing. Her thoughts started racing.

I know things haven't been good between us lately, but surely he wouldn't take Jonah? Where would he go? Where would he take him? Maybe he's at home!

Anika dialed their home number, praying that Soren would answer. With each ring, she felt her heart pounding harder. When the call went through to voicemail, she hung up and tossed her phone in the passenger seat. She fastened her seatbelt, turned the key in the ignition, and slammed the vehicle into reverse. As she backed out of her parking spot, she sensed a blur in her peripheral vision and slammed on her brakes. The other car screeched to a halt, blaring its horn at Anika. The man behind the wheel flipped her the bird, then drove on.

Anika took a couple of deep breaths, let her foot off the brake slowly, and then backed the rest of the way out of her parking spot. She jammed the vehicle into *Drive* and her SUV flew out of the parking lot, tires squealing as she turned right onto Blanshard. She headed for the highway back toward Brentwood Bay.

Rush hour traffic was heavy on the highway. It seemed to take forever to reach the Brentwood Bay turn-off. Anika's mind raced and her hands were locked onto the steering wheel as she sped along Mt. Newton Cross Road. Two more turns, and she came to their cul de sac. Anika swung into the driveway, slammed on the brakes, threw the transmission into *Park*, and flung the driver's door open, all in one motion. Her hands shook and she fumbled impatiently with her keys, trying desperately to open the front door to her home. Finally, her key seated in the lock and she turned the deadbolt. She threw the heavy door open.

"Jonah! Soren! Anybody home?" she screamed.

Anika was greeted by an ominous calm. Except for the steady ticking of the grandfather clock in the hallway, the house was silent. Anika's heart pounded. Her chest was tight and she struggled to catch her breath.

"Jonah," she whimpered. The clock ticked relentlessly and Anika's heart sank. Reality started to set in. She ran upstairs and then down the hallway to her bedroom. Her jaw dropped when she threw open the door. Soren's closet door was agape. His bureau drawers were hanging open. He'd clearly gathered up some clothes and left in a hurry. Anika ran to Jonah's room and was greeted by the same sight.

With a growing sense of dread, Anika marched down the hallway, down the staircase to the main floor, then downstairs to the basement. The basement light was already on. Her eyes were drawn to a glaring gap on their storage shelves where two suitcases had been stored. Her mind was now spinning out of control. She began to feel violated—worse than if somebody had put a knife to her throat and threatened her life—she felt angry and betrayed. Then the floodgates opened and she became overwhelmed by a flood of emotions—anger, betrayal, fear, helplessness, sadness, loneliness and guilt. But most of all, it was anger that raged inside her.

Anika felt like there was an anvil on her chest, preventing her lungs from sucking in any air. She dropped to her knees on the concrete floor, gasping for breath. Tears filled her eyes.

She sobbed inconsolably while she struggled to breathe. Time seemed to stand still. She had no idea how long she spent on her knees. Gradually, she felt the pressure easing off of her chest. Her knees throbbed. She managed to hoist herself to her feet and slowly ascended the stairs, first to the main floor, then to the upper floor. She wandered into Jonah's bedroom and sat on his bed, reaching for his favourite stuffed animal; a tattered and worn panda that Anika's parents had given him for his first birthday. She pulled it close to her body, and then curled up on the bed. Her sobbing didn't stop until she had cried herself to sleep.

SUNLIGHT streamed through the window of Jonah's bedroom. Anika's eyes flickered open. She felt herself still clinging to Jonah's stuffed panda. As she slowly became aware of where she was, and why she was there, the bitterness of her reality slammed home. Soren wasn't going to be bringing Jonah home.

Anika sat the panda against the pillow where she found it. With her head clear, she walked from Jonah's room and headed downstairs. She went directly to the telephone and dialed 911.

"Hello, I'd like to report a child abduction… yes… I know who took him… his father… Soren Kristiansen… K-R-I-S-T-I-A-N-S-E-N… yes, he's the pastor… no… neither one of them came home last night… I have no idea where he might be… I only know that he picked my son up from kindergarten yesterday morning… Jonah Kristiansen… J-O-N-A-H… yes, that's the address… I'll be waiting… thank you."

Anika hung up the phone. She walked to the den and sat down in front of the computer. Now that the police were involved, she needed the one person she knew she could really trust. The only problem was, she hadn't seen that person for years, and she didn't know how to contact him.

She began composing an email to her brother, Jan, in Calgary:

To: Jan Reurink
From: Anika Kristiansen
Subject: Dan Whitney

Hi Jan. After hearing about Dan Whitney in the news last month, I thought I'd like to contact him to see how he's doing. Do you still keep in touch with his brothers in Dallas? If so, could you ask them for Dan's contact information? Thanks.

Love, Anika

Anika sighed. While she waited for the police to arrive, she reached for the phone to call her office. She would need to make arrangements for somebody to look after her medical practice. She had an ominous feeling that she might not be back at work for a while.

JONAH KRISTIANSEN sat, cross-legged and bored, on the floor of the motel room in Bremerton, Washington, watching cartoons. The corners of his mouth were turned down and his forehead was wrinkled. His face was a portrait of sadness, loneliness, and worry that overshadowed his normally playful, carefree and bubbly nature. Without warning, he was stunned to see his mother's face speaking to him from the TV.

'Jonah, honey, I love you and miss you very much. We'll have you home very soon. Soren, for Jonah's sake, I beg you to turn yourself in so Jonah can come home…'

"Daddy, it's Mommy! She's looking for us! She wants us to come home. Can we go home now? Please, Daddy?" His face became animated and full of hope.

"I told you already, Jonah. The bad people are trying to take over Daddy's church. Now they've caught your mommy and they're making her tell lies on TV. If I take you home, they'll catch me, and then we'll all be in the hands of the devil. You don't want that, do you?"

The corners of Jonah's mouth turned down again, and the wrinkles of worry returned to his face. Tears welled up in his eyes. He made his way to the couch where Soren sat beside Beth. He climbed up onto his father's lap, putting his arms around Soren's neck. He leaned against the man's chest, sobbing.

"What's going to happen to Mommy? Is she going to hell?" the young boy sniffled.

"Not if she stays strong and keeps her faith in God," Soren answered. "We have to hope that Mommy doesn't become one of the devil's servants. That's why we can't try to contact her. Understand?"

Jonah nodded slowly as he continued to sob against his dad's chest.

"I'm scared, Daddy. Is the devil going to catch me too?"

"Not if we're all careful, Jonah. That's why it's so very important that you don't go outside unless you go with Beth. When we do go out, we all have to wear our disguises. The bad people could be anywhere, so we can't let them see you and me together," he explained.

"Is that why you aren't sleeping here with me and Beth?" Jonah asked.

"That's right. The bad people are going to be looking for you and me together. So Beth always has to stay with you, and Daddy has to keep away from you a lot."

"What about Beth? Does she have to wear her disguise?"

"Yes, I'll have to wear one too," Beth said. "Just in case the bad people know that I've helped you escape."

"But where are we going, Daddy? Are we going to live here now?" Jonah asked.

A look of consternation crossed Soren's face.

"We can't stay here, son. I don't know where we're going to live yet, but it has to be somewhere far away, where the bad people can't find us."

Soren sat upright, using both hands to lift Jonah's head from his chest.

"No more questions now. Go find some cartoons to watch on TV," Soren said, trying to lay the subject to rest.

Jonah slid slowly from his dad's lap and started walking towards the TV. After he took two steps, he paused and turned to Soren and Beth.

"Are we ever going to see Mommy again?" he asked, tears welling in his eyes again.

"Sure, Jonah," Soren lied. His face was devoid of any emotion. "We just have to hide until the bad people leave us alone."

Jonah turned away slowly and sat down on the floor in front of the TV, trying to numb the painful emotions inside. He held up the remote, clicking blindly, until he found a cartoon show. He stared through the TV, as if it wasn't even there. His world was upside-down. His small mind tried to find a way to make sense of what was happening. He choked back the tears and closed his eyes. He had to be strong.

It must be my fault. I think Mommy and Daddy are fighting about me. Maybe if I pray hard enough, God will forgive me. Maybe he'll make the Devil and the bad people go away. Then I can be with Mommy again.

Jonah bowed his head and clasped his hands together.

Dear God, this is Jonah. Please help me be a good boy. Help me and Daddy hide from the Devil and the bad people. Help me be good so I can see Mommy again. Thank you. Amen.

BACK IN his own room again, Soren sat alone, staring at a map of the world on his laptop. He was pleased with the intricacy of his escape plan. It was going to be expensive, but fortunately for him, money wasn't a problem. For a price, it was easy to make the right underworld contacts to obtain new identities for himself, Jonah, and Beth. He smiled. *You can have anything you want, if you have the money.*

He considered the map on the computer screen. It was a map of countries that had signed the Hague Convention on International Child Abduction. *They'll be expecting me to head for a non-Hague country.* He noted the areas of the world marked in grey—the clumps of countries that had not yet signed the Hague Convention. Most of them were in Africa or Eastern Asia.

They'll expect me to head west to Asia, but they won't suspect Vietnam—they've recently signed the Convention. I'll stick to Hague countries where I can hide in plain sight. But I'll head east first, where they won't be looking for me.

Soren Googled motels in the greater Atlanta area. He needed something near Hartsfield-Jackson International Airport. They'd have to change their appearance and identities in Atlanta. He chuckled to himself again.

Those fools in the church! Some of them will do anything for me, just to feel useful. He smiled as he thought about Beth, who had come to Victoria from Seattle to help him. She had rented the car and booked these rooms in her name, leaving no trace of him along their escape route.

Soren sighed contentedly and shook his head.

Organized religion—it's the perfect cover for making money! It's like a magnet for people who need to feel wanted—for people who are addicted to giving. They're hooked on taking care of others so they can feel good about themselves. The desperate ones will do anything to feel accepted. Their personality type is everywhere. All I have to do is find them and give them what they're looking for!

Suddenly, a frown worked its way across Soren's face. His forehead wrinkled as an unsettling thought distracted him.

Except for that bitch, Angela Baranyi! She wasn't a giver—she was a taker! She weaseled her way close to me, just so she could take advantage of me. The corners of Soren's mouth slowly started turning upwards. The wrinkles in his face softened, and then disappeared. A knowing smile replaced his frown. *That's okay. When I find her, she'll pay the price for cheating me.*

Soren's mind drifted back to his younger days, when he was a pimply-faced teen from a background of childhood abuse; lonely and vulnerable. He had been drawn to the idealism of the church. It was there that he finally found friends, acceptance, and a purpose —helping others. That sense of purpose helped him to push the anger that he harboured towards his parents into the far recesses of his mind. It gave him the motivation and the drive to minister to God's word. He was accepted into the Presbyterian Seminary in Austin, where he excelled academically. His sermons, along with his warmth and charm, won acclaim from his teachers and the congregations where he did placements. He was a hot prospect and he knew he'd have no difficulty finding himself a church.

An ember of anger resurfaced and started to glow in Soren's eye as he remembered his first job. He was hired as the assistant minister at the largest, most prestigious Presbyterian Church in Dallas. The current minister had served the congregation for over twenty years and was nearing retirement. The position was an ideal stepping-stone for Soren. There was only one problem. Soren soon found out about the realities of organized religion in a large, affluent church—the stuffy conservative atmosphere, and the politics and power plays amongst the church elders. He soon found out that he had little stomach for church politics and having to suck up to others. He had never played well with others if he didn't get his own way.

Rather than allow his contempt for the church establishment to surface, Soren needed to find a socially acceptable way of leaving gracefully. What better way to receive the admiration of a conservative Texas congregation than by joining the military? He laughed derisively as he remembered them showering him with praise at his send-off celebration. He'd have the last laugh on them when he finished his stint in the Air Force. As a veteran, he'd have his pick of congregations after he finished serving his country.

At least, that's what Soren had expected. Who could have predicted that he'd be sent to Lackland Air Force Base, where he would fall victim to the sadistic culture of military sexual abuse perpetuated by an elite group of officers at the base? Soren began feeling sick to his stomach. Every muscle in his body tensed as he felt his anger resurfacing. It was the same feeling that had driven him to consider suicide, or going on a shooting spree against the perpetrators, as his only possible ways out. That's when he met Helen, also a victim, who had rescued him from his hopelessness. Together, they had consoled each other and helped each other to stay strong. Together, they found a way to survive their ordeals. Even as he thought of her, he found his anger beginning to recede behind the protective barriers deep inside his mind.

When his discharge from the Air Force came through, it was Helen who urged him to start looking for a young, vibrant congregation where he wouldn't be an assistant; where he could follow his true path. Together, they searched for a church where he would be able to win his flock over with his charm and his convincing oratory. They saw the advertisement for the Victoria Gospel Temple and he applied immediately. The congregation felt privileged to have such a highly rated young preacher and ex-serviceman apply for their position. They fell in love with his irresistible appeal.

Soren smiled as he remembered being hired. The church soon thrived under his guidance. The physical structure of the church soon needed to expand to house the growing congregation. A local TV station started broadcasting his services every Sunday. His popularity and reputation spread the length of Vancouver Island, and even across the Strait of Georgia into the greater Vancouver metropolitan area.

But as the congregation expanded, Soren's lust for recognition soon outgrew the limitations of local television. He was attracted to the almost limitless potential of the Internet. After their experiences at Lackland, he and Helen were already well acquainted with a variety of web sites that satisfied their growing desire for kinky BDSM sex and pornography. They were only human, after all. But Soren was especially captivated by web sites with live, streaming video. He even invested his own money (under a pseudonym, or course) to purchase a struggling porn website. If the porn industry could stream its content, why couldn't his church? He was already learning how to turn his underground pornography hobby into a profitable enterprise. He recognized that taking his ministry to the worldwide web was the ideal way to expand his ministry, without having to build an expensive new church.

Soren recalled becoming even more popular with his congregation when he courted and wed the beautiful, single female doctor in their midst. The day he and Anika wed was a day of celebration for the entire church. He smiled proudly as he recalled that time.

That was probably my shrewdest move. It was one thing to be a brilliant, young, single pastor. But it's hard to preach family values when you don't have a family yourself. And Anika was so needy and vulnerable—so intent on starting a happy family of her own. It was mere child's play to add that last puzzle piece to my plan. It took a while to convince Helen of its brilliance, but I'm glad she finally realized how necessary Anika was to our plan and our future.

Soren felt a glow of pride as he remembered the beautiful spring Sunday in 1997 when the Victoria Gospel Temple became the World-Wide Community of Christ. The local TV broadcast was also streamed live on the Internet that day. His audience started growing exponentially. Within a year, the World-Wide Community of Christ, or WWCC as it became known, was the largest virtual church in the world. Soren's face became recognized around North America and the world. The opportunities for spreading his ministry, and of course for raising money for the church, became almost limitless.

Soren turned his attention back to his laptop computer, typing his administrator password to gain access to the WWCC website. He scrolled through the entries for the contest he had recently posted, including photographs of the families who entered. His face brightened and he stopped scrolling to examine one family's photo.

Perfect! A smug smile spread across his face as he read the family's biography. *They'll suit my purpose perfectly. P.T. Barnum was right - there IS a sucker born every minute!*

Soren looked at the time on his screen—past midnight already. *Time to get some sleep if we're going to be on the move tomorrow. It's a long drive to Atlanta.* He clicked the button on his track pad to start powering down the laptop.

Plink.

The electronic sound signalled the arrival of an email message, and then the screen abruptly turned blue while Windows took over the machine and began installing updates. Soren shrugged and walked away, feeling tired, but confident and energized at the same time.

Whoever it's from, it can wait until tomorrow. I need a good night's sleep.

If he'd known that the message was from the one person in the world who could ruin his plan—the one person he was desperate to find—he wouldn't have felt nearly so confident and calm.

CHAPTER 2

THE MORNING of Friday, April twenty-eighth dawned with an unusual overcast and a forecast for scattered rain showers in the Coachella Valley. But the weather wasn't the only unusual event in the valley that morning.

As Defense Attorney Joanna Sullivan drove Dan Whitney and Francesca Capellini past the Indio Courthouse, all three of the car's occupants were surprised to see a large group of religious protesters parading back and forth, waving large placards.

"Wow," Joanna commented. "Looks like you two have attracted a lot of attention from the religious right. Somebody's really got it out for you, Francesca. They look like they're well-organized."

Dan caught glimpses of some of the signs as they drove by. He squeezed Fran's hand and tried to read her face as she looked out the car window. She swallowed and her jaw was taut. Her hands were cold and tense. She had the same faraway look in her eyes that he'd seen on that first afternoon at Chateau Eden more than a month before. His eyes looked past Fran and out the window to the signs that were waving in the air.

Revelation 17:1… I will shew unto thee the judgment of the great whore…

Face God's Judgment for your sins!

Death penalty for the killer adulteress!

Condemn Capellini's Immoral and Depraved Acts!

"I can't believe the anger in their eyes and in their words. I've never seen anything like that before," Dan said.

"What's going on over there?" Fran asked. "It looks like an argument."

"You're right," Joanna remarked. "Look at that green sign—some of those people are demonstrating *for* you!"

Fran strained to see the poster through the crowd, as their car gradually left the protest behind.

Stop Blaming Victims of Domestic Violence!

"Welcome to conservative America," Joanna continued. "This isn't the liberal northeast, Dan. You're a long way from home. People in the south and southwest take their religion pretty seriously. And they're not very tolerant of anybody who doesn't share their beliefs, like that handful of feminists back there."

"Do you think this is going to have any effect on Fran's case?" Dan asked.

"It shouldn't," she answered. "When it goes to a Grand Jury, I can screen for religious extremists. Of course, the prosecution can do the same and screen for feminists and people with liberal views about domestic abuse. We just want to do our best to get a jury of people who are objective and will see that this is a classic battered spouse case. There's a lot of case law on our side now, so I don't see any problem."

Dan shivered. Up to now, he'd felt complete confidence in Joanna and her ability to make a case for having the Grand Jury drop all of the remaining charges against Fran. But, having seen the protest against Fran, a hint of doubt began to creep through a crack in his self-confidence.

It's nothing to worry about, Dan. It's just a few religious fanatics. They're not going to be able to swing public opinion, and they're certainly not going to have any effect on a Grand Jury. Stop looking at them, and stay positive for Fran's sake.

Dan refocused his eyes on Fran. Once again, he squeezed her hand to let her know he was there with her. He leaned over and kissed her gently on her cheek, feeling the love for her that felt stronger with each passing day.

THE INDIO courthouse was full to capacity with members of the media and curious onlookers. Fran sat at the defendant's table with Joanna. Her arraignment, on charges of first-degree murder in the deaths of her husband, Philippe Morel, and Diego and Juanita Alvarez, was to begin at any moment. Dan made eye contact with her, once again seeing anxiety etched on her face. He smiled reassuringly at her, giving a thumbs up to boost her confidence.

Beside Dan, Tim Jennings and Shelley Paul had come to lend emotional support, as they had since the deaths of Philippe and Dan's wife, Chelly, five weeks ago. Dan still had difficulty believing that Chelly was gone. It was harder still to believe the chain of chaotic events that had brought him and Fran together so dramatically. They were both still having nightmares and flashbacks of Chelly's death.

Although the events at Philippe and Fran's Palm Desert estate had thrust them together, and Dan was still living at Chateau Eden with her, Fran had been more distant and withdrawn lately. They had both been seeking treatment for their PTSD symptoms, but Dan was worried about Fran. As a psychologist, he knew that this morning's arraignment was sure to trigger some emotional memories for both himself and Fran. He had a feeling that something else was bothering her, but it was only a gut feeling, with no substance to back it up. Tim's voice brought Dan back from his worries.

"How's she doing this morning?" he asked. "Especially with those demonstrators outside."

"Not bad," Dan answered. "She says she's not worried, but I know it's affecting her more than she's letting on. She's not saying much these days."

"Well, I'm sure she has a lot on her mind," Shelley said, staring directly in Dan's direction.

Puzzled, Dan frowned. He looked at Shelley, trying to read her face. *Is she trying to tell me something?* She abruptly broke eye contact with him and looked away. *That's not like Shelley. Why won't she look me in the eye?*

"Isn't this just a formality?" Tim asked.

"Yeah," Dan answered. "They'll just read the charges to Fran, make sure she's got legal representation, and get her plea."

"Fran told us not to worry," Shelley replied. "Joanna told her it's a clear case of self-defense—battered spouse syndrome—she can't understand why the prosecution is even bothering to take it to a Grand Jury. She says they're bound to look embarrassed when this is all over."

Dan looked over toward the Prosecution table, where a middle-aged blonde woman accompanied the well-dressed young County Prosecutor, Kevin Vasquez. Vasquez was calmly reading over his notes, but Dan noticed that the woman was fidgety and anxious. He also noticed that Joanna Sullivan was glaring intently at the woman, saying something to her that Dan couldn't make out. He nudged Tim with his elbow.

"Any idea who that woman is at the Prosecution table?" Dan asked.

Tim shrugged. "I don't know. Maybe another prosecutor helping Vasquez on this case?"

A side door at the front of the court opened, and a distinguished looking silver-haired man in black robes strode to the front of the courtroom.

"All rise!" the bailiff called. "His Honor Ernest Hartley presiding." The crowd in the courtroom rose to their feet.

"Thank you, bailiff. Everybody, please be seated," Hartley announced. "What's first on the docket?"

"Riverside County versus Francesca Capellini," the bailiff announced. Judge Hartley looked up over his glasses towards Fran at the Defense table. Then he glanced to his left at the Prosecution table, giving the blonde woman a curious look, followed by a nod.

"Ms. Capellini, please rise," Hartley said with authority. "Ms. Sullivan, I take it that you're continuing to represent Ms. Capellini?"

"I am, Your Honor," Joanna replied.

"Ms. Capellini, you have been charged with the first degree murder of your husband, Philippe Morel, and with conspiracy and first degree murder in the deaths of Diego and Juanita Alvarez. Do you understand the charges?"

Fran looked anxiously toward Joanna, who nodded, letting Fran know with her eyes that it was alright to answer.

"Yes, Your Honor," Fran replied.

"Ms. Capellini, Ms. Sullivan has no doubt told you that the crimes with which you have been charged are capital offences. If found guilty, those crimes could be punishable by death. How do you plead, Ms. Capellini?"

Fran swallowed hard and opened her mouth, but only a hoarse sound emerged. She looked nervously at Joanna, who nodded and looked at Fran with reassurance in her eyes. Fran swallowed again.

"Not guilty, Your Honor," she said quietly.

"The defendant pleads not guilty," Hartley repeated. "I see that your client is free on two hundred and fifty-thousand dollars bail. I am remanding… "

Without warning, the blonde woman at the prosecution table leapt to her feet.

"Your Honor, the Prosecution would like to approach the bench, if we may," she shouted.

Judge Hartley looked over his glasses towards the woman.

"District Attorney Mulholland, it's an unexpected surprise for you to grace us with your presence today. Please approach the bench."

Mulholland's eyes strayed to the Defense table, where they were met with an icy stare from Joanna Sullivan, who also jumped to her feet.

"Your Honor, the Defense objects. This is highly irregular for an arraignment! This matter is straightforward and a date should be set for a Grand Jury hearing. Bail has already been set and there should be no reason for the District Attorney to be involved with the proceedings."

"Your objection is noted, Ms. Sullivan. Ms. Mulholland, please approach the bench."

Kelly Mulholland avoided eye contact with Joanna as she walked up to Judge Hartley. Hartley lowered his voice as he spoke.

"So what's so important that it brought you into my court to make this unusual request, Ms. Mulholland?"

Mulholland cleared her voice.

"Your Honor, the County has received new information about the possibility that Ms. Capellini may have been involved in other capital crimes in other jurisdictions. I would like to request a meeting in chambers with you and Defense counsel."

Joanna and Fran strained to hear the low-key conversation between Hartley and Mulholland. A look of worry crossed both Fran's and Joanna's faces. They looked at each other in dismay.

"Very well, Ms. Mulholland. Ms. Sullivan, will you please join me in my chambers with Ms. Mulholland." He raised his head and looked out over the courtroom. "Court is adjourned for fifteen minutes. We will reconvene at nine forty-five."

Judge Hartley slammed his gavel down, and then rose from his seat. District Attorney Mulholland, Kevin Vasquez, and Joanna Sullivan followed him into his chambers. The bailiff followed them from the courtroom, closing the door behind them.

"WHAT ARE you trying to pull here, Mulholland?" Joanna shouted.

Hartley turned to Joanna, glared, and raised his voice.

"That will do, counsellor," he said firmly. "I'll ask the questions. Ms. Mulholland, you seem to have taken over this case from Mr. Vasquez, and your request is extremely unusual. What's this all about?"

"Your Honor, we've received inquiries from NYPD about a cold case they've been trying to solve for about a year and a half. They just contacted us within the past two days. Apparently one of the portraits hanging on the wall at the Morel estate, seen prominently in the news broadcasts from the crime scene, is a portrait taken by Ms. Capellini of a woman named Angela Baranyi, who has been missing and presumed dead for eighteen months. They've requested that we hold her in custody, at least until they've had a chance to question her. I'm asking you to revoke Ms. Capellini's bail, due to the seriousness of these new allegations about her possible involvement in a third crime, which raises the possibility that we're dealing with a serial killer here."

"That's absurd! I object!" Joanna shouted. "Mulholland, all you needed to do was phone me and invite us to have a visit with some NYPD detectives. I'm sure we could clear this up within a matter of minutes, instead of jumping to grandiose conclusions. There's something else going on here that you're not telling me. This makes no sense whatsoever!"

"Your Honor," Vasquez answered, coming to Mulholland's rescue. "If new charges are warranted in this investigation, then another preliminary hearing will have to be held, and the bail issue will have to be revisited. Because of the possibility that Ms. Capellini is a multiple offender, we feel that she is a potential danger to society and should remain in custody while the new allegations are investigated."

Joanna rolled her eyes, then looked at Judge Hartley.

"Your Honor, are you going to allow this kind of legal sleight of hand in your courtroom? There is no substance to these allegations and no basis for revoking my client's bail!"

"Alright, that's enough! Both of you!" Harley snapped. "I've heard your arguments and I need some time to consider Ms.

Mulholland's request. I'll give my decision at nine forty-five, when court reconvenes. You're both excused."

As Joanna, Vasquez, and Mulholland filed out of Judge Hartley's chambers, Joanna's mind raced.

What the hell are they up to? What else is going on here that I don't know about? Her mind flashed back to the demonstrators outside the courtroom. She had an uneasy feeling that something was going wrong, but she had no idea what it was. She almost ran to where Fran sat at the Defense table, knowing she had little time to get information from her client before Judge Hartley reconvened the court.

THE HANDS on the large clock in the courtroom wound their way slowly towards nine forty-five. Dan, Shelley, and Tim sat in silence, waiting for Judge Hartley and the lawyers to emerge from Hartley's chambers. Dan's eyes met Fran's, and he shrugged his shoulders, asking her non-verbally if she knew what was happening. He saw the same fear in her eyes that he'd seen when she was massaging him at Chateau Eden, just five weeks earlier. She shrugged her shoulders in return.

The door to Judge Hartley's chambers opened, the lawyers emerged, and Joanna walked quickly to Fran, engaging her in frantic conversation. Whatever was happening, it didn't look good. Dan felt a cold chill run down his spine. He exchanged looks with Tim and Shelley.

"I'm worried," he said. "Joanna looks upset, like she's lost control over what's going on. She's normally got her finger on everything, telling us not to worry. What's the District Attorney up to?"

Shelley and Tim looked at each other and shrugged their shoulders in confusion. Tim placed a reassuring hand on Dan's shoulder. Dan gazed at the Prosecution table, where Vasquez and District Attorney Mulholland were engaged in a heated exchange.

Mulholland was visibly agitated and appeared to be putting pressure on Vasquez, who wasn't happy about whatever was going on.

Suddenly, the door to Hartley's chambers opened, and the judge emerged into the courtroom.

"All rise," the bailiff shouted. "Riverside County Court is reconvening."

"Everybody be seated," Hartley said, his voice curt and businesslike. He settled into his chair, and then removed his reading glasses to address the court. "The District Attorney has brought new information to the attention of the court about other possible charges which may be brought against the defendant. She has requested that Ms. Capellini be held in custody, without bail, until such time as the new allegations are investigated."

Judge Hartley's eyes moved to the Defense table, where they met Joanna's.

"Ms. Sullivan. I'm going to grant the District Attorney's request for an adjournment of these proceedings. The defendant's bail is hereby revoked, and she is to be held in custody until this arraignment is reconvened two weeks from today, Friday May twelfth, at one o'clock pm. Ms. Capellini, you are remanded into custody without bail. You have five minutes to meet with family behind the courtroom before you are taken into custody. Court is adjourned."

The words hit Dan like a clap of thunder. He was numb and unable to move. For the second time in only a few weeks, he was losing a woman that he loved. Overcome with emotion, his mind flew backwards in time to the pool deck at the Morel estate, holding Chelly in his arms, hearing her last words…

'She's… good… for… you… Dan… take… good… care…'

FRAN STOOD in the holding area behind the courtroom, watched closely by a female court officer as Dan, Shelley, and Tim were ushered into the room. Joanna Sullivan stood silently by Fran's side as Shelley ran to Fran and threw her arms around her neck. The two women embraced, then Shelley looked into Fran's eyes. Without exchanging a word, she was asking Fran if she'd told Dan about the baby. Fran shook her head imperceptibly, so only Shelley noticed. She was terrified to tell him, and she never imagined that she would wind up behind bars before being able to break the news.

"We'll do whatever we can to get you out of here as soon as possible," Shelley whispered. "Take care of yourself until then."

Tim joined Shelley in the embrace, wrapping his large arms around both women.

"We're here for you, Fran," he said. "We'll stay in touch with you and Joanna, and we'll visit as often as we can. Just ask if there's anything we can do."

Tim and Shelley stepped back, allowing Dan to reach out to hold Fran. She felt herself falling into the safety of his arms, remembering the night that he came back from Detroit after Chelly's funeral. She clutched him tightly, never wanting to let go. She felt fear inside—not the same kind of fear she felt from Philippe—a different kind of fear. She was terrified that Dan might leave her if he found out about their baby. But at the same time, she was also scared that he might choose to stay with her. She'd never been able to trust a man before. Could she ever truly trust Dan if they did stay together?

The whole scene felt surreal to Fran. She felt like she was outside her body, watching herself embracing Dan. From a distance, she heard his voice speaking in her ear. The touch of his lips on hers brought her back into reality.

"I can't go to Victoria. I can't leave you like this," he whispered. "I'll call Anika and tell her I can't come now."

Fran saw tears welling up in Dan's eyes. She felt his love, but she didn't know what to do with it. She felt overwhelmed, her heart torn in two. She wanted him to stay, and she was terrified he'd reconnect with Anika. She was also terrified of being loved. Her mouth opened, not knowing what she was going to say until her lips started moving.

"Go. There is nothing you can do for me here. Anika needs your help more than I do right now. Carmen and her family can manage the Chateau until you get back. I'm in good hands with Joanna. She will get this straightened out and I will be home soon."

Dan looked to Joanna, his eyes searching for reassurance.

"She's right, Dan. There isn't anything you can do right now. There's something funny going on here, and I need to do some digging to see what I can find out. In the meantime, Fran looks like she's surrounded with good support. It's your decision, but I agree with Fran."

"Where's she going to be held? When can I visit and talk to her?" Dan asked.

"She's going to be held in the jail here in Indio," Joanna said. "She's allowed to make one phone call each day, and she's allowed two visits each week, with a maximum of two people per visit. You can stay for forty-five minutes. But you have to call ahead, one day in advance, to book your visit."

Fran felt the warmth of Dan's embrace, and felt it tighten. She felt her love-starved romantic side struggling against the independent, businesslike side of her. Finally, the businesslike Fran released her grip on Dan. She put her hands on his chest, gave him one last kiss, and gently pushed herself away from him. Two guards stepped up and took her arms, locking them together behind her back with handcuffs. They started leading her away.

"I'll call you!" Dan called. "I won't be gone for more than a few days. Hopefully, Joanna will have you out of here before I'm back."

Fran's eyes darted frantically from Dan, to Joanna, then to Shelley and Tim as she looked back over her shoulder. The guards guided her around a corner, and she lost sight of them. A strange feeling, one she hadn't felt for many years, descended upon her. The pain-filled part of her that had felt so rejected, lonely, and afraid as a young girl in Manarola, started to overwhelm the strong, businesslike Fran. She began to feel small and vulnerable. Her legs trembled uncontrollably as she forced herself to walk the short distance from the courthouse to Indio's Riverside County Jail, followed closely by two prison guards.

CHAPTER 3

DAN GAZED wistfully out the window of the small Dash-8 turbo-prop. Through the window on his right, British Columbia's Gulf Islands, with Vancouver Island behind them, were silhouetted against a golden sunset. On the far side of the plane, to the south, lay Washington's San Juan Island.

He had been restless on the flight from Los Angeles to Vancouver, and his anxiety was still escalating. He felt completely helpless with Fran spending her first night in a jail cell in Indio, with nothing he could do to help her. As the plane moved nearer to Victoria, his thoughts turned more to Anika. She'd been his best friend throughout high school, and there was no doubt he'd always been attracted to her.

What's it going to be like to see her again, when I already feel guilty about what happened to Chelly, and I'm starting to fall for Fran? What if I still have the same feelings for Anika that I had back then? I should have stayed behind in Indio. At least I could have been there to visit Fran.

The plane droned onward into the sunset, which was gradually turning a golden shade of orange. Dan's ears started to pop, a sure sign that they were making their final descent into Victoria.

Maybe Fran's right. Helping Anika will give me something to do, instead of fretting about her court case. Besides, it won't hurt to talk with Anika about everything that's happened lately. We've always been able to talk about anything without judging each other. I know she won't turn on me like my family and friends in Detroit did at Chelly's funeral.

The plane bumped and bounced on the runway, nudging Dan back into reality. The aircraft's wheels settled on the tarmac. Victoria's airport terminal and hangars flew by quickly at first, and then moved more slowly as Dan gazed out the window beside him. He felt the butterflies returning in his stomach, knowing that his reunion with Anika was only minutes away. He'd always secretly dreamed for this moment. But now that it was about to happen, he was filled with anticipation and uncertainty.

DAN EMERGED from the baggage area, scanning the crowd of waiting faces before him. He recognized Anika immediately, despite her red eyes and the dark bags beneath them. Her short, wavy blonde hair had not changed much at all since he last saw her. She was thin and pale, seeming to Dan like a fragile porcelain figurine. She waved as she recognized him coming toward her, standing patiently until Dan stood in front of her and set down his bags. They stood in silence for what seemed like an eternity, as if the protocol for such an occasion was unknown to both of them. Finally, Dan reached out and wrapped his arms around her, kissing her on her cheek as they embraced.

Anika seemed to catch herself, then she let go of Dan and stepped back so they could look at each other again. A single tear flowed slowly down one side of her face.

"You haven't changed a bit," Dan exclaimed. "I would have recognized you in any crowd."

"You're just saying that," she replied. "I look like hell and you know it. Except for the first night when I realized Jonah was gone, I haven't slept since he disappeared. And I haven't stopped crying either. Come on; let's get out of here before I start up again. Can I take anything for you?"

"I'm okay, I just have my carry-on. Show me the way."

The silence was awkward as Anika led him through the terminal and the parking lot toward her SUV. She opened the rear hatch and Dan loaded the bags into the vehicle. He lowered the door, and then double-checked to make sure it was closed.

Anika opened the driver's door and Dan climbed into the passenger side. Silence continued to hang in the air, until Anika finally broke down, bursting into tears. Her head hung down and she wept uncontrollably. Sitting in the passenger seat, Dan felt helpless to console her. He reached out and put a hand on her shoulder. With his other hand, he managed to find Anika's hand and clasped it tightly. Then he waited until her wave of grief had passed.

"Thank you so much for coming, Dan," she sniffled. "I just don't know what to do or how to cope with this. You always managed to calm me down when we were young. I just knew I needed that again."

"Well, I'm here now," Dan answered. "Do you have anybody else coming to be with you? Your parents or sister?"

"Not right now," Anika replied. "Dad's having some exploratory surgery tomorrow, and Trudy's busy with her three small kids. She offered to come, but I said no—not until we get some leads. I might have to leave at a moment's notice to go and get Jonah."

"Is it anything serious with your dad?" Dan asked.

"We don't know yet, but he's been having a lot of stomach problems lately. His doctor won't say much, so I'm worried he's seen something in the scans that he isn't telling them," Anika answered.

"I hope he's going to be okay. It's been a long time since I've seen him, but I remember how kind he was whenever I saw him," Dan added.

"Thanks. I know he always liked you," Anika replied, followed by more silence.

Dan sensed that she didn't want to talk about it anymore right now. "So, what are the police doing to find Jonah?" he inquired.

"They've talked to everybody in the church office. Nobody there seemed to notice anything strange. The day before they disappeared, Soren told them that he was going to work on this week's sermon at home for a while, then go out to make his weekly visits to a couple of nearby nursing homes. He never made it to those visits."

"What about the airports and ferry terminals?" Dan asked.

"The police told me it helps that we live on the island. It limits how he could have left. They're in the process of looking through security video, but it's a big job. There's the airport and two ferry terminals. But, if he really wanted to disappear, he could easily have taken a boat across the Strait to Vancouver. That's why they've issued the Amber Alert for all of Western Canada and the Western States. They could be anywhere," she sniffled.

"Yeah, but it's pretty hard for a man to run with a small boy when everybody's seen his face on TV," Dan said. "He's got to show his face somewhere, or slip up somehow. Don't worry, he'll turn up soon."

"What if he tries to leave the country, Dan?" Anika asked.

"Do you have any reason to believe he would? Does he have relatives anywhere here in Canada or the States that he'd try to reach out to? Anywhere else in the world?"

"I don't know," Anika whispered, hanging her head.

"You don't know?" Dan asked. "Where is his family? Where does he come from?"

"I don't really know," Anika answered, looking away in embarrassment. "He told me that he was an only child, and that his parents both died a few years ago in a car crash when he was in college. He told me that it was then that he decided to dedicate his life to God and went into the ministry. He never said much about them, and he usually found a way to change the subject whenever I asked."

"Okay. Let's talk to the police and see if there's anything we can do to help. Maybe we can help with video surveillance. You might see something that other people will miss."

"What about you, Dan? How did Francesca's arraignment go this morning? When do you have to go back?" Anika asked.

Dan took a deep breath, and then released it in a slow sigh, letting go of some of the tension that had built inside during the day.

"Not good," Dan said. "They revoked her bail and held her in custody. Something about her being implicated in a missing person's case. They say Fran might have been the last person to see a missing woman alive."

"That's terrible! Why didn't you stay home to be with her?"

Dan sucked in another deep breath, and then let it out slowly before he answered.

"Well, her lawyer says there's nothing I can do right now. Fran told me to go. She says I'll be more helpful to you right now. She's probably right. Being here will give me something worthwhile to do instead of worrying. In the majority of cases like this, kids are found in the first couple of days. I'll stay here and work around the clock if you want. But I should go home to see Fran in a few days. Is that okay?" Dan asked.

"Of course," Anika replied. "I can't believe you actually came at all. Just being here for a while, until I calm down, is more than I could ever have hoped for."

She squeezed Dan's hand, and then sat up straight in her driver's seat.

"I guess we're wasting time sitting here," Anika said. "Let's go downtown to see if the police have anything new."

CHAPTER 4

ANIKA led Dan through the corridors of Victoria Police headquarters as though she worked there herself. Dan realized she must have spent almost every waking moment there since Jonah's disappearance, doing whatever she could to help with the investigation. They entered a room where three officers, two females and one male, were staring intently at computer monitors. The male officer noticed their entrance and jumped to his feet.

"Anika. I'm glad you're back. Good news! We've finally got all of the security video from the airport and ferry terminals, but we've got a lot of work ahead of us."

Dan felt the officer's eyes shift to him, scanning him quickly from head to toe. Apparently satisfied with what he saw, the officer extended his hand.

"Detective Shawn Hayward," he said. "I'm in charge of Jonah Kristiansen's case."

"Dan Whitney," Dan replied. "Good to meet you. I'm here to do whatever I can to help Anika. We're old friends."

"Thanks for coming. Anika and Jonah need all the support they can get, and I appreciate any help you can give us. I'd like you to meet Constables Hedger and Creswell. They're helping us out with the videos," he added, nodding in the direction of the female officers.

Dan shook hands with the two officers.

"Pleased to meet you both, and thanks for your help," Dan said.

"Now that we're both here, what can we do to help?" Anika asked.

"Well, as you can see, we've got a limited number of bodies available for scouring these videos. Your eyes are the most valuable, because you're going to catch things we might not see. So I think we need you to watch as much of this surveillance as possible. It's tedious work, but it's the most important thing we can do until we have a sighting of Soren or Jonah," Hayward said.

Anika nodded. "Where would you like us to work?" she asked.

"Now? It's getting late. Why don't you and Dan go home and get some sleep. You've been pushing yourself to the limit and your brains will be sharper if you get some rest."

Dan saw the emotional strain etched into Anika's face, her bloodshot eyes betraying her stress and exhaustion. He was thankful for Hayward's empathy and concern for Anika.

"As long as we're here, we might as well put in a few hours of work," Anika said, then she turned to Dan.

"You and I haven't eaten yet. Are you okay if we order in some pizza and work for two or three hours?" she asked.

"That works for me," Dan answered. "We might as well get down to work. That's why I came. Pizza would be perfect."

"Alright," Hayward replied reluctantly. "You guys can work at my terminal. I've got some paperwork I need to finish tonight before I head home. First thing in the morning, I need to go out to interview people at your church again, especially those who saw your husband last. Have you got my cell phone number in case you see something?"

"Oh,… let me see," Anika answered. Flustered, she rummaged through her purse for her phone. "I think I entered it into my phone, but I'm not sure. I'm sorry… I've been so absent-minded since all this happened."

She huffed as she searched, then finally found her phone. Flipping it open, she tried to navigate through the cumbersome menus. Her hands trembled, and Dan sensed she was struggling to keep herself together emotionally.

"There it is… yes… I've got it. We'll call you as soon as we find anything."

"Alright, if you need anything else, just ask Hedger and Creswell," he said. "I'll probably see you guys back here around noon."

"Thanks, Detective," Dan said. "We'll see you tomorrow."

Dan's eyes followed Hayward as he left the room, and then walked across an open area to his own office. The walls of the office were constructed of glass, so Dan saw the detective flop his weary body down in front of his computer terminal. He turned his eyes back to Anika, who was now seated in front of the monitor Hayward had been working on.

"Alright, let's get back to work," Anika declared. "Dan, I'll put you in charge of ordering pizza. Then I'll show you how we work our way through all of this video."

What a trooper, Dan thought to himself. *I don't know how she's managing to be so strong.*

He stood for a moment, watching his old friend. It was hard to believe he was actually standing beside her after all these years. And yet, he felt just as comfortable now as he did years ago. They had always felt completely at ease with each other. When it came to solving each other's problems, they were a team. It felt great to have that feeling back. But he also felt a growing sense of urgency inside. He knew they were running out of time. He knew that the odds of finding Jonah were growing smaller with each passing day.

RE-ENERGIZED by six hours of sleep, Dan and Anika made their way back downtown to the Victoria police station from her home in Sydney. It was Saturday morning, a full day since Francesca's nightmare court experience in Indio and three days since Soren and Jonah had vanished. Dan felt like he still hadn't wakened from the shock of the arraignment yet. It was hard to believe that he was now hundreds of miles away in Canada, immersed in the nightmare of his best friend from many years ago. Anika finally brought Dan out of his daydream and back into the present.

"I guess I need to bring you up to date on what's been happening over the past few years," Anika said as she drove. "It must be strange for you to parachute into my new life, without a clue about how things have brought me to this point."

"I imagine you're probably wondering how my life got so screwed up too," Dan answered. "You know, I always regretted not keeping in touch after we went our separate ways to different universities. I'm sorry for not doing that."

"Don't blame yourself," Anika replied. "I'm just as much to blame. I think we both needed to find ourselves. For me it was immersing myself in becoming a doctor and a pediatrician. I think the only time I've ever felt completely confident is when I'm helping somebody who is sick. I never socialized or dated much, apart from always being active in my medical community and at church. I guess I've always felt like there's been a big void inside me, but I've never really figured it out completely."

"You never dated much?" Dan asked.

"No. You were the only guy I ever really trusted or felt comfortable with. I'm not sure why. But I do know I always wanted to have a family. So, after I came to Victoria and I got my practice going, I joined the Gospel Temple in hopes of meeting a nice Christian man. And trust me, the matchmakers in the church were relentless in their attempts to fix me up with a number of eligible men. Then, out of the blue, they hired Soren as their pastor. There we were, the two most eligible and prominent unmarried people in the church. It seemed inevitable that the congregation would eventually bring us together."

"So, you fell in love with him?" Dan inquired.

"You know what? I really don't know if I did. I don't even think I know what falling in love is. I know that it felt good to be needed, and it felt good not being so alone. For a while, I enjoyed being at Soren's side for all of the church events. He's always had such great plans for the church, so I admired his faith, his commitment, and his energy. I guess I loved being part of that. We were good friends, so when he proposed to me, it seemed like the logical thing to do."

"And then you got pregnant and had Jonah," Dan added. "Now you had the family you always wanted."

"That's right. That's when I found out what real love is. I realized that my friendship with Soren didn't come close to matching my love for Jonah. I devoted myself to my son. Before long, Soren started becoming jealous of how close I was with Jonah. He was upset at how distant we were becoming, and he grew more cynical and critical. After a while, his resentment transformed into bouts of anger, and I realized he was being more verbally abusive, both to me and to Jonah. When we were in public, we both smiled and we were the perfect family. But when we got home, it turned into a living hell."

"Had you thought about leaving him?" Dan asked.

"Yes. By then, the Gospel Temple had evolved into the *World-Wide Community of Christ*, and his ministry and charities had turned into a huge financial enterprise. The church was getting more involved in real-estate investments and developments. But over the past month, Soren became much more irritable. Something was bothering him a lot. He spent more and more time in his den on his computer, dealing with financial and business issues. He spent one week out of every month in the office he opened for the church in New York. Then the rumours started. People were alleging that they were getting scammed and losing their identities after becoming online members of the WWCC."

A light turned on in Dan's memory. He recalled overhearing a conversation between Chelly and other guests at Chateau Eden, just before Philippe Morel sent their lives careening out of control.

"I remember that. He was in the newspaper in Palm Springs the week we arrived there. It was big news. Something about a big commercial development, and he was a key player. But I didn't hear any rumours about any legal issues," Dan said.

"So far, it's been just that—nothing but rumour. But the rumbling has been getting louder. He became more and more distant, and I finally had enough. I asked for a separation two weeks ago," Anika admitted.

"And he didn't take it well, I presume?" Dan asked.

"That would be an understatement," Anika sighed. She paused to take a deep breath before continuing. "Soren went ballistic. It was the first time he ever started throwing things. Jonah was terrified and wouldn't stop crying. It was the first time I'd ever been afraid of him. He didn't hit me, but he threatened. I figured it was only a matter of time. He told me that if separation is what I wanted, I'd have to leave and I'd have to fight for Jonah. He promised to fight for full custody."

Anika's voice quivered as she finished her story. She was sniffling and Dan saw a couple of tears working their way slowly down her cheeks.

"I was so afraid, Dan. I was afraid that if I left the house, I'd lose Jonah. I was afraid of going to court. I couldn't afford a custody battle against him. Because the church was becoming so prosperous, Soren started to enjoy showing off his affluence. He was driving an expensive new Mercedes. And I saw his credit card statement. He was staying in expensive New York hotels, eating in very upscale restaurants on his business trips, and now he was flying first class. I realized he could outlast me in a custody battle, and he knew it. I didn't know what to do!"

Anika's tears burst into loud sobbing as they entered downtown Victoria, nearing the police station. She struggled to keep control over her emotions as she guided her vehicle into the parking lot. As she turned off the ignition, Dan leaned over and put an arm around her to comfort her.

"I saw a lawyer, Dan," she sobbed. "He… he asked me if I thought Soren might try to abduct Jonah and take him out of the country."

Anika sniffled and tried to gulp a deep breath. Dan realized she was starting to hyperventilate.

"Slow down your breathing, Anika," Dan whispered. "You're starting to panic. Nice slow breaths."

Anika paused, trying to think consciously as she attempted to take some deeper breaths. She began sobbing uncontrollably, interspersed with gasps for air.

"I didn't ever think… he was capable of that… I didn't listen… It's all my fault!"

Dan felt overwhelmed with empathy for his old friend. He felt her fear. And while he also felt her helplessness, he realized how helpless he felt in his own life. He desperately wanted to do something to help Anika, but he didn't know how. He wrapped his other arm around her and squeezed to let her know he was there for her. He felt long-forgotten feelings from his past slowly working their way to the surface. He touched his lips to the side of her face and kissed her gently.

"Try not to worry, Anika. Everything's going to be alright."

IT WAS NEARLY eleven o'clock in the morning. Dan and Anika had been working in near silence for the past three hours, their eyes feeling the strain of staring at surveillance video from the Black Ball Ferry Company.

Dan was distracted, feeling guilty that he had inadvertently crossed a boundary that he had no right to cross, when he kissed Anika. She was still a married woman. And even if he was now a widower, he was emotionally attached to Fran, who was now languishing in Indio Prison. He wondered if Anika was angry.

Suddenly, Anika's body went rigid in her chair and she leaned closer to her monitor.

"I've got something! Look at that grey mini-van. There's something familiar about the driver's face," she said, trying to hold back the excitement in her voice.

"Do you think that's Soren?" Dan asked.

"I don't know. I can't tell for sure."

She reached for the photo of Soren that was lying on the desk beside the monitor, handing it to Dan.

"What do you think? Do you think it looks like him?"

Dan's eyes went back and forth between the monitor and the photo in his hand. The shape of the face certainly had similarities.

"I don't know, Anika," he said. "The driver is wearing a cap, so we can't see the colour of his hair. He's wearing sunglasses too, so we can't even see his eyes. And the glare on the windshield makes it difficult to see his face clearly. Is that a young child in the back seat?" She stared intently at the monitor.

"I was wondering that too," Dan said.

"I think so," Anika muttered. "But I can't see any face. Could that be a ball cap obscuring the face?"

"You're right," Dan said, excitement in his voice. "It's a Blue Jays cap!"

Instead of excitement, his last comment was greeted with silence from Anika.

"What's wrong?" he asked.

"Jonah hates wearing hats. I gave up trying to make him wear them, because it always turned into a big fight. And what about the woman in the passenger seat? It looks like the driver's wife."

Dan felt deflated by Anika's response. He tried to read the license plate on the van, but couldn't see it clearly. He looked behind them at Constables Hedger and Creswell.

"Excuse me," he said. "Can you ladies do anything to enhance this license plate so we can get the number? It's not much, but this is the only thing we've seen that's even close to looking like Soren."

"Let's have a look," Hedgewell said. "Let me have your chair for a minute. I'll make a copy of this part of the tape and send it to our analyst. We might not get it done until Monday, and then we'll have to run the plate number to find the vehicle's owner. I'll show you how to do it, in case you see something else that's promising."

Hedgewell showed Dan how to select parts of the security video, and how to email the clip from a pull-down menu. She scribbled the analyst's email address on a sticky note for Dan and Anika.

"Thanks," Anika said. "I think I overreacted this time. My eyes are getting tired and I'm starting to clutch at straws. I can't believe we haven't seen them yet. Either he's still on Vancouver Island, or he's hired a private boat and made it to the mainland already."

Dan saw hopelessness starting to creep into Anika's voice. He couldn't let her give up hope.

"We'll find them," Dan said. "We're just getting tired from doing this non-stop for the past three hours. Let's go take a walk and grab a bit of lunch—give our eyes a rest. We'll turn something up. Hedger and Creswell still haven't finished with the airport and Swartz Bay ferry video yet. And we're only about half way through the Black Ball ferry video. C'mon. Time for a break."

He put a hand on Anika's shoulder, and then withdrew it, hoping he hadn't inadvertently crossed any boundaries with her. He watched her face for any change in expression. He was relieved to see her sigh, and then give a weak smile.

"You're right. Let's go. I know a nice quiet little sandwich place close by where we can talk. I need to catch up on what you've been doing all these years."

Anika turned to Creswell and Hedger behind her. "We'll be back in an hour or so. Do you want us to pick up anything for you?"

Dan gazed at Anika's wavy blonde hair, white skin, and her deep blue eyes, as she took sandwich orders for the two constables.

It feels so good to be with her again. But I wonder when she's going to ask me about Chelly and Fran? She's not going to have good things to say about what happened in Palm Desert!

THE MOTEL owner, a scrawny, hawk-faced man in his early sixties, looked up to see a man wearing sunglasses emerging into the lobby from the darkened hallway.

"Mornin'," said the owner. "Everythin' to your likin', sir?"

"Just fine, thanks," Soren mumbled. His head was turned away, not looking directly at the owner.

Strange lookin' dude. Ah wonder why he's wearin' shades in here.

"Need me t'getcha a cab?" the owner inquired.

"No thanks. I'm just waiting for my ride," Soren answered. He sat down on a well-worn leather couch, its tan-colored leather cracked from years of constant use. He stared expectantly out through the window. The couch faced the front desk, so Soren was forced to turn his body sideways to look out the window. As he did, he made sure he turned his face away from the owner.

"You from aroun' here?" the owner asked. "Ya sorta look familiar."

Soren turned his body towards the window as far as he could, so that he was only showing the left side of his face to the front desk.

"No. Not from around here. I'm sorry, do you mind? I'm watching for my ride, and I don't really feel like talking much this morning."

"Sure, no problem," the owner said. "No problem at all."

Wonder what's buggin' him? Dude's not very sociable. Where have ah seen him before?

The owner tried to work his way down to the end of the reception desk nearest the window to get a better look, but the man with the suitcase turned his head even further away from view.

An uncomfortable silence filled the lobby as Soren stared out the window, while the owner continued to stare at him. After a few seconds, the sounds of young children running towards the lobby shattered the silence. A harried-looking couple with four young children, running and shouting along beside them, emerged from the passage and spilled into the lobby, distracting the owner from his vigil. They were all wearing swimming attire, and obviously heading towards the motel's pool.

"We want all of the towels changed while we're out," the woman whined. "And you'll have to change the sheets on one'a the beds—Jimmy here peed the bed," she said, nodding to a red-haired boy who was crawling on his hands and knees, pretending to be an elephant.

The boy put his lips close together and tried to reproduce the trumpet-like sound of the beast he was imitating. The high wailing sound that resulted caused the owner to turn his head away, and to put a hand over the ear that was nearest to the antisocial dude on the couch. He didn't notice Soren stand up and start rolling his two suitcases out of the lobby.

"Will there be anythin' else?" the owner said to the harried parents.

"No, we're good as long as you get our room cleaned up," the woman answered. "C'mon, kids. Pool time!" The woman shouted so her voice could be heard over the children's din.

The motel owner looked up at the lobby's couch, noticing that the man was no longer there. He gave a quick glance outside and saw the antisocial man walk up to a grey minivan. The driver's door opened and a woman with long blonde hair stepped out of the van. It looked like the sliding door on the far side of the van might have opened. Suddenly a young boy wearing a Blue Jays ball cap came racing around the front of the van. The owner saw the man grab the boy by the wrist and whirl his body around, so that he and the boy were face to face. The owner didn't hear the man's words, but it was obvious that the boy was being scolded.

That boy seems familiar too - where've ah seen those two before?

The woman took the boy by the arm and walked him back to the other side of the van. The owner saw the van's sliding door slide forward, then the passenger door opened and the woman climbed in. The antisocial dude rolled his suitcase to the rear of the van, opened the back door, and appeared to be trying to force his luggage into the van. When he was sure that the rear door had closed, the man walked back to the driver's door and climbed into the grey van. The van rolled out of the driveway, then turned right, heading towards Highway 16.

"Guess ah better find housekeeping' an' tell them to change th' linens on that bed," the owner mumbled to himself.

Damn. Where do I know that dude an' that kid from? he thought to himself. He walked around the end of the reception desk and began walking towards the noisy family's room, then stopped and went back behind the desk. He grabbed a remote control and pointed it at a TV set, mounted in the corner of the lobby, to turn it on. He turned his back to the TV and walked out of the lobby. As he did, photos of Soren and Jonah Kristiansen flashed onto the TV screen. The Amber Alert, now in its second day, was displayed to an empty lobby.

"CAN'T YOU do one thing right?" Soren screamed at Beth. "I told you to keep that kid out of sight, and you just let him parade around for the whole world to see! What's wrong with you?"

"I'm sorry, Soren. I didn't know he was going to get out. I just got out for a few seconds," Beth squeaked. She hung her head and didn't dare look Soren in the eye.

"And you!" Soren shouted at Jonah. "What is the one thing we told you to remember, over and over again?"

Jonah curled himself up in a ball in the back seat of the van, trying to hold back the tears that were forming in his eyes.

"Well, what did we tell you?" Soren screamed.

"I can only get out of the van with Beth," Jonah whimpered, half whispering and half squeaking his answer. "Beth got out, so I thought it was okay for me to get out too."

"No, you stupid kid," Soren screamed. "We told you to *never* get out when *I'm* outside the van too. We're not to be seen together! Remember?"

Jonah, too afraid to respond, silently sniffled in the back seat. He continued to let his head hang down. Soren pressed his foot down on the gas pedal, trying to put as much distance between them and the motel as possible. Against a background of road noise, silence filled the van. After a few minutes, Soren took his eyes off the road and glanced at Beth.

"Are you still awake?" he snapped.

"Yes," Beth answered, her voice quivering and unsure.

"Did you phone that number I gave you? Did you get the address for the new van?"

"Yes," Beth whispered. She reached for her purse and opened it. She unzipped an inner pocket, from which she produced a piece of motel stationery with an address scribbled in pencil. She handed it to Soren, who grabbed it from her extended hand. He abruptly handed it back to her.

"You know how to get there?" he shouted.

"Yes," Beth whispered, nodding her head up and down.

"Speak up, I can't hear a damn word you're saying!" Soren shouted. "Do you know how to get there?"

Beth cleared her voice, managing to produce a timid squeak this time.

"Yes, I know where it is," she answered.

"Good," Soren grunted. "Stay awake and make sure I don't make any wrong turns. We have to get there before that old fart at the motel puts two and two together and calls the cops on us!"

Soren's foot pressed down even further on the accelerator. The van leaped forward until he was matching speed with other faster traffic on the road. He was walking a fine line. He knew time and speed were of the essence. But he also knew that a speeding ticket would be a catastrophe he couldn't afford.

CHAPTER 5

DAN STRUGGLED to keep his mind focused on the news
conference. He felt his arm wrapped around Anika's upper back,
his hand resting protectively on her shoulder. The flash of cameras
and the trembling in Anika's body should have helped to keep him
more focused on the present. But his nightmare from last night
continued to resurface and preoccupy his brain. Images of Chelly,
losing precious blood and gasping for air, alternated with flashes of
her being alive and coherent, ringing the doorbell of Anika's home
and confronting Dan and Anika when they answered the door.

"What are you doing with *her*?" Chelly demanded. "Shouldn't
you be in Indio, helping Fran? Doesn't she need you more?"

Images of Fran, languishing in her jail cell in Indio, also
flashed through his consciousness, alternating with the images of
Chelly. Dan felt guilt bearing down on his shoulders and chest. His
thoughts were jumbled, one part of his brain arguing that his
friend, Anika, needed help. He owed her for being there for him
many years ago. Another part of him sided with Chelly, feeling
guilty for not being with Fran right now. Then there was the part
that still couldn't accept the events leading up to Chelly's death,
and couldn't accept that his wife was no longer alive.

The sound of Anika's voice jerked him back into reality.

"Jonah, honey, I love you and miss you very much," Anika
sniffled into reporter's microphones. "We'll have you home very
soon."

Anika went silent while she sniffled and struggled to swallow,
before she finally managed to find her voice again.

"Soren, for Jonah's sake, I beg you to turn yourself in so he can come home. And to the public, both in British Columbia and the Pacific Northwest, if you see the man or the boy in these pictures, please contact your local police immediately."

Anika broke down, sobbing uncontrollably. Dan wrapped both of his arms around her to console her, feeling her body continue to shudder with each wave of tears. Detective Shawn Hayward stepped in front of the microphone, finishing the interview by telling the public how to contact police if they recognized either Soren or Jonah Kristiansen.

The mob of reporters started to disperse, and Hayward guided Anika and Dan back to his unmarked cruiser. Dan helped his distraught friend into the back seat, and then slid onto the seat beside her, cradling her in his arms.

"You were great, Anika," Hayward said, as he slipped behind the wheel. "I know how exhausting that must have been for you."

"Thanks… thank you. I just… Jonah… I pray that he sees it," Anika sobbed.

"Don't worry, Anika. If he's watching any TV at all, he'll see it. Dan, thanks for being up there with her, she really needed your support. Where can I drive you to?"

"Anika's car is back at the station. I think I'll try to get her away from there for a while," Dan answered. "I think we both need a break."

"I agree," Hayward replied. "You guys have been putting in a lot of hours with those security videos. Why don't you call it a day? I'll call you right away if something comes up."

"Thanks," Dan said. He sensed the trembling in Anika's body starting to subside, and he felt the tension beginning to dissipate from some of her muscles. "We both appreciate everything you've been doing. Do you think the press conference will help?"

"It all depends on whether Soren or Jonah see it on TV. I doubt if it's going to shake Soren, but I'm hoping the boy sees it. Right now, I'm sure his dad is filling him with lies about Anika—telling him what a bad person she is. The most important thing is that Jonah knows that his mother still cares deeply for him. We've got to give him some hope that she wants to see him and bring him home. It's also important for the public to see how distraught Anika is. They're more likely to remember the press conference if they see the torment Anika is going through," Hayward explained.

"Well, I guess all we can do now is wait," Dan said, letting out some of his own tension with a long sigh. He felt a blanket of fatigue and silence settle over them as Hayward guided the black cruiser towards Victoria Police headquarters.

DAN AND ANIKA gazed out the window of the seafood restaurant at Brentwood Bay. A small car ferry was just slipping away from its moorings, transporting its cargo across the long narrow finger of water separating the Saanich peninsula from the main body of Vancouver Island to the west. Although slower, the ferry served as a shortcut to the Coast Highway that served the heavily populated east side of Vancouver Island.

"You're preoccupied today," Anika said, bringing Dan's mind back from watching the ferry.

"Sorry," Dan answered. "The nightmares were back last night. It's happening less often now, but I'm still getting them once or twice a week. But enough about me; how are you doing now?"

"I'm a bit better. Thanks for taking me home for some sleep. I guess that press conference was a lot harder on me than I anticipated. How do you think it went?" she asked.

"You did great," Dan said. "Anybody who sees it will be touched by your grief."

"Thanks," she answered. "I never realized I was grieving, but you're right. I think I've been feeling mostly shock and denial for the past couple of days since Jonah disappeared. But since the press conference, especially since I woke up, I'm feeling more and more angry. I knew Soren and I were having some problems in our marriage, but I never thought he would stoop that low. What kind of an asshole steals his own child away from his spouse? You're the psychologist. Can you explain it?"

"Well, without ever meeting Soren, I can only speculate," Dan replied. "But I'd venture a guess that he's quite narcissistic. He probably thrived on all the attention he got when the WWCC took off in popularity. Underneath his confident, self-assured smile, I'll bet he's really quite insecure. But he won't dare show that side of himself publicly. The face he wears in public is likely just a mask."

"I can see that," Anika said. "But why kidnap our child? How does that help him? Isn't it only going to show the public the kind of person he really is? I don't get it—if he wants people to think he's so great, why did he do something like this?"

"It doesn't seem to make sense, does it?" Dan replied. "But remember, you're assuming that his actions are based on rational thinking, and that's probably not the case here. If I was to hear his life story, I'm almost certain I'd hear that Soren missed out on something important when he was a child. It probably made him feel worthless and vulnerable, and made him feel like he was losing out, from an emotional perspective."

"So, he's trying to make sure he never loses out again?" Anika asked.

"Yeah, that pretty well sums it up," Dan answered. "And he probably feels angry towards anybody who makes him feel like he's losing, especially you."

"That explains the escalation in his anger over the past few months," Anika observed. "Every time we had an issue, he couldn't bring himself to find any middle ground. It was his way or the highway! He just didn't seem to understand the concept of compromise—giving up something to get something else in return."

"Did it feel like he was always keeping score?" Dan asked.

Anika rolled her eyes. "How did you know? He was constantly reminding me that I owed him for something."

"It was just his way of trying to make up for all of times in his life when he's felt like he's lost out to others," Dan answered.

"I guess that's why I felt like nothing I could do would ever make him happy," Anika said, starting to weep again. "But… but why did he have to involve Jonah? I just don't understand!"

Dan felt Anika's pain as he gazed deep into her eyes, past the redness and the tears that refused to stop flowing. Compassion welled up inside him. He felt his own eyes starting to water.

"Because it's the ultimate way of making you pay for making him unhappy. It's the worst kind of emotional manipulation possible—holding your own flesh and blood as ransom," Dan concluded.

"But he's a servant of God!" Anika blurted, her frustration finally getting the best of her. "I feel so betrayed—not just by Soren—but by God too! How could He let Soren do something like that? What kind of God would do this to Jonah and me?"

Seeing the pain and the tears in Anika's eyes, and feeling the depth of his compassion, Dan reached across the table and took her hands in his.

"I don't know what to believe anymore, Dan!" Anika continued. "I always admired your faith when we were young. You seemed so sure of yourself and your faith. I thought there was something wrong with me because I couldn't believe as much as you."

Dan shook his head slowly from side to side.

"That's ironic," Dan said. "I always thought *you* were the one who had the strong faith. I'm the one who was disillusioned with the church. I even left home for university so I could leave the church without having to explain it to my family and friends."

"Why didn't you ever tell me about that?" Anika asked. "I thought we told each other all of our secrets back then—all of the things we couldn't even tell our families."

"I was too embarrassed," Dan said. "Because I thought *you* were so strong, I didn't think you'd understand. So I kept it to myself."

"I guess we didn't know each other as well as we thought," Anika said, trying to stop her sniffling and pull herself together.

"Maybe that's why we were so close," Dan wondered aloud. He felt the warmth of Anika's hands and gave them a loving squeeze. "Maybe neither one of us was very confident. Maybe we both learned to rely too much on each other."

"You might be right," Anika answered. "I'm sure that's why I was so attracted to Soren. He seemed to have such a strong faith, and I envied how much strength it seemed to give him."

Anika managed to force a weak smile. "I'm just glad you're here. When I realized Jonah was gone, I felt so lost. I didn't know who else to turn to."

"You know you can always count on me," Dan said. "Besides, I owe you. You were there for me when I was feeling lost and disillusioned with med school, and after I'd caught my girlfriend cheating on me. Just being with you for coffee one night seemed to bring back my self-confidence. You helped me get in touch with myself and what I really wanted to do."

Dan felt Anika raising his hand to her lips. She kissed it and lifted her head until Dan felt the warmth of her eyes gazing into his.

"I guess it was meant to be. We're both lost and we both need somebody right now," Anika said. "Do you ever wonder why we never became a couple?"

"Yeah, from time to time," Dan replied. "I guess life just sent us in different directions to have different experiences."

"Well, we're together now," Anika said. "Do you want to talk about what happened in Palm Desert? I was so shocked when I heard you were involved with that sadistic pervert. It's just not you, Dan. That's not the way we were both raised."

"I don't know what to say, Anika. I'm still trying to make sense of it myself. Even this morning, at the press conference, my mind was drifting and I felt like I was only half-present," Dan admitted.

"What about this other woman… Fran. You couldn't possibly have any feelings for her, could you?" Anika asked. "You hardly know each other."

"It's complicated," Dan said. "On one hand, you're absolutely right—we hardly know each other. But on the other hand, it's hard to describe how that whole experience brought us together. And I don't just mean sexually. It's hard for two people not to feel close after they've survived something like that together."

"Well, I still can't understand how you got yourself mixed up in something that twisted—it's so unlike you…"

Suddenly, a commotion from the table directly behind Anika interrupted her in mid-sentence. Dan looked past Anika and saw an elderly couple at the table. The woman's face was frozen in fear and white as a sheet. A wine glass crashed to the floor beside the old man, who was making grotesque wheezing and snorting sounds. Anika wheeled around and leapt from her chair.

"Dan, he's choking! Help me get him on his feet!"

The man's wife screamed hysterically.

"He's going to die… oh my God… somebody help him… please!…"

Dan jumped from his chair and rushed to help Anika, who already had her arms wrapped around the man's torso. Together, they dragged him from his chair to an upright position. Anika manoeuvred herself so she was standing behind the man, her arms around his waist.

"Get in front of him," Anika shouted to Dan. "Get your arms under his arms and support him! And get your head out of the way!"

Before he had a chance to move, Dan felt the man's body bounce and saw his eyes bulge as Anika gave the man's diaphragm a violent squeeze. His face was turning blue. Dan moved his face so he was looking over the man's shoulder.

Dan felt the man's body bounce even higher, as Anika squeezed the man again with every ounce of strength she had inside her. He heard a large pop coming from over his right shoulder, followed by a surge of air and an object flying past his ear. The man's body shuddered. He gasped and wheezed. Gigantic breaths of life-giving air surged raggedly in and out of his lungs.

"He's breathing! Oh my God… thank you, thank you!… You saved his life!"

The elderly woman broke into tears, sobbing so hard she could no longer speak. As Anika stepped away from the man, the woman ran to her husband and threw her arms around the man, who still wore a stunned expression on his face. His wife clung to his body, realizing how close she had come to losing her soul mate.

Dan moved to Anika's side. Together, they watched the loving couple. Dan put his arm around Anika's waist and gave her an affectionate squeeze. He gazed deep into her eyes for the first time in many years. He recognized the same loving, helping Anika that he had come to know in his youth. He felt a warm glow flowing through his body and into his genitals, recognizing it as the same love and unfulfilled physical longing he'd had for her as a teen.

"You saved his life," Dan said. "You were amazing."

"It wasn't anything special," Anika replied humbly. "I just did the Heimlich manoeuvre. Anybody can do it."

"Yeah, but you did it without thinking," Dan said. "Other people might have panicked, but you didn't."

"I guess it was the doctor in me," Anika admitted. "It was just automatic."

The elderly woman turned to Anika and wiped the tears from her eyes. A look of gratitude came across her face.

"You're a doctor?" she said. "Dear God, how could we have been so lucky to have you sitting at the next table? How can we ever thank you?"

The elderly man, his breathing now more regular, stepped forward and extended his right hand to Anika.

"I'm Robert Simpson," he said quietly. "And this is my wife, Barbara. How can I ever thank you for saving my life, Doctor…?"

"Kristiansen," Anika answered. "Anika Kristiansen."

"Dr. Kristiansen," the man replied. "I hope you'll allow me to pay for your meals. It's the least I can do in return for what you did today."

"That's not necessary," Anika said. "I only did what anybody else would have done in your situation."

"Please, we insist," Simpson's wife echoed. "We owe you more than we could ever pay. Please accept it with our gratitude."

Dan gave Anika's waist a subtle squeeze, sending her a non-verbal message that conveyed his pride in her.

"Thank you," Anika said. "That's very kind of you." Dan noticed that her fair skin was flushed and pink. She was embarrassed, unused to being the centre of so much commotion and attention. She always had been the kind of person who preferred to do her helping unobtrusively, without any fanfare.

"You look familiar, dear," Mrs. Simpson said to Anika. "Have I seen you somewhere recently?" Her eyes shifted to Dan and she studied him. "You too. I've seen you both somewhere, quite recently."

Dan looked at Anika.

"You might have seen us on the news—the Amber Alert for the missing boy—that's Anika's son," Dan explained.

"Oh my, of course," the woman said. "That's so terrible. It must be such a shock for you. I'm sure you'll hear something soon. They just can't disappear, can they?"

Dan noticed redness and tears returning to Anika's eyes.

"Childhood abduction by a parent is a lot more common than you think," Dan said. "It's hard for a parent to disappear because most western countries have signed the Hague Convention, which acknowledges the legal rights in the affected parent's home country. But there are still a lot of countries, especially in Asia, that haven't signed the Hague Convention yet."

"I can't believe such things still happen in this day and age," Robert said, his breathing now back to normal. "We wish you good luck in your search. We'll pray for you and your son, Dr. Kristiansen. But we've taken enough of your time; we should let you get back to your lunch now. I'll make arrangements for your meal on the way out. Thank you once again for your timely medical intervention."

"No problem. Thank you for your thoughts and prayers," Anika replied.

"Very nice to have met you," Mrs. Simpson said, as she took her husband's arm. "Come along, dear."

Dan watched the elderly couple as they weaved their way slowly through a maze of tables, and then disappeared from the restaurant.

"Well, it's definitely been an eventful lunch," Dan remarked, as he and Anika sat down again at their table. "You were amazing —I'm proud of how quickly you reacted."

"I *am* a doctor, Dan. I *should* know how to react when somebody's choking."

"True," Dan agreed. "So what were we talking about before you saved Robert's life?"

Anika paused, her forehead furrowed in concentration.

"Oh yeah, I remember. I was asking you about your feelings for Fran."

"Right. I was telling you how confused I feel. I get overwhelmed by so many different emotions at times. Even though it was Chelly who dragged me into the swinging and BDSM with Philippe and Fran, I still feel so guilty about what happened. I knew better, Anika."

"So, why did you let it happen?"

"I guess I felt Chelly slipping away from me," Dan admitted. "If I didn't go along with her, I was afraid she was going to leave me for somebody more exciting. You have to understand how much I loved her. I would have done anything for her."

"Even compromising your own values?"

"For the love of my wife? Yes. Absolutely. I guess that's why I'm so confused. How could things have gone so badly when I did it for love?"

"That's where I'm confused," Anika said. "If you did it for Chelly, how could you have fallen for another woman? I don't get it."

"Me too," Dan admitted. "But there was something about Fran that created a connection between us, right from the start—even before Chelly suggested swinging. Maybe it's because I'm a psychologist. I think I sensed her vulnerability… that she was terrified and was being abused."

The ringing of Anika's cell phone interrupted Dan. Anika reached into her purse and withdrew the device, studying her call display. Dan saw her eyes open wide and her eyebrows raise. An expression of anxious anticipation crossed her face

"It's Detective Hayward," Anika said. "I wonder what he wants."

THE BELEAGUERED motel owner heaved a long sigh of relief. So far, this Saturday morning had not been going well. One of his cleaning staff called in sick at the worst possible time, as the motel had been full last night. Most of the guests had left already, leaving a long list of rooms that required cleaning in preparation for a busy Saturday night. Then he had to unplug the toilet in room number nine. It never ceased to amaze him how stupid people could be when it came to flushing bulky things in other people's toilets. To put a cap on it all, his front desk clerk was an hour late because her car wouldn't start. Fortunately, the morning rush of checkouts was nearing an end, allowing him to catch his breath.

He looked up at the TV screen in the lobby, noticing that Seattle's KREM news was still running the Amber Alert from yesterday.

Still no sign of that missin' boy yet.

The photo on the screen switched from that of a young boy, to that of the man who was suspected of abducting him. The beleaguered motel owner noticed the man's broad smile, making a mental note that it seemed phoney.

Mamma always said, 'Never trust no one who smiles too much.'

Something about the man seemed vaguely familiar and it was tugging at his subconscious. Suddenly, the images from the TV screen made a conscious connection in his brain.

"Damn!" he cursed aloud. "That's the guy who spent the night here! And that's the kid who got out of that grey van this mornin'!"

The motel owner stared at the face on the TV screen.

But the guy was different from his picture... I know... he weren't wearin' that smirk on his face... he din't want to talk... he wouldn't even look at me. That's it! He was tryin' t' hide his face!

He reached for the phone, quickly dialing 911.

"Police?" he blurted. "This here's the owner of the Belfair Motel in Bremerton. It's about that Amber Alert on the TV..."

"A GREY mini-van?" Anika asked. She paused while her mind processed the information Detective Hayward had just passed along to her. "Oh my God! How could I have been so stupid! That was them at the Black Ball Ferry!... Where are you?... We have to get back to the station to watch that security video again..."

Dan noticed tears building in Anika's eyes as he listened to her conversation with Detective Hayward. The expression on her face had now changed from concern to shock and disbelief.

"We're out in Brentwood Bay... we'll meet you there as soon as we can... thank you... bye."

Anika burst into tears and rested her head on her arms on the table. She wept inconsolably.

"What's the matter? What's happened?" Dan asked.

Anika wouldn't answer. She pounded her fist on the restaurant table. "Stupid, stupid, stupid… I'm so stupid…" She continued sobbing.

"What about the ferry, Anika? What's going on?"

Anika jerked her head upright at the word *ferry*. She sniffled loudly and wiped the tears from her eyes in an effort to compose herself. She reached into her purse and grabbed her car keys. "Come on. We have to get back to the police station. Somebody spotted Soren and Jonah at a motel north of Seattle this morning!" She pushed her chair back from the table and leapt to her feet in one motion, then she started running for the exit.

Dan felt a surge of hope shoot through his body, followed by a sense of urgency. He leapt to his feet and ran after Anika.

"They took the Black Ball to Port Angeles?" he called.

"Yes," Anika shouted. "Remember the grey mini-van we saw in the security video? It must have been them. We have to look at that video again—we need that license plate number. We have to get back to the station."

They reached Anika's SUV and jumped in. Anika slammed it into reverse. The vehicle's tires squealed as she raced out of Brentwood Bay towards the highway to Victoria.

"When were they spotted?" Dan asked.

"This morning. They stayed at a motel and the manager recognized them from the photos on the Amber Alert."

"So they must be close to the motel," Dan said.

"No. They got one or two hours' head start. The manager didn't connect their faces with the Amber Alert until later."

"Well, it's still hopeful. The Olympic Peninsula isn't that big, and there are only a few roads in and out. Somebody's going to notice them again sooner or later."

"But I'm so stupid!" Anika shouted. "If I'd noticed them on that video, we would have known they were in Washington yesterday."

"Take it easy on yourself," Dan said. "We both missed it. You were looking at hundreds of faces on those videos, and you were looking only for shots with a man and a boy—two specific faces. They disguised themselves well."

Anika paused. "That shouldn't matter. I should have been able to recognize my own husband!"

"Wasn't there a woman in the front seat?" Dan said. "Maybe that's what confused us. Soren's clever. He added a third face, a woman's face, knowing we would only be looking for him and Jonah. And he made Jonah wear that ball cap too. He knew that would throw you off. Any idea who the woman is? Was it anybody from your church?"

"I don't know," Anika answered. "We'll have to look at the video again. I can't remember."

Question after question raced through Dan's mind.

"Does Soren have any family in the States?" Dan asked. "Anybody he might contact for help?"

Anika went silent. She began sobbing again.

"I… I don't know." She sniffed. "I'm not just stupid because I missed them at the ferry terminal. How could I marry somebody without knowing anything about him? I was married to him for six years and didn't know him at all. How stupid and sad is that?"

"You've got to stop beating yourself up," Dan answered. "The most important thing is finding Soren and Jonah right now. It's going to be hard for them to run, now that they've been spotted. I'm sure somebody else will notice them again soon."

"That's why we have to get that van's plate number off that video, as soon as possible," she replied. "We can also send out new pictures to the press, showing what their faces look like now."

Dan felt the vehicle braking as they approached the intersection with the Trans-Canada Highway. The light was red, but Anika barely stopped long enough to look for ongoing traffic before tromping on the gas pedal again. Dan felt his body being forced back into his seat as they accelerated to highway speed, and Anika started overtaking every car on the road into the city center.

DETECTIVE HAYWARD met Anika and Dan at police headquarters.

"Good news, Anika," he reported. "Hedger and Creswell already have the tech people trying to enhance the video, so we can get the plate number and send it to the police and media in Seattle."

Anika was still trying to catch her breath after running from her SUV into police headquarters.

"Thank you… Detective… I don't know what else to say. Is there anything else we can do to help?"

"No need to say anything," Hayward answered. "And not much you can do right now. We've got everything pretty much under control at this end."

"I need to get to Seattle," Anika blurted. "I need to be there when they find him." She burst into tears and began crying again. Dan put his arm around her shoulder and pulled her trembling body against his.

"We'll get you there soon enough," Dan answered, turning to Detective Hayward. "Thanks for everything that you, Hedger and Creswell have done."

Dan turned back to Anika and spoke softly into her ear. "Why don't we get you home so you can get some rest? Don't you also have to talk to that lawyer in Vancouver? This might be a good time."

"You're right," she sniffled. "I almost forgot. I need to find out more about what my parental rights are, and what I can do to get Jonah back into my custody."

"After you've done that and had some rest, then you can pack a bag so you're ready to travel as soon as Soren and Jonah are sighted again."

Anika's head snapped up from against Dan's chest and she stared into his eyes. Dan saw the sense of panic in her eyes.

"You're coming with me, aren't you?" she cried. "I can't go alone. Please tell me you're coming with me."

"I'll have to see," Dan replied. "I'm supposed to phone Fran in Indio tonight. I only get to call her a couple of times each week. It depends on how she's doing. You'll understand if I can't go?"

Dan saw a look of hurt, then panic, in Anika's eyes and etched on her face. He took both of her hands in his and gazed into her eyes.

"You know I'll do whatever I can to help you," Dan said, trying his best to reassure her. "If Fran needs me, I might have to go back to California for a few days. I'll know better after I talk with her tonight. But I'll be back to help, if you need me."

"I'm so afraid, Dan," Anika said. Tears continued to drip steadily from her eyes onto her cheeks. "I feel so alone and so afraid. I need you."

"I know," Dan sighed. He pulled her body close, held her tightly, and felt her warmth as their bodies pressed against each other. He realized how good it felt to have her in his arms after all these years. "We both need each other right now."

CHAPTER 6

FRAN'S THOUGHTS wandered as she lay on the narrow bed in her cell in the Indio Jail. She sighed, then swung her legs over the side of the bed and sat up. Lifting her bright orange prison smock, she rubbed her hands back and forth over her belly, which was becoming tighter each day. Fortunately, the bulky prison uniform was hiding her bulge, but Fran knew it wouldn't be long before she showed. Her thoughts continued to wander as she rubbed herself.

How am I going to tell Dan I'm pregnant? Should I tell him? What if he doesn't want to be a father? How do I even know we are going to stay together? We hardly know each other. Can I raise a child on my own? What will happen if Joanna loses the case? What will happen to my child...?

Lost in her silent reverie, Fran didn't even notice the sound of footsteps coming down the hallway towards her cell. Suddenly, her mind was jerked back into reality by an authoritative female voice.

"Capellini! Incoming phone call for you in five minutes. Come on, git up an' let's go."

Fran pulled down her smock, but not before two guards reached her cell and saw her. The two women were like night and day. One of them was a short, slim, Caucasian woman with a mousy face, her silvery brown hair pulled back into a ponytail. Her tiny stature made her appear younger than her real age. The other guard was a tall, heavy-set African American woman with short, jet-black hair. Her hair was obviously dyed, making her look younger than her probable age. Fran heard a click and the hum of a motor as the cell door slowly slid open. The heavy-set black woman entered, carrying handcuffs and shackles.

"Well lookee here," the guard said. "Y'all got a bun in the oven, Capellini? How far 'long, girl?"

Fran's eyes stayed focused on the floor. "About six weeks," she mumbled.

"'Bout six weeks? You not sure? Yer baby daddy even know yet?" the guard asked, laughing.

Fran remained silent, just shaking her head from side to side.

The guard's laughter bellowed through Fran's cell and echoed down the corridor. "I bet you got yerself knocked up cuz'a all that shit that went down at y'alls fancy mansion? Am I right, sweetheart? C'mon, let's get these cuffs on you."

"Is that really necessary?" Fran said. "I am not going to run away."

"Yeah, that's what they all say. You know the drill, honey," the guard replied.

Fran stood, legs slightly spread and extended her arms as the other woman quickly snapped the restraints around her ankles and wrists.

"Okay, sweetheart, let's go," the guard commanded.

Fran shuffled her way out of the cell, hearing the jingling of the metal shackles and feeling their weight as the two women escorted her, one on either side. She felt humiliated as other female inmates glared at her or smirked as she moved reluctantly down the hallway. She waited while another door of steel bars slid open at the end of the corridor. Once through that door, they turned right and started down another long hallway. Fran knew the way. There was a room at the end of the corridor with a row of small cubicles equipped with phones. She was thankful that Shelley or Tim had called her every day since Friday's nightmare in court to check on her.

They reached the room with the phones and the mousey guard directed Fran to an open cubicle, helping her into a chair.

"You get fifteen minutes, Capellini," the slim woman said, then turned and left Fran to herself. Fran's thoughts started drifting again, wondering whether it was Shelley and Tim, or if it was Dan who was calling her. She felt her heart beating and her chest tightening as she thought of Dan.

What am I going to say if it's him? Can I tell him?…

Her thoughts were cut short by the ringing of the phone in front of her. She tried to slow her breathing, without much success, and reached for the phone.

"Hello," Fran said timidly.

"Hello… Is that you, Fran?… It's Dan, how are you?"

Fran felt an uneasy silence as she searched for words.

"I'm okay," she answered tentatively. "How are you doing? How is Anika? Have you found her son yet?"

"I'm fine," Dan said. "I miss you."

Silence hung in the air, as Fran remained silent.

"We haven't found Jonah yet, but we just got our first break a couple of hours ago. Soren and the boy were spotted north of Seattle, in Bremerton, but the police weren't notified in time to stop them. They can't go very far now that the authorities are watching for them. Anika wants to go to Seattle right away, so she can be there when they find him."

Dan waited expectantly for Fran to say something.

"Is everything alright? Is something wrong?" Dan asked.

Fran felt her heart pounding and her chest getting tight. She knew she needed to tell Dan, but she couldn't force herself to do it.

"I'm fine," she lied. "Just tired, that's all."

Another uneasy silence hung in the air before Dan responded.

"Anika wants me to go with her. I told her that you're my first priority. I have to find out how you're doing and make sure you're okay before I even consider going. I'm hoping it will be over soon for her, so I can be with you."

Fran waited while Dan paused again. She felt the anxiety and the hesitancy in his voice.

"What's happening with your defense? Has Joanna figured out why they're so obsessed with prosecuting you?" he asked.

"The police in New York are sending somebody to interview me next week. Do you remember that black and white portrait you like so much—the one of the woman on the street in Los Angeles?"

"Yes," Dan said. "What's that got to do Philippe's drowning or the Alvarez couple?"

"Apparently the woman in that photo disappeared from New York City about eighteen months ago. She was a single mother from Cleveland who was working in New York. Her name was Angela, or something like that."

"I still don't understand," Dan answered. "What's she got to do with anything?"

"It might just be a coincidence, but who do you think she worked for in New York?" Fran asked.

"I haven't got a clue," Dan said. "It could be anybody."

"Soren Kristiansen," Fran replied. "Your friend Anika's husband."

"What?" Dan blurted. There was a long pause on the other end of the line. "You've got to be kidding. Now I'm really lost. Why are the police interested in you?"

"Because, apparently, I am the last person to see this Angela alive. And before my photo went public, Soren had been the last person to see her the night she disappeared. He is still a person of interest in her disappearance."

"So nobody knew when the picture was taken—whether you took the photo before or after the woman disappeared," Dan surmised. "If it was before, Soren is still a suspect in her disappearance. If it was after, Soren obviously didn't kill her."

"I guess so," Fran answered.

"Can you prove when you took the picture?" Dan asked.

"Yes, I catalogue all of my negatives in binders with dates."

"Then why couldn't they just ask you to produce the binder and ask you whether you ever saw her again?" Dan asked. "It still seems like overkill—sending an NYPD detective all the way out here for something that could have been done over the phone. It doesn't make any sense, unless there's something going on that we don't know about. Is Joanna worried?"

"No," Fran whispered. "She thinks this will all go away once they find out I only saw her once. She still thinks that the Battered Spouse Syndrome defense is going to be hard for them to beat."

"Well, that's encouraging," Dan said. "Are you sure everything's alright? You're awfully quiet—you don't sound like yourself."

There was more silence while Fran searched for what she was going to say next.

I need to tell him about the baby—I can't hide it much longer —he is sure to find out soon...

"Dan… I am…"

"You're what?" Dan asked

"… I am just very tired," Fran lied. "This whole thing has been exhausting for me. I hope you understand."

Why didn't you tell him? What are you afraid of? What is wrong with you?

"I'm sure you are," Dan replied. "I can't imagine being in your position. I'll tell Anika that you need me, and I'll come home right away. She's doing better now that the initial shock has worn off. I can still keep in touch with her from Palm Springs."

Fran felt a surge of panic growing inside. She didn't know why, but she wasn't ready to see Dan yet or tell him about the baby. There were still too many unanswered questions in her mind.

"It's alright, Dan. I am fine… really. Tim and Shelley are phoning each day. And Shelley has a few days off, so she is coming to visit me tomorrow. I am only allowed two visits each week, so there's not much you can do here anyway. You would be much more help for Anika right now."

Fran heard Dan pausing, hesitating.

"Are you sure?" Dan asked. "You really don't sound so good. And I really miss you. I mean that, Fran."

He misses you. You know he's a good man, and you know you miss him too.

Fran felt herself struggling with her conflicting feelings. Part of her needed Dan desperately, but there was another part deep inside that was overcome with the *fear* of needing him. For the moment, that part of her was prevailing.

"I miss you too, Dan," she whispered. "I know they will find Jonah and you will be home soon."

Home.

That word reverberated through Fran's consciousness. She began to realize that that single, small word was the big problem. On one hand, having a home with a loving man like Dan was the one thing she wanted most in the world. But it was also the one thing that scared her the most.

What if he falls in love with Anika and leaves me alone with a child, like Papa did to Mamma? Will I turn into a bitter, resentful woman like her? Will my child's home be the same as my childhood home?

"I can't wait to be home too," Dan said. "Tell you what. I'll give it another two or three days. If they find Jonah, I'll be on the first plane home. Otherwise, I'll make sure Anika's alright, and I may stay a few days longer. Will you be okay until then?"

Fran felt the weight starting to lift from her chest. Her heart responded almost immediately. She no longer felt it pounding, and she heard herself sigh.

"That will be fine," she said. "I'm sure I will be okay for a few more days.

"One more minute!" the mousey prison guard shouted in the background. "Time to say your goodbyes, Capellini."

"They say I have to go, Dan. Thank you for calling. Goodbye."

Fran hung up the phone abruptly. She couldn't bear a prolonged goodbye. It would only make things more difficult.

DAN'S cell phone went silent. He stood in the parking lot outside Victoria Police headquarters, feeling a flood of different emotions. Despite her reassurances, Dan had the uneasy feeling that there was something Fran was holding back. He had grown so close to her in the five weeks since Chelly's death and the events in Palm Desert. He could tell something was wrong, and he longed to be with her again.

He replaced his phone in the pouch on his belt and gazed towards police headquarters. He felt a wave of guilt as he thought of the woman inside that building—a woman who had been his best friend as a young man—a woman to whom he still felt a strong attraction. He pushed the conflicting thoughts aside and re-entered the building, walking to the situation room where Detective Hayward was briefing Anika on the recent events. Her face brightened as Dan returned to the room.

"Detective Hayward tells me that the entire State of Washington is on the lookout for the grey van. A woman, Elizabeth Daley, using a B.C. driver's license, rented the van. She rented it from Thrifty at SeaTac and paid with cash."

"We're just running the woman's name and checking out the address to see if they're real," Hayward added. "We've alerted Thrifty to contact police if Kristiansen or the woman try to return it or rent another vehicle."

"How is Fran doing?" Anika asked.

"She says she's doing fine," Dan answered. "But I'm not sure she's telling me everything. There isn't much I can do for her right now. Everything's in her lawyer's hands. But she told me something that was very odd."

"Odd?" Anika said, her eyes narrowing and her forehead wrinkling.

"Yeah. She said that NYPD is sending somebody to question her about one of the portraits she had hanging in their estate in Palm Desert. Apparently somebody recognized the woman in the photo as a person who disappeared from New York eighteen months ago. Angela somebody. But the really strange part is that she worked for Soren at the time."

Anika's face went white, her puzzled expression abruptly replaced with a look of shock.

"Her?" Anika blurted. "The tramp that was with Soren the same night she disappeared?"

"You've heard of her?" Dan asked.

"Heard of her?" Anika shouted. "So did the whole world. They found her cell phone on the floor in the back seat of Soren's care. It was in all the tabloids and on all of the entertainment shows. The rumours were awful—claims that Pastor Soren of the *World-Wide Community of Christ* was having an affair with one of his employees. There were unnamed sources who said that Soren's semen and the woman's vaginal fluids were both found on the front seat of Soren's car. It was humiliating!"

Dan saw Anika's eyes growing red. Tears were pooling. He knew he'd just opened an old wound.

"It was the beginning of the end for us," Anika sniffled. "It confirmed what I'd suspected for a long time—that he'd been with other women when he was on the road. We had a huge fight about it when he got back from New York and his big Mission Tour. He just laughed it off as being sensationalistic reporting. He admitted they'd had a business meeting over dinner, but he denied they had sex. He admitted to driving her home after dinner, and claimed she must have dropped her phone. He just wasn't the same after the news broke. I knew he was worried about people questioning his reputation and his Ministry, but he refused to let it show."

"I guess I get the wrong newspapers," Dan said, laughing. "I hadn't even heard of Soren, except for an article that was in the Palms Springs paper a few weeks ago. The article was something about the WWCC looking for real estate in the Coachella Valley. It didn't say anything about the scandal."

"It's old news now," Anika said. "That was eighteen months ago. When there was no sign of the woman for a few weeks, it disappeared from the top of the news. But what does this have to do with Fran?"

"That's what I can't figure out. The only thing Fran and I came up with is that NYPD wants to know if Fran took that photo before or after this woman disappeared. We'll find out more in a few days when NYPD interviews her. Until then, there's not much I can do to help her."

Anika glanced at Hayward, then back at Dan.

"I'm flying to Seattle tonight, Dan. I have to be there when they find Jonah. Can you come with me? I don't know how I would have got through the last few days without you. Did you ask Fran?"

"Yes, she told me I'd be much more help to you right now. Do you think there are any seats left on the flight?" Dan asked.

"So you'll come with me?" she repeated.

"I'm in this with you all the way," he replied. "Until you get Jonah back with you, safe and sound."

Dan saw the relief sweeping across her face, replacing the sadness and worry that had been there only seconds before. For the first time in days, she had the hint of a smile on her face. The Anika he knew and loved in the past was trying to come back.

"I was pretty sure you'd say yes, so I made a reservation for you. I hope you don't think I was being presumptuous. You'll just have to confirm."

IT WAS ten-thirty p.m. by the time Dan and Anika claimed their bagged and cleared U.S. Customs. A young woman wearing a smart-looking grey suit, bearing a sign with Anika's name, greeted them. She smiled warmly at Anika and Dan when they raised their hands to acknowledge their host.

"Doctor Kristiansen?" the woman said.

"I am," Anika replied, trying her best to smile and hide her anxiety. "Please call me Anika. This is my good friend Doctor Dan Whitney. He's been helping me over the past few days."

"Pleased to meet you both," the woman replied. "I'm Detective Marilyn Moulder, Seattle Police. My car is just outside. I've reserved rooms in a hotel close to the airport and the I-5. I'll bring you up to date while we're on our way to the hotel."

As Detective Moulder led the way, Dan and Anika's weary legs had difficulty keeping up with their athletic-looking host. As they emerged from the terminal, the detective motioned to an unmarked cruiser and helped load their luggage into the trunk. Anika sat in the front beside the detective, while Dan sat in the back. Detective Moulder broke the ice once they had merged into traffic and were on their way out of the airport.

"So, tell me what you knew when you left Victoria," Moulder said. "Then I'll fill you in on what's happened since then."

"Well, we know that Soren has a woman helping him—I think her name was Daley—and she rented the minivan using a B.C. driver's license. Detective Hayward said they were running her name before we left. We hadn't heard anything more from him before we took off."

"Okay, then that's the first bit of news. Detective Hayward called about half an hour ago to let us know there's no Elizabeth Daley at the address on the driver's license. The license is a fake. We may have to assume that your husband is travelling with fake ID as well. We've asked Homeland Security at Port Angeles for the passport information for all of the passengers in that van. Once we get that information, it's going to be tough for them to leave the country by air, and his driver's license is going to pop up if he's stopped anywhere by police."

Dan saw the look of deep concern etched into Anika's face.

"So you haven't found them yet?" Anika asked.

"I'm sorry, Anika. Not yet. That's the second piece of news. But they can't get far in that van, and every hotel in the Pacific

Northwest has been alerted to watch for them. We've got extra security at the airport, bus depot, and train station. We'll get them. It's just a matter of time before they're seen, or your husband slips up and uses a credit or debit card."

"So how can we help, Detective?" Dan said from the back seat. "We didn't come down here to be cheerleaders. We want you to put us to work."

"I know, Hayward told me you were a big help with the security video from the ferry. We'd like your help with the video from the airport—he'll have to fly eventually if he's trying to get to Asia with your son. It's an enormous job and we need every set of eyes we can get, especially yours, because you know your son and husband," Moulder said.

Dan looked at Anika, seeing an overwhelming sadness in her eyes. He smiled at her and took her hand.

"We'll be happy to help. We learned a lot from watching the ferry video. We'll be watching more closely for disguises and misdirection this time, won't we, Anika?" He squeezed her hand again in a gesture of reassurance.

The emotion in Anika's eyes was beginning to transform from sadness to angry determination. Every muscle in her face was tight.

"Damn right we will," Anika replied. "He's not going to slip past me again! When do we start?"

"Bright and early tomorrow morning. We should have yesterday's video from SeaTac by then, and we'll put you to work. Can I pick you up at six o'clock?" Moulder said to Anika.

"You can pick us up anytime you like," Anika said, looking to Dan for confirmation. He nodded his agreement and squeezed her hand again as the police cruiser turned into their destination.

As they climbed from the car, Dan extended his hand to Detective Moulder.

"Thanks for everything, Detective," Dan said, shaking the officer's hand. "We'll try to get as much sleep as we can tonight. I have a feeling it's going to be a long day tomorrow."

TRUE to her word, Marilyn Moulder picked up Dan and Anika promptly at six a.m. Seattle had decided to greet them with an ominous black sky and heavy rain. They listened in silence to the sound of wet tires on pavement, interspersed with the sounds of splashing as the cruiser raced through puddles, sending waves of spray on either side of its path. The black sky resisted any attempt by the sun to break through. It was still dark when they arrived at the Seattle Police Department's 12th Precinct at six-twenty. Within ten minutes, Dan and Anika were scanning the security videos from SeaTac, concentrating on the one central location where every potential passenger had to show their faces—the TSA security checkpoint.

"So, what did we learn the first time, and what are we going to do differently today?" Dan asked Anika.

"We check every adult travelling with a child," Anika replied. "Male or female. We know he's trying to mislead us, so I wouldn't be surprised if Soren separates himself from Jonah and that bitch that's helping him."

"Good," Dan said. "That's what I was thinking too. And we have to watch for disguises—fake beards and moustaches, wigs, hats—they may even have a new cap for Jonah to throw us off."

Ten minutes later, an officer showed up with two Grande Starbucks coffees and breakfast sandwiches for Anika and Dan. They settled into the routine of watching face after face after face file slowly past the security camera. It was painstaking, mesmerizing work. They took turns taking short breaks to go outside to stretch their legs and catch some fresh air; they needed to keep their brains alert. This time, their hypervigilance produced a number of possible hits, all of them eventually ruled out. It was almost noon when the door flew open and Detective Moulder ran into the room. She was puffing and struggling to find breath. Her face was illuminated by excitement.

"We found the grey van," she blurted, followed by sucking a large breath of air into her lungs. "… Abandoned… only about five blocks from SeaTac… in an industrial area… "

"Near the airport?" Anika interrupted. "That means we're on the right track. They must have gone to the airport!"

Moulder was beginning to catch her breath.

"Not so fast. It raises that probability, but we can't jump to conclusions. They still needed to get from the minivan to the airport—we're checking the cab companies to see if they made any pickups in that area yesterday. Or they could have taken another vehicle. The crew from the crime lab is all over the van right now. They'll call me as soon as they find anything useful, especially if it gives us any clue as to where they might be going."

"Well, if they did go through the airport, I'm going to find him," Anika said. The muscles in her face and neck were taut, giving her face a look of dogged determination. "Let's get back to work."

Spurred on by Anika's renewed determination, and fuelled by a pizza they ordered for lunch, she and Dan viewed and reviewed at least thirty possible sightings in the security tapes throughout the afternoon. There was always something to rule each sighting out—either the boy in the clip wasn't the right height, or the man or woman had obvious tattoos, or they were too heavy, too thin, too tall, or too short. By late evening, when Marilyn Moulder returned to check their progress, they had analyzed all of Saturday's tapes, with nothing to show for their efforts. Anika's frustration was beginning to show. She let out a huge sigh.

"I just *know* Soren's going to try to take Jonah out of the country. He never does anything halfway—if he's going to take Jonah away from me, he's going to make it as difficult as possible for me to get him back!"

Dan saw her eyes beginning to turn red again. Tears of sadness and frustration were welling up in Anika's eyes.

"I've got all of today's video up until six o'clock," Moulder said.

"What about the train station and bus depots?" Dan asked.

"Nothing," Moulder replied. "The number of passengers is much lower and we've gone over all of that video twice. There's no chance he took the bus or train yesterday."

"You mentioned another vehicle. Do you think he could still be on the road?" Dan asked.

"Anything's possible," Moulder answered. "If they are, they'll slip up somewhere—he'll use his plastic or somebody will recognize them. If we're patient, something will turn up."

The detective turned to Anika.

"You can't give up. That's one thing about this job—you get used to being methodical and patient. In the end, we'll find something—they have to show their faces somewhere."

THE PRE-DAWN sky over Boise Idaho was still dark, obscured by a heavy overcast that portended impending precipitation. The late May morning had a definite chill. Soren hoisted the last of their few bags into the truck and slammed the rear hatch of the black Cadillac Escalade. He rubbed his chilled hands and blew into them. He looked towards the motel's office and noted that it was still deserted. Even if somebody was still at the desk, the Escalade shielded their room from sight. He hurried back into the motel.

"Are you and the boy ready to go?" he hissed at Beth.

"Your son has a name; and yes, he's ready to go," Beth snarled in return.

"Then shut your mouth and run him out to the truck as fast as your fat ass can move. Understand?" Soren snapped. "We need to put as many miles between us and Seattle as possible today."

"Why won't you tell me where we're going?" Beth asked.

Soren wheeled and slapped Beth across the side of her head. She stumbled, tripping over the corner of a bed, and fell to the floor. A small voice squealed from the rear of the room.

"Stop it! Stop it, Daddy!" Jonah cried.

"Shut up, boy!" Soren snapped. His angry eyes burned into the young boy like lasers. "This is between me and Beth." He reached down and grabbed Beth by her long blonde hair, pulling her to her feet.

"Shut your mouth and stop asking question," Soren snapped, the words spitting off his tongue like venom. "The less you know, the less you can tell the cops if they catch you. Now get the boy into that van so I don't have to hit you again!"

Beth looked at Jonah and tried to smile at the terrified boy.

"Come on, Jonah. It's time to go. Take my hand and we'll go put a video on in the truck. What do you wanna watch this morning?"

"I don't care. You pick one for me," Jonah whimpered. He walked slowly toward Beth, cowering and doing his best to avoid his father. He reached out to take the woman's hand. Beth picked up Jonah's Blue Jays cap and put in on his head, carefully pulling the brim down over the boy's face.

"Okay, Jonah," she said. "I'll go out and open the door of the truck. When I do, I want you to run out and jump up into the back seat as fast as you can. Can you do that for me?"

"Okay," Jonah answered meekly.

Beth opened the door, and then picked up the cooler full of sandwiches, drinks and fruit she had purchased at Wal-Mart the night before. As Soren stood and watched, she went to the van, opened the rear hatch, and made room for the cooler. She carefully closed the hatch and then went to the passenger side of the truck, opening the door.

"Okay, Jonah," she mouthed, motioning to the boy with her finger to join her. He ran quickly from their room and jumped quickly into the truck, disappearing to the far side of the vehicle. Beth climbed into the back seat beside him.

A moment later, Soren walked slowly and deliberately to the driver's side of the large black SUV, opened the door and climbed in. The heavily tinted black glass obscured the faces of the three passengers inside.

Soren started the engine, backed away from the building, then turned the wheel and drove past the office towards the highway. He noted with satisfaction that the office was still deserted. As far as the motel staff knew, the man and woman who checked in late last night were gone by dawn.

Soren made a right turn onto the highway and pressed his foot down on the accelerator, steering the vehicle towards the east.

By tonight it should be safe enough for us to stop at a hotel with free Internet. I've been off the grid far too long. I need to check my email and send a message to Helen.

Soren pondered his next moves as he accelerated down the highway, away from the motel and Boise. His mind began working faster and the truck's big engine began to hum. The taillights of the black SUV grew steadily smaller and more faint. Finally, they disappeared into the inky black pre-dawn darkness, gradually leaving Boise and the Pacific Northwest far behind.

CHAPTER 7

IT WAS late Monday afternoon when the unceasing monotony of Fran's existence in the Indio Jail was broken by the hum of a motor and clanking steel, as the door at the far end of the corridor rolled open. Two pairs of footsteps approached and a voice shouted.

"Capellini! Visitor. On your feet!"

Fran recognized the heavy-set African-American guard, but the other one, a redhead, replaced the usual mousey-looking officer.

"Okay, honey, you know the drill," the heavy-set woman commanded. She carried the usual handcuffs and manacle as she marched into the cell. Fran held out her hands and spread her legs slightly again. Once again, she heard the jingle-jangle of her chains as she did the march of shame down the corridor, towards the visitors' area. She had made the march for phone calls four times since her arrival at the jail on Friday, but it didn't get any easier.

Once again, she was ushered into a small booth containing a phone. The wall in front of her was all glass. She saw her friend, Shelley Paul, waiting for her on the other side of the glass. Shelley was the first person, besides her lawyer Joanna Sullivan, to visit since her unexpected incarceration. Fran felt a rush of pure joy at seeing her first friendly face in four days.

Shelley, along with her partner Tim, had been a regular visitor at Chateau Eden ever since Fran and her now-deceased husband, Philippe, had opened their boutique nudist hotel two years ago. Over time, Fran had given Shelley many massages in her capacity as a part time massage therapist at the clothing-optional resort. The daughter of a researcher from India and an English mother,

Shelley's flawless light brown skin, fine features, and exceptional figure also made her one of the most beautiful women Fran had ever known. Not only was Shelley beautiful on the outside, she was the warmest, friendliest, and most genuine person Fran had ever known.

Fran picked up the phone in her booth as she saw Shelley reach for hers.

"Hello, Shelley. Thank you so much for coming. You have no idea how good it is to see a familiar face."

"I'm sorry it took me three days to visit you in person, but I had prior commitments at the San Diego office. I have a few days off before I have to fly back to Switzerland. How are you holding up, girl?" Shelley asked, with concern etched in her voice.

"I'm okay," Fran said, trying her best to disguise her exhausted, haggard appearance with a brave face.

"What are you doing to keep yourself occupied?" Shelley asked. "Do you have any books or anything? Do you get a chance to get some exercise? You have to care good care of yourself."

"There is a library, but I haven't been there yet. There is also a small exercise yard where we can walk a couple of times each day. It feels good to get fresh air and some sun, but the time is so short."

"I can bring you some books the next time I visit," Shelley said.

"Thank you. I would like that very much. I haven't felt much like reading over the past three days. I'm spending too much time in my own head. I'll make myself crazy if I don't find something else to do."

"No doubt," Shelley replied. "I don't know how you're managing, and I'm not sure I could do it. But you're strong, Fran. I know you'll get through this. Have you heard from Dan yet?"

"Yes. He phoned me yesterday from Victoria. Somebody reported seeing Anika's husband and son just north of Seattle. He and Anika went there last night, to help with the search."

"That poor woman," Shelley said, shaking her head from side to side. "I can't imagine the nightmare she's going through."

Shelley paused, then looked straight into Fran's eyes.

"Did you tell him about the baby yet?" she asked.

"Almost… I mean, I tried… but I couldn't find the words," Fran said. Just thinking about telling Dan about their future child made her feel anxious.

Shelley shook her head back and forth again.

"You know you're going to have to tell him soon. You're going to start showing."

"I know," Fran replied. "It is not an easy thing to do over the phone."

"Can I ask you something?" Shelley asked.

"Of course." Fran answered.

"How did you get pregnant? Weren't you taking precautions?"

"I was on the pill. But I was so upset and distracted after Philippe killed the Alvarez couple, I was in a total daze. I sometimes forgot to take my pills. By the time I noticed, I had probably forgotten to take three or four of them. I started taking them again, but I didn't know where to start. I wasn't taking them properly when Dan and Chelly were staying with us at our estate."

"And you weren't using condoms?" Shelley asked, raising her eyebrows.

"We were," Fran replied. "Every time except one."

Fran bowed her head, feeling ashamed at her lapse and the predicament she found herself in.

"I understand," Shelley answered. "I can't imagine the stress you must have been under - carrying around that terrible secret! And I know how difficult it must be to tell Dan. Do you think he'll be back sometime this week?" Shelley asked. "If he is, you'd better save your second visitor's pass this week for him. I can have Tim bring my books to you next week when I'm away."

"I should know in two or three days if he is coming back this week. If not, can you or Tim visit again?"

"Of course," Shelley replied. "I still can't believe they only allow you two visitors each week. Save the last pass for Dan—you guys have to talk."

Fran paused and an awkward silence began to build. She felt the tension and anxiety building in her body and looked away from Shelley, feeling self-conscious.

"Is it something about Dan?" Shelley asked. "Are you afraid of him?"

"No. He isn't the problem," Fran answered.

"So if not Dan, what are you afraid of?" Shelley asked.

Fran swallowed hard. She hadn't told anybody outside of her home in Manarola, Italy, about her dysfunctional childhood.

"I am afraid to bring children into this world," Fran said, her voice soft and barely audible. "I don't want them to grow up like I did."

"Why? What happened?"

"My father was a sailor and a drunk who was never home. When he did come home, all he did was drink and beat Mamma. She had to work hard to raise two children, so she was never at home either. And she resented me. By the time my older sister, Giulia, got old enough to help in Mamma's restaurant, Mamma thought her hardships were over. Then Papa made her pregnant with me. She and Giulia ignored me, unless they needed me to take care of Giulia's two boys," Fran said. She was speaking louder and with a bit more confidence now.

"I'm so sorry," Shelley said. "That must have been terrible for you."

"Not as terrible as when Giulia's husband, Paulo, started leering at me and touching me. It became worse over time. Finally, he started whipping me… with his belt," Fran said, the words sticking in her throat.

"Oh dear," Shelley gasped, tears starting to flow down her cheeks as she listened to Fran's tragic tale. "I had no idea you had to endure that."

Fran sniffled twice to pull back a few tears that threatened to escape from her eyes.

"I learned to be strong. I found a way to end it, but I couldn't wait to be old enough to leave Manarola," Fran said.

"Is that where Philippe came into the story?" Shelley asked.

Fran nodded affirmatively.

"He was so charming and worldly. He offered me everything I ever wanted—travel, an education in both massage and art—never having to worry about having money. I was so young and naive. I should have known better," Fran admitted.

"He was an abuser, Fran. People like Philippe prey on vulnerable young women like you. You mustn't blame yourself for what happened."

Fran shrugged.

"I know that now. But how can I ever trust another man again? Every man I have ever known has either abused or neglected me. How do I know if Dan is any different? How do I know if he is going to leave me to raise a child alone, just like my mother?" Fran asked. She felt her voice beginning to crack and tears beginning to glisten in her eyes.

"That's just it, Fran. You can't ever know for sure. All you can ever do is give somebody like Dan a chance. It's up to you to learn whether you can trust him, or whether you have to leave. You should really talk to Tim about this. He had a childhood just like yours. He admitted the same thing to me—that he didn't know whether he could trust me to stay with him. But I stuck with him, and I kept showing him that I wasn't about to leave him. Gradually, he learned that he could trust me to keep loving him. He's one in a million, Fran. And I think Dan might be a keeper too."

"You really think so?" Fran asked. "How do you know?"

"Do you remember the weekend when Dan and Chelly first arrived at the Chateau?"

"I don't think I'll ever forget the events after they arrived," Fran said. "That's when Philippe started to go crazy."

"Well, that morning, Chelly went for her usual run, so Dan joined us for our morning hike. The three of us had a long talk about relationships and life during that hike. He was particularly worried about how to make his marriage with Chelly work better. He seemed very open, honest, and genuine. Both Tim and I saw that in him. He and Tim had another long talk that night, and Tim told me how impressed he was with Dan," Shelley explained. "Tim doesn't usually make friends that quickly with anybody."

"So you think I should give him a chance?" Fran said. It was both a statement and a question rolled into one.

"I can't answer for you, Fran. But from what I know about Dan, I think I'd give him a chance."

"What about his friend, Anika?" Fran asked. "He was in love with her once. What if he falls in love and decides to stay with her?"

"Well, that's something you can't control. I think you're doing the wise thing by letting him help her. But you're going to have to trust him to do what he thinks is best for him," Shelley replied.

"And if he decides to stay with me and the baby?" Fran asked.

"Then you have a decision that you *can* control. You can either decide to give him a chance, or not. You can always choose to give up on him in the future if he proves himself untrustworthy. But I do know one thing for certain," Shelley said.

"What is that?" Fran asked.

"You'll never have a chance to be happy if you don't take the risk of trying."

Fran was silent as she pondered Shelley's words.

"My head says you're probably right," Fran replied. "But the part of me that remembers my childhood is still terrified. Do you understand that?"

"Yes, I do. I never had to endure the kinds of things that you and Tim went through in your childhood. I can only imagine what it was like. So I do understand what you're struggling with."

"One minute!" Fran's heavy-set guard shouted from behind Fran's tiny booth.

"Thanks for understanding, Shelley. The guard says I have to go now—I can't believe our half hour is over. I look forward to the books, and I will let you know if Dan will be visiting this week." Fran felt tears starting to trickle down her cheeks as reality set in. Shelley was going to have to leave, and she was going to be alone with her thoughts in her cell again.

"Stay strong, Fran! You can do it," Shelley implored over the phone. "We're all thinking about you every minute you're in there. Keep us in your heart, Fran."

The guard stepped forward and grasped Fran's elbow, guiding her to her feet and away from the window. Fran wept freely until she arrived back in the corridor where her cell was located. She sniffled twice and sucked a deep breath into her lungs. She dug deep, and somehow managed to find the strong, independent Fran that her old mentor, Susan Keaner, had seen in her so many years ago in Manarola. The young timid parts of Fran that had been feeling so afraid and so lonely, only minutes before, began to recede into the background. Instead, she heard only a strong, independent voice speaking to the whole of her identity.

You've been through worse than this before, Fran. Shelley is right. You can do this. Just get back to trusting yourself, like you did in the old days before you met Philippe. You will survive. Before you can trust Dan or anybody else, you must get back to trusting yourself!

IT WAS already three days since Anika's son, Jonah, had disappeared. By early afternoon, Dan's eyes were beginning to feel like sandpaper from too many hours of staring at security videos on computer monitors. He resisted the urge to rub his eyes, reaching instead for the bottle of eye drops in his pocket. He tipped his head back to administer the drops. He heard Anika release a long sigh of frustration beside him. Dan blinked his eyes to clear his vision, and then turned to look at Anika. She sniffled, and he saw tears running down each of her cheeks, leaving glistening trails of moisture in their wake.

"Nothing!" Anika announced, sniffling once again as her frustration started to boil over. She pushed her chair back forcefully, causing it to fall over backwards as she rose to her feet. "We've gone over a full two days of video—Saturday and Sunday. Where the fuck did that bastard go with my son!"

Dan's eyes opened wide, his eyebrows lifting in surprise. He couldn't ever recall hearing Anika—usually calm, collected, prim and proper—raising her voice in anger. Never mind hearing her use the 'f' word. He stepped forward and wrapped his arms around her in a show of empathy, holding her close to his body.

"I know you're frustrated," Dan whispered in her ear. "We both are."

Anika pushed Dan away and glared at him, her eyes searing with anger.

"How do you know what I feel?" she shouted. "That bastard has taken everything in the world that was important to me—my son, my marriage, and my faith in God! How could anybody's God do this to a human being! Don't you dare try to tell me that you know how I feel!"

The trail of tears on Anika's cheeks was now a river. Her normally alabaster skin was red and her eyes were swollen and puffy. Her blonde hair was stringy. The stress of the last three days had finally broken her down. She wept uncontrollably. Without warning, she bolted from the room and ran down the corridor toward the West Precinct's main exit.

Dan jogged after her, shock and concern written all over his face. He pushed open the main door of the police station, following Anika out into the street. It was teeming with rain again for a second continuous day in Seattle. Dan looked right, then left. He saw her about twenty yards away, confused and already soaked to the skin. She stood in one spot, turning in circles, seeming to be lost and trying to get her bearings. Dan walked up to her slowly and reached out to her.

"Let's go back inside," he said, taking her hands in his. "You're going to catch your death of cold if you stay out here."

Anika allowed Dan to wrap one arm around her shoulders. He guided her back towards the entrance, ducking into a covered alcove to get out of the rain.

"What are we going to do now? We've lost him!" Anika wailed.

"Calm down. Just take some slow breaths," Dan said. "We aren't going to find him by standing out here in the rain. Let's go back inside and find Detective Moulder. Let's find out if they've had any other leads, or if there's anything else we can do to help."

He waited to give Anika a chance to calm herself. Her sobbing gradually ebbed, becoming more intermittent as she slowly wrested some control over her emotions.

"Let's go back inside," Dan said, putting gentle pressure on Anika's upper back with his arm, guiding her gently back onto the sidewalk and out into the rain again. They walked slowly, Anika seemingly oblivious to the rain. Dan realized she was in a state of shock from acute stress. Her mind was someplace else, losing touch with her present reality. He needed to get her away from the investigation for a while—anyplace that might help her to anchor herself back into the present.

As they entered the station, Detective Moulder, who had heard Anika's outburst and had gone after the couple, met them.

Moulder took over from Dan, wrapping her arm around Anika and guiding her towards a corridor.

"Let's go into my office and have a cup of hot chocolate," she said in a soft, soothing voice. She glanced at Dan, who read the message in her eyes.

"I'll go get the hot chocolate," he said, leaving the two women alone while he went in search of some hot drinks.

"I FEEL your frustration, Anika," Moulder said, once the two women were alone. "I can't imagine what I'd feel if one of my kids went missing. We *will* find the bastard, Anika. We just have to be patient. He's going to slip up somewhere, sometime. And when he does, we'll be all over him. It might not be today. Maybe not even tomorrow. But we'll find him. We'll get Jonah back to you."

"What do we do now?" Anika whimpered.

"Why don't you and Dan go back to the hotel for a while and get some rest. Maybe it's time we did a press conference later today to keep the public interested and alert. Soren needs to hear your voice and how determined you are to get Jonah back. Jonah needs to hear that too. Do you think you're up to it?" Moulder asked.

Anika sniffled once, and then pulled herself up so that she was sitting more upright in her chair. She sucked in a long breath of air.

"Sure," she said. "He needs to know that I'm not going to just give up and go away."

Dan knocked on the door and Moulder let him into the office. He was carrying a tray with three Styrofoam cups of hot chocolate. Anika looked up at him as he set the tray on Moulder's desk.

"Detective Moulder thinks we should do another press conference later this afternoon," Anika said.

Dan glanced at Moulder, who confirmed with her eyes.

"That sounds like a good idea," Dan replied. "Do you think you're up to it?"

"I guess I have to be up to it, don't I?" Anika answered. She looked across the desk at Moulder and her eyes met with the other woman's eyes. "Arrange it, and we'll be there."

"I'll call a cab to take you back to your hotel," Moulder said. "I'll arrange to have the press conference at the hotel, so I'll call you and let you know the details."

"Thank you, Detective," Dan said, reaching out to shake Moulder's hand. Anika did the same.

The trio sat quietly as they sipped on their hot chocolate. Anika began to shiver, the cold from her soaked clothing finally beginning to take a toll on her body. Dan watched as Moulder reached for her uniform jacket, draping it across Anika's back.

"Call me Marilyn," Moulder replied. "Please. I'm a mother too. I want to catch this guy just as much as you do."

Tears welled up in Anika's eyes again as they connected with Marilyn Moulder. She allowed herself to feel the other woman's empathy, knowing it was genuine. She knew that they shared something that Dan would never be able to feel—the bond between a mother and child that only women share. She knew that Dan could only imagine what it must be like for a woman who carried a child inside her for nine months—who felt it moving inside her, who gave birth to that child, and who nursed it until she could finally wean that child—and to have that child torn away from her.

I wasn't myself earlier. I don't even know if he'll ever be a parent, so how could he ever imagine what it's like to have my child abducted? I'll have to apologize to Dan when we get back to the hotel.

"WHAT ARE you doing after the press conference, Dan? There's not much more we can do here until there's some sign of Soren or Jonah," Anika said.

Dan gazed at his friend, who was sitting on the edge of one of the room's two queen-sized beds. He felt overwhelmed by his compassion for her, and for what she was enduring. He felt a warm feeling working its way through his body. He walked across the room and sat down beside her, putting his arm around her waist.

"I don't want to leave you alone," Dan said. "You're still so fragile. I'll come back to Victoria with you for a few days, if you want. Just to make sure you're okay."

Anika turned her body to face Dan. She took his face in both hands and leaned forward, planting a gentle kiss on his lips. The combination of compassion for Anika, along with the touch of her hands on his face, caused Dan to feel a familiar stir in his genitals. He kissed her back, and then wrapped his arms around her body, pulling himself closer so their torsos were pressed firmly against each other.

Anika went limp in his arms. It was the first time he had felt her relax since he landed in Victoria three days before. He realized how many years it had been since he had held her this way. He allowed himself to savour the moment—neither one of them moving—each of them enjoying the safety of each other's embrace. Finally, he kissed her again, waiting to see what her response would be.

Her lips responded, tentatively, and she returned his kiss. He felt her hands moving over his head, her fingers gently massaging his scalp as her lips teased his. Dan felt his arousal growing. He moved his hands to her head, his fingers working their way through her hair and massaging her scalp beneath. His hands moved slowly down over her neck and onto her back, at the same time that their tongues began making quick, tentative explorations into each other's mouths. His hands made ever-widening, slow rhythmic circles around her back and her waist. He felt her breathing quicken.

Suddenly, Anika broke off the kiss and pulled away.

"This is wrong," she said. "I'm still married and you've got Fran. I can't do it. It just doesn't feel right."

Dan felt confused by the mixed messages.

"It didn't feel right to you? It certainly felt right for me," he answered.

"Don't get me wrong," Anika answered. "I needed to feel your arms around me. More than anything, I realize how much I need to feel human warmth and connection. But I can't make love with you, Dan. It's not the kind of closeness I need right now."

She took Dan's hands in hers.

"Until I get some solid news about Jonah, I have to get back to whatever remains of my life. I have to get back to work. I need to lose myself in taking care of other people's children. It's the only sense of purpose I have left right now."

Dan nodded to confirm that he understood.

"And you have to get back to Palm Springs to support Fran. You need to go back and sort out where you stand with her. I still don't understand how you got involved in the kinky sex, and I don't understand how it could be enjoyable. But that's for you to figure out. Right now, she needs your support. I can't imagine what it must be like for her to be thrown into jail, after everything that you two have been through."

"I'm sorry," Dan said. "You're right. I think I've got a weakness for vulnerable women. The feeling is overpowering—what I felt for you just now was so much like what I felt with Fran when we first met. But you're right; Fran and I need to get to know each other for real. And I need to figure out where my own life is going."

"Don't be sorry, Dan. Your empathy and compassion are the best part of who you are. And it felt so good for you to hold me. Let's just appreciate it for what it was, okay?"

"Okay," Dan answered, pausing to think. "I suppose we'd better make ourselves presentable for the press conference. Detec… I mean Marilyn, will be here in about half an hour."

He felt Anika's lips plant a short kiss on his cheek. Then she stood up and took a deep breath.

"Okay. Let's do this," she said.

THE ELEVATOR door finally slid closed, shutting out the din from the relentless press mob that had followed them all the way from the podium.

"Thank God," Anika said. "I was feeling claustrophobic. I couldn't breathe!"

Dan felt the gentle tug as the elevator began its ascent to their rooms.

"You were great, as usual," Dan said. "I'm sure you got your message through to Jonah. Let's hope they're letting him watch TV and he sees it. And I'm sure you also got the message through to Soren that you're not going to give up." Dan felt the subtle jerk of the elevator as it reached their destination. The door slid open.

"Do you want to come in for a few minutes before we have to catch our flights?" Anika asked.

"Are you sure?" Dan asked, wondering if it was such a good idea after their earlier close encounter.

"I'm sure," Anika said. "We don't have much time to say goodbye, but I want to make sure we say goodbye as friends."

"Good idea," Dan replied. Anika slid her key into the lock for her room. The green light flashed and the lock beeped, then Anika pushed the door open. Awkward silence ensued as the pair walked into small room. Dan finally broke the silence.

"What are you going to do when you get back to Victoria?" Dan inquired.

"My staff cancelled my appointments for this week, so I won't be going back to work until next Monday," she answered. "I've got an appointment Wednesday morning with the lawyer in Vancouver. I need to find out what my rights are, and what the authorities can do to get Jonah back, now that we know they're in the U.S. where Soren is a citizen."

"I didn't know that," Dan replied. "I hope that doesn't make a difference."

"Me too," Anika said. Dan heard a quivering in her voice that belied her worries.

"What are you going to do?" Anika asked.

"I'm going to go visit Fran as soon as possible," he answered. "It's only been three days since they locked her up and I left Palm Springs. So much has happened in those three days. It almost feels like a month since I left. I need to find out how she's doing and be there for her any way I can."

Another heavy silence descended on the room. Neither he nor Anika had mentioned their earlier kisses. This time, it was Anika who broke the silence.

"I hope I didn't give you the wrong message by kissing you earlier," she said. "I'm feeling so lonely right now, and we've been working so closely for the past three days. I guess I just needed to feel close to somebody. I'm sorry," she said.

Dan noticed that she was looking down at the floor, embarrassed by her earlier actions.

"Don't blame yourself," he answered. "We're both vulnerable and we both need somebody right now." He paused, wondering if he should leave it at that. He decided against it.

"You know I always loved you when we were young, don't you? Being with you again is bringing all of those old feelings to the surface. With everything that happened between Chelly, Fran, and me in the past few weeks, I'm feeling very confused right now. I hope you understand," he said. He let out a deep breath as he unburdened himself of his secret.

Anika's fair skin turned bright red, unable to hide her self-consciousness.

"I know," she said, trying to look into his eyes while taking his hand in hers. "I've always felt closer to you than anybody else. It's confusing for me too. I'm glad you finally told me. Do you think we can just be friends while we're searching for Jonah? If you don't think it will work, and you want out, I'll understand."

Dan paused for a couple of seconds, weighing both sides of the issue in his mind. It seemed like minutes were ticking away. He came to his conclusion.

"We've always been just friends," he said. "I'd hate to lose that. So I'm still here for you if you need me."

Anika reached her arms out and wrapped them around Dan's waist, bringing him close to her. Dan felt the warmth of her body against his, then felt her lips on his cheek, giving him a quick kiss to confirm their friendship.

"Thank you, Dan," she whispered. She released her grip on his waist and stepped back. Dan saw tears, but realized that they were tears of gratitude instead of sadness. "I'll be sure to call you just as soon as there are any developments, okay?"

"Make sure you do," he said. "I'd better get started on packing my bag. My flight leaves before yours."

"Yeah, I don't want to be the cause of you missing the last flight of the day."

Dan leaned close and kissed Anika on the cheek.

"Be sure you call me. Bye for now," he said.

Dan turned and walked away from the first love of his life. He knew he couldn't turn around to look at her again. In their current vulnerable state, he knew he might not be strong enough to keep walking if he did.

CHAPTER 8

THIRTEEN hundred miles away, in a hotel room on the outskirts of Denver, five-year-old Jonah Kristiansen sat on the floor, transfixed, as he watched his mother's message on TV.

"... Soren, we know you're out there, and it's just a matter of time before we find you. Do the right thing and turn yourself into the authorities. Think of Jonah and what he's going through. You and I can work things out so Jonah can be a part of both of our lives.

"And Jonah, if you can hear me. Mommy's not going to stop looking for you. I love you so much and I'm praying every night for you to be safe at home soon."

Jonah rose to his feet and walked to the TV, then turned it off. His head hung low and his eyes looked downwards at the floor. He wandered into the motel's bedroom, where Beth was resting.

"I don't want to watch TV anymore. It makes me sad."

He stood silently by the bed for a moment, gazing at the blonde woman on the bed and wishing that it was his mother instead. He climbed up on the bed and curled up beside her.

"Beth?" he asked.

"Yes, Jonah. What is it, honey?"

"I'm confused. If Mommy is looking for me, why is she one of the bad guys?"

"It's… it's confusing, dear," Beth stammered, searching for words to give the boy an answer that wouldn't make Soren angry. "The bad people are tricking your mommy into helping them. She doesn't know they are bad people yet, so she's still helping them. She really does love you and wants you back. It's just not safe to go home, because the bad people want to trick you and your mommy into helping them find your daddy."

"Oh," Jonah said. "I don't like seeing Mommy cry. It makes me sad too. Who's taking care of Mommy when she's sad? Is it that man who had his arm on her shoulder?"

"That's one of the bad men, Jonah," Beth answered.

"But he doesn't seem bad. He's trying to make Mommy happy," Jonah observed.

"Tsssk…," Beth huffed. "Remember, the bad people are trying to trick your mommy. That man is pretending to take care of her, but he's really trying to trick her."

"I don't think so," Jonah said. "He looks like a good people."

"*Person*, Jonah. Not *people*. No, he's one of the bad people, but he's trying to trick you too. You must try to remember that."

"Okay, Beth," Jonah answered. "Can I go to bed now? I'm sleepy."

"That's a good idea, Jonah. I'll get your PJ's out of the bag for you," she said. She got off the bed and scrounged through the suitcase with the boy's clothes.

"Here you are, sweetie. Do you need any help?"

"No. I can do it myself," Jonah said. "Beth?"

"What is it, Jonah?"

"Why is Daddy so mean? Is he one of the bad people?"

Beth's mouth hung wide open, but no words came out. She was lost for words—unable to say something that wouldn't get her into trouble with Soren.

Anika:

This is your last warning. You are messing with forces that are much larger and more dangerous than you can imagine. Don't think I don't see that pervert, Dan Whitney, lurking in the background. If both of you don't stop broadcasting your press conferences and your lies on TV for Jonah to see, I will have no choice but to take him somewhere where you will never find him or see him again. Your lives are in danger, and I will not be responsible if you ignore this warning, and if you don't stop searching for me now!

Soren

Soren hit the *Send* button, transmitting the email through a convoluted path of servers scattered around the world, that would make the message virtually untraceable. He turned his attention to the TV behind him. He sneered as the images of Anika, Dan, and Detective Moulder faded away and the Denver news anchor moved on to the evening's next news item.

"You're full of shit, Anika. You and the cops don't have clue where I am right now, or it would be all over the news. The cops have their heads so far up their asses, they can't even see daylight right now," he said aloud, as if he was talking to Anika on TV.

He pointed the remote control at the device to mute its sound, turning his attention back to his laptop. It felt good to be back online again.

"Time to let Helen know I'm okay," he muttered. "Hmmm… new mail… wonder if it's from her…"

Soren looked at the name attached to the message in his Inbox. His eyes grew wide. The muscles in the side of his face grew tense and his jaw started to clench. Anger spread like a black storm cloud over his face.

That bitch—she's alive!

Instinctively, Soren's finger moved the cursor on the laptop's track pad over top of Angela's email and he clicked on a video that was attached to the message. Before his eyes, he saw himself greeting admirers during his ministry in Los Angeles. The video was captured by Angela, who had been disguised in the crowd, carrying a video camera.

Yet, while his eyes were glued to the video and his anger reached a boil, Soren was oblivious to what was happening in the circuits beneath his fingers. He had unwittingly unleashed Angela's Trojan, so new and unique, that the virus-scanning program on his computer didn't detect it. It embedded itself deep within his Windows Registry and began its work. When it was complete, it would have removed virtually all traces of its presence, beginning with erasing its attachment to the video file in Angela's email. In the meantime, the Trojan had connected to Angela's laptop over the Internet, and it was now sending a mirror image of Soren's drive to Angela.

Unaware of Angela's unwanted and unseen invasion, Soren's eyes began reading the seemingly harmless surface message contained in her email:

To: Soren Kristiansen
From: Angela Baranyi, IT Dept.
Subject: I'm watching you.

Hello Soren. I'm sending you this message as a friendly reminder that I'm always watching you. I just want to make sure you are keeping your end of our bargain. I hope you are continuing to do everything in your power to make sure that Julia, Nicholas, and my parents stay healthy and safe. I think the attached video clip will impress upon you how easy it would be for me to harm you any time I wish.

Regards,
Angela.

"The nerve of that little bitch," Soren said aloud to himself. "She thinks she can stalk me, threaten me, and get away with it? How stupid does she think I am?"

Still fuming with rage, Soren closed his email and opened up his web browser, going to an obscure web address hidden deep within the U.S. government's website.

"You think you can play games with me? You have no idea who you're messing with!" he hissed.

He clicked on the page's login screen and was redirected to a top-secret Pentagon server. After entering his username and a very long, elaborate password, he was asked to answer a long list of security questions. Finally, when the secret server was satisfied with his request, it logged him into an email server with no identifying features. He began typing his message:

To: Helen
From: Socrates
Subject: Dan Whitney, and Francesca Capellini

If you have been watching the news, you will know I'm now in hiding. I have gone underground and I'll be travelling for a few days. I will contact you with details of my new location when I arrive. In the meantime, please order complete security checks on the two people in my subject line. I want a complete life history on each one of them. I will be forwarding an email message for you to trace. I have already scanned it to make sure it's clean. Find the server and ISP where it originated and leave a message here when you find her.

Proceed with plan Atlanta and notify me of the drop location and contact information. I must have this by midnight tomorrow (Tuesday, May 2). In case of emergency only, my new disposable mobile number is 564-226-0808

Socrates.

Soren clicked the *Send* button, directing the message to the agent known only by the code name *Helen*. Because it was sent internally from within the agency's server, and because Soren's connection from the outside was highly encrypted, nobody outside the agency would ever know that the email existed.

He logged out of the government site, his business complete for the night. He clicked on the button to shut down Windows and waited for the machine to shut down. A message appeared, telling him that updates were being applied to Windows. The process seemed longer than usual, so Soren left the machine on its own while he started running water for a shower. Unwilling to wait for the updates to finish, he stripped and returned to the bathroom for his shower.

While Soren lathered up his scalp with shampoo, Angela's virus finished logging the files it had copied, ready to resume copying Soren's hard drive the next time he logged onto the Internet with his laptop. With the log complete, Windows went into its normal shutdown routine, and then the screen went blank.

THE LIGHTS of Las Vegas sparkled in the west as Angela gazed out through the windows of her tiny East Tropicana office in Las Vegas. She had just returned from an evening out on the town with Ricki Marshall and a couple of her girlfriends. Following dinner at *Batista's Hole in the Wall*, Ricki and the girls had taken Angela to see Cirque du Soleil's *Zumanity* at *New York, New York*. Apart from her first night out to see the *Showgirls of Illusion* with Ricki, this was her first night out in public in two years. It was the first time she'd been able to relax and be herself in a public place. It felt good to allow herself to laugh hysterically with Ricki and the other girls.

Her introduction to Cirque du Soleil was inspiring. The artistry, grace, and strength of the gymnasts created a visual feast for the eyes, as did the sensual choreography and suggestive costumes of the performers. She was surprised that it left her feeling aroused again, just as the *Showgirls of Illusion* had done a few nights previously.

Maybe Ricki's right. Maybe I do need to get myself laid.

Angela's curiosity was aroused by the women's friendly banter during dinner and after *Zumanity*. Ricki's two girlfriends raved about the physiques of both the male and female performers in the show, making lewd suggestions to Angela about the kinds of sexual positions at which each performer might excel. On the other hand, Ricki wasn't as vocal, and Angela sensed a masculine side of Ricki that she hadn't sensed during their first night out.

I wonder if Ricki's gay? I couldn't get a good read on the other two. They both seemed turned on by the men—but then again, they seemed just as enthusiastic about the female performers. Bisexual? Oh well, it doesn't matter to me. They made me laugh and I had fun.

Angela was startled by an alarm from her laptop. It took her by surprise because she wasn't expecting the unique alarm to sound so soon. She moved quickly to her computer table and noted that her Mac's *Console* window was open. It displayed the execution log of the Trojan virus she had sent Soren. A smile spread across her face. He had taken the bait!

So, my friend. Where are you? How long are you going to be online tonight? How long before I can start watching what you're doing? When will I know where you're hiding?

Angela heard the external hard drive spinning continuously as it stored the binary bits of information being downloaded to it over the Internet.

Now for part two of my plan.

Angela opened up her web browser and entered a search for major Detroit hospitals. The search was a long shot—her chances that the email account she was looking for was still active were slim. The list of hospitals was discouragingly long. Angela set to work, systematically searching each hospital, one at a time. While she was on the fourth hospital on the list, the unique alarm on her Mac sounded again.

Damn! Soren's logging off his laptop already. This might take longer than I thought.

She turned her attention back to the task at hand. She finally struck pay dirt on her seventh try—*Henry Ford Hospital* in downtown Detroit. The name she was searching was still listed, along with an email address. She copied the email address and switched to her mail program. She carefully typed a message to the recipient and clicked the *Send* button, listening to the *whoosh* of the email program as the message hurtled into cyberspace. Seconds later, she heard the familiar *plink* of her email's Inbox.

Shit! Auto-response. He's away and won't be responding to that account. Okay, I guess I need to do a little fishing.

Angela returned to her browser, typing *Chateau Eden* in the search box. The nudist resort's website popped up in her browser and she went right to the *Contact Us* page and typed a message:

Hello.

I understand from TV news reports that Dan Whitney is currently living at your hotel. Please tell him that both he and Francesca have seen me, but don't know me. Please understand that I can't reveal my identity right now. I am in great danger, as is Francesca, Dan, and his friend, Anika. Like them, I am also searching for Soren Kristiansen. Please believe me when I say I am Dan's friend. I will soon be able to watch over him from a distance and warn him of any dangers from Soren. Please pass this message along to Dan or Francesca as soon as possible.

Your Guardian Angel

Angela pressed the *Submit* button on the website and sent her inquiry to Chateau Eden. She smiled to herself, knowing that her message would eventually grab Dan's attention. Satisfied with the night's accomplishments, she went to her bar fridge and opened a small hotel-sized bottle of California Malbec with a screw top lid. She poured it into the only wine glass she owned, then wandered back to the wall of windows at the front of her office.

She gazed out at the sparkling cityscape with a renewed sense of hope. Things were starting to fall into place. The hunt would soon begin, and she would be taking her first step toward venturing back out into the world to reclaim her life.

CHAPTER 9

BETH AND JONAH were finally sleeping soundly. Soren finished checking his email, satisfied that Helen had carried out his request and the drop had been made. He left his laptop on, unaware of Angela's Trojan and its clandestine disk-cloning activities going on behind the scenes.

Soren took the bag containing the items Beth had purchased for him at Wal-Mart, and he retreated into the suite's small bathroom. He looked at his face in the mirror, satisfied with his scruffy appearance. "I may be blond," he said to himself, "but it's a good thing I've got a heavy beard."

He pulled a can of shaving gel and his razor from his travel case and began running hot water into the sink. He soaked a facecloth and then covered his face, allowing to steam to soften his skin and beard. After repeating the process, he covered the soft facial skin with gel and began the careful process of shaving the five-day growth from his face. He was careful to leave the moustache and goatee areas untouched. When he was finished, he looked in the mirror, satisfied that he had sufficient hair growth on his face for a good-looking Van Dyke.

Next, Soren removed the box of red hair dye from the Wal-Mart bag. This wasn't the 'For Men Only' touch-up dye—it was the full-strength formula for women. He took time to read the instructions, and then settled into massaging the dye carefully into his hair and the Van Dyke. As he massaged, his thoughts began to wander. He found himself brooding again about the email message from Angela Baranyi.

I need to increase the surveillance on her friends and family. If she's bold enough to re-surface and contact me, she might be stupid enough to try contacting one of them.

Soren felt his entire body tensing as he thought about how Angela had played him.

How dare that bitch come onto me and make me look like a fool! Then making it look like I made her disappear! If I was going to do that, I'd make damned sure she was never seen again!

Momentarily distracted by his anger, Soren brought himself back to the tasks at hand. So far, his plan was unfolding almost perfectly, apart from that damned motel manager who wouldn't mind his own business. *That stupid Beth! If only she'd kept Jonah in the van, then he never would have seen all three of us.* But, things turned out okay in the end. They got out of Washington State without being noticed again.

The trick is to keep letting the cops catch an occasional glimpse of our faces to distract them. He found himself laughing out loud as he gazed at his facial transformation in the mirror. *They get so obsessed with what they see, that they're blind to our new faces! I'll be able to walk right through their security cameras, and nobody will be any wiser. The best place to hide is always in plain sight—nobody expects it!*

Soren's mood was lighter now, his angry thoughts of Angela replaced by a deep sense of satisfaction at the grandiosity of his plan to take Jonah from Anika.

So you thought you'd divorce me and destroy my family, did you, Anika? Well, who's destroying who now? You don't deserve Jonah. You never did. You don't know the pain of somebody who can't bear children. Now he's finally going to have a mother who truly appreciates and loves him. He'll finally have the perfect family!

Soren felt himself smiling with satisfaction. He brought his mind back to the task at hand. He would pick up Helen's package tonight after his hair was dyed. He would sleep well. Tomorrow was going to be a big day, and he would have to be sharp. Everything would go well, as long as nobody slipped up again.

So far I've only made one careless mistake, but I'll be covering my tracks by tomorrow night. I won't let it happen again.

Soren checked his watch. It was time to rinse the carrot-red hair dye from his hair and Van Dyke. He watched the orange water swirl in the sink and disappear down the drain, the intensity of the orange colour gradually diminishing as he continued rinsing. Finally satisfied that no more dye was leaching out of his hair, he turned off the taps and gently blotted his hair and face dry with a towel.

Soren stood back and analyzed the results carefully. Satisfied with his new face, the corners of his mouth gradually turned upwards and his facial muscles lifted. The sparkle returned to his eyes.

It's perfect!

Soren gathered up the evidence of his hair-dying project and wrapped it up in the Wal-Mart bag. He donned his shirt, then tiptoed carefully through the darkened room, being careful not to trip and waken Jonah or Beth. Finally in the outer part of the suite, he closed the door so that he was by himself. He reached for his leather jacket to protect against the chilly Midwest spring evening, and then he made sure he had the keys for the Escalade in his pocket. He donned his ball cap and pulled it down low to shield his new face from security cameras until he was ready to show it tomorrow.

Soren turned off the light and slipped quietly out of the room, into the corridor, and down the stairwell. At the bottom, he pushed on the bar and opened the *Exit* door, stepping out into the night and making his way to the Escalade. In a matter of seconds, the black SUV's taillights disappeared into traffic and into the night. Soren made his way through the darkened streets of Little Rock to the drop site, where his package from Helen was waiting.

DAN WAS disoriented as his eyes opened to the new dawn. His eyes darted around the room, taking in the light, modern decor and pastel shades of the paintings of Italy on the wall. It took a few seconds for his mind to register that he was back in the Italian-themed room at Chateau Eden. The paintings had an immediate calming effect on Dan. He was now at the point where the room no longer reminded him of the three days he had spent here with Chelly before the tragedy in Palm Desert. Now, almost six weeks later, the room was beginning to feel more like home to him.

He rubbed his eyes, then he threw the bedcovers aside and climbed out of bed onto the room's cool white tiled floor. He slipped on his flip-flops, rubbing his face with one hand and scratching an itch on his back with the other.

I need to shave today if I'm going to visit Fran.

Dan's mind wandered while he shaved and showered, jumping back and forth between his past three days with Anika and his growing affection for Fran. He felt a discomforting emotion growing in his guts—guilt over living with Fran, so soon after Chelly's tragedy—and guilt over the feelings for Anika that were resurfacing after all these years. He managed to refocus on the present as he dried himself, then he searched through the room's small bureau for a pair of shorts and a clean sport shirt. He surveyed the tranquil courtyard of Chateau Eden through the room's glass doors. The morning sun was shining from behind his room onto the rooms on the other side of the pool and the courtyard. Empty white lounge chairs were arranged neatly around the courtyard, awaiting the hotel's nudist sun worshippers and another hot day in the Southern California sun.

Dan exited the room and turned to his right, where the entrance to the lobby was only steps away. As he entered, a short, dark-skinned Hispanic woman smiled at him.

"Good morning, Señor Dan," the woman said. "It is good to have you back."

"Good morning, Carmen. It's great to be back. How is everything at the hotel?"

"Everything is good, Señor. I mean… as good as it can be without Señora Francesca. How is your friend? Did she find her son yet?"

"Not yet. Her husband has managed to elude the police for now. We both decided to go home until we hear any new information. Have you heard from Fran lately?" Dan asked.

"*Si*. I talked with her yesterday. I only wanted to tell her that everything at the Chateau is fine. She does not need to worry about anything," Carmen replied. "Will you be going to see her soon?"

"Yes, I was going to arrange a visit for later today, if I can," Dan answered. "You can tell your husband that I'll take over all of the routine maintenance as long as I'm here. Make sure you thank him for taking my place. I'd forgotten how relaxing it is around here—I'm looking forward to a quiet morning of vacuuming the pool and tending to the spa. I'm going to grab a coffee and some breakfast, and I'll be on the patio behind the office if you need me," Dan said.

"Oh, forgive me," Carmen said. "There is one more thing. Somebody sent you a very strange email yesterday. The person who sent it didn't give their name, but they said that they know you and Señora Francesca."

Dan frowned, his face reflecting concern. It wasn't the first unusual email received by the hotel. But Dan remembered that the last one in February of this year from Diego Alvarez had started the chain reaction of tragic events in Palm Desert—events that eventually almost cost him his own life.

"You still have the email?" Dan asked.

"Si. Of course, Señor. I will show you."

Dan followed Carmen into the small, cramped business office behind the front desk. He read the message that Carmen had brought up on the screen for him.

FACES

Hello.

I understand from TV news reports that Dan Whitney is currently living at your hotel. Please tell him that both he and Francesca have seen me, but don't know me. Please understand that I can't reveal my identity right now. I am in great danger, as is Francesca, Dan, and his friend, Anika. I am also searching for Soren Kristiansen. Please believe me when I say I am Dan's friend. I will soon be able to watch over him from a distance and warn him of any dangers from Soren. Please pass this message along to Dan or Francesca as soon as possible.

Your Guardian Angel

"She says that you and Señora Francesca have both seen her, but don't know her. What does that mean?" Carmen asked.

"I don't know. It could mean anything. Maybe it's somebody who is well known, but neither one of us has met him… or her. There's nothing to say whether this is a man or a woman," Dan replied.

"Could it be the police?" Carmen asked.

"I suppose," Dan answered. "Maybe one of those two female detectives, Dixon or Jameson, I suppose. If not them, one of the hotel's guests?"

Carmen raised her eyebrows and shrugged her shoulders. It was clear that she didn't know who sent the message either.

"Well, I guess there's only one way to find out," Dan said. "Let's see if they answer me back."

Dan's fingers went to work on the keyboard, making numerous typing errors as his fingers stumbled over the unfamiliar keys. It didn't help that his hands and fingers were quivering with apprehension over the strange message and its implied dangers. He reviewed his reply:

Thank you for your concern about our safety. Where have we seen you and how do you know us? Please tell us who you are and why you are stalking us. How do you know that we are in grave danger? Why are we in danger? Give us some information so we know we can trust you.

Dan Whitney

Dan hit the *Send* key and the computer's mail program confirmed that it had been sent.

"Okay," Dan said. "Now we wait and see what happens next."

AFTER checking in at the Indio Jail, Dan was led to a small room with a row of small three-sided booths, each constructed with dividers on two sides and a glass window in between. A telephone was mounted on the right-hand wall in each booth. Two of the booths were already occupied when he arrived. He saw Fran waiting for him at the booth on the far left when he entered the room. He sat in the chair on his side of the glass and picked up the receiver. He couldn't avoid hearing the voices of the other two visitors in the background. He resigned himself to the fact that there wasn't going to be much privacy for his conversations with Fran.

"Hi, Fran. It's great to see you. How are you holding up?" he asked. He thought he saw a spark of happiness in Fran's eyes, but it was short-lived, replaced by a face that was expressionless.

"Hello, Dan," she answered. "I'm fine. Thank you for coming. How are you?"

That's it? 'I'm fine. Thank you for coming.' Something's wrong!

"You don't sound fine, babe," Dan said. "Are they treating you well? Are you eating and sleeping well?"

"The food is okay," Fran replied. Her voice, like her facial features, was also flat and expressionless. "I have not slept well. I keep trying to find an answer for why this is happening and why I am here. I ask the same questions over and over. I can't stop them. How are you? How is Anika?"

"I'm fine," Dan answered. "Anika's doing as well as can be expected, but she's not sleeping much either. She's exhausted."

"Have they found her son yet?" Fran asked.

Dan shook his head slowly from side to side.

"Not a sign after that sighting in Bremerton," Dan said. "Then they just vanished into thin air. They abandoned their van near the airport in Seattle, but we don't have a clue where they went after that. We went through all of the security video from the airport and didn't come up with anything. There's nothing more we can do right now."

"I'm sorry," Fran said. "It must be terrible for her… " Her voice trailed off. Dan noticed her eyes becoming distant and her face going blank.

"Fran! Are you there?" Dan asked. Her eyes seemed to snap back into reality at the change in volume of Dan's voice.

"What's going on, Fran? What were you thinking?"

"I was just thinking about her son… how hard it must be for her to be alone right now… how terrible it must be for her son… "

Fran's voice trailed off again.

She's preoccupied about something. It happened when she mentioned Jonah—about Anika being alone.

"Is there something bothering you, Fran?" Dan asked. Her eyes made fleeting contact with his for a moment, and then she looked down. Her mouth opened as if she was going to say something. Then it closed and she fell silent. He was about to ask her if she was depressed, when she opened her mouth to speak.

"How are things at the Chateau? Are Carmen and her husband holding things together while we are gone?"

"They're doing fine," Dan answered. "Everything is normal… except… well, the oddest thing happened this morning."

"Odd? What do you mean?" Fran asked.

"An odd email—a comment, really," Dan explained. "Somebody left it in the comment box on the Chateau's website. Whoever left it was trying to contact me. He or she never left their name, but said that you and I have both seen him or her, but we don't know the person. Do you have any idea who that could be?"

Dan was relieved to see that the expressionless look on Fran's face was replaced by one of puzzlement. She frowned and pursed her lips as she wracked her brain for somebody who might fit the clues to Dan's puzzle. After a few moments, she shook her head slowly from side to side, then shrugged her shoulders and gave Dan a blank look.

"I don't know," she said. "Did they say anything else?"

"Only that he or she couldn't reveal their identity because they were in grave danger. But they also seemed to think that you, me, and Anika were in danger too," Dan added.

"They know Anika?" Fran asked. The puzzled look returned to her face.

"Who knows you, me, and Anika?" she continued. "I can't think of anybody who knows all three of us. Can you, Dan?"

"I'm stumped too," Dan admitted. "The list of people who know both you and me is extremely small to begin with. But I can't think of anybody on that list who knows Anika too."

"What are you going to do?" Fran asked.

"He or she left an email address referring to herself as our 'Guardian Angel'," Dan replied. "So I sent a reply, asking them to tell us why we should trust them. I guess we'll have to wait and see if they respond."

Fran changed the subject and told Dan all about her visit with Shelley. She became more talkative and was taking control of the conversation.

Why do I get the feeling there's something she's not telling me?

Dan's thoughts were interrupted by a voice coming from the background on Fran's end of the line. The voice was telling Fran that they only had a minute left in their visit. He noticed a small, mousey-looking guard hovering behind Fran, the movement of her lips matching the background voice on the phone.

"We only have a minute left," Fran relayed to Dan. "I have to go now. When will you be coming next?"

"Probably in two or three days. But I promise to phone every day. I miss you," Dan added. He felt a large lump in his throat and tears were welling up in his eyes.

"I miss you too, Dan," Fran replied. "Goodbye."

Fran's voice was expressionless again, and Dan noticed that her eyes were watery and red. The line went dead as he saw her hang up the receiver. The guard pulled up on Fran's elbow, getting her to stand up, then guided her backwards and out of her cubicle and out of Dan's sight.

Dan sighed and frowned, his deep concern for Fran etched into his forehead and facial muscles.

What's bothering her? What is she hiding from me?

CHAPTER 10

SOREN, Jonah, and Beth had already crossed the Mississippi River at Memphis, and were nearing Birmingham by nine o'clock Thursday morning, when Francesca returned to her cell from having breakfast in the prison cafeteria.

But as she neared her cell, another body clad in prison orange became more visible with each step. A feeling of panic surged through her body. Fran's worst fear was realized—she could no longer isolate herself from the other prisoners. She was going to have to share her cell with another inmate.

As she drew nearer, Fran made out more features of the person who was sitting at the foot of her bunk, intruding on her solitude. She estimated that the other woman was no more than five feet tall. Her orange prison attire was slightly too big, causing her orange smock to slide off her left shoulder. Fran's eyes were drawn to a tattoo of a black widow spider on the left side of the woman's neck. The woman's hair was blonde, but Fran realized right away that it was a wig—it didn't fit with the woman's dark brown eyes and her complexion.

But it was the woman's eyes, not her physical stature, that had an instantaneous intimidating effect on Fran as they followed her into the cell. The deep brown irises and jet black pupils were confident and calculating, making Fran feel like they were stripping her naked—seeing right through her. She felt weak and vulnerable, trembling in the other woman's presence and doing her best to avoid eye contact.

"I was beginning to think I was going to be all alone here," the woman said. "You look surprised. What's your name?"

"I'm Fran. They didn't tell me I was going to have company."

The other woman laughed sarcastically, making no attempt to introduce herself. Her laughter resonated through the concrete and metal building.

"Well, who do you think *you* are, honey? The First fuckin' Lady? Nobody has to tell *you* anything around here."

The woman stood up and stepped directly into Fran's personal space, staring directly into her frightened eyes.

"Sit down," the woman commanded. "Take a load off your feet and relax." Her eyes directed Fran to the other bunk, where Fran now felt small and insignificant as the new arrival stood over her. The woman's intimidating presence demanded submission. An awkward silence followed, as Fran tried to think of something to say.

"So, what are you in here for?" Fran asked, her voice quavering.

"That's none of your business," the woman answered. "I'm the one asking the questions. And the big question is, what are *you* doing here?"

Fran felt her heart pounding. Every muscle in her body was trembling and her mind was racing? *What does she want with me?* She felt like time was suspended while her new cellmate seemed to be deciding her fate.

Suddenly, a sickly smile appeared on the woman's face.

"You can call me Helen," she said sweetly. "Let's just say that you really don't want to know the kind of pain I can cause for people. Okay?

Fran felt Helen's cold, domineering eyes through the insincere smile, still trying to penetrate through her. Her entire body was rigid with fear, not knowing what to expect from this unexpected and strange intruder into her world. But there was something else in Helen's look. Fran had an eerie feeling she had seen that face before—like she was seeing an apparition through a distant fog.

"Do I know you from somewhere?" Fran asked.

Helen laughed aloud.

"Honey, where in the world would we have met? You, from Spain or France, or wherever you come from—and me, a poor American girl from the wrong side of the tracks. Don't be ridiculous. Like I said, I'm just a girl who has always caused other people pain."

"But, you don't have to worry about me," she said, changing the subject. "As long as you answer my questions. So, I'll ask you again. What are you doing in here?"

Fran swallowed and tried to speak. Her mouth and throat were dry. Nothing emerged but a weak croaking sound on her first attempt. She swallowed once more.

"I have been charged with murdering my husband. I didn't do it. I mean… well… I did… but it was self-defense," Fran answered.

Helen's roar of laughter reverberated through the cellblock.

"Sure, Fran. That's what they all say," she managed to say, between bursts of laughter.

"I suppose you're going to tell me that he was abusing you too. Are you all lawyered up? I'll bet your pretty ass that you can pay for the best. Am I right?" Helen pressed.

"My lawyer, Joanna Sullivan, has a good reputation," Fran answered meekly.

Helen's eyes narrowed and she stared hard at Fran again. Fran had never felt so vulnerable, even in all the years that her husband, Philippe, was controlled and abused her. The intensity of Helen's stare made her feel as if she was transparent—like she wasn't even there.

"Well, well," Helen replied, appearing to recognize Joanna's name. "Aren't you the one who's been on the news lately? The one they say was into all that kinky S and M sex?"

Fran felt her face burning from embarrassment. She didn't have to say a word. Her answer was written all over her face in red.

"Well, I'll be damned. You're a celebrity!"

Helen's eyes narrowed again.

"A beautiful, rich girl like you—and your fancy lawyer can't even get you out on bail? What's with that? Have you got something else you're hiding? Helen asked.

Fran felt torn between answering Helen's probing questions, and keeping her cards close to her chest. She didn't like the idea of making an enemy of her new cellmate, so she chose the former.

"They want to know about a photo of a street person I took last year in L.A. Apparently, the woman in the photo disappeared from New York and was presumed killed about eighteen months ago. I guess they want to know if I had anything to do with her disappearance. They're sending a detective from New York to interview me here tomorrow," Fran admitted.

Helen looked pensive. "Really? So, did you have something do with it?"

"Of course not," Fran answered. "I had never seen her before. I stumbled upon her somewhere in East Los Angeles one day when I was taking pictures. I'm an amateur photographer. I never saw her again after that."

"You're sure about that?" Helen asked.

Fran nodded her head up and down.

"Do you want to hear some good advice?"

"Okay…," Fran answered hesitantly.

"You make sure you tell them everything they want to know, do you understand?" Helen bristled. "Because, if they convict you of murder, you're not going to be staying here in Indio. You're going to State. And if the rest of the girls in there hear that you like rough sex, they're all going to want a piece of your pretty, rich ass and a taste of your nice pink pussy. You're going to be a star inside State, honey!"

Fran shuddered with fear from Helen's description of her possible life in State prison. For the moment, the cat had her tongue.

Helen leaned over, grabbed Fran by the head, and brought them together, nose to nose.

"You listen to me. You tell those New York cops everything they want to know. Understand?"

Fran struggled to swallow. She nodded her head slowly up and down in Helen's hands, letting her know that she understood completely.

"So," Helen pressed. "Is there anything else you're not telling me?"

"No, I swear," Fran replied, desperation and panic starting to sweep through her body.

"You'd better be sure now," Helen responded, waving a finger to admonish Fran. "If I hear that you've been lying to me, I promise I'm going to give you rougher sex than you've ever had. Am I making myself crystal clear?"

Fran's tongue went mute again.

"One more thing, Fran," Helen added. "This conversation never happened, right?"

Fran nodded, silently affirming Helen's words. She needed to get out of the cell—away from this new threat—any way she could. Fortunately, she knew she was scheduled to meet with Joanna Sullivan at eleven this morning. The meeting was still over two hours away, but those two hours couldn't go fast enough for her.

"THEY PUT another prisoner in with you this morning?" Joanna asked, raising her eyebrows. "Can you remember her name?"

"It was Helen… something… I don't think she gave a last name," Fran answered.

Joanna scribbled Helen's name on her notepad, then looked up at Fran.

"Did she say much to you?" Joanna asked.

Fran paused, unsure about how much she should tell Joanna.

"She just wanted to know why I was here," Fran replied. "Oh, and she thought it was funny that I was being held without bail. She asked me if I thought they were looking for something else."

"She did?" Joanna replied. "And what did you say?"

"I told her about all of the questions about the portrait of that street person—Angela, or whatever her name is—the one I took in L.A," Fran said.

"And what did she say to that?" Joanna inquired.

"She just told me to make sure I told them everything I knew. She warned me that things could be very… difficult… if I'm convicted and go to State prison," Fran answered.

"Oh, she did, did she? Did you feel like she was threatening you?" Joanna asked.

Fran paused again, swallowing nervously.

"Yes, her words felt threatening," Fran answered.

"Your friend Helen was probably a plant," Joanna said. "You can bet our old friend, the D.A., is probably up to her old tricks again. She likely traded a lesser sentence to Helen… or whatever her name is…, in return for having her put the fear of God into you. Or she may not have been an inmate at all. They want to make sure you're not keeping anything from them."

"Can they do that?" Fran asked.

"Legally? No," Joanna answered. "But it's your word against theirs. We'll never be able to prove it. I'll make a friendly call to Ms. Mulholland anyway, just to let her know that we know what she's up to. I'll reassure her that it's in the D.A.'s best interests to make sure that your friend Helen makes your safety her first priority. I wouldn't be surprised if Helen's already served her purpose and won't be around much longer. Try not to spend too much time worrying about her."

"Are you sure?" Fran asked.

"I'm sure," Joanna answered. "Now, let's get down to business and talk about this interview with NYPD tomorrow. Why don't you tell me everything you know about this Baranyi woman?"

"There is hardly anything to tell," Fran replied. "Philippe and I were in Los Angeles for a couple of days, entertaining a client from Europe. Philippe never let me sit in on his business meetings, so I often went out with my camera for the day to relax. I took a cab into East Los Angeles, and I was taking photos of people who were living on the street. The Baranyi woman caught my eye—there was something too different about her, compared to the other street people. She was too alert and too refined. She was wary and afraid—I saw it in her eyes. She was in a small park where there was only one way in and out. By the time she realized I was taking her picture, there was no place for her to go except right past me. I only got the one shot before she got to her feet, ran by me, and then out of the park. She ran down the street and was gone in seconds. I never saw her again."

"That's it?" Joanna inquired. "All this fuss is about thirty seconds of contact you had with this woman? Why?"

"She was very afraid of something," Fran said.

"Or somebody," Joanna added. "She must be so afraid of somebody in New York that she found her way to the other side of the country to live on the street. The big question is *who*? Do you have any idea who might want her dead?"

"Not a clue," Fran answered. "I'm just as curious about this person as everybody else, but I have no idea who would be looking for her."

"Well, whoever it is, they must be important to be exerting so much pressure on Kelly Mulholland. When we find out who's searching for Ms. Baranyi, we'll know who's pulling the strings behind our D.A.," Joanna concluded.

"Can't we just ask the D.A.?" Fran asked.

Joanna threw her head back and allowed herself a good laugh.

"I wish we could, Fran," Joanna replied, recovering from her brief departure from her usually reserved demeanour. "Unfortunately, we can't just walk in and ask Ms. Mulholland to tell us who is paying her to obstruct justice. We have to be able to prove it first. And to do that, we have to find the person who is playing puppet master."

"So what do I do tomorrow?" Fran asked.

"Just tell them what you told me today," Joanna replied. "Those NYPD dicks are going to be pretty pissed off when they find out that they flew all the way across the country to hear your short little story. I can't wait to see the looks on their faces. Mulholland is going to look like a fool tomorrow. After that happens, she's going to start getting pressure from the mayor about what she's doing. We'll find out what's going on sooner or later. We just have to sit back and watch it all fall apart on her."

"And meanwhile, what about me?" Fran asked.

"Just tell the truth tomorrow, then wait patiently until their case falls apart. And trust me, Fran; this one is going to fall apart on them. They're just bluffing. And sometime soon, somebody important is going to ask to see their cards."

THE EASTERN sky was still dark as Soren wakened Beth and Jonah at four-thirty a.m. They still had an eight-hour drive to Atlanta and it was time to get back on the road. Soren grinned broadly as he saw the looks of surprise on Beth and Jonah's faces.

"Why is your hair all red?" Jonah asked meekly.

Soren's eyes shifted towards Beth, then back to Jonah.

"We need to wear clever disguises so the bad people and Mommy don't find us," Soren answered. "See, I got a new disguise for you too!"

Soren reached into a plastic Wal-Mart bag and pulled out a new baseball cap and t-shirt, both with Atlanta Braves logos emblazoned on them. He pointed to a large new child's backpack on the floor beside the room's TV stand. It also had the Braves logo on it.

"I got this for you too—it's your own backpack so you can carry your own things through the airport and onto the airplane," Soren said.

Jonah's eyes went wide with excitement for a second, in anticipation of going on an airplane. Then, just as quickly, they went dull as he understood what this meant.

"We're going on an airplane?" he asked. "Where are we going? Are we going to meet Mommy somewhere?"

Beth's eyes darted quickly from Jonah's new backpack to Soren, becoming narrow as she spoke.

"Yes, where *are* we going, Soren?" she asked. Her eyes opened wide as she guessed the answer to her own question. "You don't really think we can get on a plane and leave the country without being caught. You really think that dyeing your hair will fool them?"

"Why don't you just shut up," Soren snapped. "You'll know soon enough where we're going. And as long as you both shut your mouths and do as I say, nothing's going to go wrong. Now, get yourself and the boy ready. I want you both in the van in fifteen minutes!"

Soren went to a desk in the corner of the motel room, where he had been sending an email to Helen. He clicked the machine's track pad to start the shutdown process, and then turned to packing his own bag.

"What about me, Soren?" Beth asked. "If they found the van in Seattle, they'll be looking for me too. How will I disguise myself?"

"Just get the boy ready and get him into the van," Soren sneered. "Then come back up to the room. I've got something for you too."

Soren watched Beth gather up her few articles of clothing and pack them into her small suitcase, then watched approvingly as she gathered up Jonah's few belongings, packed his suitcase and his new backpack, and then herded him into the bathroom to use the toilet and brush his teeth. Beth quickly changed into clean clothes while Jonah was in the bathroom. Soren grabbed Jonah's freshly packed bags and his own suitcase, exiting the room and quickly opening the Escalade's rear hatch. He wasted little time throwing the bags into the back of the truck, then re-entered the motel room to minimize the chance of being seen.

Beth and Jonah were putting on their jackets to ward off the morning chill when Soren returned.

"Okay, get Jonah in the truck then come back into the room. It'll only take a minute. Get going, woman! We don't have all day!" Soren snapped.

Beth guided Jonah toward the doorway, and then stopped him briefly while she opened the door and peered outside to make sure they wouldn't be seen. Then, quickly, she herded Jonah to the side of the Escalade that was hidden from the motel office and helped him scamper up into the back seat.

"We'll only be a minute," Beth said. "You make sure you stay in the truck. You don't want to make Daddy angry again, do you?"

Jonah shook his head silently from side to side.

Beth closed the vehicle's door, making sure to do it as quietly as possible so as not to waken anybody. She hurried back into the motel, looking for Soren.

"Soren, where are you?" she whispered loudly, not wanting to waken their neighbours.

"I'm in the bedroom. Get in here for a minute so we can talk," Soren hissed.

Beth moved quickly toward the bedroom at the back of the suite. As she passed the bathroom, Soren slipped out of the darkness. She didn't hear a thing as Soren fell in behind her. Quickly and silently, he dropped his looped belt over her head. She had time to emit a surprised gasp, and to bring her hands up to her neck, before Soren yanked the belt viciously around her throat. There was a large thump as he threw her to the ground and pinned her with his body. He held his breath, waiting to hear if any of their neighbours reacted to the loud thump of Beth's body hitting the floor. With all his strength, he restrained Beth's squirming body and thrashing limbs, keeping the deadly tension on the leather loop around her neck.

The struggling only lasted about twenty seconds before Beth lost consciousness and Soren felt her body go limp. He kept her body pinned, and he kept the belt tight around her throat while he watched his watch and the life drained from her body. It seemed like an eternity for Soren as he watched the second hand makes its journey around the face of his watch three times. Finally, he loosened the belt and removed it from Beth's throat. Her body remained motionless. Feeling a surge of power and confidence, Soren stood and reinserted his belt into the loops on his pants, cinching it into place.

That was easier than I expected.

He closed the bedroom door and walked calmly through the room and out the front door, placing the *Do Not Disturb* sign on the handle before turning his back to the door and walking to the Escalade.

As Soren climbed into the truck, Jonah's small voice piped up from the back seat.

"Daddy, where's Beth?"

"She decided not to come with us, Jonah. She wants to go back home to Seattle, so it's up to you and me to hide from the bad people now."

Soren looked into the rear-view mirror. He saw Jonah's eyes beginning to water, and then saw him sniffle.

"I didn't get to say goodbye," Jonah squeaked from the back seat. "I wish Mommy was here."

"I know, Jonah. But the bad people would follow Mommy. If they find us, they'll try to keep us from spreading God's word and doing God's work. We can't let that happen, can we?"

"Would God be angry with us then?" Jonah asked. "Would we go to hell?"

"Maybe. And we don't want that to happen, do we?" Soren asked.

"No, Daddy," Jonah said, his timid little voice barely audible from the back seat.

Soren started the engine and guided the Escalade down a ramp onto Interstate 40. Gradually, the lights of Little Rock began to thin behind them. He thought briefly of Beth, lying lifelessly back in the motel room. He liked the adrenaline and the feeling of power that was surging through his body right now. He was glad he remembered to put the *Do Not Disturb* sign on the door as he left. That should buy him more than enough time. He redirected his thoughts to the contents of the package that Helen had sent him, and to Atlanta.

This was the day for which he had been waiting for weeks. The adrenaline continued to pump through his veins. His self-confidence was growing and he felt invincible. He would finally be in Atlanta today, and he would no longer need the World-Wide Community of Christ. By the end of today, his plan would be put in motion and nobody could stop him.

CHAPTER 11

HAVING JUST checked into the Best Western Hotel just off Interstate 75 in Atlanta, Soren walked down the corridor towards the back of the hotel where he had parked the Escalade. He was now officially Magnus Larssen, thanks to the new United States passports that Helen had delivered to the drop in Little Rock. Jonah, now official known as John Larssen, was waiting nervously in the back seat of the truck, safely hidden behind the vehicle's heavily tinted windows. Soren exited the hotel, walked to the vehicle, and climbed in.

"Okay, Jonah. I want you to listen carefully before we go into the hotel. We have new pretend names again. Your first name is still John, so that's easy to remember. Do you understand?" Soren asked.

Jonah nodded his head up and down to acknowledge his new instructions.

"And my name is now Magnus Larssen, can you remember that? What is Dad's new name?"

"Mag… Magnus… Larssen?" he answered, unsure of his response.

"That's right," Soren replied. "Good boy. Now, I want you to put on your new baseball cap, and then we're going to get our bags and walk into the hotel, just the two of us, okay? Make sure you keep looking down at the floor. Don't look up, because we don't want any TV cameras to see our faces. Understand?"

"Okay, Daddy," Jonah answered, reaching for his new cap and reluctantly placing it on his head.

Soren climbed out of the truck and opened Jonah's door, helping him out. He retrieved their luggage from the rear of the vehicle, then the pair walked calmly into the hotel through the same rear entrance that Soren had used before, their luggage rolling along behind them. Soren guided Jonah along the hallway toward the elevator, then into the first car that came along. When the door closed and they were alone, Soren repeated his instructions.

"Good boy. Remember, don't look up."

The elevator opened at the third floor and they proceeded down the hallway to their room. Soren inserted his key card. The door lock flashed green and beeped. Father and son entered the room and closed the door behind them. Soren turned the TV on for Jonah.

"Daddy has to make some phone calls now. If anybody comes to the door, don't say a word. Let Daddy answer the door, and you hide in the bathroom. Understand?" Soren said.

Jonah nodded again. Soren was worried. He didn't need the boy getting nervous now at this critical stage of the plan. He looked at his watch and reached for his cell phone. He opened the package of papers from Helen, found the phone number he wanted, and dialed.

"Hello, is this Lucy? This is Magnus. Do you have the address?" Soren said. "That's right. I'll meet you in the lobby. Remember, we're husband and wife, and we haven't seen each other for a while. You're the actress, make it look good."

"Ten minutes? Good, I'll be downstairs waiting." Soren added, pressing the button to finish his call.

Soren put on the Braves cap that he'd bought for himself to match his new Braves t-shirt. It was important that he and Jonah look like a father and son on a pilgrimage to see their favourite baseball team.

"I have to go downstairs now, Jonah. Remember; don't answer the door for any reason. I'll be back in about ten minutes. Understand?" Soren asked.

"Yes, Daddy." Jonah said. "I won't say a word and won't answer the door."

"Make sure you don't," Soren said. He exited the room and made his way down the hallway to the exit, taking the stairs down to the lobby. He found a chair from which he could see cabs stopping in front of the hotel entrance, and then he kept his head low. Occasionally, he raised his head, peering from beneath the brim of his Braves cap, and being careful not to look up in the direction of any security cameras. Before long, he saw a Prius cab stop in the driveway. A slender Asian woman climbed from the back seat of the vehicle. The driver removed her bags from the rear hatch and a porter helped the woman bring them into the lobby. Soren met her just inside the sliding doors.

"Lucy!" Soren said in a loud voice. "I'm so glad to see you. How was your flight?"

"Magnus!" Lucy shouted, dropping her carry-on bag and jumping into Soren's arms. Soren felt her body pressing against his. Her lips pressed found his, giving him a long, intimate kiss.

She is *a good actress*, Soren thought to himself. He had fleeting thoughts of what it might be like to take her sleek young body to bed. He'd watched the porn film in which she'd recently made her starring debut. He remembered how hard he'd become at seeing her engaged in all kinds of kinky sex acts.

Stop it, Soren! Helen didn't hire her for you to screw. Don't get sloppy and lose your focus. There will be plenty of time after we've reached safety to have her.

Their lips parted. Lucy smiled at Soren and he smiled back. Anybody who saw their reunion wouldn't doubt how happy they were to see each other.

"JONAH, this is Lucy. She'll be taking care of you now that Beth has gone home. You must pretend that Lucy and Daddy are married, okay? You have to pretend that she's your mommy too."

"Hello, Jonah. I'm Lucy," the young woman said. There was genuine warmth in her voice. She extended her hand to Jonah. "Glad to meet you, young man."

A confused look came over Jonah's face as he shook Lucy's hand. Soren watched as Lucy smiled back reassuringly at the boy.

"If anybody asks, Jonah's mother died in childbirth, and you adopted him as your son when we got married. Got it?"

"Sure, Mister…,"

"Not *Mister*!" Soren hissed at Lucy. "Magnus! We're married. You're supposed to be an actress. Get into your role—I'm Magnus and *you* are Lucy Larssen, my wife and young John's mother. If you make one mistake, Jonah goes back his mother. And if that happens, she wins and I lose everything. Because of you, I'd end up in jail. And remember, you're an illegal alien. How would you like to get shipped back to a Chinese prison?"

Lucy lowered her eyes in submission.

"I'm sorry. I slipped up. It won't happen again," Lucy said. She raised her eyes until they met Soren's, signalling her understanding and her submission to his orders.

"That's better," Soren snapped. "Okay, both of you. It's time for us to go, so listen carefully. We're going to the airport and we're going to be taking a four-fifteen Delta flight to Dallas. Lucy, you and Jonah… I mean John… will take a cab to the airport. You'll check in separately. I'll be taking a separate cab and I'll check in later. When I get there, I won't sit near you. It's important that you pretend that you don't know me. We'll also be sitting far apart on the plane."

Soren knelt down so that he was face to face with Jonah.

"Don't be afraid. Lucy has flown on airplanes many times and she knows what she's doing. You don't have to be afraid," Soren said, turning to Lucy. "It's going to be an adventure and Lucy is going to make sure it's lots of fun, aren't you, Lucy?"

"Absolutely," Lucy said. She knelt down so that her face was at the same level as Jonah's. "It's going to be a fun adventure, isn't that right, Jonah? We're going to have fun together."

Once again, Lucy reached out and took Jonah's hand. Soren noted the immediate calming effect that the young woman had on the boy. Jonah smiled and took a step towards Lucy, throwing his arms around her shoulders and giving her a huge bear hug.

"That's my boy," Lucy said, smiling back at Jonah.

Soren looked at his watch.

"Time to get going," he said to Lucy. "Make sure you go to the Domestic Terminal. Here's cab fare."

Soren knelt down, took Jonah's hand, and spoke to him one last time.

"It's very important that you pretend that it's only you and Lucy travelling together. You must pretend that she's my new wife, and she's your new mom. And if you see me, you have to pretend that you don't know me. Understand?"

"Yes, Daddy," Jonah answered. "Lucy is my mom, and I'm going to Dallas with her."

"Good boy," Soren said. He turned to Lucy.

"Make sure you keep your hats on and your heads down as soon as you get out of the cab. We can't have your faces showing on any security videos."

"I'll watch Jonah. Don't worry," Lucy answered.

"Good," Soren said. "Now grab your bags, get yourselves downstairs, and get yourselves a cab."

THE NONDESCRIPT Caucasian woman with shoulder-length blonde hair and pale white complexion emerged from the women's restroom at Hartsfield-Jackson Airport's International Terminal. She stopped momentarily, smoothing the creases in her smart-looking American Airlines uniform. Helen felt the handle of the black leather briefcase on wheels, cradled in her right hand. She bent down and removed a black leather folder from the briefcase that contained all of the vital documents she needed. She took one last look to ensure that her airport identification badge was clipped to her uniform, and then headed in the direction of the American Airlines check-in desk.

As she approached the area, she began scanning the crowd, looking for a family of three who would be waiting near the meeting place. It took only a few seconds to spot her targets lingering near the check-in line, looking around nervously and obviously waiting for somebody. The family was composed of a blond-haired man and his heavy-set, blonde wife, accompanied by a young boy with blond hair like both of his parents.

Helen was amazed by the resemblance to Soren, and to the photos she had seen of Beth Andersson and Soren's son, Jonah. At first she'd thought Soren's plan was far-fetched. Now, seeing the family, she was beginning to think it was a stroke of genius. She approached the bewildered trio of tourists.

"Are you the Smith family?" Helen said, extending her hand as she spoke. "I'm Helen Harper, American Airlines Public Relations."

Relief spread across the faces of all three members of the family as Helen introduced herself.

"Hello, Ms. Harper. I'm Dwayne Smith and this here's my wife Tina and son Jason."

"Pleased to meet you," Helen replied. "I'm very excited to be here today. Unfortunately, the WWCC representative couldn't be here because of a family emergency, so I'm going to handle everything for them today. I'll need your passports in order to get you checked in. Do you mind?"

Dwayne and Tina Smith handed Helen the family's passports. Helen opened her leather case, laying the passports inside. She flipped some pages back and forth, making it look like she had lost something.

"Now, where did I put those tickets?" she said aloud.

She flipped the papers a couple more times then flipped to the back of the folder, where three tickets and three passports were neatly concealed in a pocket of her folder.

"Oh, here they are. Just wait over here for a few minutes while I take care of all the paperwork."

Helen strode confidently to the check-in desk, flagging down the first free agent she could find.

"Good afternoon. I'm Helen Harper with American Public Relations," she said, identifying herself to the check-in agent, a young man who appeared to be in his early twenties. "I'm from the office downtown. I have the contest winners that you were told about."

A bewildered look crossed the young agent's face.

"Contest winners?" he said. "I'm not sure I know what you're talking about."

"Didn't you get the notice from our department about the World-Wide Community of Christ contest winners? You know. The original contest winners had to back out at the last minute, so the church picked some new winners to take their place at the church's mission in Ecuador."

"I'm sorry," the agent replied. "This is the first I've heard of this."

"You didn't? Well, at any rate, I'm here to make sure that our new winners get checked in properly. Here are their tickets and passports." Helen pointed to the Smith family, who were standing off to the side of the check-in desk.

"Certainly, Ms. Harper, I'll take care of that." Helen went over to the Smiths.

"Don't be confused if the agent gets you mixed up with the original winners, the Daleys. All of the paperwork will be changed to Smith during the check-in process. Take your luggage up to the desk, and the agent will get you checked in."

The Smith family stepped up to the desk, and the young man checked in each family member. Dwayne Smith was the last to check in. As the agent finished, Helen stepped forward and intervened.

"I'll walk them through security to their gate. I'll return their passports and boarding passes to them."

The agent complied and handed the documents back to Helen.

"Okay, everybody, follow me," Helen said, waving for the Smiths to follow her. She led Dwayne, Tina, and young Jason around the long, winding security line-up so that they were standing at the head of the line. The eyes of hundreds of other jealous passengers followed them. Helen handed the paperwork to the TSA security officer in charge, a handsome Hispanic-looking man with a black moustache and dark black hair, and smiled at the agent.

"I'm accompanying three special guests of American Airlines to their departure gate," Helen said, making sure to show her security badge to the TSA agent. "Here are their passports and boarding passes."

Helen waited, smiling at the Smiths to hide her anxiety, as the agent checked their paperwork. After looking up to verify the identity of Helen's three guests, he gestured with his left hand to the frequent flyers security line.

"You can use the line on your left," he said, smiling at the Smiths. "Remove your shoes, belts, and all objects from your pockets. Please take any laptops out of their cases and put them in a plastic bin. You know the routine, Ms. Harper. Shoes, your belongings, and your security badge in one of the plastic bins."

Helen smiled at the agent, and then she led the Smiths through the line and up to the metal detector. As she walked through the large metal frame, it beeped loudly. Another female TSA officer stepped up to her.

Helen felt her breathing quicken and she began to feel hot. She told herself to take a couple of slow breaths to quickly gather her wits.

"Boarding pass?" the agent inquired.

"I'm with American Airlines Public Relations, my ID badge is in the bin with my shoes," Helen answered.

"Raise your arms in the air," the agent commanded, brandishing her hand-held metal detector. She waved the instrument all over Helen's body, pausing over Helen's bra when the detector started beeping.

"Metal in the bra?" the woman asked. Helen nodded in acknowledgement. The agent looked at a plastic bin that had just emerged from the X-ray machine, containing a pair a shoes, Helen's leather folder, and her ID badge. "Is this yours?" she asked.

"Yes," Helen answered. She stepped to the side and plucked her ID badge out of the bin, handing it to the TSA agent, who glanced at it casually, then handed it back to Helen."

"Thank you, ma'am. Have a good day," the woman said. Helen clipped the badge back onto her uniform jacket, smiling. She took a few steps, inhaled a slow calming breath, then turned and waited patiently for the Smiths to make their way through the metal detector. She watched as the family of three gathered their belongings and replaced their shoes, oblivious to the storm of attention they were going to attract by the time they landed in Quito. Despite looking outwardly calm, Helen felt a growing sense of urgency inside.

Two major hurdles cleared, just one more to go! As long as I can get them on that plane before Homeland Security notices those passports, everything should be okay.

HELEN LOOKED anxiously at her watch as she and the Smiths waited in the departure lounge, only a few feet away the check-in desk. Precious time was passing. The flight to Quito, originally scheduled to board at four-ten pm., was already fifteen minutes late. Her hands felt sticky with sweat. She looked up at the check-in desk and smiled at the agents. Fortunately, nobody had questioned her authority or her ID so far. Helen turned her head and looked down at the Smiths, who were joking and laughing with each other, unaware of Helen's anxiety. A voice behind Helen interrupted her silent vigil.

"Ms. Harper, we'll be ready to pre-board our guests as soon as I make the announcement. You can tell them to gather up their carry-on bags," the agent said.

Helen put on her best calm, professional smile and turned to Dwayne Smith and his family. In the background, the agent was beginning to announce the boarding process.

"Okay, Dwayne and Tina—you too, Jason—gather up your bags. They'll be ready to pre-board you in just a minute."

Helen pulled the three boarding passes and passports from her folder, making sure to keep the documents away from the Smiths for as long as possible. She waited for the agent to finish her announcement, and then she made her way to the desk and handed the paperwork to the young woman. Helen motioned for the family to join her at the desk as the agent scanned the barcodes on the boarding passes and glanced quickly at the three passports. Helen found herself holding her breath.

The agent looked up at the Smiths and handed the boarding passes and passports back to Dwayne Smith.

"Here, Tina. Put the passports into your purse so we don't lose them."

"Sure, honey," Tina answered. She dropped the documents into her purse without looking at them. "C'mon Jason, they're ready for us."

Dwayne extended his hand to Helen. "Thanks for the VIP treatment. I've never made it through the security line so fast in all my life. Make sure you tell the WWCC people how grateful we are to go to Ecuador and to help them with God's work."

"I'll be sure to do that," Helen answered. Tina Smith stepped forward and threw her arms around Helen, embracing her in a tight bear hug. "I hope you enjoy your mission, Tina."

Tina released her death grip on Helen, who reached out and shook Jason's hand.

"Enjoy your trip, young man. I'm sure this will be a trip you'll never forget," Helen said, the true meaning of her words known only to herself. "Now get going, you three, we're holding up people behind you!"

Helen watched as the Smiths made their way through the door and down the ramp towards their plane. Jason turned and waved to Helen. As soon as they were out of sight, Helen spun around and began walking away from the gate at a steady pace, being careful to remain calm and unhurried. She kept her head down, trying as much as possible not to show her face to the network of security cameras in the terminal.

Once outside the security zone, she made her way to the nearest washroom. Inside, she locked herself in a cubicle, carefully removing a thin plastic shopping bag from the pocket of her American Airlines jacket. She removed her security badge, then carefully rolled up the jacket and placed it in the bag. For a more casual look, she unfastened the two top buttons of her white blouse.

Finally, Helen removed her blonde wig. She opened her large handbag, first removing a pair of dark-rimmed glasses, and then hiding the wig in her bag. Opening the door to the cubicle, she found an open space at the sinks and removed some makeup from her purse. She carefully applied the makeup, giving her face a healthy pink glow and making her deep brown eyes stand out. She stood back and admired her transformation in the mirror, nodding her approval. She was pleased by the alluring hint of cleavage, her short, dark brown hair, and the suggestive glimpse of the black widow spider tattoo, barely visible on the left side of her neck. In contrast to the blonde, pale, nondescript Ms. Harper from American Airlines, she was pleased with the confident, professional, yet sexy face she now presented.

Helen gathered her handbag, replaced the leather folder in the rolling briefcase, and grabbed the plastic bag containing the jacket. She strode confidently from the washroom, merging into a crowd of people and making her way through the terminal towards the exit. At the first large garbage bin, she calmly dropped the shopping bag containing the jacket into the bin, saying a final goodbye to her Ms. Harper identity. Without breaking stride, she merged back into a small crowd of people and continued to an escalator, where she descended to the arrivals level. There, the attractive brown-haired businesswoman blended in with a large group of middle-aged French tourists. She walked slowly with the group as they made their way to the terminal exit, and toward their tour bus.

Once outside Hartsfield-Jackson's International Terminal, Helen separated from the group of tourists and flagged a cab. As the driver closed the door and she sunk into the back seat, she let out a long sigh of relief and smiled to herself. It wasn't the first time she had stepped outside the strict discipline of her job and broken the law. But knowing the implications of what she had just accomplished, it was the biggest thrill she had felt yet. Had she failed, it could have led to the discovery of their entire network.

Somewhere, deep in the recesses of Helen's mind, she heard another voice—a voice of duty and discipline—questioning what she'd just done.

"What are you doing?" the voice shouted from a distance. "Do you have any idea what will happen if you get caught?"

"Oh, shut up and don't be such as pussy!" Helen answered out loud.

"Pardon me?" the cab driver answered, clearly confused. His voice jolted Helen from her reverie.

"I'm sorry… just talking to myself," she said to the driver, still somewhat disorientated. She fidgeted with the new silver bracelet on her right wrist. She knew it was brand new, a recent gift from Soren. Feeling it helped her to refocus on the success of her mission inside the terminal.

I have to hand it to Soren. He's a smart man. His plan worked just like he said it would. I'm pleased with him. As long as he remains undetected for the next few hours, we should be in the clear!

SOREN SAT quietly by himself in the departure lounge, waiting for their Delta Airlines flight for Dallas to board. Three rows of seating away from him, he could see the back of Lucy's head and the top of Jonah's ball cap. He was thankful that they were sitting with their backs to him, making it difficult for Jonah to see him. It minimized any temptation for the boy to look at him. He felt restless, his clammy hands fidgeting with the magazine he had purchased in the airport bookstore. The pages clung to his sticky fingers. He was worried. He hadn't heard from Helen yet. She was supposed to text him to tell him whether she'd been successful or not.

Suddenly, his cell phone buzzed in his pocket. He struggled to get his sticky hands into his pocket, impatiently retrieving the phone and flipping it open. He held his breath as his eyes scanned the brief message from Helen:

Mission successful.
Decoys safely aboard and on their way.

Soren felt the air escaping from his lungs, unaware that he'd been holding his breath. Helen's part of the plan was the most difficult to execute. They had to hope that nobody questioned her identity or her position. Then they had to get that family on the plane before Homeland Security realized that the passports of the wanted Dailey family had just been used.

Slowly and deliberately, Soren looked down at the ground while he removed his Braves ball cap, exposing his head of red hair to the prying lenses of security cameras. With an exaggerated sense of purpose, he wiped his sweaty forehead with hand, making sure that the cameras had a good long view of his short red hair, without capturing his face. After about fifteen seconds, he slowly and deliberately replaced the ball cap and leaned back in his seat. He opened his *People* magazine, pretending to be interested.

Moments later, a man's voice echoed through the terminal's PA system. Soren heard their flight number and looked up at the check-in desk. He saw the young gate agent speaking into a telephone handset. Despite being told that this was only a pre-boarding announcement, and that the plane would board by row number, passengers began getting to their feet and lining up like sheep.

Soren remained in his seat, watching Lucy and Jonah show their passports and boarding passes to the gate agent. They pre-boarded the plane ahead of the herd of passengers behind them.

"Fools!" Soren muttered silently to himself. "They act like they're going to be left behind. Why bother sitting in those cramped seats for half an hour before we even take off?"

He waited until the crowd had thinned before getting to his feet, moving patiently towards the end of the long line-up, always keeping his head low to avoid security cameras. He was amongst the last of the passengers to reach the check-in desk, handing his boarding pass and passport to a female gate agent.

"Thank you. Have a good flight, Mr. Larssen," the woman said, smiling. She tore off her portion of the boarding pass and handed the documents back to Soren.

He made his way casually down to ramp to the aircraft, then down the narrow aisle towards seat 30D. He spotted Lucy and Jonah to his left, near the front of the plane, but he avoided eye contact by looking up towards the back of the aircraft. He waited patiently while people stowed their belongings in the overhead bins, finally reaching his seat. He was the last passenger to take his seat.

The flight crew wasted no time. They were moving down the aisle, performing their head count, before Soren even had his seatbelt fastened. Two of the flight crew had taken their positions in the aisle and were beginning their well-rehearsed pantomime along with a pre-recorded safety message. The moment they were finished, Soren heard the whine of first one, then the other turbine, climbing in pitch as they picked up speed. He felt a bump as the aircraft was nudged backwards, away from the gate. He leaned back in his seat and allowed himself to relax.

The plane taxied across the tarmac, bumping in rhythm as it bounced across cracks that separated the giant concrete slabs that collectively created the vast expanse of Hartsfield-Jackson's airfield. Finally, the rhythm slowed and the plane slowly rotated until it was in position for take-off. After a pause of about twenty seconds, the pitch of the engines grew steadily higher as they roared to life. Finally, the pilot released the brakes and the plane started rolling. Soren felt himself being pressed back into his seat as the aircraft accelerated down the runway. He looked out the window at the enormous airport, one of America's largest, which was now moving past his window at increasing velocity. He felt the nose of the plane start to lift. Then, abruptly, the bumping of tires on runway seams ceased, and the plane lifted into the air, pressing Soren back further into his seat as the giant jet engines continued to roar and they climbed towards cruising altitude.

Soren closed his eyes and exhaled slowly. He suddenly became aware of the tension throughout his entire body. He had been on high alert since he woke up early that morning in Little Rock. His mind drifted back to the hotel room, and how the adrenaline had been pumping through his veins as he pinned Beth to the floor. He could still feel her body thrashing. And in his mind, he could see remember seeing their struggling images in the mirror on the wall of the motel room, his mind reliving those moments while he waited for Beth's life to drain slowly from her body.

He gave his head a brief shake, jerking himself back into reality. There was nothing more he could do now, except wait until they landed in Dallas. Only a few more hours to wait until he and Jonah would leave the U.S. behind, their faces disappearing from sight. Anika and the authorities would have no idea where to look for them. He would be free, leaving his identity as Pastor Soren Kristiansen, leader of the World-Wide Community of Christ, behind him. The church had served its purpose. He could now devote his energies to other, more lucrative enterprises. No longer needing to be constantly on guard, he allowed his eyes to relax and close for some much needed rest.

CHAPTER 12

FRAN SHUFFLED down the corridor in her institutional orange attire, the manacles on her legs jingling as she walked, her hands cuffed in front of her. She was oblivious to the guard who held her by the elbow, guiding her through the corridors toward the interview room.

Conflicting thoughts continued to swirl in Fran's mind, the different sides of her fragile identity jockeying for control. She replayed this morning's phone conversation with Dan in her head.

"Anika's husband and son used their fake passports to take a flight from Atlanta to Ecuador yesterday. They landed in Quito late last night. We're hoping that the authorities will deny them entry into the country, and they'll put them on the next plane back to the U.S."

"That's great news, Dan," she said. "I can't imagine what a nightmare this is for her. I hope she'll have Jonah home with her soon."

"She's flying to Atlanta to meet with the authorities there as soon as possible," Dan answered. "She's flying through LAX later this morning and wants me to join her. Is that okay with you? I'll probably only be gone for two or three days, so I'll be home long before your arraignment next week."

"Of course. She needs your support. Has she heard anything from her family about her father yet?"

"Yeah, it's not good." Dan said. "They found a large tumour and had to remove part of his colon. It turned into a big surgery and it was hard on him. The news was hard on the family too. I know Anika wants to be there, but they all told her that she needs to be focusing her energy on getting Jonah back."

"It's okay, Dan. Go with her. I understand. There is still nothing you can do for me right now, anyway. I have my interview with NYPD this afternoon, and Shelley will be coming to Indio to visit on Friday. I will be okay until you get back."

"Are you sure? I feel guilty leaving you like this."

"Don't worry about me. I will be fine," she lied. She wasn't fine. She was still afraid to tell Dan that she was pregnant with his child. The thoughts swirling and the different parts of her identity continued to battle with each other inside her mind.

A nurturing, loving side of Fran that had emerged as a young girl in Manarola, when she was caring for her sister Giulia's twin sons, had re-emerged after discovering that she was pregnant, and after spending the last month living with Dan. And the long forgotten romantic side of her—the part that desperately craved being loved, that had emerged so long ago when she met Philippe —had also resurfaced since meeting Dan. But other parts of her— especially an overpowering part that desperately feared being abandoned, were pushing back against her desire to be loved and to feel close to Dan. The independent, businesslike side of Fran was determined that she could survive and raise her unborn child on her own. It was telling her that she didn't need a man to take care of her, and that she was better off on her own, like she when she was working for Susan Keaner as a young woman in Manarola.

And if her inner conflict wasn't bad enough, another side of Fran continued to persist, after the shooting death of Dan's wife, Michelle, and the drowning of her own husband, Philippe. Deep feelings of worthlessness and guilt continued to grip Fran. She couldn't stop feeling that Chelly's death was her fault, and that Dan would always hold her responsible for it. The feeling that she was unworthy of Dan's love continued to plague Fran, making it even more difficult to resolve the struggle between her desire for love, and her need to remain independent.

Feeling the tightening of the guard's grip on her arm, Fran wakened from her daydream. They were slowing and approaching the interview room. Joanna Sullivan, her lawyer, was waiting in the corridor and she nodded to Fran as she walked past her and into the room. Fran's guard finally broke the silence.

"We're here, Capellini. I'll take off the cuffs once we're in the room, but the manacles stay on. I'll be right behind you during the interview, in case you decide to act up. Understand?"

It was only then that Fran realized that she hadn't seen this particular guard before. She had red hair and the whitest skin that Fran had ever seen, much like Dan's wife Michelle. But unlike Chelly, who was short and solidly built, this new guard was tall and slim, with solid, well-toned muscles.

"Are you ready for this?" Joanna asked.

"I suppose so," Fran answered. "But I still don't understand why my photograph is so important to them."

"Don't worry about a thing," Joanna replied. "Just tell them exactly what you told me yesterday, and this will all be over in a matter of a few minutes. There's nothing you said that can justify them holding you without bail any longer. Just tell the truth and you'll be fine."

Joanna nodded to the guard, who opened the door and ushered them into the room.

"Hold it right there," the guard said. "Hold out your arms." The tall redhead moved in front of Fran and unlocked the cuffs.

Fran felt a sense of relief at not having the metal rings chafing at her skin. She raised her head and surveyed the room. In front of her was a table, with four chairs on the opposite side. There were also two chairs on the near side, presumably for herself and Joanna. On her far left, a tall, dark-haired man with touches of grey, wearing a black suit, stood imposingly. Standing in front of the two seats on the far right, Fran recognized the two female detectives, Julie Jameson and Beverly Dixon, who had interviewed her before and after Philippe and Chelly's deaths. Immediately in front of her stood District Attorney Kelly Mulholland, who stepped forward to make introductions.

"Ms. Capellini, Ms. Sullivan," Mulholland said, turning her body and gesturing towards the man in the black suit. "This is Detective Morosco from NYPD. He's come here today to ask a few questions regarding a missing person case he's been investigating." The District Attorney took a step to Fran's left, then turned her body to face the two female detectives. "I believe you already know Detectives Jameson and Dixon. They're here to determine if our discussions have any bearing on the current charges you are facing. Any questions, Ms. Sullivan?"

"Not yet, Ms. Mulholland," Joanna replied, feigning courtesy to her counterpart. In reality, Fran knew that Joanna was more than just a little irritated by the need for today's proceedings.

"Very well. Shall we get down to business?" Mulholland said, gesturing to the two chairs in front of Fran, and then moving around the table to the empty chair on the other side. Detectives Morosco, Jameson, and Dixon took their seats. Detective Morosco opened a leather folder and removed an 8 by 10 black and white photograph, which he placed on the table in front of Fran, clearing his voice as he did so.

"Ms. Capellini, this photograph is a frame from the CBS news broadcast from your home, taken on the afternoon of Thursday, March twenty-third, just a few hours after the deaths of your husband and Michelle Whitney. Do you recognize this photograph, hanging on the wall in the background?" he asked, pointing to a large black and white portrait of a blonde-haired woman.

"Yes. This is a candid portrait I took of a woman who was living on the streets of East Los Angeles," Fran answered.

"When you say *candid*, does this mean you took the picture without the subject's knowledge?" Morosco inquired.

"Not exactly," Fran replied. "It means I didn't ask her to pose. I was using a long lens to take pictures of people from a distance, in their natural setting—trying to capture them the way they are. If I ask them to pose, then I don't capture their natural essence. In this case, the woman saw me and tried to hide her face. I captured this shot when she looked up to see if I was still following her."

"I see," Morosco replied. "And when did you take this photo, Ms. Capellini?"

"I took it just over a year ago, sometime in March 2005. I was in Los Angeles with my husband, who was meeting with a client regarding some financial business. I never attended those kinds of meetings, so I often took my camera and I would spend the day taking candid photos of people in their natural environment. It's always been a way for me to relax."

"Did you find out the woman's name? Did you talk to her after you took the photo?" Morosco asked.

"No, sir. She ran away after I snapped the picture. She was very frightened—as though she was hiding and was afraid that somebody was going to find her. I don't know if you can see it, but look at her eyes. They are full of fear," Fran said, pointing to the woman's eyes.

"So you have no idea who the woman was?" Morosco asked. His words were becoming clipped, and Fran sensed that he was becoming impatient.

"No, sir," Fran replied. "I had never seen her before, and I never saw her again."

Fran heard Detective Jameson clear her voice. She turned towards the female officer, making eye contact with her.

"Did you try to talk with the woman when she bolted? Did you try to find out her name?" Jameson asked.

"I'm sorry, Detective. But the woman was sitting with her back to the wall in a small park. There is only one entrance into the park, and I was between her and the exit. She was so frightened that she ran right past me and ran across the street. Then she disappeared into the crowds on the street. I am sure she was hiding and didn't want to be found. I could see it in her eyes."

Fran heard Detective Morosco taking a deep breath, aware that he had another question. She turned her attention back to him.

"Have you ever hear the name Angela Baranyi?" Morosco asked.

"No, sir. Should I?" Fran asked.

Morosco pulled another 8 by 10 photo from his folder. This time it was a colour photo of a striking blonde-haired woman. Fran realized immediately that it was the same person as the street lady in her photo.

"We believe that the woman in your portrait is this woman, Angela Baranyi. She was originally from Cleveland, Ohio, but she was working for the *World-Wide Community of Christ*, an online evangelical church, in their New York office. She was working as a special assistant to this man, Pastor Soren Kristiansen, the founder and spiritual leader of the WWCC. Is this the same woman, and do you recognize Pastor Kristiansen?"

"Yes, sir. The woman in this photo certainly looks like the person in my portrait. But I have never seen Pastor Kristiansen before. In fact, I had never even heard of him until he came to visit Palm Springs a couple of months ago. I saw his name in the newspaper. I believe he was there on business—something about looking for real estate for his church."

"In that case, I'll fill in the blanks for you, Ms. Capellini. Maybe it will refresh your memory," Morosco said.

"I object," Joanna Sullivan interrupted. "My client has already told you that she's never seen Ms. Baranyi before, and she has only seen Pastor Kristiansen's name on one occasion. I fail to see what any of this has to do with the charges against my client."

District Attorney Mulholland jumped into the fray, clearly upset by Joanna's interruption. The muscles in her face were tight.

"Will you be patient," Mulholland snapped. "Let Detective Morosco finish. Give him a chance to show the connection!"

Joanna turned to Detective Morosco.

"Alright, Detective. Please continue, but get to the point," she said sternly.

"Okay," Morosco replied. "Ms. Baranyi disappeared suddenly from New York at the end of August, 2004. Her disappearance was suspicious, since she was a single mother with two young children in Cleveland who were living with Ms. Baranyi's parents. Her family didn't notice anything suspicious or alarming when they last talked with her. She disappeared without saying goodbye. The evidence indicates that she went out for dinner with Pastor Kristiansen to one of *the* chic restaurants in New York. They attracted the attention of the paparazzi, and this picture appeared in *The Enquirer* a few days later."

Morosco pulled yet another photo from his folder, showing Angela Baranyi, elegantly dressed in a sexy evening gown, posing together with Donald Trump in the restaurant.

"Then Ms. Baranyi disappeared. Her cell phone was left on and was tracked to Pastor Kristiansen's car a couple of days later. The forensic squad went through the car with a fine-tooth comb. They found mixed semen and vaginal fluids, and some of Ms. Baranyi's blood. But she was never found. Pastor Kristiansen admitted to having a sexual encounter with her in the car, but denied that anything else happened. He claimed he dropped her off at her apartment building and never saw her again. Although he remains a person of interest in her disappearance, we don't have enough evidence to press any charges against him. The allegations tainted his reputation briefly, but the public has a short memory. He appears to be as popular as ever," Morosco explained.

"I still don't understand," Joanna interrupted. "What has Ms. Baranyi's disappearance got to do with my client and her photo?"

"If your client is telling the truth, Ms. Sullivan, then she took that photo more than six months after Ms. Baranyi disappeared. It shows that she was still alive in March 2005, and it supports Pastor Kristiansen's story that he took her home and never saw her again."

"I *know* that!" Joanna snapped, turning her attention to District Attorney Mulholland. "So that also means that no crime has been committed, and it has no bearing on the charges against my client. So explain to me why my client should continue to be held without bail, like she's some kind of mass murderer!"

Fran saw Mulholland's face turn pink with embarrassment. She noticed Morosco glaring at Mulholland, as if he wanted to hear why she had dragged him all the way across the country for nothing.

"We didn't know that," Mulholland answered defensively. "We only heard that from Ms. Capellini today. And we still don't know why she disappeared. I'm sure that Pastor Kristiansen is interested in putting the rumours and innuendo about a possible murder to rest, and in restoring his good reputation."

"That's a big stretch, and you know it, Kelly!" Joanna said, wagging her finger accusingly at the District Attorney. "You and I both know the connection between my client and Ms. Baranyi's disappearance is tenuous, at best. And I'm sure that Pastor Kristiansen has other more important things in his life right now, given that he abducted his own child and is the focus of a national manhunt at this moment."

Fran saw Morosco's eyes growing wide. His eyebrows and forehead lifted in unison as he realized what was happening. He was obviously unaware of what had been happening in British Columbia and Washington State over the past five days—unaware that the good pastor was the subject of an Amber Alert, and was now on the run from authorities. Joanna continued her verbal barrage at District Attorney Mulholland.

"There's something else going on here, Kelly, and I intend to find out what it is. When I do, I guarantee that it's going to make you look like a fool."

Fran saw Detectives Jameson and Dixon look at each other and roll their eyes in unison. They looked at Fran, shaking their heads sadly from side to side. Fran connected with each of the women's eyes, sensing compassion and empathy for her plight from both of them. She got the distinct feeling that they were not onside with District Attorney Mulholland and how she was handling her case.

Joanna turned to Detective Morosco and began speaking to him.

"If you don't have any further questions, Detective, then my client and I are finished here." She turned her head back to the District Attorney again, as she gathered up her papers and began rising to her feet.

"Drop the charges and stop this farce, Kelly. You and I both know you don't have a case. I don't know what else is going on, but drop it. If this goes to trial, you're just going to embarrass yourself!" Joanna warned sternly. "Come on, Francesca. We're finished for today." She took Fran by the arm, helping her manacled client out of her chair and to her feet. Joanna guided her towards the exit, where they were met by the imposing figure of the redheaded guard.

"Let's see your arms, dear," the guard said. She locked the metal rings to Fran's wrists, and then took over control of her arm from Joanna. She opened the door and the trio of women moved into the hallway. As the door closed behind them, Joanna turned to Fran. She felt the warmth of the older woman's hand squeezing hers. Without saying a word, Joanna was conveying her human side—her understanding and compassion for Fran's plight.

"I'll be talking to Mulholland before we meet on Wednesday. She knows damned well that your case will meet the Dyas Standard for proving Battered Woman Syndrome, and we won't have any problem finding expert witnesses that will testify on your behalf. So far, she hasn't provided a stitch of evidence to prove otherwise. All of this bullshit about your portrait of the Baranyi woman is just one big distraction. I'll try one more time to convince her to drop the charges before the arraignment reconvenes next Friday," Joanna promised. "Until then, be sure to phone me if there's anything else you need."

"Thank you, Joanna. I know you're doing everything you can for me. I will be fine," Fran answered, not fully believing the words she was saying. The guard grasped Fran's elbow and started guiding her back down the corridor towards her cell. Fran looked back over her shoulder to see Joanna giving her a small wave, and nodding to affirm her commitment to her.

Fran's thoughts began drifting again as she lost sight of Joanna. She was confused. Like Joanna, she didn't understand why her portrait and the link to the Baranyi woman were so important. Her head filled with unanswered questions.

Who was causing the woman to be so afraid that she left her life and her children behind to live on the streets? And Anika's husband was the last person to see her? Is that just a coincidence? Is that who Angela was so afraid of, and are Anika and Dan in danger too?

Fran's nurturing, loving, and romantic sides were starting to surface. Her feelings of empathy and compassion for Anika and Jonah were bringing her close to tears. And she could also feel her feelings for Dan growing stronger—she felt her need to be with him again, to feel him making love to her. But just as quickly, she started feeling afraid. Afraid for Dan's safety, afraid of getting too close to him. She was desperately afraid to feel the sadness and loneliness of ever losing him. She was afraid to tell him about their unborn child, in case he walked away from her. And in addition to fear, she felt guilt rising in her stomach, making her feel nauseous —guilt over her role in Chelly's death, and for taking her from Dan. The swirling mixture of emotions was almost overwhelming her. Then gradually, through her confusion, she felt the independent, businesslike part of her identity coming to her defense, slowly rising above her confusion and gradually taking charge. It was the part of Fran she had always relied upon to survive. Now it was telling her that she could take care of herself again—that she didn't need Dan to take care of her, or to help her raise their child. It was telling her that it was better for her if she pushed him away now.

Fran sensed that her independent side was the only part of her that was keeping the rest of her identity glued together, however fragile that adhesive might be. She replayed the logic of her businesslike, independent side, over and over again, until she felt like she was starting to believe it.

It doesn't matter if Dan stays with Anika. They were meant to be together long before he met me. I can do it on my own, just as I did when I worked for Susan in Manarola. If I did it then, I can do it now. I'll tell him when he returns from Atlanta. Better now than later, before his feelings for me get any stronger, and before he grows too close to our child.

THE GENTLE electronic chime signalled that the pilot had just turned off the *Seatbelt* sign over the passengers' seats. Dan loosened his lap belt, still keeping it buckled in case of sudden turbulence.

He let out a long breath, finally able to relax. Once he had talked to Fran and received her okay to join Anika, he booked a standby ticket, packed a small carry-on bag, and jumped into Fran's Prius, praying that the freeways between Palm Springs and LAX weren't clogged. Even without traffic jams, making it onto Anika's flight had been tight. He'd run through the terminal, fidgeting anxiously as the security line-up seemed to creep more and more slowly, the nearer he got to the TSA security check. He finally reached the departure lounge just as the plane was boarding.

Now that they had reached cruising altitude, there was nothing left to do but relax. He had passed Anika on his way toward the rear of the plane, getting only a brief chance to say hello before he moved to the rear of the aircraft and squeezed past two other passengers into his cramped window seat. A male flight attendant, who had been walking up the aisle, stopped beside his row. Another passenger, a slim young woman, came trailing up behind the attendant.

"Dr. Whitney?" the flight attendant asked. Dan nodded in acknowledgement. "This lady is from 14B, beside your wife. She's willing to change seats so you two can sit together."

Dan smiled. Anika must have asked the attendants if they could move 'her husband' so they could sit together.

"That's very kind of you," Dan said, speaking to both the flight attendant and the young woman at the same time. The two passengers beside Dan got out of their seats and moved grudgingly into the already crowded aisle, allowing Dan to extricate himself from his cramped quarters, and allowing the slim young woman to take his former seat. Dan smiled at the two passenger, and then at the young woman as she passed in front of him.

"Thank you, ma'am," he said. "I really appreciate this."

"No worries," the woman said, with a delightfully sweet Aussie lilt to her voice. "I'm by myself, so it doesn't matter where I sit. I know you'd like to sit with your wife."

The other two passengers gratefully climbed back into their seats beside the young woman, making room for Dan to walk down the aisle towards the front of the cabin. He tapped Anika, who was seated in the aisle seat, on her shoulder. She unbuckled her seatbelt and leapt to her feet, throwing her arms around Dan's torso in an emotional embrace. Dan saw a look of relief and tears of joy in her eyes.

"I'm so glad you're here!" she whispered into Dan's ear. "Thank you so much for coming."

"I'm glad to be here," he answered. "You know I'll always do what I can to help you."

Anika released her grip and allowed him to slide into the middle seat. His seatbelt fastened once again, he raised the armrest between them and turned to Anika.

"How's your dad doing?"

"Thanks for asking. Trudy says he's recovering, and he took the news well. They're going to be doing some radiation and chemotherapy as soon as he's recovered and is strong enough. The good news is that they didn't think it spread to any nearby organs, especially his liver," Anika said.

Dan reached over and held her hand in his, feeling its warmth and feeling her relax at the same time.

"I'm glad to hear that," he said. "That must be a big relief."

"That's for sure," Anika replied. But I still feel so guilty, Dan —I feel guilty about *everything*! I feel guilty about not being there with Dad, even though everybody still insists that I stay focused on finding Jonah. And I feel so guilty about letting Jonah down. I should have suspected Soren would do something like this. I should have warned the school to call me if Soren did something unusual. I should have known he was capable of doing this!"

Tears welled up in Anika's eyes. She leaned on Dan's shoulder, trying to hide her sobs from other passengers.

"Shhhhhh…," Dan whispered softly. "You guys hadn't talked about separation or divorce. And he never threatened to take Jonah, did he?"

"No," Anika whimpered softly. "He always denounced separation and divorce. He preached that it went against family values and God's plan for husbands and wives."

"So, you had no reason to suspect he'd do anything like this, even if your marriage wasn't going well. Right?" Dan reasoned.

"I suppose," Anika whispered, sniffling back some tears.

"Okay, then," Dan said. "Stop beating up on yourself. You're not to blame here—Soren is. So start putting the responsibility for all of this where it belongs—squarely on Soren's shoulders."

Dan wrapped his arm around Anika and gave a firm squeeze of reassurance.

"So, let's get focused on finding Jonah. What's the story? Soren tried to take him to Ecuador?"

Anika sat up, sniffled, and then blew her nose into a tissue. She took a breath to gather her composure.

"This is all I know so far," she began. "Detective Hayward called me early last night to say that the authorities in Ecuador contacted Interpol when the plane landed in Quito. Apparently, Soren tried to enter the country with the same fake ID that he used at Port Angeles. Fortunately, the passport numbers and the Amber Alert were already on record with Interpol, so they were going to set off alarms in any country. I can't believe Soren didn't know that."

"Well, lucky thing he didn't," Dan said.

"Detective Hayward gave me the number for the FBI in Atlanta," Anika replied. "They're sending somebody to meet me once we're through U.S. Customs."

"Will they be sending Soren and Jonah back on the next plane?" Dan asked.

"I don't know yet," Anika answered. "We won't know anything more until we land and the FBI brings us up to date."

"Did you talk to a lawyer about the custody issues? Even if they fly Soren back to the States, he's still outside of Canada," Dan said.

"Yes," Anika said. Dan saw her take a deep breath and exhale slowly. "I've retained that lawyer in Vancouver—Rashad Ramsay. He specializes in International Child Abduction. I've only had a chance to talk with him on the phone, so he only has the bare bones of my situation."

"So, what did he have to say?" Dan asked.

"Well, the good news is that if they bring Soren back to Atlanta, the U.S. has signed the Hague Convention. It's the international treaty about child abduction. All signing countries agree to abide by the Family Law of the jurisdiction where the child and custodial parents live. So, for me and Jonah, that means the British Columbia Family Law Act."

"And the bad news?" Dan asked.

"Because Soren and I weren't separated or divorced, there aren't any court-ordered custody documents to enforce. Soren and I have equal custodial rights to Jonah."

"Ouch," Dan answered. "So Soren has just as much right as you to take Jonah anywhere he wants?"

"Absolutely not," Anika blurted. "It means that one parent can't take a child away from the other parent without their permission. In B.C., Soren would have to give me sixty days' notice before he could legally take Jonah anywhere. I would have to do the same for him. But because he took Jonah without my consent, I can apply for a court order for custody. If the order is granted, I can apply through the Hague Convention Central Authority in the States to have Jonah returned to B.C."

"It doesn't sound like a simple process," Dan remarked. "So what did Mr. Ramsay advise you to do right now?"

"I've already contacted the RCMP and the lawyer for the Ministry of Justice, who is the Hague Convention Central Authority in B.C., to advise them that Jonah has been abducted and taken outside Canada. Rashad is preparing an application for a court order right now, and he'll be applying to have it heard in court as soon as possible. I may have to talk to the judge via teleconference on a moment's notice."

"So if Soren brings Jonah back to the States, it shouldn't be too difficult getting Jonah back to Victoria," Dan surmised.

"Maybe,… maybe not," Anika said. Dan saw her eyes getting red and beginning to well up with tears.

"What's wrong?" Dan asked.

Anika burst into tears and buried her head in Dan's shoulders, trying to hide her crying from nearby passengers. After a moment of sobbing, she lifted her head and looked into Dan's eyes.

"Oh, Dan. I'm so stupid and naive," she sniffled. "I hardly know anything about Soren's past! He's told me about his days in the seminary, and about his first church in Dallas. But he never said anything about his family, except to say that he's from

Minnesota—that he was an only child, and both his parents are dead. Any time I tried to ask more questions, he just got irritated or angry. He said he's happy now with his church and his family, and that's all that's important."

"So he's probably an American citizen," Dan said. "Does that make a difference?"

Anika's eyes remained red. She sniffled and looked into Dan's eyes and shrugged.

"It shouldn't, if both the States and Ecuador are Hague Convention signees. But even if Ecuador sends him back to the States, Soren could use his U.S. Citizenship and the U.S. legal system to slow the whole process down for a long time. I might have to hire a lawyer in the States to keep the process moving along. It could end up costing me a small fortune."

"Wow, I had no idea that child abduction had so many legal complications. So, what do we do now?" Dan asked.

"We hope and pray that Ecuador put him on the next plane home, and that Soren is taken into custody until I can get my court order," Anika said. "I'm supposed to meet the FBI once we're through U.S. Customs, so they can update me on what's been happening in Quito. After that…"

Anika shrugged her shoulders, then clutched Dan's arm. Dan saw both fear and desperate hope behind the redness and tears in her eyes. He wrapped his arm around her, bringing her against his chest and into the safety of his arms. Anika curled up like a small girl and wept until her breathing slowed and she had finally cried herself to sleep.

THE LAYOVER at Dallas-Fort Worth International Airport had been uneventful. Soren had purchased the tickets for the Atlanta-Dallas leg of their journey separately to make their trail more difficult to follow. He made sure that Lucy understood that they needed to claim their baggage, and then check herself and Jonah in with American Airlines for the next leg of their flight. He had purposely avoided using American Airlines in Atlanta, the same airline on which he had sent the Smiths on their wild goose chase to Ecuador. Since nobody suspected that he and Jonah were in Dallas, Soren felt safe. He followed well behind Lucy and Jonas, who were nearing the front of the long, winding line-up.

Soren allowed himself to smile at how smoothly everything had gone, so far. But only for a few seconds. This was no time to get overconfident. He saw Jonah turn around a couple of times, trying to find a glimpse of him, despite Lucy chastising him and warning him not to do it. Fortunately, Lucy managed to distract the young boy and keep him calm.

That girl's good. I may have to think about keeping her around longer than I'd planned. Who would have guessed that a hooker and porn star would be so good with kids?

Soren felt the stirring in his loins again, temporarily distracted as he remembered her role in the porn film where he'd first seen her. Just as abruptly he brought his mind back into the moment, watching her take Jonah's hand as they took their turn at the check-in counter.

Don't be stupid, Soren! Don't start mixing business and pleasure. There's plenty more like her where she came from. You can't afford to be seen anywhere with her and the boy. Helen would be furious if you screwed up now.

Finally at the front of the line, an agent wrapped baggage tags through the handles of Jonah and Lucy's luggage. Lucy dumped the two bags on the conveyor and they disappeared from sight. Lucy took Jonah by the hand and led him away towards the security line-ups.

Soren realized he was holding his breath again. He let it out slowly and focused on getting his breathing back to normal. He removed his hat and wiped the sweat from his forehead, once again allowing the security cameras to see his red hair, but looking down to prevent the cameras from getting a good view of his face.

Finally, it was Soren's turn. He stepped forward to the desk, hoisting his luggage onto the scale.

"Destination, sir?" a young man in an American Airlines uniform asked.

"Brisbane," Soren answered, handing the agent his passport and e-ticket.

"Do you have your Australian visa?" the agent asked.

"Yes, it's there in the passport," Soren answered. He watched the agent check the visa carefully. He knew the visa was good. Helen had done an excellent job in obtaining their new fake identities. With her highly placed connections, the quality of his passport was unsurpassed, and he knew she could get visas from any U.S. ally within a day. There had been no problems with the visas for Jonah and Lucy, so Soren felt confident.

"One bag?" the agent asked rhetorically, as he glanced at the weight that was displayed on the scale's digital readout. Soren nodded in acknowledgement, keeping his head low and his face obscured from security cameras.

"There you go," the young man said, smiling. He handed Soren his passport, visa, and boarding pass. "Enjoy your flight, sir."

Soren watched as his baggage slid onto the conveyor, and gradually disappeared from sight.

"Thank *you*," Soren said to himself. He felt a lightness in his step as he headed in the direction of the security line-up. Only one final hurdle with the TSA security line-up, then he'd be in the air over the Pacific, safe for the time being.

A few more hours, then I can lie low in Australia for a while until the search dies down. After that, I can take Jonah somewhere secluded, but civilized, so I can grow my businesses and stay out of sight. Somewhere Anika will never suspect, and will never think to look for Jonah or me!

CHAPTER 13

IT WAS early evening, Eastern Time, when the flight from Los Angeles hit the tarmac in Atlanta. Dan watched Anika gather her belongings, then fidget nervously as the plane made its way towards the terminal.

As soon as the plane stopped, she jumped to her feet, throwing open the overhead bin and dragging her overnight bag down before any other passengers were out of their seats.

Dan knew how badly she needed to make contact with the FBI, to find out if Jonah was back on American soil. But they were at the mercy of the crowd of people in front of them on the aircraft. He watched as Anika flipped open her cell phone, looking anxiously for any messages. There were none. He felt her helplessness as she stood impatiently, waiting for the crew to open the doors, and for the passengers to slowly file out of the plane. But he also shared her sense of hope—hope that Jonah was safe and that she would be able to see her son shortly, even if it took some time to return him to Canada.

"You go ahead," Dan said. "I'll have to wait until everybody's off the plane before I can go back and get my bag. I'll meet you at the top of the ramp."

Ten minutes later, he found Anika waiting impatiently, waving her arms at him. Another woman, wearing an airport security badge, stood beside her.

"Hurry up, Dan!" she shouted. "This lady's going to take us right to Airport Security."

The woman directed them to a staircase that descended to the tarmac. When they exited the terminal, a white SUV with a flashing yellow light on top waited for them. They threw their bags in the rear hatch of the SUV, and then jumped in the back seat.

"I'll be driving you directly around to the North Terminal," the woman said. "The FBI are waiting for you, and will bring you up to date."

He reached for Anika's hand, feeling her tension. Her jaw was clenched tight, her eyes looking straight ahead, focused only on reaching their destination as quickly as possible.

It took less than five minutes for them to reach the North Terminal. They jumped out of SUV and grabbed their carry-on bags. Their guide inserted her security card in a slot, opening a door that allowed them to enter the terminal.

"Follow me," she said, leading Anika and Dan to an elevator. The door closed and Dan felt the elevator start moving upward. When they reached the third level, the elevator opened and the woman led them down a corridor until they came to a door labelled *Airport Security Division*. As they entered, a tall African-American man in a dark suit rose to his feet and walked towards them.

"Agent Garrett Robinson, FBI," the man said. "Ms. Kristiansen?"

"Agent Robinson," Anika resounded. "Please call me Anika. This is my good friend, Dr. Dan Whitney. He's been helping me since Jonah disappeared."

Dan reached out with his hand, feeling the man's strong, confident grip as the two men shook hands.

"This way please," Robinson said, showing them towards an office with an open door. "Airport security is letting us use their office for this operation."

Dan and Anika followed him into the office, where Agent Robinson pointed to a seating area with a couch and two chairs.

"Is he here?" Anika blurted. "Have they sent my son back from Ecuador yet?" Anika's eyes were riveted on the tall dark man as he took his seat in one of the vacant chairs. Robinson paused.

Dan sensed that the man was searching for words. An ominous feeling grew in Dan's gut.

"Ms. Kristiansen… Anika… There's been some confusion regarding your son… "

"Confusion!" Anika shouted. "What kind of confusion? Where is he? Here? Ecuador?"

Dan reached for Anika's hand, trying to help calm her.

"Please, let me explain," Robinson said. "This may be difficult to understand."

Anika glanced quickly at Dan, and he saw panic in her eyes. He put his arm around her shoulders, pulling her closer to him as he sensed bad news coming.

"Three people answering the descriptions of your husband, your son, and the woman who crossed into Washington with them, boarded a flight from this airport to Quito late yesterday afternoon. They were using the same passports that were scanned in Port Angeles, Washington, when your husband got off the ferry from Canada. There was confusion when they landed in Quito. They claimed to be a family of three, last name Smith from Atlanta, who were winners of a contest sponsored by your husband's church. They came up with a crazy story about being chosen at the last minute, when the original contest winners had to pull out. Both Mr. and Mrs. Smith told a similar story about a woman with blonde hair, apparently an American Airlines PR rep, who did all of their check-in paperwork for them. It seems like she managed to swap the passports your husband used in Washington, for the Smiths' passports. They didn't even notice until they got off the plane in Quito. They seem to be genuinely shocked by what happened. Representatives from your husband's church in Ecuador knew nothing about an alleged contest. From what we've gathered so far, your husband must have a female accomplice who is very skilled and knowledgeable about airport security. Do you have any idea who that could be?"

Anika, stunned with disbelief, couldn't find any words. Dan felt her gasp for air. Her entire body started to shake. Dan spoke up for her.

"So where are these three people—the Smiths—right now?" Dan asked.

"Still in Quito," Robinson said. "It's going to take a couple of days until we verify their identities and get new passports for them… "

"Where's my husband… and my son!" Anika screamed.

Robinson glanced at Dan, and then he gathered himself to face Anika.

"We don't know, ma'am," he said. "But there's been another unexpected development. A woman who answers the description of the woman who rented the mini-van used in your son's abduction, using the name Elizabeth Andersson, was found strangled in a motel in Little Rock, Arkansas yesterday afternoon. We have to wait for forensics, but we suspect that your husband and son may have been staying there as well."

Dan saw Anika's eyes go wide and fill with fear.

"You think Soren did it?" Anika asked, her eyes now riveted on the FBI agent.

"We don't know yet, Ms. Kristiansen. We can't rule it out and we don't have any other potential suspects at this time."

"So what do we do now?" Dan asked. "If they were heading in this direction, do you think Soren and Jonah could have flown somewhere else from Atlanta?"

"It's a distinct possibility," Robinson said. "We're thinking it may have been an elaborate diversion."

"If that's the case, time is working against us," Dan reasoned. "Can we help in any way? Have you looked through the security videos?"

"We have," Robinson said. "But we don't really know what we're looking for. If she can, we'd like Anika to have a close look. We'll only have to look at the images from the few cameras in the security area, since all passengers are funnelled through there." He looked at Anika for her response.

Without hesitation, Anika answered.

"What are we waiting for? Time's wasting."

"That's what we thought. We have everything set up in the control centre," Robinson said. "Follow me."

"I DON'T understand!" Anika cried. Her frustration had finally boiled over. Her eyes were shiny and glazed, and tears once again gathered in her eyes.

"We've been through these clips three times between last night and this morning. We've looked at every possible clip with a young child! Why can't we see them?" she sobbed.

Dan took her in his arms, trying to console her.

"Soren's already shown that he's got at least one accomplice. If he can lay his hands on fake passports that easily, he's probably also getting help with disguising their identities. We could be staring right at them, but we don't know what we're looking for. Remember how I told you that Soren is like a chameleon?" Dan asked.

"Yes, but you were talking about his personality, weren't you?" Anika asked.

"I was," Dan answered. "But I'm starting to think it may be true about his physical appearance too. And somehow, he's probably finding ways to disguise Jonah as well."

"We looked at so many children, Dan. And so many of them looked the same. Why can't I even recognize my own son?"

Anika continued sobbing in complete despair.

"We don't even know if they were at the airport, Anika. If it was an elaborate diversion, and I'm beginning to think it was, Soren could have gone anywhere. There are any number of airports within a few hours of Atlanta. He could be anywhere by now," Dan said.

"He's right, Ms. Kristiansen. He hasn't used any credit or debit cards. If the motel in Little Rock is any indication, he's using cash. He's not leaving a trail we can follow. He had this planned extremely well before he even took your son."

"Is that supposed to make me feel better?" Anika shouted, her frustration finally getting the best of her. "I'm the stupid wife who didn't even notice that her husband was planning on kidnapping her son! Some mother I turned out to be. I don't even know my own husband, and I can't keep my own son safe!"

Dan turned to Agent Robinson.

"Can you give us a few minutes?"

Robinson nodded, leaving Dan and Anika alone in the office.

"You've got to stop second-guessing yourself, Anika," Dan urged. "That's exactly what Soren wants. He wants you to think you're not worthy of being Jonah's parent. He's counting on you giving up eventually, because you don't feel you deserve to find him. But if you give up, he wins. Is that what you want?"

Anika's sobbing continued. Gradually it became more subdued. Finally, she gathered herself, sniffling one last time. She took a deep breath and looked into Dan's eyes.

"What do we do now?" she asked.

"Well, I suppose we ask Agent Robinson if there's anything else we can do here in Atlanta to help the FBI. If there isn't, I guess we go back home to wait for news," he answered.

"I don't know if I can do that again," Anika said. "After I got back to Victoria from Seattle, I couldn't stand the emptiness in the house. I saw traces of Jonah everywhere. I couldn't focus or concentrate on what I was doing. I can't go back to work. It's not fair to my patients, or to my staff. I have Dr. Patel as a locum. She's willing to stay on for a while if necessary. I think I just need to get away for a while."

Dan paused, taking a long sip from his cup of coffee.

"I have an idea," Dan said. "Why don't you come back to Palm Springs for a while with me? You can meet Fran, Tim, and Shelley, and just relax in the sun for a while."

"Are you crazy? Me? Stay at that nudist resort?" Anika said. Her face turned red, breaking into an embarrassed smile. "You know I couldn't do that!"

"I know," Dan said. "But you don't have to go nude. The dress code is *Clothing Optional*—you wear as little or as much as you feel comfortable wearing. You just have to get used to seeing the guests without their clothes. It's the most relaxing place in the world—I promise! What do you say?"

Anika's face was still crimson. Dan couldn't tell if she was upset with him, or just embarrassed by his suggestion.

"I don't know," Anika said. "What would everybody else say— my family and the church members?"

"What could be worse than what they're saying already?" Dan asked. "Besides, you don't have to tell them anything about where you're staying. It's none of their business. You're just on a holiday, getting some sun and relaxation."

Anika's eyes were cautious as they met Dan's. Her face was still red. She managed a tentative smile.

"I'm not sure how I feel about seeing you naked. All these years and we've never done that, have we?"

This time, it was Dan's face that turned red.

"No, we haven't. If it embarrasses you, I'll wear clothes— unless I'm in the pool or the spa Come on, it will do you good to get away. You said so yourself."

Anika hesitated. Dan hoped she would say yes. He knew she'd like Fran and his new friends in Palm Springs. Secretly, he knew she'd probably enjoy the clothing optional atmosphere of the hotel, if she just gave herself a chance.

"Okay, I'll try it," Anika said. "But you have to promise not to tell a soul!"

Dan tried to hide his delight. He held up his right hand in true Boy Scout fashion.

"I promise," he said. He was glad that his long-time friend wouldn't be alone, and would have a chance to meet his new friends.

Anika's smile disappeared, once again replaced by worry.

"Let's get Agent Robinson in here and find out if he needs us to stick around in Atlanta," she said.

Dan caught Robinson's eye through the office's window, indicating that he should rejoin them.

"Everything okay in here?" Robinson asked.

"I'm fine," Anika answered. "Is there anything more I can do here in Atlanta to help?"

"I'm afraid not, Ms. Kristiansen. Until we have something more concrete about your son's whereabouts, you might as well go home. Did you give me a phone number in Victoria where I can reach you?"

"You have my cell phone number. I may be going back to California with Dan to relax for a few days, but I'll keep my phone on twenty-four-seven," Anika replied.

"That's a good idea," Robinson said. "We need to be able to reach you at all times."

Dan saw Anika swallow and then acknowledge Robinson with a nod. Then she turned to face Dan again.

"Then I guess we might as well get back to the hotel and book some flights to Palm Springs," she said.

"To L.A.," Dan said, correcting her. "I had to drive Fran's car and park it at LAX in order to make our flight to Atlanta. So we won't have to take the commuter flight to Palm Springs."

He turned to Agent Robinson and extended his hand.

"I want to thank you for everything you've done for us while we've been here," he said. As the handshake ended, Anika stepped forward and shook the agent's hand.

"Me too," Anika said. "Thank you for all of your efforts."

Agent Robinson held Anika's hand as he began to respond.

"I'm sorry things didn't turn out this time," he answered, his face smiling and full of warmth and compassion. "But we'll find him if he's anywhere in this country. And if he's not, we'll be working with Interpol to track him down, wherever he tries to go. You just keep that cell phone charged. Hopefully, we'll be talking with you again real soon."

Anika turned to Dan. She couldn't hide the disappointment and worry in her face.

"Let's call a cab and get back to the hotel, Dan. I'm exhausted. We can still catch a late flight to L.A., is that okay?"

"Absolutely," Dan replied. "No sense sticking around in Atlanta if we don't need to. We can catch some sleep on the plane. The last twenty-four hours have been a blur. The sooner we get back to Palm Springs, the sooner both of us can wind down and relax."

THE FLIGHT from Hartsfield-Jackson airport in Atlanta to LAX was still ascending towards cruising altitude. The flight crew had already dimmed the cabin lights, and many of the passengers had turned off their reading lights and closed their eyes, hoping to get some sleep.

"Let's not talk about Soren or Jonah anymore tonight," Anika said. "It just makes me feel angry, and I don't have the energy for that right now. Tell me more about Fran," she said, changing the subject.

"What do you want to know?" Dan asked.

"What's she like? Do you love her? Do you think she loves you?"

"Whoa, one at a time," Dan said, chuckling. "Is this an inquisition?"

"You could say that," Anika said, allowing herself a slight smile. "I'm just watching out for my friend. You've been burned once, so I don't want to see you burned again, that's all. So c'mon, talk to me. What do you see in her?"

Dan paused, staring out the window at the flashing navigation lights on the aircraft's wing. He turned his head back to face Anika.

"Well, I see somebody who is afraid to let herself love anybody. But I also see another part that's capable of loving—that desperately wants to be loved. She's terrified to let that part out," Dan explained.

"So, in other words, she's damaged goods," Anika answered. "You're a psychologist. Isn't that a bad sign for any relationship?"

"It can be," Dan answered. "Especially if I wasn't aware of it, or if my expectations for her weren't reasonable. But she's never had anybody who showed her any love, Anika. There's never been anybody she could trust to love her. I think she deserves a chance, don't you?"

"Not even anybody in her family?" Anika asked.

"Especially her family," Dan answered. "Her dad was a drunk who was never around, and her mom and older sister mostly ignored her, except for using her for babysitting. And then there was some serious sexual and physical abuse from her sister's husband."

"That's awful!" Anika said. "No wonder the poor woman wanted to leave Italy. Too bad she ended up with a psychopath like her husband. What was his name again?"

"Philippe," Dan said. "It was a classic case of a narcissist preying on somebody who was needy."

Anika remained silent, gazing pensively at Dan.

"Do you love her?"

Dan paused and closed his eyes so he could think. He took a long, slow breath then opened his eyes and his eyes met Anika's again.

"That's hard to answer," Dan said. "We share a lot of interests—swimming and photography—and we've shared a life-changing event together. I know there's a lot of danger in being close, just because of what we survived. But she saved my life, Anika. I owe her the chance for us to get to know if we really love each other. And in the end, if we don't, I hope she at least learns to trust the next guy who really does love her."

"Do you think she loves you?" Anika asked.

"Another hard question," Dan answered. "Like I said before, on one hand I think she really longs to be in love. But on the other, I think she's terrified. She's torn. But I think there's something else."

"Something else?" Anika said. "What do you mean?"

"I can't put it into words—it's just a gut feeling—there's something else bothering her, but she's holding it back from me."

"But you have no idea what it could be?" Anika said.

Dan shook his head and shrugged.

"So, that wild card aside, which part of Fran do you think will win out in the end?" Anika said.

"That's the million-dollar question, isn't it?" Dan replied. "But, I'm willing to give her a chance. I mean, what am I going to do with my life after we find Jonah? I'm a widower now. My family, Chelly's family and even our friends won't talk to me. I'm not ready to go back to work in Detroit yet. I think I feel just as helpless as you feel about finding Jonah. Fran's sitting in a cell in Indio right now, and there's nothing I can do to help her."

"I think I understand that," Anika answered. "But there's one thing I still don't understand. How could you let yourself get caught up in all of that kinky S and M stuff? That's not the Dan I know. What were you thinking?"

"I don't expect you to understand, Anika. And by the way, they call it BDSM now—not S and M. I'm not sure I understand one hundred percent how it happened myself. I know that Chelly had more sexual fantasies than she ever admitted to me—maybe even to herself. And I know that Philippe was a predator who hunted for people like her to fulfill his own perverted sadistic fantasies. Most of all, I know that Philippe was incredibly clever. He managed to get Chelly on his side. Together, they used my own logic to trap me into joining them. And at the time, I was willing to do anything to keep Chelly. I admit it," he said.

"Okay, I think I get that. But you're still doing it with Fran, aren't you? Didn't you learn your lesson? Or has Fran got you so wrapped around her finger that you're thinking with the wrong head right now?" Anika asked.

Dan laughed at Anika's play on words. He paused and sighed.

"I won't deny there's a powerful sexual attraction between us," he said. "It was there almost from the moment we met. And I have to admit that I've learned to enjoy some of the things she's taught me. We certainly don't carry it to the extremes that Philippe wanted us to do. But I can assure you that it heightens the senses and makes sex more intense."

"So you admit it," she said under her breath. "You're just like Soren and every other man. All you care about is making sure you get laid!"

"Shhh…," Dan whispered. "Do you want to wake up everybody on the plane? And that's not fair—comparing me with Soren. I would never treat you or any other woman that way, and you know it!"

Dan saw Anika's anger begin to dissolve. Tears were forming in her eyes. Her hands reached for his arm and pulled him closer to her.

"I'm sorry, Dan," she said softly. "I shouldn't have said that. I know you'd never treat Fran or me the way that Soren or Philippe would. I guess I'm just jaded and raw right now. Forgive me?"

Dan put his arm around her and drew her closer to him. He felt confused again as he gazed into Anika's teary eyes. He was trying so hard to commit to his new relationship with Fran. Yet, there in front of him he saw those big blue eyes that he'd loved so much in the past. He felt the sadness that he saw in them. He felt himself being drawn back towards Anika, both emotionally and physically.

At that moment, he just wanted to hold her as close as he possibly could. He placed his lips gently on hers.

He felt Anika hesitate. Then, for a moment, he felt her give in. Her lips relaxed and responded to the gentle, tentative touch of his kiss. He felt her body melt into his own for a few seconds. Then, suddenly, she stiffened and pulled away from him. He stared into her eyes, seeing fear and confusion in them.

"I'm sorry," Dan whispered. "I didn't mean for that to happen."

"Me neither," Anika replied softly. "I'm still technically married, remember? And I don't want to get in between you and Fran. Do you understand?"

"Yes, I think so," Dan answered. He felt confused emotionally, since the stiffness in his pants still wanted to be as close as he could get with her.

"Still friends?" Anika asked, gazing into Dan's eyes.

"Still friends," he answered, glad that he hadn't scared her away. The last thing he wanted to do was lose her as a friend.

"Let's try to get some sleep," he suggested. "It's going to feel like the middle of the night when we reach L.A."

Anika raised the armrest between them and nestled into Dan, resting her head on his shoulder. At that moment, Dan realized how much they needed each other's support and friendship at this point in their both of their lives. He felt grateful that she had sought him out and put her trust in him after all these years. He still felt confused between his growing love for Fran and his love for his old friend. But for now, Dan was relieved to have Anika beside him, holding her close and feeling the warmth of her body against his.

CHAPTER 14

FRAN FELT a gigantic knot in her gut as she looked through the glass at Dan. There were so many things she needed to tell him. She knew she needed to unburden herself. Her hand clenched the telephone receiver as she held it to her mouth and ear. She tried to swallow, but her throat felt so dry it was like trying to eat sand. Finally, she found the strength to speak.

"Thank you for coming," she said. "You have no idea how lonely it is being in that cell. I think it's starting to get to me."

"I thought you had a new cellmate," Dan said. "Is she not there anymore?"

"No, she was only there for a few hours. I think Joanna may have been right. She thought the D.A. might have planted her there to prise information from me. Anyway, she wasn't very good company. Her tone became threatening when I couldn't answer all of her questions. I'm glad she didn't stay long."

"Have Shelley or Tim been to visit you this week?" Dan asked.

"No, they are going to be coming up Monday. They're having a big rally in Orange County on Sunday for Tim and Richard's charity. You remember? The one about sexual abuse in the military."

Dan thought for a moment, then a hint of recognition lit up his face.

"Isn't that how Tim met Shelley? When Pam invited her to speak at one of their rallies?"

Fran nodded. "You've got a good memory."

Dan became quiet and distant. Fran realized that he was remembering the weekend that he and Chelly had spent at Chateau Eden, before the nightmare in Palm Desert.

"So, tell me," Fran said, changing the subject. "How did it go in Atlanta? Did Anika get Jonah back yet?"

"Things didn't go well, I'm afraid," Dan admitted. "It looks like Soren created an elaborate diversion at the airport, then he disappeared with Jonah. And it looks like he may have strangled the woman who helped him kidnap Jonah from Victoria. The people at Quito airport—the ones the FBI thought were Soren, Jonah, and the other woman—were just unsuspecting pawns in a big ruse. It wasn't really Jonah who was in Quito."

"What about Anika?" Fran asked. "How is she doing?"

"She's a mess," Dan continued. "She doesn't know what to do next, so I convinced her to spend a few days in Palm Springs to relax. She doesn't have much support back in Victoria, and her father just had surgery. She's probably going to fly to Calgary to visit him after she leaves here. I gave her the Italian room at the Chateau for the time being, and I'm sleeping wherever there's room. I was really hoping she could meet you."

Fran felt the knot in her stomach growing more pronounced. She didn't want to feel jealous, but the feeling was there, nonetheless. She couldn't help it. She felt confused. On one hand, her independent side knew it would be simpler just to let Dan be with Anika. But, deep down, her long repressed romantic side just couldn't let Dan go. What if Dan was falling for his old girlfriend? She didn't know what to think right now.

"Oh, I am so sorry to hear that she didn't get Jonah back. That's so terrible! Of course, I'd like to meet her. Can you bring her with you the next time you visit?" Fran asked.

"I'd like that," Dan said. "I don't know how long she'll be staying, but if she's still here next time I visit, I'll bring her. She's coming with me to the Orange County rally tomorrow. She's looking forward to meeting Tim, Shelley, Pam, and Richard."

"So she's staying at Chateau Eden?" Fran asked, raising her eyebrows. "You told her it's a nudist resort, didn't you?" She noticed Dan smiling and chuckling to himself at her question.

"Yeah, she knows. Right now, she's sitting by herself under the orange tree on the back patio, beside the spa. She's wearing a bikini, but she liked the idea of trying topless tanning," Dan said, smiling. "She probably waited until I left, so she wouldn't feel self-conscious. We'll see how she does when the sun goes down and everybody makes their way to the spa without any clothes."

So Dan and Anika haven't seen each other naked? They've never been intimate?

Fran paused, digesting this new piece of information. She knew she absolutely had to talk about some difficult things with Dan. The pause in their conversation seemed like an eternity. She felt her face getting hot, her breathing becoming labored, and her heart pounding. She had to find a way to tell him now.

"Dan, there are some things I need to tell you," Fran said. "Things about what happened at the estate before Chelly died. I've been meaning to tell you, but I just have not been able to find a way. I have to tell you now. Please don't hate me."

"Hate you?" Dan exclaimed. "Why would I hate you? What could you have done that is so terrible?"

"Those nights we were all together in the spa with Chelly and Philippe, do you remember how relaxed everybody felt? How easily everybody was aroused?" she asked.

"Sure, I remember. We'd all had a lot of wine," Dan admitted. His face became grim as the conversation returned to the events at Palm Desert.

Fran felt her face turning crimson. She felt tension building inside. It was now or never—she had to tell him, or it felt like she might burst.

"It wasn't just the wine, Dan," she said. "I put Ecstasy in your wine—everybody's wine. Philippe made me do it. He wanted everybody to feel more aroused. He wanted to make you and Chelly feel more relaxed about having sex with me and Philippe."

She watched Dan's face for his reaction. His face was frozen. He was shocked by what he'd just heard.

"There's more," Fran admitted. "Philippe was worried that you would try to leave the estate to use your cell phone, and he refused to let that happen. He blocked your cell phone signals, and he ordered me to put GHB in your orange juice at breakfast that one day to make you sick. I'm so sorry. Please don't hate me!"

The dam finally burst. Fran let her tears go, the flood of liquid blurring her vision so that she couldn't read the stunned look on Dan's face. She waited for the outrage she knew would follow.

But the only thing she heard over the phone was silence. She wiped the tears from her eyes, trying to see Dan's face. His head was bowed. He was biting his lip nervously. Finally, he raised his head and looked into her eyes. Fran felt herself being gripped by fear. She had to force herself to keep looking into Dan's eyes. What she saw shocked her. Instead of anger, she saw pity and sadness— and she also saw tears in his eyes. He swallowed, and then she heard his voice.

"He ordered you to do that?" Dan asked. "He was that controlling? Did he ever make you do that before?"

Fran found herself nodding her head up and down.

"Many times. More than I can count," she answered. "Starting when he first ordered me to have sex with his clients in Paris. He knew drugs would help me not to care. And he was right—it helped me endure it. He demanded it whenever we had sex with other couples, and I did it for the Alvarez couple too. I'm just as guilty as Philippe in their deaths, just like the D.A. says."

She lowered her head in sorrow. She felt the knot in her stomach, and in that moment, she knew where it came from.

It's my fault—everything has always been my fault. The lack of interest and love from Mamma and Giulia, the sexual advances and beatings from Paulo, Philippe's control and abuse, and the deaths of Chelly and the Alvarez couple—it's all my fault! I'm nothing but a despicable person. What can Dan possibly see in me?

When she looked up again, all she saw was pain and the compassion in Dan's eyes. And she also saw love. She felt herself being drawn into his eyes. At that moment, more than anything else in the world, she wanted to feel the warmth of Dan's empathy, and to feel him inside her, making love to her. Yet, at the same time, she felt completely unworthy of his love. She felt confused. The inner struggle between the romantic part, independent, and worthless sides of her identity was overwhelming her. Then, suddenly, Dan's voice broke the silence.

"It's not your fault, Fran. You've got to believe that," he pleaded. "None of those things are your fault. Joanna is going to prove that it was Philippe's abuse and coercion that led you to do the things you did. I don't blame you for Chelly's death. It was her choice to get involved with Philippe. And in the end, it was my choice too. We were just as much to blame as you. You've got to believe that, Fran. You've got to believe in yourself. I believe in you. And I love you!"

Fran's loving side wanted so much to believe those words. Even the independent, businesslike part of her couldn't argue with Dan's argument. But in that moment, the worthless side of her was still winning the three-way inner battle. Nothing Dan could say—not even the compassion and love in his eyes—could convince her that she wasn't worthless.

How can I ever be a good wife? I don't deserve a man like him, and I will only make him miserable. How can I tell him about our child, and then tell him I can't be with him?

She knew she still had that one huge secret left to tell Dan. It was what she wanted most to tell him today. But the knot in her stomach continued to grow. She began to feel nauseous. She still couldn't force herself to tell him.

"I love you too," Fran answered half-heartedly.

"I'm worried about you," Dan said. "Have you asked them if you can continue your therapy sessions with Dr. Torres while you're here?"

"Joanna did not think I would be here long enough to need that. But she's going to ask now, because she thinks the D.A. is trying to drag this out as long as she can. I hope I'm not here much longer, but if I am, I would like to see Dr. Torres. I think the longer I'm here, the more depressed I'm feeling."

"I agree," Dan said. "Would you like me to phone Joanna for you?"

Fran noticed Dan's eyes looking up over her shoulder. She sensed her guard moving in her direction. She knew their visit was almost over.

"I think it's time to say goodbye," Fran said. "Make sure you bring Anika when you visit next. I really would like to meet her. Please help her feel at home at Chateau Eden. Let her know she is welcome to stay there as long as she wants."

"Thanks, I will," Dan replied. "Make sure you take care of yourself. I'll call you on Monday after we get back from Orange County. I love you!"

"I love you too," Fran answered.

She felt her guard's hand on her shoulder. It was time to go. Her eyes locked with Dan's, not wanting to let go. Finally, she felt more pressure on her arm, turning her body and guiding her away from the visiting area, and from Dan. As Fran felt the handcuffs snap shut on her wrists, she felt an overpowering weight descending upon her shoulders. Once again, she couldn't force herself to tell Dan the most important thing she needed to tell him. She was surprised he had not noticed her weight gain. Now she knew she would have to live with that burden, along with her inner conflicts, for yet another week. She shuffled down the corridor towards her cell, and her mind began dissociating into the conflicting parts of her identity. Her thoughts picked up speed and were soon spinning out of control.

Before long, Fran's mind was someplace other than the Indio Jail, working feverishly to find some sort of resolution to her mind's inner war. She shuffled back to her cell on autopilot, failing to notice anything else along the way. Before she knew it, she was back in her cell.

After sitting down on her cot, her mind gradually found its way back to reality. When it did, she came to a realization. It was easier to believe that everything *was* her fault. It helped to ease the sense of helplessness she felt when she dared to be hopeful, and when she dared to look forward to her release. It was easier to give up, and to resign herself to her current situation. It was easier to just lose herself in sleep. She lay down on her back on the cot and closed her eyes.

THE GLOW from the LCD screen of Angela's laptop illuminated her face in the darkness of her Las Vegas office. She stared out over the screen at the neon circus in the distance, trying to remain patient. Still no contact with Soren Kristiansen's laptop for the past four days.

What is he up to? Where the hell is he?

Angela's fingers typed Soren's name into her web browser. There was no shortage of search results. She clicked her mouse on the most recent CNN report. A video news report by an African-American reporter came to life on her screen.

... The FBI confirmed today that the woman whose body was found in a Little Rock, Arkansas hotel room has been identified as forty-four-year-old Elizabeth Andersson of Seattle, Washington. The victim had apparently been strangled. Andersson matches the description of the woman who rented a minivan that was used in the recent unsolved abduction of Jonah Kristiansen by his father, Pastor Soren Kristiansen. An FBI source has told CNN that Pastor Kristiansen is definitely a person of interest in the death of the Andersson woman. The disappearance of Jonah Kristiansen took

another bizarre turn today, when it was discovered that three unidentified U.S. citizens attempted to fly to Quito, Ecuador on Thursday, using the same fake passports allegedly used by Pastor Sorenson, his son, and Elizabeth Andersson, when they entered the U.S. at Port Angeles, Washington. Sources say that the three unidentified people, a family from Atlanta, may have been the innocent victims of an elaborate diversion created by Pastor Sorenson. Our sources say that Interpol has been alerted to the possibility that Pastor Sorensen may be attempting to leave the United States, and may be making his way to a country where the Hague Convention on International Child Abduction has not been signed, such as Japan or other Asian countries.

In another related story, the FBI are searching for an unidentified woman in her late thirties or early forties with shoulder length blonde hair, who was allegedly posing as a Public Relations representative for American Airlines at Hartsfield-Jackson Airport on Thursday...

Angela started working out the time frame of the events. It made sense. If Soren was flying to Asia, he might not have any easy access to the Internet from his computer for a couple of days.

You know he's got his porn business based in Asia, Angela. It makes sense that he'd try to go there. If his flight left late Wednesday or Thursday, he should have landed in Asia by now. You can probably expect to see some activity almost any time now, as soon as he gets settle somewhere. Be patient. He'll show himself sooner or later. Then you can start working on getting the boy back to his mother.

Another thought burst into Angela's mind. Her fingers tapped out another Google search, looking for any new reports on Soren's wife, Anika, and her friend, Dan Whitney.

Nothing new to report since her last press conference in Seattle.

Angela's fingers tapped out another search.

Francesca Capellini. The woman who caused all of the problems with that damned portrait of me. Any new developments?

Once again, Angela was disappointed to find there were no new developments in Capellini's case. Her arraignment wasn't due to reconvene until Friday, another five days from now.

The bright glow on Angela's face vanished as she closed the lid of her laptop. It was replaced by a dull reflection of the garish Las Vegas light show. She had learned to seek comfort in the dark after arriving in Las Vegas a few weeks ago, first in her dark refuge in the floodways beneath the city, and then under cover of darkness. She had spent as little time as possible being out during daylight hours, only going out for a couple of hours each day to scout properties that might make good investments for the 4.7 million dollars she stole from Soren. Eventually, she had learned to enjoy going out and enjoying some of the Las Vegas nightlife with her new friend, Ricki Marshall, and Ricki's girlfriends.

I wonder if Ricki is gay? Angela said to herself. The thought came to her totally out of the blue. She shrugged her shoulders. *No big deal if she or her friends are, I suppose.*

Angela heard herself chuckle aloud.

Maybe that's why I like hanging out with them. They're safe! After my terrible marriage to David, and after the harassment from Soren, maybe I've had enough bad experiences with men for a while. It's more fun having a night out on the town with Ricki and the girls!

Angela looked at her watch.

Speaking of Ricki and the girls, I'd better start getting ready. This might be my last night out on the town for a while if Soren's laptop checks in soon.

Angela looked through her meagre wardrobe, deciding to dress up a little for their night of stand-up comedy with Jay Leno. Her choices were limited. She reached for the short, sexy black dress she wore on her first night out with Ricki. For some reason, she felt sexier tonight, and the dress matched her mood.

It's been a long time—maybe I do just need to get myself laid! Who knows, if we go out for drinks afterwards, maybe I'll let this little black number work its magic if I see some hunk with a six-pack.

Angela slipped out of her jeans and tank top and stepped into her half bathroom. She ran some hot water into the sink for a sponge bath. She soaked a facecloth and started washing her face, basking in sensations of the warm facecloth on her face. Her thoughts started drifting.

That poor Anika Kristiansen. I know what she's going through, not being able to see her son.

Angela looked in the mirror. Her eyes were moist, not from the facecloth or the water in the sink. Without warning, she felt overcome by a sense of overpowering loneliness and emptiness.

Julia. Nicholas. I miss both of you so much! Can you ever forgive me for leaving you like I did?

Angela found herself weeping uncontrollably, sobbing so hard that she had difficulty catching her breath. On top of her grief, she felt intense anger rising in her gut—anger at Soren Kristiansen and how he harassed and threatened her. But he didn't stop there; he had threatened the most important people in her life—her children.

The anger grew so intense, along with her sadness, emptiness, and loneliness, that Angela felt herself shutting down. She felt her brain blocking out the emotional pain and her body going numb…

… Distant images and painful sensations filtered randomly through her mind… images of the look in Soren's eyes while he was making advances… the touch of his hand on her thigh… a young girl… a distant teenage face… Michael Farkas… painful sensations… fear and shame… feeling numb… more images of Soren… surprise on his face… pushing him away…

From somewhere far back in her consciousness, Angela started feeling herself gradually growing stronger. She started to remember… a part of her that managed to survive after she left

David… that managed to push Soren away… to outsmart him and escape…

Angela… my name is Angela Baranyi… I've survived so much… I am a survivor… I will survive…

Two images now filled Angela's consciousness—Julia and Nicholas. And with the images, Angela felt herself growing stronger from within—gradually feeling more like her own self. Through the images of Julia and Nicholas, she saw the image of herself growing stronger with each passing second. She saw herself in the bathroom mirror, facecloth in hand. She was coming back into the present. She stared into her own eyes—Angela's eyes —and she began speaking to herself.

Only one thing matters now, Angela. You have to help Anika. You must help her and the police find Jonah… and Soren! If things go well, you'll only have a few more weeks of pretending to be Anna Benz. But you have to find Jonah. It's the only way you'll ever be free to see Julia and Nicholas again!

Her sponge bath now finished, Angela hung the facecloth on the towel rack to dry. She focused on her reflection in the mirror, returning to the task at hand—getting ready for a night on the town. She dried her face, and then started her makeup, immersing herself in the process of applying blush, eyeliner and mascara. She finished by applying a shade of bright red lipstick. Thoughts of Julia and Nicholas, together with all of the painful emotions, were once again relegated to the far recesses of her mind. She surveyed the finished product in the mirror, nodding her head in approval. For the first time in a long time, she liked what she saw. In fact, she thought she even looked downright sexy.

Angela's mask of self-confidence and happiness was back in place, at least for this evening.

Have fun tonight, girl. Who knows what you'll be doing, or where you might be, tomorrow.

HELEN WATCHED the CNN news reports of Soren Kristiansen's possible involvement in the Andersson woman's death in Little Rock, feeling a deep glow of pride swelling inside her. So far, their plan had worked to perfection! Soren had carried out his part with military precision. But then, she expected nothing less than perfection from him.

She laughed inwardly as she recalled her role in their diversion. Not a single American Airlines employee thought to question her bogus airport ID or her identity as a Public Relations agent from their downtown Atlanta office. She laughed aloud when she recalled the Smith family.

What a bunch of naive clowns!

Helen tried to imagine the family's shock when they realized their own passports were missing, and the passports they were carrying were forgeries that were already being used by someone else—Soren, Jonah, and Beth.

The CNN report, with nothing new to report, was now summarizing the events of Jonah's abduction in the background. Helen tried to visualize the gestalt of their elaborate plan. So far, Soren's part, Jonah's abduction, had gone exactly as predicted. She moved on to other key aspects. For her own part, she had done nothing to raise any suspicions about herself or her past. Anika Kristiansen wasn't likely to cause any significant problems. Despite the strange coincidence of involving Dan Whitney in her search for Jonah, Anika and the police were so far behind in their investigation, that they weren't causing any significant problems.

The only fly in the ointment was Angela Baranyi. Helen didn't like loose ends. In fact, she didn't like anything that wasn't under her control. She didn't like that Baranyi was out there somewhere and she didn't know where. It was too much of a wild card. So far, the only lead to that bitch's whereabouts was Whitney's new girlfriend, the Capellini woman. Helen and Soren had called in District Attorney Mulholland's past debts to her and Soren, counting on her to use her position to find some credible information about Baranyi. But so far, Kelly Mulholland was not producing results, and Helen was far from pleased with her efforts.

Helen sat down to her computer and logged into her personal email program. Unlike most people's laptop computers, Helen's employed state of the art technology for bouncing her emails through clandestine servers around the world. Even when using a common, everyday Gmail account, her messages were virtually untraceable by all but the most knowledgeable Internet security geeks. She checked her inbox.

Still no news from Soren. He hasn't sent me an Australian mobile phone number yet, so he must not be settled or feel safe enough to contact me.

Helen went to her bookcase and pulled down an anthology of Emily Dickinson's poetry. From a pocket on the inside cover, she removed the key to her filing cabinet. Inserting the key in the cabinet, she opened the middle drawer and removed a disposable cell phone. She sat in her leather reading chair and put her feet up on the matching ottoman. She dialed a number using autodial and listened to the phone ring, waiting for an answer.

"Hello, Kelly here."

"Good evening, Madam D.A.," Helen answered.

"What do you want?" Mulholland replied, her voice suddenly curt and cold as ice.

"Is that any way to greet an old friend, Kelly? Let's try again, shall we?" There was a momentary silence on the District Attorney's end of the line.

"Good evening, ma'am," Mulholland said, this time much more contritely. "How may I please you?"

"Much better, Kelly. Now, tell me—have you got any more information from the Capellini woman after my little visit with her? Has she changed her story? Did she reveal anything to you? By the way, how was your day in jail?"

"I'm sorry, ma'am," Mulholland replied. "She's sticking to her story that she took the picture over a year ago in East L.A. If anything, you just frightened her and she just got defensive. She hasn't wavered a bit. Both Kevin and I tend to believe her. We think we've reached a dead end. I still think we have a decent chance at convicting her on the conspiracy charge, but I'd advise you to compromise on denying her bail. I don't think we can make that stand."

"Don't ever give me advice!" Helen screamed. "Is that clear?"

"Yes, ma'am. I didn't mean…"

"Listen to me, Ms. District Attorney," Helen said sharply. "Do you happen to remember the favours that I've done for you? Do you remember those videos from Lackland? And what about the money you owe me? How do you think your porn video and your gambling debts would look to the good people of Riverside County? You don't really want that kind of information on the Internet for the whole world to see, do you? And what do you think your husband and children would think? Have you told your husband about your extracurricular sexual adventures? I bet he'd enjoy seeing that tape," Helen said coyly. Once again, there was silence on Mulholland's end of the line.

"Please, ma'am. Please don't…"

"Stop begging," Helen ordered. "It's unbecoming of somebody in your position. Just do as I say! Capellini must have met others in East L.A. There must have been others who would have known Baranyi if she'd been living on the streets for months. You've got five days until the arraignment reconvenes, Kelly. Get me some credible information, and then maybe you can drop the bail demands. But if you don't find out anything new from Capellini, then I make an anonymous call to the local media. Understood?"

"Yes, ma'am," Mulholland answered, her voice trembling and barely audible.

"Louder, Kelly. I didn't hear you!" Helen commanded. She felt a familiar, powerful surge rising in her body.

"Yes, ma'am," repeated Mulholland, her voice much louder this time, but still trembling with fear. Helen heard a voice in the background on Mulholland's end of the line.

'Who are you talking to, Kelly? Who's on the phone?'

Helen listened nervously, hearing a long silence on Kelly's end… wondering how the D.A. would explain herself.

"It's just the mayor, dear. She just wants me to bring her up to date on the Capellini case. We'll be done in a minute."

"Are we finished?" Mulholland whispered, her voice back on the line with Helen.

"Well done, Kelly," Helen said, with a mocking tone. "You're getting good at the lying game, aren't you? Let's just hope you keep up your end of the bargain. We wouldn't want to expose some of those lies, would we now? We'll be watching, dear, so don't disappoint us. Now, have yourself a good night. Go and see what that nice husband of yours wants."

Helen hung up her phone. Leaving the comfort of her reading chair, she opened the filing cabinet drawer and deposited the phone back in its hiding place. She locked the cabinet and replaced the key back within the safe confines of Emily Dickinson's pages.

Living by herself, it was unlikely that anybody was going to find her disposable phone. But Helen had built a career on secrecy, and on being hyper-vigilant and in control at all times. It had served her well. She knew that bad things only happened when she let her guard down. She learned that during her childhood, and again as a young woman in training back at Lackland Air Force Base. But she vowed she would never let it happen again.

CHAPTER 15

DAN MET Anika outside the Italian room on Chateau Eden's pool deck. The morning sun had just risen over the east side of the hotel, bathing the pool and the west side of the enclosed compound in golden rays of early morning California sunshine. The San Jacinto Mountains loomed crisp and clear above the hotel's west side in the cool morning air.

Dan noticed some colour in Anika's face from yesterday's afternoon in the sun. She was casually dressed in white shorts and a yellow tank top.

"You look well rested. Have a good sleep?" Dan asked.

"Yes, thanks," Anika replied. "I left the window open last night. That cool, fresh desert air is wonderful. It's the best sleep I've had since… well, you know."

Sensing her discomfort with the topic of Jonah's abduction, Dan changed the subject.

"You're all ready to go?" Dan asked.

"Yup," she answered. "How long is the drive?"

They exited the courtyard through the massive pine door in the high, vine-covered wall that concealed Chateau Eden's private courtyard from the street.

"It's only about an hour and three quarters," Dan answered. "As long as the freeway isn't too clogged when we get closer to Placentia. At least it's Sunday, so we don't have to contend with rush hour. But the traffic can still be bad on weekends."

"I'm sure glad I live in Victoria and don't have to contend with Los Angeles traffic," Anika said, as they climbed into Fran's Prius.

"I try to avoid L.A. whenever possible," Dan answered. "It's so tranquil here in the valley. It's hard to believe we're that close to the big city."

"I see that. I'm starting to see why you like staying at the Chateau. It's just as peaceful and quiet as you described it," Anika said.

"Even with the naked bodies?" Dan asked.

Anika's face blushed a rosy pink colour, her fair skin unable to hide her embarrassment.

"Well, that might take some getting used to," she answered. "But you'll be proud of me, I did some topless tanning yesterday afternoon, and I kept my top off with a couple of women in the spa, too."

Dan raised his eyebrows and smiled as he guided the Prius out of Palm Springs.

"You're right. I *am* proud of you. What would you have done if any guys joined you?" Dan asked.

"I don't know," Anika answered, laughing. "I guess I would have crossed that bridge if I came to it. The ladies shared their wine with me, so I'm guessing that helped me to relax. The women were very nice. They didn't say anything about me wearing my bikini bottoms."

"I told you," Dan said. "Remember, it's *clothing optional*. Everybody who comes to Chateau Eden was a nudist virgin at some point in their lives. So they understand if you're nervous. That's why I think you'll like Shelley, Tim, Pam, and Richard. They let Chelly take things at her own pace when she first arrived, and they welcomed her with open arms."

"So, tell me more about your friends, Dan. What do they do when they're not naked at the Chateau?"

Dan smiled and chuckled.

"Well, Tim spent years in the navy, but he decided to go into social work when he left the service. He grew up in a tough neighbourhood in L.A., so he wants to help other kids in similar situations. He's actually working now in the same area where he grew up," Dan said. "Shelley works for a big pharmaceutical company based in Switzerland. Their U.S. head office is in San Diego, but she moved to Placentia so she and Tim could live together."

"That's so sweet," Anika said. "How did they meet?"

"They met at a rally for military sexual abuse victims, just like the one we're going to this afternoon. Tim, Richard, and Pam were the organizers, and Shelley represented her company after Pam recruited them as sponsors. Tim and Shelley hit it off right from the start, and the rest is history," Dan said.

"What about Pam and Richard?" Anika asked. "What do they do?"

"Richard was in the Marines for many years. Now he owns a security company that does contract work, mostly for big corporations, in places like Iraq and Afghanistan. He and Pam have been together for years. She's a realtor in Orange County."

"So, how did Richard and Tim get involved in the military sexual abuse cause?" Anika asked.

"As Tim tells it, many of the ex-military personnel who work for Richard are women. A few of them had told Richard and Pam their stories, and about how they're trying to raise awareness of just how big a problem it is for women in the military. Because Richard was one of the few black kids growing up at Lackland Air Force Base in Texas, he has a real soft spot for anybody who is bullied or abused. Pam and Richard told the women's stories of military abuse to Tim. Together, they decided to help women draw attention to their cause," Dan replied.

"They sound like an interesting group of people. I'm looking forward to meeting them—preferably with their clothes on!" she said, laughing. "Maybe that will make it easier for me if I meet them at the Chateau sometime."

"Didn't I tell you?" Dan said. "You're going to get the chance this weekend. Tim and Shelley are going to visit Fran at Indio tomorrow, so all four of them are coming down tonight and they'll be spending most of the day at the Chateau."

"No, you didn't tell me," Anika said. "Were you going to keep that a secret from me?"

"No," Dan replied. "I knew Tim and Shelley were coming to visit Fran, but they didn't book rooms at the Chateau until late yesterday. Carmen just told me this morning. Don't worry, just wear whatever feels most comfortable and enjoy the company."

"Well, that's easy for you to say," Anika said, laughing nervously. "I guess we'll see how things go tonight, and how I feel tomorrow. Any other secrets you haven't told me yet?

Dan went silent, trying to decide whether to tell Anika about his email from his *'Guardian Angel'*. His silence gave him away.

"Dan, what is it? What aren't you telling me?"

"I didn't know if I should tell you this or not. It might not be anything. And I didn't want to get your hopes up if it turns out to be a hoax," he responded.

"Tell me what?"

"I got an email about a week ago," he admitted. "It was anonymous, from somebody who claims to be our 'guardian angel'. He or she claims they're my friend, and that they're also looking for Soren and want to help us. He or she also implied that we could be in danger, and that he or she will be watching us from a distance."

"Danger? From Soren? What kind of danger, Dan?"

"I don't know," he replied. "Didn't say. He or she just left an email address, but I haven't replied yet. I didn't want to do anything until things calmed down and I had a chance to talk to you. What do you think we should do? Should we reply?"

Anika went silent.

"What if it's Soren? What if it's a trap?" Anika asked aloud.

"I wondered that too," Dan answered. "How would we know?"

Once again, Anika grew pensive. Finally, she sighed and began to speak.

"Let's think about it for a couple of days," she said. "There's no urgent reason to contact him or her, is there? Let's wait to see if there's any new sighting of Soren or Jonah in the next couple of days. If we haven't heard anything new, then what do we have to lose?"

"Good question. I can't think of any reason, can you?"

Anika shook her head slowly from side to side.

"Then I agree. Let's sit on it for a couple of days," Dan said.

A hush descended on the car as the traffic grew busier and they drew closer to Orange County. Anika checked her cell phone for new calls or email from the police about Jonah. From her sigh, Dan suspected that there was no news. She turned her head and gazed out the window, lost in worry about Jonah. Dan left her alone with her thoughts. He was glad she'd come with him to Palm Springs. So far, it had been a good distraction for her, and he looked forward to introducing her to his new friends. He hoped she could relax, even just a little bit, for a couple of days.

"THERE IT IS, next exit," Anika said, pointing to the large shopping centre off to the left of the highway.

Dan took the off-ramp and made his way towards the Imperial Center.

"It says to watch for a big stage in the middle of the parking lot," Anika said, reading from the printed directions Dan had given to her.

After driving for about thirty seconds, Dan spotted a raised stage with a crowd congregated around it.

"That must be it," he observed. He guided the car into a parking spot about a hundred yards away. He and Anika left the car and walked towards the stage. Dan scanned the crowd for familiar faces. Before long, he spotted the familiar black hair and dark skin of Richard Holloway's head standing out above the crowd.

"There's Richard!" Dan said to Anika. "The tall black fellow over there."

"You're not kidding he's tall," Anika remarked. "And look at that body! The guy's built like a brick you-know-what. Don't tell me—he's the one who does security work, right?"

"You got it," Dan answered, grinning. "And you haven't even seen him in the spa yet!" Anika's face turned pink. Dan had no doubt that she was imagining sharing the hot tub with this black Adonis and his ripped body—in the flesh, no less.

Richard made eye contact with Dan. Strangely, Dan felt self-conscious and looked away briefly. He realized he hadn't seen Richard or Pam since the awkward ending to their flirtatious night in the spa at Chateau Eden, almost two months ago. They hadn't seen each other since Chelly's death in Palm Desert six weeks earlier. Dan's eyes reconnected with Richard's. The distinguished looking African-American man flashed his usual friendly smile, featuring a perfect set of ivory-colored teeth. Dan allowed himself to smile back. He felt himself starting to relax.

"Whitney! Good t'see y'all, bro," Richard drawled, as he made his way toward Dan and Anika. He grabbed Dan's right hand and squeezed firmly, not letting go. "I can't tell y'all how sorry I was to hear about what happened to Chelly. Pam and I… well, we were completely shocked. How are y'all doin'… you and Fran?"

"As well as can be expected, I guess," Dan answered. "It still feels strange not having Chelly around. I still have some dreams about the shooting, but not nearly as often now. And I'm trying to keep myself busy… that helps. I'm not so sure about Fran, though. I went to Indio to visit her yesterday. She seems depressed."

"I just got back from Iraq a couple of days ago, so Pam and I haven't had a chance to visit yet. Since she only gets a couple of visits each week, we want to make sure you get every chance to see her," Richard said. His eyes suddenly lit up when he saw Anika standing behind Dan.

"You must be Anika," Richard observed, stepping past Dan and extending his hand. "Charmed t'meetcha. We're so glad y'all decided to visit with us for a while. So sorry that it had ta be under these circumstances. We've been thinkin' of y'all since Dan told us 'bout your situation."

"Thank you," Anika answered. Dan watched her try to swallow. He knew she was trying not to think about Jonah this afternoon, but he realized what a struggle that was for her. "Dan's told me so many good things about all of you."

"Well, any friend of Dan's is a friend of ours," Richard drawled. "C'mon, the others are up by the stage. They'll be so happy to see y'all."

Dan and Anika followed Richard's head as it bobbed through the crowd, which was well represented by members of all branches of the armed forces in uniform. Dan noticed that a majority of them were women.

As they neared the stage, Dan was able to make out three more familiar faces: Shelley, Tim, and Richard's wife, Pam. Shelley spotted Dan first and came running towards him. She greeted him with a warm hug, then turned to Anika, her hand extended.

"Hi, Anika. I'm Shelley Paul. I'm so pleased to finally meet you. The last couple of weeks must have been horrific for you. I hope you've had a chance to get some rest at the Chateau," Shelley said.

"Hello, Shelley. Thank you." Anika replied. She smiled and even managed a chuckle. "The last two weeks *have* been exhausting. And I am starting to relax a bit at the Chateau. But I have to admit it's not easy making eye contact while talking to naked strangers!"

Dan and Shelley laughed along with Anika, helping to lighten the mood for her. As they laughed, Shelley's partner, Tim, approached the group.

"Anika, I'd like you to meet my better half, Tim Jennings," Shelley said.

"A pleasure to meet you," Tim said, first shaking Anika's hand, then pulling her towards him and kissing her, European style, on either side of the face. He turned to Dan. "Good to see you again." The two men, who were fast becoming good friends, shook hands. As they did, a tall, voluptuous African-American woman emerged from the crowd. Richard's wife, Pam Holloway, headed straight for Dan. She pulled him firmly into her arms and against her ample chest.

"Dan," Pam shouted. "It's been too long." As Dan felt the warmth of her sincere embrace, he felt her warm breath against his ear. She whispered a private message for him.

"I hope you'll forgive Richard and me for any misunderstandings at the Chateau," Pam said softly. Dan pulled his head back so he could look her in the eye. Under his breath, he whispered.

"Nothing that happened is your fault," Dan said. "What went down was between Chelly and me. I'm sorry if we made you feel uncomfortable. If the lights had stayed on another thirty minutes, who knows where things would have gone?"

Pam smiled at Dan. He felt any remaining apprehension about seeing Pam and Richard evaporate. He had forgotten how beautiful and sexually alluring Pam was. Suddenly, he remembered Anika standing beside him. Turning to her, he placed his hand on her shoulder.

"Pam, I'd like you to meet my good friend, Anika Kristiansen," he said.

"We're so pleased you came to visit us," Pam said. "I can't tell you how disgusted I was to hear about your son's abduction. I hope you're able to chill out a bit while you're at the Chateau. How are things going for you? I know it's not easy being a newbie at a nude resort. I was terrified my first time!"

"I'm settling in fine. I had a couple of glasses of wine on the patio, beside the spa, while I was reading. I managed to take my top off and get some sun. Then I shared a couple of bottles of wine with some ladies in the spa. I felt *really* relaxed by the time I got out," Anika said, smiling.

"Yeah, the alcohol will tend to do that, won't it, Dan?" Pam said, winking suggestively at him. "Anyway, I hope you'll join us all in the spa tonight when we go back to the Chateau. I'm sure we can find another bottle or two of wine to help you relax some more!"

Pam paused, her face becoming more solemn.

"But seriously, Anika, we're all stunned by what has happened to you. I'm glad that Dan's been available to help you. I can't imagine going through what you're going through, and having to do it by yourself."

"Thank you, Pam. I appreciate everybody's kind words. Dan's lucky to have friends like you. And I'm lucky to have found Dan again, after all these years," Anika said.

Pam turned and looked towards the stage, her eyes searching, until she spotted what she was looking for.

"I'd like you two to meet somebody. Dan, you remember that I'm helping Richard and Tim in their efforts to get more support for veterans who have PTSD? We've become active advocates for both women and men who've been sexually abused by superior officers while serving in the military. Our guest speaker is the assistant to the Director of Public Affairs for the Air Force. She's heard of you, Dan, and she wants to meet you."

Dan raised his eyebrows and wrinkled his forehead in surprise.

"Me?" he asked. "Where has she heard of me?"

"Don't be so bashful. You were in the news a lot after the events in Palm Desert—not just because of the deaths, but also because you're a psychologist and you deal with PTSD," Pam said. "She saw your interview on CNN. C'mon, she's over here."

Pam led Dan and Anika through the crowd. As they approached the stage, Dan got a rear view of a woman in a dark blue skirt and jacket, and a dark blue flight cap. From the epaulettes she wore, Dan realized that she was an officer. She was talking to three women—a medium-height blonde, a taller redhead, and an imposing, muscular woman with short blonde hair. The first two women were both dressed in surplus fatigues and khaki tank tops. Their eyes shifted towards Pam, Dan, and Anika as they approached.

Seeing the first two women's eyes shift, the uniformed woman turned to see who was approaching her from behind. As she turned, Dan thought he saw a look of shock appear briefly in the officer's eyes. When he looked again, he second-guessed himself. The woman's face wore a broad smile as they walked up to her.

"Dan, Anika, this is Major Teri Taylor. She's the Assistant to the Director of Public Relations for the Air Force. These two fine women here are Miriam Fox and Gwen Parks. They both work for the security company with Richard." Pam explained. "Ladies, this is Dr. Dan Whitney and his friend, Anika… Anika Kristiansen."

"Pleased to meet you, Dr. Whitney… Anika," Major Taylor said enthusiastically, focusing her attention on Dan. "I saw your interview on CNN with Anderson Cooper a couple of weeks ago. I'm glad to see your special interest is in treating PTSD. It's a big problem for our veterans, and we need more people with specialized training like yours."

Noticing the third woman in the group, Pam switched her attention to the tall blonde woman. "I don't believe we're met. I'm Pam Holloway, one of the event organizers."

"I'm sorry," the blonde replied. "My name is Ricki Marshall. I'm a freelance journalist who's following the whole MSA issue. I'm hoping to interview Major Taylor after her presentation."

"Pleased to meet you," Pam answered. "We're pleased that you could attend the rally today. If there's anything at all we can do to help you bring awareness to our cause, please let me know."

"Thanks," the journalist replied. "I'll be sure to do that."

Pam turned her attention back to her guest speaker.

"Major Taylor, Anika, is the mother of the young boy who is the subject of the recent Amber Alert. Dan is helping her in the effort to find her son," Pam explained.

Dan's eyes surveyed Major Taylor as she shifted her attention towards Anika. She wasn't as imposing as he might have expected from a military woman in such an important position. She was probably no more than five foot two or three. She had short, dark brown hair that was brushed back into a smooth wave on either side of her head. She had dark brown eyes, pale skin, and small thin lips covered with a soft pink shade of lipstick.

Initially, Dan saw a stern, businesslike look on Major Taylor's face. Her eyes seemed to be scanning Anika like a hawk, as if she was trying to cram as much information into that first look as possible. But within seconds, he noticed that the Major's look softened dramatically. Her face now wore a look of compassion and empathy in her eyes as they studied Anika.

"Ms. Kristiansen. I can't imagine what you are going through right now. It must be every parent's nightmare—having your child taken from you. And by your husband, no less! Please accept my wishes for the speediest of recoveries of your son. The FBI are involved, I assume?"

"Thank you, Major Taylor. Yes, the FBI, the RCMP, and Interpol are all involved. So far, there's no further sign of Soren… er, my husband… so we're hopeful that he's still here in the U.S.," Anika explained.

The tall redheaded colleague of Richard's stepped forward.

"Everybody in America is thinkin' of y'all, ma'am. Our hearts go out to both you and your son. I'm Gwen… Gwen Perkins. Honored to meet y'all."

"Me too, Ms. Kristiansen," said her shorter, blonde-haired colleague. "I'm Miriam Fox. And if you'll pardon me for saying so, I'd make sure that bastard never fathered another child again if I caught him!"

"Miriam!" Gwen exclaimed. "You're talking about Ms. Kristiansen's husband!"

"It's okay, Gwen," Anika interjected. "I probably feel the same as Miriam towards him right now."

"Well, it's disgusting," Miriam expounded. "It's just another form of manipulation. It's just as much a form of domestic abuse as if he was beating you. I'm hoping the bastard wasn't doing that to you and your son too, was he?"

"No, I guess we were lucky in that way, if you can call it lucky," Anika replied.

"I suppose it's all related to the cause that we're here to support today," Major Taylor said. Her face had a soft, compassionate look. Dan noticed that the woman was skilled at summarizing the conversation. He was impressed by the fact that she didn't flaunt her rank. Her appearance and her sense of authority might be understated, but she was definitely used to taking control of situations.

She's no pushover. She didn't just make it to the rank of Major on good looks or by being compassionate.

"Dr. Whitney. I hope I can talk with you later, after I finish my speech," Major Taylor said. "I would like to pick your brain about how we could integrate your kind of skills and training into our programs for veterans."

"I'd be more than happy to," Dan answered.

"No offence to Major Taylor," Miriam interrupted, turning her attention to Dan and ignoring Major Taylor. "But we feel the military isn't doing near enough to end the epidemic of MSA. Richard has told us a lot about the work you do. Gwen and I both watched the video of your CNN interview too, and we'd love to talk with you about how you can help our cause."

"MSA?" Dan asked.

"Sorry," Gwen replied. "Military Sexual Abuse. We're all so used to talkin' about sexual abuse in the military, that we just use the acronym now. Miriam and I would really appreciate if we could have a few moments of y'all's time after you've talked with the Major."

"Sure. I didn't think I'd be in such demand today," Dan said, chuckling. "I'd be happy to talk with all of you afterwards."

"I don't mean to interrupt," Pam chimed in. "But it's two o'clock. Miriam and Gwen—time to get your butts on stage and kick off this event. You remember the schedule?"

"Yes, ma'am," Gwen replied, rolling her eyes. "After we talk about the MSA cause, we introduce Major Taylor here, then we introduce the survivors, then we let people know about our initiatives, an' finally we talk to the crowd about how y'all can get involved. Of course we remember the schedule. Geez, Pam. Sometimes I think you're as anal as ole' Richard over there."

"Good. You girls can talk to Dan all you want later. Did Richard invite you to Chateau Eden to spend the day tomorrow?" Pam asked.

"He did," Miriam answered. "He's been bugging us to come out there and skinny dip with you guys forever. We figured if we stayed at the Chateau tonight, he'll finally shut up about it."

"So you girls are newbies at this nudist thing like me?" Anika asked.

"Absolutely," Gwen confirmed. "And I can tell you, it's not an easy thing to contemplate for anybody like us with an MSA history."

Anika nodded in agreement.

"I'll bet. If it's that scary for me, it must be even more frightening for you and Miriam," Anika said, pausing to think. "Tell you what. If you two are strong enough to face your fears and bare it all, then I guess I can do it too. And I'll be happy to share a few glasses of wine with you too, if it makes it any easier. What the heck—we only live once, right?"

Dan raised his eyebrows and forehead in surprise. He exchanged a smile with Anika. He looked at Miriam and Gwen for their reaction.

"You've got yourself a deal," Miriam replied, looking to Gwen for moral support.

"What the hell," Gwen responded. "We'll see you and Dan in the spa tonight!"

"Okay, enough!" Pam shouted. "On stage you two—get going!" She turned to Dan.

"This better not be another game of *Truth or Dare*, because you know I'm not going there again, right?" Her eyes locked onto Dan's, demanding his acknowledgement. Anika wore a look of confusion on her face.

"Who said anything about *Truth or Dare*?" she asked, watching Dan's reaction for a clue as to what he and Pam were talking about.

Dan just nodded his head up and down, slowly and silently, to acknowledge Pam. He had trouble swallowing. Pam didn't need to remind him of what happened the first time they played *Truth or Dare* in Chateau Eden's spa, and how things turned out.

SOFT, yellow incandescent lighting from the back of the hotel, and from a decorative post-mounted lantern beside the orange tree, bathed the courtyard patio at Chateau Eden. An eerie aquamarine glow from the foaming waters of the spa illuminated the faces, necks, and bare shoulders of the eight occupants of the hotel's spa. Stars twinkled in the dark desert sky and a light breeze whispered through the leaves of the orange and grapefruit trees in the courtyard. Bottles of wine ringed the edge of the sunken hot tub. The nude bathers had their glasses raised in a toast.

"To Anika!" they all chanted.

"No longer a skinny-dipping virgin!" Pam Holloway toasted. The others laughed and saluted the newest member of their nude circle.

Anika's face turned a subtle pink as she acknowledged her seven new friends. Dan was proud of her. After half an hour in the water, she seemed more embarrassed by the extra attention from the others, than by being totally naked in the presence of these people. They were no longer strangers and were fast becoming Anika's new friends.

"I just want to thank all of you for being so friendly and supportive. It made skinny-dipping seem natural. I see now that it isn't such a big deal. I wonder what the folks in the *World-Wide Community of Christ* would say if they saw the good pastor's wife now," Anika added, laughing.

Anika's mini-speech was saluted with yet another cheer of alcohol-fuelled enthusiasm.

"What happens at Chateau Eden stays at Chateau Eden." Richard Holloway's voice boomed over the group's laughter. Plastic glasses clicked in the air once again, as the group echoed his salute.

Gwen Perkins, sitting off to Dan's right, brought down her glass and turned her attention to Dan. The underwater spa lights reflected in her deep green eyes, bringing out the carrot-red hue of her hair, which was already a deeper red from being completely wet.

"So how did y'all's chat with Major Taylor go?" Gwen asked Dan.

"Very well," Dan answered. "She asked me a lot about the EMDR therapy I use for treating PTSD, how long the treatment takes, and how much training is involved in learning it. She was very nice, and she seemed quite sincere."

"Don't let her fool you," Miriam Fox interjected. "Remember, PR is her job, and she's damned good at it. When all is said and done, she's a master at making the military sound empathic, but she keeps spouting the same old rhetoric."

While he watched Miriam speak, Dan's mind wandered.

Why does Miriam's face look so familiar? She looks like somebody, but I just can't put my finger on it. Who else do I know who's blonde... and wary... like Miriam?

Frustrated, he brought his mind back to the conversation.

"I didn't sense that," Dan said. "What rhetoric?"

Tim jumped into the conversation.

"The biggest problem with investigating sexual abuse in the military is that the people who are often the abusers, are also the people who are in command and responsible for investigating the abuse. It's a huge conflict of interest. When women like Gwen and Miriam tried to report their abuse, it was swept under the carpet by the old boys' club."

"What we're pushing for," Pam added, "is for independent judicial investigations into military sexual abuse. It has to be completely at arm's length from the military chain of command."

"That's why we're organizin' rallies, like the one we had today, all 'cross the country. We hav'ta wake up the rest of the country, not just to the sexual abuse epidemic inside the military, but 'specially t'abuse of power in the chain'a command," Gwen drawled.

"Yeah, and we hav'ta encourage the men and women who are still bein' abused to come forward and report their abusers," Richard said. "Every time we have a rally like today's event, I keep hearin' more rumours about MSA, 'specially at Lackland, where Gwen an' I come from. The true extent of the problem is startin' to become truly disturbin'. "

"Okay, enough!" Pam interrupted. "Anika's our guest tonight. Can we please talk about something else?" She turned towards Dan. "You saw Fran yesterday. How is she holding up?"

"Thanks for asking. I'm getting worried about her. She's getting more distant. I'm afraid she's starting to get depressed. What would you say, Shelley? You've visited with her—what do you think is going on?"

Shelley shifted in her seat. Dan felt like she avoided his eyes for a moment. There was a short, but palpable silence before she answered.

"You might be right, Dan," she said. "Something seems to be troubling her. She hasn't said anything to you?"

"No, she hasn't. I thought she might have said something to you," he answered.

"You guys were seeing a psychologist after Chelly died, weren't you?" Shelley asked. "Do you think Fran should keep seeing her while she's in custody?"

"I talked with her lawyer, Joanna, about that," Dan replied. "At first, we thought the charges would be dropped, or at worst, she'd be out on bail within a day or two. We didn't ever think that having to bring a psychologist into the jail would be an issue. But we may have to rethink that now. You and Tim are going to be seeing her tomorrow. Do you want to ask her if she'd like us to arrange for Dr. Torres to see her?"

"Sure, we could do that," Tim answered. "It might not be an issue after her arraignment on Friday. But there's no harm in asking, just in case things don't go her way in court."

Dan saw Miriam in his peripheral vision. Suddenly, talking about Fran and seeing Miriam jogged his memory.

Fran's portrait! The one of the homeless woman. I can't believe how much Miriam looks like the woman in the portrait!

He realized he was staring at Miriam. His eyes met hers. She was looking at him, warily.

"I'm sorry if I'm staring, Miriam. All night I've been trying to figure out who you look like, and I just figured it out. You could be a twin to somebody in one of Fran's portraits. Your face, your hair, and especially your eyes—they're almost identical. You're sure you don't have a twin who's living on the streets?" he said, smiling at Miriam.

The wary frown melted from Gwen's face. She smiled and relaxed, becoming less guarded as she realized why Dan had been staring.

"Well, they say everybody's got a twin," she said, smiling. "But as far as I know, I've only got two brothers."

"Thank God," Richard drawled. "I could only put up with one Miriam, ain't that right darlin'." He flashed her a good-natured wink.

At that moment, Anika sat upright in her seat, catching Dan's attention with her eyes.

"I don't want to break up the party, but I think I'm going to call it a night," Anika announced. "I haven't had much sleep over the past week. Thanks for being so patient and encouraging about the skinny-dipping… and for being so supportive about Jonah. It's meant a lot to me. Dan was right—I really needed to get away to relax for a while. You guys and Chateau Eden are just what I needed."

"We understand," Shelley answered. "Hope you have a good sleep. We'll see you out by the pool tomorrow afternoon, after we see Fran."

"It's been great getting to know you," Pam added. "We still have most of the day to relax tomorrow, before we all head back to the city. What do you say, Richard? Do you think we should retire to our room too?"

Dan chuckled as he saw Pam wink suggestively at Richard. Some things never changed.

"Sure, darlin', I reckon we could have our own l'il party back in the room," he said, winking suggestively at the rest of the bathers. "Don't let us stop y'all from partying."

"Well, just make sure you two keep the noise down," Tim said, laughing. "Last time we were here, you kept Shelley and me awake half the night with your mating sounds!"

"Then you'd better prepare yourself," Pam said. "He's going back to Iraq in a couple of days, and you know he's going to keep mamma up late every night until he's gone."

"Yeah, I gotta git me as much o' this fine woman as I can while I'm home," Richard said, laughing. "Women in Iraq ain't much ta look at, if y'all know what I mean."

Richard winked at his two female coworkers, both of whom would be flying back to Iraq with him in two days.

"Present company excepted, of course," he added.

Dan made eye contact with Anika. She nodded in return. Dan climbed onto the deck, took Anika's hand and helped her from the spa. He reached for his towel on the patio, and began drying himself. As he did, he saw all of Anika's slim, naked body, with her delicate white breasts, fully exposed for the first time in his life. He felt a familiar tension in his genitals, and immediately wrapped his towel around his waist. He watched as she quickly reached for her towel and self-consciously wrapped her body and her breasts in one swift movement.

It's one thing to be naked in the water, where people can't really see you. But it's another to walk around completely nude in front of others for the first time. But I'm proud of her. She did better than I thought she would.

Dan took Anika's hand and escorted her between two of the old motel's bungalows, turning to the right and walking the few steps to the Italian room, where she was staying during her visit.

"Thanks, Dan," she said. "It's been a good day. It's probably the first day since Jonah disappeared that I haven't spent every waking minute thinking about him. And tonight was fun—they're a good group of people. I can see why you like being with them."

"You're welcome," Dan replied. "I hope it translates into a good night's sleep for you. I'll be helping Carmen set out the breakfast tomorrow, so I'll see you then."

He reached for Anika and pulled her close, embracing her warm body and giving her a chaste kiss on the cheek.

"You too, Dan. Have a good sleep," she whispered. She stepped back out of their embrace and opened the door to her room. Through the translucent white fabric covering the inside of the glass door, Dan saw the lights come on. He saw the shadow of her slim body moving around. The chill on his damp skin, evaporating in the chilly desert air, brought his mind back into the present. He walked into Chateau Eden's lobby and into the office, where he sat on the narrow couch that doubled as his bed while Anika used his room at the hotel.

He rummaged through his shaving kit and found his toothbrush and toothpaste. While he started brushing, and as he wandered into the office's small kitchen to use the sink, his mind started thinking of Fran, with images of her trying to sleep in her lonely cell at the Indio jail. Soon, he was contemplating tonight's conversation with Shelley about Fran.

What is going on in Fran's mind? What's bothering her, and why is she keeping it from us?

He finished rinsing his mouth in the sink, and then wandered back into the office, unwrapping the towel from around his waist. He pulled two sheets from a stack of blankets and linen and began preparing the couch for sleep. Finally, he turned out the light and climbed in between the sheets. Multiple images surfaced—first of Fran laying in her cold, sterile jail cell—then of Anika's pale, slim, naked body—filling his mind with conflicting emotions. He recalled the feeling of that impulsive, desperate kiss that he and Anika shared in Seattle. Then he found himself remembering what it was like to make love to Fran. Before long, his mind drifted off to sleep, still trying to resolve his emotional dilemma and filling his sleep with restless dreams.

CHAPTER 16

TUESDAY morning, May ninth. The warm morning sun climbed over the stuccoed wall that surrounded the peaceful patio behind Chateau Eden's office. Dan and Anika sat at a small table beneath the grapefruit tree, sipping coffee and enjoying items from Carmen's daily breakfast buffet. The leaves on the tree were barely moving. It was going to be a hot May day in the Coachella valley.

"I'm glad to see you're spending a few days with your family in Calgary," Dan said. "What's the latest word on your dad?"

"He's at home now, recovering from his surgery. They'll be starting him on chemotherapy in a couple of weeks, once he's had a chance to recover some more."

"How's your mom doing?" Dan asked.

"As well as can be expected," Anika answered. "But she can use some help taking care of Dad. Trudy has enough on her plate with her own kids. I thought I'd spend about a week in Calgary… unless I get a call about Jonah."

"Still nothing?" Dan inquired, taking a long taste of coffee. Anika let out a frustrated sigh. The look of dejection on her face said it all.

"Nothing," she said. Silence hung in the warm morning air.

"Any word on what's happening with the custody issue?" Dan asked.

"Rashad's assistant told me that they're taking my motion to court this afternoon. That's why I have to get to Calgary as soon as possible today, so I can be available for a teleconference if the judge wants to talk to me. Rashad doubts if that will be necessary, since it's such a high profile case, but he wants to cover all the bases," Anika said.

"That sounds hopeful. Phone or email me as soon as you know anything, okay?" Dan asked.

Her mouth full of cantaloupe, Anika nodded in agreement. They continued eating breakfast in silence, Dan scooping yogurt from a small individual serving container, and Anika carefully removing a tea bag from a small teapot.

"How's Fran doing?" Anika asked, as she set aside the spent tea bag.

"About the same," Dan answered. "Shelley didn't say much about their visit, but Tim said Fran was unusually quiet. Apparently, Joanna is having trouble figuring this case out. She seems to think there's something else going on with the D.A., but she just can't figure out what it might be. Ordinarily, this should be a straightforward case of Battered Spouse Syndrome."

Dan paused, leaving another awkward silence suspended in the air.

"What?" Anika asked. "Is there something else going on?"

"Well, sort of," Dan replied. "Tim said he felt like Fran and Shelley weren't talking much because he was there—like they both wished he hadn't come along. He just felt uncomfortable being there."

"Sometimes women just want time for girl talk, Dan," Anika said. "Trust me, if there's something Fran really wants to talk about, let Shelley visit by herself next time."

"Hopefully, there won't be a next time after the arraignment on Friday," Dan said. "Even if they don't drop the charges, I'm sure she'll be a lot happier if she's granted bail."

"Yes, let's all pray that happens," Anika said. She held her warm teacup between her hands, enjoying the heat being given off by the cup. Dan busied himself with putting some jam on a piece of toast. When he was done, he put down his knife, then took another sip of coffee.

"We still have something we have to do before you go," Dan said. "What do you want me to say to our mysterious 'guardian angel'?"

"I've been thinking about that," Anika said. "We could just send a message to see if he or she is still out there. Maybe we could ask if we're in any kind of immediate danger, and what the danger might be. What do you think?"

"I'm okay with that," Dan replied. He reached down beside his chair and lifted his MacBook out of its carrying case. He pushed his breakfast to one side, and then set up the screen so Anika could look over his shoulder. "Come around here and help me compose the message."

Anika picked up her teacup, holding it between both hands, and walked around the table while Dan opened his mail application. He opened the message he had forwarded to himself from the Chateau Eden computer, allowing the message to fill the screen.

Hello.

I understand from TV news reports that Dan Whitney is currently living at your hotel. Please tell him that both he and Francesca have seen me, but don't know me. Please understand that I can't reveal my identity right now. I am in great danger, as is Francesca, Dan, and his friend, Anika. Like Anika and Dan, I am also searching for Soren Kristiansen. Please believe me when I say I am Dan's friend. I will soon be watching over him from a distance and warning him of any dangers from Soren. Please pass this message along to Dan or Francesca as soon as possible.

Your Guardian Angel

He clicked on the icon to start a new email message, and then he cut and pasted their anonymous protector's email address into the new message. His fingers went to work, efficiently tapping out a draft message:

To: Guardian Angel
Subject: Your recent message

Hello. We're intrigued by your recent message to me. Can you be more specific about what kind of danger we might be in? If the danger is Soren Kristiansen, is Anika in danger too? If so, what kind of danger are we in? Can you tell us something more about you that will let us know that you can trust you? How do we know that you aren't Soren himself? We look forward to your reply.

Dan, Francesca, and Anika

"What do you say?" Dan asked when he was finished typing.

"Can you ask him or her if they know if Jonah is safe?" she asked.

"Sorry, I forgot to say that," Dan said, his fingers typing again, appending the line: *'Can you tell us if Jonah is safe at the moment'* to the end of the message. "There, how does that look?"

"Perfect. Let's send it and see what happens," Anika said. Dan moved the mouse cursor and clicked on the send button. A *whoosh* sound emanated from the computer, letting them know that their message was being delivered to some unknown destination.

"That's it," Dan said. "All we can do now is wait. I'll let you know the minute I hear anything from our mystery man or woman."

"Thanks, Dan. Not just for this, but for everything—going to Seattle and Atlanta with me, letting me stay here at the Chateau and introducing me to your friends—just for being there for me. I don't know what I'd do without you," she said, her eyes growing red and glistening with telltale tears. Dan closed the cover of the laptop and rose to his feet, taking her into his arms.

"You know I'd do anything to help," he reaffirmed. "Let me know the minute you know anything. I'll meet you wherever you need me. If it's on Friday, I'll get back to you as soon as the arraignment is over."

Anika pulled out of the embrace and held Dan by the shoulders.

"Fran comes first, Dan," she said. "Don't let my problem with Soren get in the way of what you need to do for her. Understood?"

"Yes, ma'am," he said, smiling and wiping a solitary tear that had just escaped from her right eye. He took a quick glance at his watch. "Time to get you to the airport to catch your connector."

"Okay, after I brush my teeth. And I must say goodbye to Carmen. Fran is lucky to have her taking care of the Chateau for her. She's a real sweetheart," Anika said.

"You're right about that," Dan said. "I don't know what Fran would have done without her while I was back in Detroit after Chelly's death. She's definitely a keeper. Let's get these dishes back inside."

While Anika finished getting ready and packed her bags, Dan helped Carmen in the kitchen. The Chateau was quiet, since most of the guests had returned to L.A. on Sunday evening. Tim, Shelley, Richard, and Pam had also returned to Orange County. The few hotel guests who remained had finished breakfast and were waiting for the sun to move higher in the sky before venturing out of their rooms to gather around the pool.

Anika emerged from her room, one bag in each hand. Hearing her door open and close, Carmen and Dan emerged from the office to meet her.

"Thank you so much for everything, Carmen," Anika said. "I hope I'll be able to come back and see you soon."

"*Gracias*, Señora. It has been a pleasure meeting you. We hope you enjoyed your stay with us."

"Surprisingly, I did," Anika said, laughing. "I wouldn't have believed how relaxing it is here, unless I'd witnessed it myself. I won't be afraid to come back the next time."

Dan looked at his watch again.

"Time to go," he said. "It's only ten minutes away, but you don't want to miss your connection at LAX if you want to be in Calgary by lunch." He picked up Anika's bags, while she and Carmen gave each other a parting hug.

"All ready?" Dan asked.

"Let's go," Anika replied. She went ahead of Dan, pulling open the massive pine door. Dan carried her bags through the door and out into the parking lot. Seconds later, the huge door clicked shut behind them, leaving Carmen standing by herself in the early morning serenity of Chateau Eden's courtyard.

KEVIN VASQUEZ felt like his head was going to explode. His frustration with District Attorney Mulholland was threatening to cause him to do something he had never done—he was about to lose it on his superior.

"Kelly, even if I agree that Capellini might be a flight risk, we don't have anything to support that. Hartley is going to laugh us out of his courtroom. We'll both look like a couple of amateurs."

"Listen, Kevin. You were in that interview with NYPD last week. She didn't tell us dick. She's hiding something big, and you know it!"

"Let's assume you're right, Kelly. What is she hiding? All she told us was that Pastor Soren didn't kill that Baranyi woman, because she's seen her in the flesh. There is no crime, Kelly! Or at least no crime that we know of."

"Oh, shut up!" Mulholland shouted. "If you can't get on board and support the goals of this office, then you might as well walk out that door and never come back. And if you do, I guarantee you'll be finished as a prosecutor. You'll be back doing legal aid like you were when I found you! How would you…"

Mulholland stopped abruptly in mid-sentence.

"What did you just say, Kevin?"

"When?" Vasquez replied timidly. "I wasn't talking, you were."

"A minute ago—you said something about Pastor Soren— about there not being a crime," Mulholland recalled.

"Yes, I said we don't have a crime if Baranyi is alive," Vasquez repeated, clearly frustrated with his superior's dogged determination to make a case out of nothing.

"But we do!" Mulholland shouted. "Soren Kristiansen is one of the most wanted people in the country right now. He abducted his own son! And there's an unknown blonde female accomplice at large—possibly Baranyi! All we have to do is raise a reasonable doubt that Capellini knows both Baranyi and Kristiansen, and that she's keeping quiet to protect both of them!"

"That's a gigantic stretch and you know it, Kelly," Vasquez pleaded. "Hartley will never fall for it."

"Well, it's your job to sell it and make sure he does, Kevin. *Your* job depends on it!"

"Can I just ask one question, Kelly?" Vasquez asked.

"It better be good. What is it?" Mulholland answered.

"I heard Joanna Sullivan asking you if there's anything else going on. Is that true? Are you keeping something from me? Because, if I'm going to win this case, I need to know everything," Vasquez demanded.

Before Kevin Vasquez had even finished his question, he knew it was a mistake. Mulholland's face had turned crimson. Every muscle in it was strained to its limit. Her head looked like it was ready to explode.

"You grandiose little prick! How dare you question my motives? The outcome of every case in this office rests on my shoulders, and I approach every case with the idea that I'm going to win it for the people of Riverside County. Don't you ever dare to suggest that I have any other motives. Do I make myself clear!"

"Yes, ma'am," Vasquez said contritely. "I'm sorry if I implied anything else."

"You'd better be sorry. Anything else, Mr. Vasquez?"

"No ma'am," he replied.

"Then get out of here and figure out how you're going to sell Hartley on the idea that Capellini is holding back on us and Baranyi could be involved. Get out of here!"

Vasquez turned quickly on the heels of his expensive Italian leather shoes, relieved to be leaving his boss.

I've taken impossible cases before, and I haven't lost one yet. That's why Kelly hired me. If I've done it before, I can do it again. But this time…

Kevin Vasquez had less than three days until Capellini's preliminary hearing. And for the first time in his life, he didn't have any idea how he was going to find a convincing argument.

ANGELA'S EYES fluttered open as her apartment's ancient air conditioning groaned and rattled to life. She tilted her head for a look at her clock. It was eleven-fifty Wednesday morning. The second floor office was already feeling the effects of the unforgiving rays of desert sun. She swung her legs over the side of her pullout couch, yawned, and stretched her arms. Heaving a big sigh, she leaned down and scooped her panties and bra off the floor, digging deep for the motivation to get through another endless day.

It was taking more and more effort to get herself motivated with each day that passed, waiting for contact with Soren's laptop. She knew she was sinking into a depression, but she felt powerless to stop the downward emotional vortex. Still naked, she shuffled over to her TV and clicked it on.

'... temperatures in the valley today will creep close to the one-hundred-degree mark for the first time this year, as a high pressure system moves into place over most of the American Southwest...'

More of the same, just hotter, she said to herself. She shuffled her naked body over to her desk, automatically flipping open the lid to her laptop. She glanced idly at the control panel window for a progress report on the synchronization with Soren's computer. Robotically, as she had done each morning for the past week, she turned to walk away from the machine, still carrying her worn panties and bra in her hand. Suddenly, she stopped dead in her tracks. The panties and bra fell to the floor. Her eyes darted back to the screen. She stared at the control panel and blinked her eyes.

Synchronization Complete.

It took a few seconds for the words to sink in. She pulled her chair up in front of the computer, and plopped herself down on the chair in front of the screen. She began typing commands in the control window.

"Where the hell are you hiding, Soren?" she said to herself as she typed. She stopped typing and waited while her machine started tracing the connection between their two computers. The seconds ticked by, seeming like minutes to Angela. As the length of time increased, she smiled.

So, that's the way you're going to play—you're re-routing yourself through multiple servers around the world.

Her fingers went to work again, typing commands to modify the search parameters in her control panel. Progress was painstakingly slow. Angela realized it was going to be more difficult to pinpoint Soren's exact whereabouts. Her cloning program would keep fine-tuning its search over the next few hours to home in on her adversary.

While her laptop worked away silently in the background, she skipped her nude body over to the office's tiny closet, finding herself suddenly energized. She quickly pulled on a pair of clean panties and a fresh bra, then a pair of capris and a clean tank top. She rushed back to her desk.

Unable to pinpoint IP Address: Nearest approximation—Australia.

"Yes! Australia!" Angela shouted aloud, unable to restrain her enthusiasm. Her mind was now up to speed, running through the ramifications of this new piece of knowledge.

Watch out, Soren. I'm coming to find you!

Angela's mind began racing, trying to think of everything at once. Instinctively, she took a deep breath and let it out in a long sigh. Gradually, she regained control over her thoughts.

Okay, Angela. You've got to get your butt 'down under' as fast as possible. It will be easier to pinpoint his location once you're there!

Her mouse clicked away furiously, bringing up the *Travelocity* website, searching for flights between LAX and Sidney. She selected a flight that departed the next evening.

"Shit!" she muttered. "I need a freakin' visa?" She emitted a frustrated huff. Once again her mouse and fingers went into action, bringing up the website for the Australian government. She set to work, completing the online application form. Abruptly, she pushed back her chair and leapt across the room to a counter beside her closet, grabbing her purse and leaping back to her chair in one fluid motion. Rummaging through her purse, she finally found her wallet, flipped it open and withdrew the Visa credit card bearing her alias: Anna Benz. Her fingers flew over the keys, paying the exorbitant expedited fee and completing her application. She hit the *Return* key.

Angela felt her heart pounding in her chest. She realized that she'd been holding her breath while typing in her credit card information. In the last half hour, her sluggish brain had surged back into high gear. She felt a flood of mixed emotions racing through her—excitement that was fuelling her with renewed motivation and energy—frustration at having to wait for the

Australian visa before she could begin the physical hunt for Soren —anxious anticipation of becoming a chameleon and putting her Anna Benz identity to work. But most of all, her mind leapt ahead in time, dreaming of what it would be like to walk up to the front door of her parents' small house in Cleveland, and to take Julia and Nicholas into her arms again.

She jerked her mind back to reality, refocusing her attention on the clone's control panel. Her fingers typed out another command. The prompt blinked rhythmically for a few seconds. Suddenly, a large new window opened on Angela's desktop. A huge sigh escaped slowly from her lungs as the reality of what she was viewing sunk in—she was staring at the mirror image of the desktop of Soren's laptop. She looked at her control panel and noted that the last transmission from Soren's machine was just over three hours ago. She brought up a time-zone map of the world, calculating that he must have last used his machine in the hours after midnight in Australia—early tomorrow morning Australian time.

Angela rose from her chair. Calmly she filled her kettle with water, flipping on the switch and hearing the appliance hiss to life. She readied her coffee mug by spooning some instant coffee into the vessel. She poured some muesli into a bowl then retrieved a container of strawberry yogurt from her tiny bar fridge. After pouring yogurt over the muesli, she sliced some fresh strawberries into the mixture and stirred them together. She took the bowl over to her desk and slowly began spooning breakfast into her mouth. While she chewed the grains, she began the slow, painstaking process of searching through the file structure of Soren's hard disk. Her first priority was to search his email messages, hoping they would give some clue as to his current location. It might save her the work of having to trace his IP address. If that didn't work out, she would study his recent browser history.

Angela opened Outlook on Soren's clone. He had two accounts: one for his Pastor Soren account on the WWCC server, the other a personal Yahoo account. Her heart sank as she searched through the mailboxes for each account. There were no recent messages, either sent or received, for almost two weeks. He had not been using either account.

The whistling of the kettle and the click of the auto-shutoff distracted Angela. She went to the countertop that served as her makeshift kitchen and poured boiling water over the instant coffee in her mug. After giving it a thorough stir, she carried it back to her desk and plopped herself down in the rolling chair. She carefully took a small sip of the steaming hot fluid, then sat back and took a deep breath. It looked like it was going to be a long day.

Deep inside, Angela began to feel her motivation and determination coming back to life. She had a goal and could now see a light at the end of the tunnel. She was going undercover to find Soren Kristiansen. More importantly, she was going to find Jonah and reunite him with his mother. And in the process, she was going to expose Soren and finish him for good. If she was lucky, and this all worked out, maybe she could finally have her life back, and maybe Julia and Nicholas could have their mother again.

Feeling her new energy and motivation coursing through her body, along with the warm glow from her coffee, she opened Soren's web browser and brought up his history. Taking one more long breath, she reached for her mouse and started clicking on links, one at a time. She felt an adrenaline rush—the thrill of becoming a voyeur into the life of the man who wanted her dead. The tables had turned. The prey had now become the hunter, and Angela felt herself getting high on the thrill.

Game on, Soren—who's chasing who now? Now let's see which one of us is best at hiding like a chameleon. Don't fool yourself. You may think you can hide from me forever. But I promise I'll find you. You can't escape Angela's Eyes!

PART FIVE: LOVE TRIANGLE

CHAPTER 17

"ALL RISE! Riverside County versus Francesca Capellini," the bailiff shouted once again. "His Honor Ernest Hartley presiding." The crowd in the courtroom rose to their feet for the continuation of Fran's arraignment.

Dan saw Fran turn around, looking for her support group—Shelley, Tim, Pam, and himself. The orange jumpsuit Fran was wearing made her look wider and heavier than Dan remembered. She nodded her head to acknowledge him and the rest of the group, but she didn't smile. To Dan, she seemed numb and her eyes were vacant.

"Everybody be seated," Hartley announced. He looked up over his glasses at Fran and Joanna Sullivan at the Defense table. Then he glanced to his left, acknowledging prosecutor Kevin Vasquez and District Attorney Mulholland.

"Mr. Vasquez, Ms. Mulholland. This arraignment was adjourned in order to allow some time for detectives from New York to interview the defendant before I make a final decision on the granting or denial of bail. What do you have for me?" Harley asked, getting right to the point.

"Thank you, Your Honor," Vasquez replied, rising to his feet. "Ms. Capellini was interviewed by detectives from NYPD, in the presence of myself, the District Attorney, and Ms. Capellini's counsel. She steadfastly refused to provide any information about the woman in question, one Angela Baranyi, apart from stating that she had taken a candid portrait of Ms. Baranyi. She claimed that it was the only time that she had ever seen this woman. Your Honor, Ms. Baranyi was an associate of Pastor Soren Kristiansen, a man who is currently a fugitive from the law for alleged kidnapping, and who appears to have at least one female accomplice. Ms. Capellini is the only person known to have had contact with Ms. Baranyi, who could very well be the mystery woman who recently helped Pastor Kristiansen disappear in Atlanta. Furthermore, it is public knowledge that Ms. Capellini's husband, the late Philippe Morel, was a business associate of Pastor Kristiansen, making it very likely that Ms. Capellini knows the Pastor and is withholding vital information. Therefore, based on Ms. Capellini's lack of cooperation, the prosecution feels there is a high probability that she is withholding vital information to protect herself from involvement in even more crimes than those of which she is accused. Given that Pastor Kristiansen is still on the run, we continue to feel that Ms. Capellini is a potential flight risk as well, and we ask that she be denied bail."

Joanna Sullivan rose to her feet, but Hartley quickly turned his head, his eyes meeting hers before she could speak.

"Ms. Sullivan. What do you have to say?" Hartley asked.

"Your Honor. The prosecution is trying to argue that their inability find any credible evidence of alleged wrongdoing is the fault of my client. If they have evidence to show that Ms. Capellini is colluding with known criminals, then I demand that they show it!" Joanna shouted.

"Counsellor, you know as well as I do that it is not the mandate of this arraignment to determine if there is enough evidence to take your client to trial. That will be up to a Grand Jury. Our task today is to decide whether your client should, or should not, be granted bail while she awaits a Grand Jury hearing," Hartley stated.

The judge lowered his head and began writing something. Apart from one or two coughs from the gallery, a hush descended on the courtroom. Hartley finished writing, and looked up once again over top of his glasses towards Fran.

"Ms. Capellini, please rise," Hartley said with authority.

Fran rose slowly to her feet, her head hanging down. She turned and looked behind her, in Dan's direction. Dan read both sadness and helplessness in her eyes. He knew she was feeling defeated, even before the courtroom heard Judge Hartley's decision. A sense of foreboding came over Dan, not just for Hartley's decision, but also for Fran and his future with her. She turned her head back toward Hartley to receive his latest decision.

"Given that your late husband knew Ms. Baranyi's employer, Pastor Kristiansen, and that Ms. Baranyi was a trusted assistant to this man, I find it hard to believe that you had no other knowledge of Ms. Baranyi, apart from a random meeting in East Los Angeles. Therefore, I'm going to agree with the prosecution that there is a significant chance that you are not cooperating, and that you could be a flight risk. I'm remanding you back into custody at the Indio Jail, without bail. A Grand Jury will be scheduled for Tuesday, June twenty-seventh, 2006 in this courtroom, to determine if there is enough evidence for this case to proceed to trial. I presume that gives both the prosecution and defense enough time to prepare your cases?" Hartley said sarcastically. He peered over his glasses, first at Joanna Sullivan, then at Vasquez and District Attorney Kelly Mulholland.

"Next case, bailiff!" Hartley ordered. His gavel slammed onto his desk. Dan felt like an anvil had just landed on his chest, forcing all of the remaining air from his lungs. He waited in shock for Joanna to protest, but soon realized that there was nothing she could add after being put in her place by Hartley's last comments. He looked at the Prosecution table and saw a look of relief spread across the face of District Attorney Mulholland. She shook the hand of Kevin Vasquez, congratulating her peer on his successful argument. Her eyes met Dan's for only a split second, and then she quickly turned away. But it was enough time for him to see the guilt in her eyes.

Dan watched helplessly as two court officers escorted Fran from the courtroom. He waited, wishing for one more chance to kiss her, to gaze into her eyes, and to tell her that he loved her. Instead, Fran's head hung down and she didn't look back. He felt the distance between them growing exponentially by the day. In that moment, he felt a mixture of overwhelming sadness and empathy for her. He felt Shelley and Tim wrapping their arms around him as tears filled his eyes.

SOMEWHERE OVER the middle of the Pacific Ocean, somewhere in the middle of a night that spans two days, a middle-aged woman, her normally long blonde hair sheared short for Australia's heat, sat quietly aboard the giant *Qantas* Boeing 747. The lights were dim and the shades were all pulled down. Most of the aircraft's hundreds of passengers were doing their best to catch a few winks to minimize the inevitable jet lag. But Angela's mind wouldn't turn off.

She had adapted quickly to the brown-tinted contact lenses that concealed her distinctive hazel eyes—a complete giveaway to anybody who knew her. Besides, the gifted graphic artist who Photoshopped the photos she had supplied for her two bogus passports, had changed her eye colour from hazel to brown. She didn't need any keen immigration agents noticing the difference. For anybody who asked, Anna Benz had just undergone chemotherapy for breast cancer. She was fulfilling the item at the top of her bucket list—a trip to Australia to visit the Great Barrier Reef.

Angela's mind continued to revisit the things she'd discovered on Soren Kristiansen's laptop computer. His browsing history only raised more questions. The most puzzling was the many trips he made to a U.S. Department of Agriculture (USDA) website. The IP address for the website didn't match that of any other USDA sites, and Angela was sure it wasn't an official part of the USDA. But if not the USDA, what was it? Her mind jumped to the most extreme of possible solutions.

Does he work for the CIA or the NSA? But if he does, how do I explain the kidnapping of his son, Jonah? Or maybe he's in the Witness Protection Program? Maybe Jonah wasn't kidnapped. Maybe he and Soren needed to disappear for their own safety?

Angela shrugged. At least that last option might explain why Soren had been able to vanish inside the U.S., and catch a flight so easily to Australia with his son. How else could they get on a plane together without raising any questions?

Angela was frustrated. Her cloning program, as clever and revealing as it was, had significant limitations. It couldn't track Soren's every move in real time. Instead, it only tracked changes to his hard drive's file structure, taking snapshots in time of his desktop whenever any changes occurred. Even worse, she suspected that he might have an email account inside the questionable USDA server that he could access over the Internet, rather than using his Outlook mail program. Without Soren's username and password for the mystery website, she was never going to be able to tell who he was contacting, or what he was saying to them.

The one thing I can do is estimate when he's usually active on his computer. He seems to be accessing the USDA account between midnight and two a.m. or three a.m. every night. I'm going to have to adjust my schedule to monitor my clone of his computer every night between those times. At least I'll get snapshots of what he's doing anytime his computer saves anything to file.

Angela started to make a mental list of things she needed when she arrived in Sydney. She'd already taken care of the most important item on that list—booking a hotel room with free high-speed Internet in Sydney for three days. If she didn't have any luck finding Soren in that time, she'd have to look for some less expensive accommodation that met her needs. Next on her list, she needed to get an Australian mobile phone plan for the new Blackberry smartphone she'd purchased before she left Las Vegas.

More importantly, she needed a data plan so she could send emails and do research on the fly from anywhere.

Angela's mind started wandering again. Like somebody trying to fit sections of a jigsaw puzzle together, she knew she'd managed to fit together many pieces from the *World-Wide Community of Christ* side of Soren's life. She was just beginning to fit a few pieces together from another more mysterious part of his life. How many other secrets did he have? What if those mystery areas were keys to Soren's life that linked all of the other clumps of puzzle pieces together?

Angela wracked her brain, trying to find ways to connect the things she had discovered about Soren while she was working for him—his online pornography enterprise, with its central servers located in Vietnam and Thailand—the laundering of that money through the South American affiliates of the WWCC. But as hard as she tried, she couldn't come up with any ways to explain the mysterious USDA website, or to connect any of those pieces to Jonah's abduction.

Another random thought jumped into her mind.

What will you do if you accidentally run into him, face to face?

The thought terrified her. Her mind drifted eerily to the times when Soren had made his creepy advances—placing his hand over hers at their first business lunch—trying to kiss her during the meeting in his office—and the nightmare of having him threaten to harm Julia and Nicholas, while he kissed her and tried to grope her breasts. Finally, she recalled the night she set up her disappearance —letting him caress her thighs, teasing his cock with fleeting touches from her body and hands—leading him into heavy foreplay.

Angela's body shuddered. She felt as if it was all happening again. Her sense of disgust from letting him use her body was battling against a totally unexpected sexual longing that was taking control of her body.

Shocked by her sudden loss of composure, Angela quickly refocused her thoughts on Julia and Nicholas. They were the only reason she had managed to pretend to give herself to Soren that night.

She rummaged through her carry-on bag, looking for the book she'd purchased in the airport bookstore. She forced herself through the first chapter, struggling to keep her thoughts focused. A number of times, she realized she hadn't comprehended the last page she'd read, having to go back and re-read it. Before long, Angela's mind succumbed to the constant drone of the huge jet engines and the cabin's darkness. Her head jerked involuntarily as she caught herself falling asleep.

Don't fight it, Angela. Get some sleep. Something will show up on his computer sooner or later.

She put the book back in her carry-on bag. Instead of trying to distract herself, she purposely changed her thoughts, focusing on happier times with Julia and Nicholas after her divorce. The corners of her mouth slowly turned upward. Her face transformed into a soft smile as she drifted gradually into a peaceful slumber.

THE GLOW from Soren's laptop illuminated his face like a ghastly apparition—a head, seemingly separated from the rest of its body, seemed to float ominously in the inky darkness of the hotel room.

His fingers finished typing. He sat back and reviewed the contents of his message, making sure not to reveal any information that would reveal his true identity. Helen was strict about that. They were lucky that she was able to pull strings and get them accounts on the NSA's secure internal server. They couldn't afford to have somebody find out who they were, or who had given them access. His eyes scanned the text one last time before hitting the *Send* button:

To: Helen

From: Socrates
Subject: Progress Report

Things are going according to plan. I'm renting my hotel room on a weekly basis. As far as the hotel knows, I'm a mining engineer who will be going back and forth to the Ranger uranium mine. I think we will probably be staying here in Darwin for another two or three weeks. That will allow me to organize the next stage of the plan with our contacts in Vietnam, and to arrange for a fast means of escape in the event that we're recognized here.

I was able to rent an apartment for the boy and Lucy on a month-to-month basis. It's about three blocks away from the hotel. I'm being careful that all three of us are not seen together. Don't worry about Lucy. She seems to be good with the boy and she knows enough to keep her mouth shut unless she's spoken to.

I hope you are pleased with how well I've executed our plan. I can't wait until we can be together again. I long for those days during our training, when we endured so much and only had each other. Being without you over these past few years has been almost more than I can bear. Being together on those precious rare occasions has only made me want to be with you, and made me want to please you more every day.

I'll keep you updated through the secure server every couple of days. Did you get my last message with my Australian mobile number? As per your wishes, I will only use my phone in case of an emergency.

Forever your servant,
Socrates

Soren clicked the track pad's button, sending the message out into the great void of the Internet. Reading the message made him miss Helen. He felt a familiar stirring in the genitals. He redirected the track pad's cursor over the search window of his browser, typing in a familiar web address. He logged in with his administrator's password, going to the area where new files were uploaded for review before being posted on the site. As he scanned thumbnails of the content of each new video, he felt his arousal growing.

Soren spotted one clip that seemed especially promising, and he clicked on the clip's thumbnail. Once the window opened, he clicked the *Play* arrow on the screen. A masked dominatrix with flowing dark hair was toying with a middle-aged white male. His arms were suspended in the air by ropes and his legs were held apart by a spreader bar. Soren watched as the woman expertly alternated her touch—sometimes teasing and stimulating the man to keep him erect, and sometimes using floggers, whips, and other instruments to inflict pain over the victim's entire body. He set the laptop on a coffee table in front of him, not taking his eyes off the video. Watching the submissive man in the video, seeing how the woman dominated him completely, Soren felt his engorged organ starting to throb. He envisioned himself as the Sub and Helen as his Dominatrix. He unzipped his fly, finally freeing himself from the confines of his clothing…

CHAPTER 18

DAN STARED at the large clock behind Joanna. It was the only object on the stark grey wall, apart from two small windows located six feet above the floor, covered in bars and too small for anybody to squeeze through. It was nine-fifteen a.m.—he and Fran had only been in the room with Joanna for fifteen minutes, but it already seemed much longer to Dan.

"If we try to figure out what game they're playing, we'll drive ourselves crazy," Joanna declared. She sat across the table from Dan and Fran in the Indio Jail meeting room.

"You don't have any idea what's going on with the D.A.?" Dan asked. "Why she keeps denying Fran bail? She's like a dog with a bone."

"I've only heard rumours," Joanna answered. "And even if they're true, it's nothing we can address in court."

"Rumours?" Fran said, her voice devoid of any emotion.

"What rumours?" Dan demanded. "What have you heard?"

"I was talking with some of the people in my firm the other day," Joanna replied. "They've heard rumblings that politics are involved—maybe even as far up as the State Department."

"The State Department?" Dan said, incredulously. "Why would they be involved?"

"The rumour my colleagues heard was that the Columbian government might be calling in favours and putting pressure on the U.S. to find out who killed the Alvarez couple. There's a lot of pressure from their families to find out what happened. They had money, Dan. And who knows who they were connected with, either through politics or business, if you know what I mean."

"You mean drug cartels?" Dan asked.

Joanna shrugged her shoulders. "Possibly, or government, or maybe even both, for all we know," she answered. "Just because he made his money in cellular networks doesn't mean he didn't have his fingers in other pies. But that's the point. We don't know anything for certain. It's nothing but speculation."

"Is there any way we can find out if any of it is true? Fran asked.

"No. But that's exactly the kind of thing Mulholland would love to see us preoccupied with," Joanna continued. "She knows she hasn't got a case. That's why she keeps trying to throw us off guard—to see if we'll abandon our game plan. Our case is solid, and we can't let her do that."

"So, we stay with the battered spouse defense," Fran stated quietly.

Dan tried making eye contact with Fran, but she did her best to avoid looking at him. Despite the natural olive shade of her skin, Dan noticed that she was growing pale. Her face was lifeless, lacking any emotional expression. And she was putting on weight and growing more out of shape. Once again, he had the gnawing feeling in his gut that something was wrong—that she was sinking further into depression. Even worse, instead of letting him help, he increasingly felt her pushing him away. Suddenly, Dan made a connection. He recognized the feeling in his gut as helplessness.

"Exactly!" Joanna replied, bringing Dan back from his reverie. "No matter what kind of spurious connections they try to make between your deceased husband, Soren Kristiansen, and Angela Baranyi, we continue to argue that all of your behaviour was a response to Philippe's continued abuse."

"You're sure that Fran's testimony will convince the Grand Jury?" Dan asked.

"By itself, it would be shaky," Joanna admitted. "There wouldn't be any evidence apart from her story. But, combined with your testimony and what you witnessed during your time at

Chateau Eden and their estate, it will confirm her story. We can't allow ourselves to play their game instead of our own."

Dan glanced at Fran for a reaction, but she continued to show little emotion.

"So, let's get down to business, Fran," Joanna continued. "Let's go over the things we want you to emphasize during your testimony—how he coerced you into swinging against your will—how he made you use alcohol and drugs to make you more compliant…"

The talk of swinging suddenly triggered Dan. Memories from the tragic events in Palm Desert flooded into his consciousness. Within seconds, he was immersed in them, unaware of what Fran or Joanna were saying in the present. Memories of Philippe, charming Chelly during their stay at Chateau Eden—the nights in the hot tub at Fran's and Philippe's estate—the freely-flowing wine —Chelly lying beside the pool, her life bleeding out of her, hearing her last words—the nights he and Fran spent in each other's arms after the deaths of Chelly and Philippe…

"… and be sure to emphasize how Philippe manipulated Diego and Juanita Alvarez in exactly the same way he manipulated the Whitneys," Joanna said, her loud voice drawing Dan back into the present.

"Is that all?" Fran asked.

"That should be more than enough," Joanna replied.

Dan looked up at the clock behind Joanna to remind him where he was. He had to remind himself that it was May 2006, almost two months since the traumatic events at Fran and Philippe's estate in late March. His eyes grew wide. His eyebrows and forehead raised in surprise when he noticed the time. It was nine twenty-five5. He had been stuck in a dissociative trance for over five minutes.

"Sorry if I was ignoring you, Dan," Joanna said. "I just wanted to make sure that Fran is prepared to tell her story to the Grand Jury. Is there anything else you wanted to add?"

"Uh,… no," Dan mumbled, having been caught off guard. "I can't think of anything at the moment."

"Then that's about all we can do for now, unless something new comes up. It's still almost six weeks until we go before the Grand Jury. We won't meet again until about a week before that, so I can prepare Fran for the kinds of questions she'll face under cross-examination. In the meantime, is there anything else I can do for you, Fran?"

Fran shook her head slowly from side to side. Sadness overcame Dan. He saw Fran shrinking back into herself as the meeting ended. Then a thought occurred to him.

"There's just one more thing," he said. "Fran and I were both seeing a psychologist for help in dealing with the trauma we experienced in March. If Fran's going to be spending six more weeks in custody, can we arrange for Dr. Torres to visit her so she can continue her treatment? I'm concerned about her."

He looked sideways at Fran, this time catching her eyes and making contact with them. Once again, he read helplessness and sadness. But even worse, he caught a glimpse of a part of her that was angry—angry with herself. From his clinical experience, he knew that inwardly focused anger could be the most damaging emotion of all to Fran's fragile identity at this crucial time in her life.

Frightened by the intimate eye contact, Fran turned her gaze away from him, looking down at the floor instead.

"I can't see why not," Joanna said, turning her attention to Fran. "I'll talk with the warden on my way out. I'll see if Dr. Torres can work you into her schedule as soon as possible."

"Thank you," Fran whispered.

Joanna stood up from the table and a guard stepped forward to help Fran to her feet. Dan gave her one last embrace, not wanting to let her go.

"I'll be flying to New York this afternoon," he said, pulling her close. "Anderson Cooper asked me to do an interview on PTSD in the veterans coming back from Iraq and Afghanistan. I'll be back by late tomorrow night, so I'll call you sometime on Wednesday. I love you."

Dan sensed Fran relaxing and falling into his arms for an instant. Then her body went rigid again, and he felt her pulling away.

"I love you too," Fran said, her voice still flat and emotionless. Dan felt almost as if she were a robot, with the words programmed into her. The effect was devastating. He felt like the air had just been sucked from his lungs. He wanted so much to commit himself to a relationship with Fran. But when Fran pulled away, it felt just like his marriage to Chelly, all over again.

Can I go through that again? Can I keep giving my love to somebody who can't give back? But I can't leave her. Not now. Not with everything she's going through.

Before he knew it, Dan found himself thinking of Anika.

Maybe she's been the right person for me all along, but I never realized it.

Dan was vaguely aware of Joanna shaking his hand, and then leaving the room. Fran's guard took her by the elbow and escorted her into the corridor. Soon she was out of sight, leaving Dan standing alone in the meeting room. Another guard motioned that she would escort him from the facility.

Dan felt his feet moving, but his mind was still somewhere else, trying to make sense of his conflicting thoughts and feelings for Fran and Anika. He loved both of them in completely different ways. He felt his identity being torn in two by the need to decide between them.

EVEN THOUGH he had already been in CNN's New York studios for his previous interview with Anderson Cooper, Dan still felt like a fish out of water. An eager young female intern named Zoe escorted him through a corridor towards the Green Room.

"That's where you'll be waiting until it's time for your interview," Zoe said. "Mr. Cooper's doing a two-part program on U.S. involvement in Iraq and Afghanistan. The first part will be from a political perspective, while your segment will be from a human perspective—the toll it's taking on our servicemen and women. I understand that you're an expert on Post-traumatic Stress Disorder?"

"It's the area of psychology I'm most interested in, if that's what you mean," Dan answered.

"Awesome," the young woman said. "Mr. Cooper said that you'll be talking about two different sources of PTSD in the military?"

"That's right. I'll be talking about the servicemen and women who are traumatized by battle. But I'll also be mentioning another kind of trauma that's coming to the surface these days—sexual abuse within the military itself," Dan said.

"Sounds interesting," Zoe said, as they reached the Green Room. "Mr. Cooper told me that you've been here before, so I don't need to describe the Green Room. I'll introduce you to his first guest, and then you'll have to wait about thirty minutes until it's your turn. You'll be on just after eight-thirty."

Zoe swung the door open and they walked into the Green Room. A familiar, distinguished-looking African-American woman, accompanied by two men in black suits, rose to greet them.

"Dr. Whitney. This is Secretary of State Rice. Madam Secretary, this is Dr. Dan Whitney," Zoe said.

Dan's eyes opened wide, and his eyebrows and forehead lifted in dismay, giving away his sudden surprise at being introduced to the Secretary of State.

"I'm pleased to meet you, Dr. Whitney," Secretary Rice said. "Please, relax and dispense with the formalities. Call me Condoleezza. May I call you Dan?"

"My pleasure, Madame…, er, Condoleezza. Dan is fine. You'll have to pardon my surprise. Anderson told me that he was going to be talking with a politician, but he didn't say it was going to be somebody as important as you."

"That's quite alright," she replied, laughing. "I've grown accustomed to just about every kind of response from people I meet. Before they rush me onto the set, I just want to tell you how much I admire the kind of work you do for people with PTSD. It sounds fascinating. I wish I had more time to talk to you about it today."

"Thank you," Dan answered. "I'd enjoy that very much if we get a chance."

"Oh, and by the way, Dr. Whitney. Mr. Cooper told me all about your recent misfortune. Please accept my condolences on the loss of your wife, and for everything that happened in Palm Desert."

For the second time in the last few minutes, Dan was again taken by surprise. He felt his face growing red, feeling self-conscious about how much the Secretary of State seemed to know about the circumstances of Chelly's death. Then, out of the blue, Dan remembered Joanna Sullivan and the rumour about possible State Department involvement in Fran's murder case. Before he had time to think, Dan heard words escaping from his mouth.

"Thank you, Condoleezza. The State Department is aware of what happened?"

"Of course," she said. "It was all over the news, Dan. I'm sorry that you and Ms…"

"Capellini," Dan said, filling in Fran's last name for the Secretary. "Francesca Capellini. She may be charged with Capital Murder and Conspiracy to Commit Murder because of those events, even though her husband abused her for years. I'm sure you're aware of the details."

"Yes, I've been watching the case with interest," the Secretary said. "It would appear to be another tragic case of self-defense by a battered spouse. I find it rather surprising that the charges haven't been dropped."

Dan was puzzled by Secretary Rice's comment. His forehead wrinkled and his eyebrows dropped. His eyes squinted.

"You do?" Dan said. "We had heard rumours that the State Department might be involved due to pressure from the Columbian government."

Secretary Rice smiled and gave a relaxed chuckle at Dan's remark.

"That's what you heard?" she said. "You really must pay less attention to rumours, Dan. We've had no such pressure, I can assure you."

"Oh," Dan said, suddenly lost for words. His face and ears felt hot again. "I appreciate you putting that rumour to rest."

"It's alright," Secretary Rice said. "No need to be embarrassed. But I agree with you that there's something odd about Ms. Capellini's case."

She leaned closer to Dan and lowered her voice.

"I can only speculate myself, Dan. But if you're looking for pressure from high places, my bet is that somebody else is putting pressure on your District Attorney. Trust me, I don't have any idea who that might be, but that's what I would suspect."

Dan paused and swallowed, giving him time to digest this new piece of information.

"That makes sense," he answered. "But who would be putting pressure on a District Attorney?"

"That's the million-dollar question, isn't it," Secretary Rice replied. "I can't help you out, Dan. But when you find out, I'll be just as interested as you are in knowing who it is."

The door to the Green Room opened and Anderson Cooper entered the room, smiling as he greeted his two guests.

"Secretary Rice, Dr. Whitney. I'm delighted that you're both here today. Has Zoe briefed you on the kinds of questions I'll be asking you today?"

Both the Secretary and Dan acknowledged the young intern's help. Cooper turned to Dan.

"I'll be going on set right now with Secretary Rice. You can watch the interview on that screen," he said, pointing to a flat screen mounted on the wall. "Zoe will come back for you about five minutes before you go on air."

Cooper turned to Secretary Rice.

"Madame Secretary. This way, please."

The Green Room door closed and Dan found himself alone. He took a seat, staring at the TV monitor, but not really seeing. His mind started spinning, wondering who could possibly be putting pressure on District Attorney Mulholland, and what possible motives they would have for keeping Fran behind bars.

Before he knew it, the door opened and Zoe the intern had come to fetch him. He scrambled to bring his thoughts back to reality, and to the questions that Anderson Cooper was going to be asking of him in just a few moments.

"All ready, Dr. Whitney?" Zoe asked.

"Ready as I'll ever be," Dan replied. He pushed aside the unanswered questions about Fran's charges from his mind. Instead, he got himself back into his role as a psychologist, and followed Zoe the intern onto the Anderson Cooper 360° set.

ANGELA glanced at the time on her laptop's screen - it was already one thirty-five a.m. For nine days, she had scoured the file directories on her clone of Soren's hard drive. Frustration and boredom were starting to set in.

He's smart; I'll give him that. The only thing changing on his computer is the search history on his web browser. Nothing but a couple of porn sites—the ones he's running himself—and that damned USDA site! Still no sign of what he's been up to, or where he's staying. If something doesn't happen soon, I'm going to have to sharpen up my hacking skills. I may have to try breaking into that USDA server.

Without thinking, Angela hit the keyboard shortcut again to re-sync her computer with Soren's. She waited impatiently for the view of his desktop to change.

Suddenly, the screen changed dramatically. Angela sat upright in her chair, her body suddenly energized. Her eyes zoomed in on a string of email messages on her screen.

Holy shit, he's reading his email! And he's not using Outlook, either. Oh, my God—he's reading webmail on that USDA website!

Angela took a screen shot of the current screen and saved it to her desktop. Then her eyes went to work, searching the string of messages for clues to Soren's whereabouts.

To: Helen
From: Socrates
Subject: Re: Progress Report

I'm glad you're pleased with me! You know I'll always be your faithful servant, as I have since we made our pact those many years ago. I've done everything you've asked of me—following a career in the ministry to gain the respect of others, so that nobody would ever suspect our true mission in life. Our positions of responsibility have earned the respect of everybody. How stupid all those morons have been! They have been so blinded by the masks we wear, that they have followed us mindlessly!

It's such a relief to finally take off my mask. You have no idea how exhilarating it feels to be free—not having to pretend to be what everybody wants me to be! Despite having those idiots chasing me, I feel liberated. I wish I could have seen you in action in Atlanta. I know you must have shared the same feeling of power I felt when I saw the look of surprise and terror in Beth's eyes, and when I felt the rush of adrenaline.

But I will be patient. I realize it is not yet time for you to take on your true identity and to be free.

Forever yours.

To: Socrates
From: Helen
Subject: Progress Report

You have indeed executed my wishes well, and I'm most pleased with you. I worried that you wouldn't be able to go through with silencing our first accomplice, but you've exceeded my expectations! I wish that you could have watched me at the airport too, working my magic on those fools who thought they'd won your contest! I wish we could have been together to celebrate our successes.

Be patient, Socrates. Like you, I constantly remember those days when we had no choice but to submit to the wills of those animals. We only had each other to keep us strong. You and I will be together soon enough. Then we will finally have our son and the family we have always wanted, and we will finally be free from the wills of others.

Continue to be vigilant! I will let you know if I see or hear anything on my end that threatens our mission. I look forward to your next progress report.

Lady Helen

To: Helen
From: Socrates
Subject: Progress Report

Things are going according to plan. I'm renting my hotel room on a weekly basis. As far as the hotel knows, I'm a mining engineer who will be going back and forth to the Ranger uranium mine. I think we will probably be staying here in Darwin for another two or three weeks. That will allow me to organize the next stage of the plan with our contacts in Vietnam, and to arrange for a fast means of escape in the event that we're recognized here.

I was able to rent an apartment for the boy and Lucy on a month-to-month basis. It's about three blocks away from the hotel. I'm being careful that all three of us are not seen together. Don't worry about Lucy. She seems to be good with the boy and she knows enough to keep her mouth shut unless she's spoken to.

I hope you are pleased with how well I've executed our plan. I can't wait until we can be together again. I long for those days during our training, when we endured so much and only had each other. Being without you over these past few years has been almost more than I can bear. Being together on those precious rare occasions has only made me want to be with you more, and made me want to please you every day.

I'll keep you updated through the secure server every couple of days. Did you get my last message with my Australian mobile number? As per your wishes, I will only use my phone in case of an emergency.

Forever yours.

Angela stared at the messages, her eyes wide open in dismay.

You bastard! So being Pastor Soren was just a big act for you —taking advantage of gullible people like me. And you ruined my life, all in the name of your sick plan!

Angela began shaking with rage—she had never felt anger like this before, even when her frustrations with David and her marriage were at their worst. The feeling was so intense it frightened her.

Get a grip, Angela. Take some deep breaths and relax.

Gradually her breathing slowed. Her eyes returned to the email string to re-examine it. The tension in her muscles began to ease, and she felt herself starting to regain control over the logical part of her brain. The rest of the information in the email messages started to sink in.

So you're in a hotel in Darwin... for at least two or three more weeks!

This was the break Angela had been looking for. She hit the shortcut key to refresh the screen. The new view of the laptop's desktop was clear. The string of emails had disappeared.

"Fuck! He's logged off!" she muttered aloud.

Angela opened the screen image of the emails and read them again. She looked at the times when the emails were sent, noticing that Soren was just typing the final words of his last message to Helen when she had synced her computer with Soren's. She realized how lucky she'd been to refresh her view of his desktop in the brief period of time he was online, otherwise she might have missed him again. She made a mental note to make sure she refreshed and captured his screen more often every night. She reviewed the messages one last time to see if she'd missed any crucial information. When she was satisfied, she opened her browser and started checking for hotel rooms and flights for Darwin.

Angela's mind continued to process the email messages as she multi-tasked and made reservations for Darwin. She wouldn't be able to get on a flight until later tomorrow.

Who is this Helen? It sounds like she has some kind of weird control over Soren—like he's her servant or something. If that's true, who is she in real life?

Angela felt herself shiver. This new piece of information was unsettling. It added a big element of uncertainty to her quest to find Soren. She didn't like that there was a wild card out there somewhere—Soren had an ally and nobody, including herself, knew who she was.

I'm going to have to be extra careful. And I'd better make sure I tell Dan and Anika to keep looking over their shoulders too.

Weariness descended upon Angela's body. She had adopted a schedule of staying up half the night and sleeping late, instead of settling into a normal daytime routine. Her eyes were weary and she allowed them to close, hoping that this would send the message to her brain to shut down for the night.

Unfortunately for Angela, her brain didn't get the message. It continued to churn, trying to digest the new bits of information from Soren's emails—sifting through her memories of her time at the WWCC. She was searching for clues—any clues at all—to the possible identity of the mysterious woman she now knew only by the code name Helen.

CHAPTER 19

"HAVE YOU told Dan that you're pregnant yet?"

The middle-aged woman, notepad and pen in hand, sat in the uncomfortable metal prison chair at a ninety-degree angle to Fran, gazing into her eyes. Fran felt uneasy. She watched as the other woman uncrossed her left leg, shifted in her chair, and then crossed her right leg over. She smoothed the shiny polyester fabric of her dress over her full-figured hips and thighs. She flipped a stray clump of her black hair away from her eyes and her round face. She waited patiently for Fran to respond.

"I'm sorry, Dr. Torres," Fran finally answered. "I haven't been able to find a way to tell him. We are always talking about other things—my court case or his friend's abducted child—it never seems to be the right moment."

"Are you afraid?" Dr. Torres asked.

Fran nodded, averting her eyes from her psychologist and looking down at the floor.

"What are you afraid of? Are you afraid of how he's going to react?"

"Of course," Fran answered. "Wouldn't you be afraid if you were in my shoes? We have only known each other for two months. Why would he stay and help me raise a child, when he could go back to his old girlfriend instead?"

"Do you know if he wants children?" Dr. Torres inquired.

"Yes… I think so. That was one of the things he and Chelly… his wife… were arguing about when they came to the Chateau. He wanted children and she did not."

"So, you know he wants children. What else are you afraid of?"

Fran fidgeted with her hands, looking down at them, and she shifted positions in the uncomfortable institutional metal chair. This whole discussion was getting too personal. She didn't want to tell Dr. Torres about how almost every other important person in her life either ignored or abused her. She didn't like to talk about it. It was something she preferred to keep safely hidden behind the walls in her mind. It was frightening enough that Dan had been able to see through those walls and get close to her.

"Do you love him?" Dr. Torres asked. "Are you afraid of letting yourself get too close to him?"

Fran felt her face getting warm. She knew it was giving her away. Dr. Torres already knew what she was going to say.

"I understand," the psychologist said, her voice calm and reassuring. "It feels scary falling in love with somebody, doesn't it? What if I trust him with my heart and he lets me down, just like everybody else in my life? What about my child? What if he leaves and breaks my child's heart?' You know what that feels like, don't you?"

There it was. The frightening truth was out in the open—Fran felt more exposed and vulnerable than if she was naked.

"Do you think he's the kind of man who would abandon you and your child?" Dr. Torres asked.

"No… I think he is different," Fran said. "When he looks into my eyes, he sees what I am feeling. I can't hide anything from him."

"I see," the psychologist said. "And you've never known anybody who has understood what you're feeling, have you? Tell me something. When you were young, did you ever want somebody to know what you wanted, what you needed, and what you were feeling?"

"Of course," Fran replied. "That's all I ever wanted."

"But you never had a chance to learn what it feels like to be emotionally close to somebody. Not with your childhood history. It's not too late to learn, Fran. But you have to take a chance on trusting somebody—somebody like Dan—if you're ever going to learn to feel comfortable being close to somebody."

Fran was quiet, slowly digesting Dr. Torres' words. It made sense logically. But she still felt the slow churning feeling of anxiety in her gut that had plagued her since she found out she was pregnant.

"One more thing," Dr. Torres said. "How do you think your children will learn how to be intimate with another person, if they don't learn it from you?"

"I suppose they would learn it from their parents," Fran replied.

"That's right. If they don't, then the cycle will continue and they'll grow up being afraid of getting close to other people. It's up to you, Fran. I understand how afraid you are of trusting yourself to Dan. But what about your children? Don't they deserve a chance to have a loving father who can teach them how to love?" Dr. Torres asked. She looked at her watch, made a notation in her notepad and then closed it. She paused, letting her last remarks float in the silence between the two women.

Dr. Torres' words lingered in Fran's head, with no other competing thoughts to dislodge them. Her romantic side desperately wanted to take a chance on letting Dan in—to try learning how to be intimate with him. But her strong, independent, businesslike part wanted just as much to protect her from any emotional pain. And the more those two sides of her identity battled against each other, the more Fran felt the churning in her stomach.

"We didn't get a chance to spend much time talking about how you're coping with the events surrounding Chelly's death. We still haven't talked much about your feelings of guilt. Are you okay with focusing on that next week?" Dr. Torres asked.

"I think so," Fran said, her voice still flat and devoid of any emotion.

Dr. Torres stood up, smoothed her dress over her hips, then walked to the door of the meeting room and tapped on the window. A guard outside acknowledged her knock and opened the door.

A familiar dark-skinned face with black hair poked out from around the door.

"All finished in here?" she asked, as the rest of the guard's heavy-set body appeared from behind the door. She walked over to Fran, who stood up in front of her chair with her arms extended in front of her, waiting for the inevitable handcuffs.

"That's it, honey," the guard said. "Let's go."

Fran shuffled her way towards the door, which was being held open by Dr. Torres. As Fran exited the room, the psychologist followed her into the hallway.

"I'll see you next week at the same time, Fran," Dr. Torres said, resting her hand gently on Fran's shoulder. "Think about the things we discussed today."

Fran nodded, her expressionless face still trying to hide her inner turmoil. She turned and walked away. Only when she was shuffling down the corridor towards her cellblock, did Fran allow one or two tears to escape from her eyes.

DAN SAT silently in the dim aircraft cabin, the unceasing drone of jet engines making it difficult for him to fall asleep like most of the other passengers. He had boarded the redeye flight from JFK at one-thirty a.m. and would be landing at LAX at about four a.m.

Dan was still trying to digest the information from his unexpected encounter with Secretary of State Rice. He had another successful interview with Anderson Cooper, and he was thankful for that half-hour distraction. But once the interview was over and he left the studio for the airport, Dan's mind was hard at work again.

Did Secretary Rice know who might be applying pressure to District Attorney Mulholland, or was she just guessing like everybody else? Who could be pressuring Mulholland, and what does it have to do with Fran?

His mind came full circle to where it had started this morning, before his conversation with Secretary Rice. He couldn't shake his concern that Fran was sinking further into depression. He knew it was part of her PTSD symptoms after the traumatic events at Palm Desert. But he couldn't shake the feeling that there was something else going on.

I know she's scared. I know she's a victim of abuse and neglect by Philippe and her family. I know she's probably afraid of committing to me. And I know it can't be easy to be locked up in jail for so long. I'd be feeling helpless and depressed too if I was locked up for no reason. But what else is going on?

Commitment.

That word triggered Dan to remember Anika and his deep friendship with her.

How can I expect Fran to commit to being with me, when I still have strong feelings for Anika? So far, the only thing Fran and I have in common is that we've shared a terrible life experience together. And the great sexual connection we made during that experience is keeping us together. But how long can that last? Do we have anything else in common? Is she really the right woman for me?

Dan tried to put on his psychologist's hat for a minute. He knew what he would tell any other person in his situation. 'You have to give yourself a chance to grieve your loss before you're ready to move on with somebody else'. He knew it was too soon for both himself and Fran to make any commitments to each other. But without his psychologist's hat, Dan also knew that he was feeling the beginnings of a deep emotional connection with Fran, the likes of which he had never felt before. And he knew how rare that kind of connection could be.

Yet another side of Dan started speaking to him—a compassionate, caring side that was human and not clinical at all. That compassionate, caring voice urged him to take a chance with Fran—it told him there was only one way to find out for sure if he and Fran were right for each other.

But what about Anika? He couldn't deny that he had always been romantically and sexually attracted to Anika.

Why else would I have had that recurring dream over so many years about making love to her? We've always been best friends. Isn't that what true love is? Being best friends and finding a lasting romantic and sexual connection?

Dan felt himself being overwhelmed by the three-way conflict in his mind. Fatigue was setting in. He closed his eyes, but all he saw were the images of Secretary of State Rice again.

Who could possibly be putting pressure on Mulholland?

Once again, Dan forced himself to go back to the beginning of Fran's court case. He remembered driving into Indio. Both Fran and he were completely confident that the charges would be thrown out on the basis of her history of being emotionally, physically, and sexually abused by Philippe. Suddenly, he felt an ominous darkness coming over him. Other images began clouding his thoughts.

He remembered the protesters outside the courthouse in Indio on the morning of Fran's arraignment. He recalled his shock at the verbal attacks against Fran on the protestor's signs.

Can't they see that she's a victim of abuse—that she was only acting in self-defense?

Then he remembered Joanna's words. 'This isn't the liberal northeast. You're a long way from home, Dan. People in the south and southwest take their religion pretty seriously.'

The religious right? Could they be applying pressure to keep Fran behind bars, and maybe even to have her convicted of Capital Murder?

The thought gave Dan a chill. Were there unseen forces at work that were much larger than he imagined? And how can you fight back when you don't even know whom you're fighting?

Suddenly, a sickening thought struck Dan.

Soren Kristiansen. The World-Wide Community of Christ. Is it even possible? Is there any way that Soren could be involved in this? He's on the run, and what possible connection does he have with Fran? His fight is with Anika—and he abducted Jonah before he knew anything about what happened at Palm Desert. It doesn't make any sense.

As much as Dan tried to reassure himself that Soren couldn't possibly be involved, he couldn't shake the nagging feeling in his gut. He couldn't shake the thought that somehow, in some unknown way, Soren Kristiansen could be the force behind District Attorney Mulholland's relentless prosecution of Fran.

DAN WATCHED, separated by a thick pane of glass, as a guard escorted Fran into the visitor's booth where Dan was waiting. He waited for her to pick her phone, and then did the same.

"Hi, I've missed you," Dan said. "How are you doing?"

Fran shrugged her shoulders.

"Okay, I guess," she replied. "How are you? Any news about Anika's son yet?"

"Nothing yet," Dan said, shaking his head. "It's not good that it's been a month since Jonah disappeared. He could be almost anywhere by now. Anika has resigned herself to going back to work after she spends some time with her family. It's driving her crazy—sitting around, feeling helpless, and continually beating herself up for not being a good enough mother. I'm glad she's going back. It will be a good distraction for her."

"Any more news in the past week from Joanna?" Dan asked. Fran moved her head from side to side, not saying a word. Dan began to feel alarmed. His concern for Fran was deepening by the minute. There was even less emotion in her voice or expression on her face today. Her face was getting round and he saw that she was clearly gaining weight, despite the baggy orange jumpsuit she was wearing. This wasn't the Fran he knew. Even when he and Chelly arrived at the Chateau, and Fran was struggling with the deaths of the Alvarez couple, she hadn't appeared this depressed.

"I'm concerned about you, Fran. You're not yourself. Have you seen Dr. Torres yet?" he asked.

"Yes, I saw her last week and I'll be seeing her again this afternoon," Fran answered.

"So, what did she say?" Dan asked. "Does she think you're becoming more depressed?"

An uncomfortable silence hung in the air. Dan waited for Fran to respond. He saw her having difficulty swallowing. The muscles in her face were tense. She looked down quickly when she saw Dan looking at her.

"I'm pregnant, Dan," she answered meekly.

The words hit Dan with the force of a body punch to his midsection, leaving him speechless. He was instantly overwhelmed by a whirlwind of emotions, unable to make sense of any of them in that moment. What had been an awkward silence before, turned into an ominous cloud—a storm of emotions like Dan had never before experienced.

"Are you disappointed?" Fran asked quietly, her voice bringing him back to reality.

"Disappointed? Of course not," he said, having difficulty finding words to express himself. "I'm just… shocked… I never expected this would happen to me… becoming a father, I mean."

A look of confusion crossed Dan's face.

"You were on the pill. How could it happen?"

A hint of a smile appeared on Fran's face.

"You know how it happened, Dan. We made love—many times. It was beautiful, and we both made a choice not to lose that moment—not to use condoms."

"But you and Chelly were both on the pill." Dan said, still not understanding.

"Yes, I was," Fran answered. "But after what happened to Diego and Juanita, I was so shocked… it was like I was in another world… I lost track of time. When I got to the end of my cycle, I realized I had some pills left over. I must have missed some days."

Dan became distant, his mind going back to the nights he shared with Fran at the Palm Desert estate. He remembered the moment when they were about to join their bodies together in lovemaking, and he reached for a condom. He heard her words, saying that she trusted that he was healthy. They both made the decision to have unprotected sex. They were both adults. They knew what the possible results of their actions could be.

"You didn't answer my question," Fran said, breaking the silence. "Are you shocked about being a father, or shocked that you are having a child with me?"

Tension hung in the air while Dan searched frantically for words to express the whirlwind of thoughts and emotions that were racing through his mind. Finally, he opened his mouth, not really knowing what was going to emerge.

"I'd be lying if I said I expected that you and I would have a child together. I always thought it would be with Chelly."

Dan swallowed with difficulty. He felt his eyes starting to water as he remembered how desperately he wanted to feel closer with Chelly while she was alive, and how much he wanted to start a family with her.

"But I'm also feeling relieved in a way—and happy too—that I'm finally going to have a chance to be a father. I'm starting to see that I have a future—a brand new beginning with you and our baby," he said.

Dan was starting to feel more calm and beginning to accept his new reality. But that initial sense of calm disappeared just as quickly, as he watched Fran. Her head continued to hang down against her chest, refusing to look at him. He became aware of an ominous fear rising in his gut.

"Fran. You do want the baby, don't you?" he asked, waiting anxiously for some kind of a response from her.

After an agonizing pause, Fran finally lifted her head and made brief contact with Dan's worried eyes. Her eyes darted anxiously from side to side, unable to focus on Dan's for any length of time.

"Of course," Fran finally answered. "When I was with Philippe, I never thought I wanted to bring a child into this world. The last thing I ever wanted was for the same things that happened to me in childhood, to happen to another child. I never wanted to get pregnant. But now that I am, I could never end it, Dan. I have to keep the child… with or without you."

"Without me?" Dan said, a new fear growing inside of him. "I assumed we'd be raising the child together… that you and I would be starting a new life. You don't want that?"

Fran bowed her head again. Dan felt a sense of alarm—a sense of helplessness was emanating from Fran. He felt like she was giving up on him. Silence and tension continued to hang in the air. Dan felt his heart pounding. He was perspiring and he became aware that he was holding his breath.

"I don't know, Dan," she said finally. She lifted her head and her eyes finally locked onto Dan's when she spoke. "We hardly know each other. What if we learn to resent each other, rather than growing closer? It might be better for a child to never know its father, rather than having two parents who resent each other because they conceived a child together."

"Is that what you think?" Dan answered desperately. "That I'm just doing this for the baby? That I don't want to be with you? That I'm not falling in love with you?"

Fran shrugged, her face not showing any emotion. Dan wondered if he saw her eyes starting to water, but they quickly looked down at the floor again.

Then Dan felt a growing sense of guilt. He realized that Fran was referring to his friendship with Anika. She wasn't just expressing her doubts about herself—she knew instinctively that he had conflicting emotions about his feelings for both her and his old girlfriend. A feeling of sadness settled over him. He felt tears forming in his eyes as he searched for words.

"I see," he said, dejectedly. "Maybe both of us do need some time to let this sink in. Since there's been no word about Jonah, and since Anika is going back to work, I guess I need to start thinking about where I'm going to live and work too."

An uncomfortable silence began filling the room again. Unable to think of anything to add to the subject, Dan changed the subject.

"I feel pretty foolish," he said. "I guess I should have noticed the signs that you were pregnant. How far along are you? How are you feeling?"

"I'm about nine weeks," she said. "My stomach feels upset in the mornings, but I haven't been sick. I just feel more tired than usual. It could be the pregnancy, or it might just be boredom. I don't know."

"I've been so worried about you," Dan said. "I thought you were depressed—I'm still worried. I don't like how you keep beating up on yourself. Chelly's death wasn't your fault, Fran. I hope you're still going to be seeing Dr. Torres."

"Yes. We are going to continue meeting each week, as long as I'm still in here," Fran said. She steered the conversation away from herself. "Will you be coming to visit again next week?"

"Of course," Dan said. "That is, if you still want me to come. Will Tim or Shelley be coming too?"

"Just Tim," Fran answered. "Shelley has to make her monthly trip to her head office in Switzerland. You can still come to visit if you want. What if you hear something from Anika?"

"Everything's changed, Fran. Now that you're pregnant, I can't just leave you and go running around the world on the spur of the moment. I'll have to tell Anika I can't go with her."

"No, you have to go and help her," Fran said. "You are only able to visit me once or twice a week anyway. There is nothing you can do here for me until the Grand Jury convenes. Have you not heard anything I have said to you today? You are better off without me, Dan. You must go and help her if she needs you."

As soon as he thought of Anika, Dan felt guilty again. His mind went back to that awkward moment of sexual tension he and Anika had felt in the hotel room in Seattle. He felt a flush in his face, knowing that Fran must see his embarrassment and sense his guilt.

"Are you sure?" he asked again.

Fran nodded unconvincingly, her eyes once again avoiding Dan's.

"Thank you for coming, Dan. I feel better, now that I have told you everything."

"I'm glad you did," he admitted. "It must have been terrifying for you to tell me."

Dan still felt tension between them. He didn't want to end the conversation, but he couldn't think of anything else to say. It was Fran who finally ended the silence.

"Goodbye, Dan. I'll see you next week," she said.

She placed her handset in its cradle. Dan heard a click as their connection went dead. He saw tears forming in Fran's eyes, but she quickly turned her head and stood up, signalling a guard that she was finished. Dan couldn't bear to see the guard put the handcuffs back on her. He stood and walked quickly from the room.

Multiple emotions resumed swirling around in Dan's mind. His confusion returned. He felt tears quickly filling his eyes—tears of joy at knowing he was going to be a father—tears of sadness at the thought that he and Fran might not be together to raise their child—but mostly tears of confusion about the strong feelings he harbored for two wonderful, but very different, women in his life.

CHAPTER 20

"COME, JONAH," Lucy said. "Do you want to go outside and do some exploring? Maybe we'll see some kangaroos!"

"Daddy said we shouldn't go out," the boy replied. "He'll be mad if he finds out."

"Then we'll keep it a secret, shall we?" Lucy said, her sly smile hinting at a conspiracy between them. "It's too nice and sunny outside for us to be staying inside in the dark. There's a park across the street. I saw it when I went out yesterday. There are swings and a playground!"

Jonah felt torn between his fear that his daddy would find out, and his boredom, sadness, and depression. He missed his mommy so much. And even though Daddy told him that she was with the *Bad People*, somehow he still couldn't believe it. He liked Lucy. As long as his mommy wasn't here, he was glad he had her to take care of him.

Jonah's sense of adventure and his natural childish need to have fun finally won the battle within his mind.

"Okay, Lucy. Let's go. Will you push me on the swing? I want to go so high I touch the sky!"

"Alright, Jonah. I promise I'll push you as high as I can. But first we have to put some sunscreen on you. The sun is very hot in Australia."

Lucy smiled at Jonah. It made him feel good. Then she squirted sunscreen into her hand and started rubbing it onto his face. It felt cool and he couldn't wait to be outside. Finally, she placed a new sun hat, one that protected his bare neck, on his head. This would be the first time he'd been outside since they came to

Australia. It had been fourteen days. He knew because he had secretly counted the days since they took the long plane ride.

Lucy finished and took Jonah by the hand.

"Okay, let's go have some fun!" Lucy said. She locked the apartment door and they walked down the dark hallway of the tired old apartment. Jonah didn't like the hallway—it felt creepy and made the hair stand up on his neck. He walked so fast that he was almost running. Finally, they went through a glass door into the lobby. He saw the bright sunshine outside for the first time in two weeks.

"Wow, are those palm trees?" Jonah asked. "I've never seen palm trees before!"

"Shhhh!" Lucy said. "Remember, we can't be loud. We don't want any of the bad people to know where we've come from, do we?"

"No," Jonah whispered. "And we don't want Daddy to be angry."

"Let's go," Lucy said. "See the park across the street? That's where we're going." She took Jonah by the hand and they exited the lobby.

"It's hot," Jonah exclaimed. "It feels like the bathroom when it gets all foggy."

Lucy chuckled. "That's right, Jonah. It's a lot like the shower. We're very close to the equator here in Darwin. Do you remember what the equator is?"

"It's the big circle that goes around the middle of the earth. That's where the sun is closest to earth and it gets really hot!"

"That's right. And because it's so hot and we're near the ocean, the water gets very warm and lots of it goes into the air—just like the fog in the bathroom. It's called evaporation. Come on, let's cross the street."

Jonah liked Lucy. She knew lots of interesting stuff and she liked teaching him things she knew.

They crossed the Esplanade to the large green space that stretched for blocks. Jonah saw Darwin harbour, down the hill from the park. He smelled the fresh air coming from the ocean at the same time that he saw the swing set. He broke into a run, with Lucy trailing far behind him.

Jonah plopped his butt on the swing and started pumping his legs back and forth. The swing started a slow, pendulum-like motion, rapidly picking up momentum. As he went backwards and started moving forward, he felt both of Lucy's hands on his back, pushing and adding to his forward momentum. He kept pumping his legs forward and leaning backwards, rapidly gaining height. It was exhilarating. For the first time since his daddy came to school to pick him up and they took the ferry to America, he felt free. He soared back and forth for so long that he lost track of time. After a while, he heard Lucy's voice.

"Jonah, if you want to play in the rest of the playground, you'd better do it now. You know we can't be away from home for too long."

Lucy's words brought him back to reality. He started using his body to slow his momentum, the arc of his pendulum gradually becoming shorter and shorter. The swing slowed and Jonah started feeling brave. As he moved forward and started another ascent, he let go of the swing and flew through the air, feet first. He felt like he was flying as he soared through the air. He braced himself for impact. His feet hit the ground. Jonah let his feet move forward with his momentum, gradually slowing himself and remaining standing. He threw his arms into the air.

"I did it! I was flying!" He ran to Lucy and gave her a gigantic hug. "Thank you for bringing me to the park, Lucy!"

"You're welcome. Now, come with me and we'll go over and see the rest of the playground."

As they walked, Jonah noticed other people in the park—some of them in groups and some of them in pairs or sitting by themselves. They had very dark skin, curly hair, and they were speaking a very different language that seemed to be coming from deep in their throats.

"Lucy, who are the dark people?" he asked.

"They're Aboriginal people, Jonah. They lived here long before the white people came to Australia from England."

Jonah carefully eyed one particularly large group as they walked past. He could tell that they were families—mothers, fathers, and children, like him. Most of them were barefoot, the lighter soles of their feet callused and hard from years without wearing shoes. One older man, his black hair turned mostly to grey, lifted a long, hollowed-out length of wood, painted with traditional art. He puffed his cheeks and started blowing. A low, deep growl resonated from the log.

"What's that?" he asked.

"It's called a didgeridoo," Lucy replied. "It's a traditional Aboriginal music instrument. Do you want to listen for a while?"

Jonah nodded his head up and down. "It sounds spooky, but I like it. They stood quietly and listened for a few moments, before Jonah started feeling restless. "C'mon, I want to go on the slide now!"

He dragged Lucy to the climbing fort then let go of her hand and immediately began scaling a ladder to the upper level of the wooden structure. He ran across the upper level to the top of a large plastic tubular slide. He shouted to Lucy.

"Catch me at the bottom!"

"You're too big to catch, Jonah. I'll sit on the bench and I'll watch."

"Okay… here goes!"

Jonah shot down the long tube, screaming with joy the whole way. He landed on his feet at the bottom and headed straight back to the ladder.

At the top of the climbing structure, Jonah slowly turned in a circle, surveying the world around him. A large freighter crept slowly into Darwin harbour. As Jonah rotated his body slowly, he looked out over the park. In the distance, the deep moan of the didgeridoo throbbed and a group of the Aboriginal men danced and clapped along in rhythm. Jonah realized why he liked the sound of the instrument—it sounded sad and lonely, just like him. Anxiously, Jonah looked to his left at the park bench, making sure that Lucy was still there. He exchanged smiles with her. He was glad she was taking care of him until he could be with his mommy again.

ANGELA watched out the window as the Boeing 737 made its descent over the Northern Territory toward Darwin. She saw plumes of smoke floating into the sky in the distance, not just from one location, but from three. As the plane descended, getting closer to its destination, she was shocked to see more smoke, this time much closer to the plane.

What's going on? It looks like they have some wildfires. I hope that's not going to be a problem while I'm here.

The smoke and flames were soon behind the plane. She craned her neck and saw the tarmac and buildings coming up on the right. Within seconds, they had flown over a fence and an array of red lights and were over the airfield. The jet dropped quickly, the nose tipped up, and then she heard the whine of the jet engines drop away. The aircraft bumped once, then gave a smaller secondary bump, before the front tire settled on the runway. She felt the brakes starting to slow the plane's momentum.

When the plane reached the end of the runway and turned around for the taxi to the terminal, Angela saw smoke in the hills southeast of the city. It seemed dangerously close to the airport. In the distance on her right, she saw hangars with military aircraft. She realized how expansive the Darwin airfield really was. The aircraft's intercom clicked on and the Captain's voice lofted over the passengers.

"G'day, everybody. On behalf of myself and the crew of Qantas flight 842, I'd like to welcome ya to Darwin. Present temperature is thirty-six degrees Celsius, but with the humidity, it's going to feel more like forty-five. If ya look outside yer window, ya might notice how big the airfield is. In fact, it's the largest airfield in the world, being shared by commercial airlines and the Royal Australian Air Force. We'd like ya to remain in yer seats…"

Angela's mind wandered as the 737 bumped its way over the tarmac, making the long trek back to the terminal. Self-doubt grew inside her as the reality of being in Australia sank in.

What am I doing here? Why didn't I just contact the police and pass along my information about Soren's whereabouts?

As the plane bumped along over the tarmac, images of Soren from two years ago in New York flashed back in her mind like a kaleidoscope—the family photo with Jonah and Anika in his office while Soren's hands strayed onto her body - the evil glare in his eyes while he threatened her children's safety—the feeling of revulsion in her body while she pretended to give herself to him in his car.

A bigger than normal bump on the runway jolted her mind back to the present. She realized her heart was racing and her breathing was ragged. In that instant it became totally clear why she was in Darwin. It was totally personal, on both an emotional and visceral level. She felt her fear and her disgust for Soren filling her body. She knew she wouldn't be able to rest until she saw Jonah back in Anika's arms, and saw Soren in custody. She forced herself to bring her focus back to the problem at hand.

Apart from knowing that Soren was staying in a hotel somewhere in Darwin, and that Lucy and Jonah were living separately in an apartment about three blocks away, she didn't have any other clues as to where she would find Soren or Jonah. She'd booked herself a room in a hotel on the Esplanade, in the city's central core. Her plan was to spend a couple of days exploring the city, getting her bearings. In her purse, she carried photos of Soren and Jonas. If she failed to spot them on her own, she'd start showing the photos to see if anybody had seen them around town.

The aircraft finally came to a stop. A few moments later, Angela felt a bump as a mobile staircase made contact with the side of the jet. The crew opened the hatch, and almost immediately, the cool air-conditioned air inside the plane rushed out the door, quickly replaced by hot, humid tropical air. When it was finally her turn to leave the plane, Angela was hit by a blast of even hotter air. Almost immediately, she felt her blue jeans, heavy cotton blouse, and her bra sticking to her skin.

Damn! I'm clearly overdressed and didn't pack right for this climate. Looks like my first order of business is doing some clothes shopping.

The arriving passengers had to walk about a hundred and fifty yards beneath a covered outdoor passageway to the terminal. When she finally walked through the door into the terminal, a wall of refreshingly cool dry air greeted Angela.

As she stood beside the luggage conveyor, a good-looking young man with a short, well-maintained beard came up beside her. He had sandy hair and was dressed in hiking attire. He looked at her and smiled.

"G'day, miss. Where ya from?"

So absorbed was Angela in her mission in Darwin, she was startled by the man's thick Australian accent.

"I'm sorry," she apologized. "My mind was somewhere else. Where am I from?"

"Yeah. Yer not from 'round here. Ya from America? I'm Derek —Derek Hardy. Pleased t'meetcha," he said, extending his hand.

"You're right, I'm from the States—Las Vegas, actually," she said, shaking Derek's hand. "Anna Benz. Nice to meet you."

"All the way from Las Vegas? So whatcha doin' ere in Darwin, Anna Benz?"

Angela started to panic. She hadn't had a chance to think about a cover story for being in Darwin.

You're here to visit somebody—your husband who works at the mine—no; you're not wearing a ring—somebody else…

"I'm here to visit my brother. He's an engineer and he's been doing some consulting out at the Ranger mine," she lied. "We thought it would be a good chance to do some exploring together and to see some of Australia."

"Ahh, yer brother, ya say. For a minute I was afraid that maybe ya was comin' to see a bloke. Well, there's lots for ya t'do with yer brother. What are ya plannin' on seein'? Maybe I can give ya some suggestions," Derek said with his thick accent.

Angela realized she needed to change the subject quickly to stop this guy from coming on to her.

"No plans yet, Derek. Hey, maybe you could explain something to me. When we were approaching Darwin earlier, I saw lots of fires in the areas around the airport. But I don't see any concern on the ground. What's going on? Are there wildfires in the area?"

Derek laughed and smiled at Angela.

"No worries, Anna. It's just the Aboriginals. They're doin' controlled burns of the bush at the end of the wet season, before things get too dry. They learned thousands of years ago that it's fire that regenerates the vegetation. The fires'll burn 'emselves out," he said, chuckling.

"Oh my God," Angela said. "I was worried I might be evacuated from the city in the middle of the night!"

"I wouldn't worry about that. We haven't had to evacuate Darwin since Typhoon Tracy, back in '74."

"You seem to know a lot about this part of the world. What do you do for a living?" Angela asked.

"I'm a pilot. I work fer Territory Air Services. We have a hangar right here at the airport. We're a small charter airline, so I've flown to almost anyplace in the territory that has a small airstrip. I've met lots of interesting local people. Learned lots from 'em, too," Derek added.

"Sounds like a fascinating job," Angela said. She looked up to see her bag coming down the conveyor.

"Oh, there's my little bag," she said.

Before she could reach out to grab it, Derek beat her to the punch, lifting her carry-on bag from the conveyor, setting it down beside her. He extended the bag's handle.

"There ya go, Anna," he said. "Any chance I might see ya while yer in the area?"

Oh my God. He's hitting on me. That's all I need right now.

"Probably not. I don't have much time, and I'll be spending most of it with my brother. But it was really nice meeting you, Derek. Thanks for explaining about the fires. Now I can relax and enjoy my vacation!" she said with a smile.

Derek pulled a card from the breast pocket of his shirt and handed it to Angela.

"Here… take my card," he said. "If you and your brother really wanna see the real Kakadu, ring me up. I'd be happy t'give ya a tour."

"Thanks, Derek," she said, reaching out to shake his hand. "I appreciate the offer. It was nice meeting you. Can you tell me where I can find the hotel shuttle?"

"Nice meeting you too, Anna," he said. His blue eyes sparkled and a broad, friendly grin spread across his face. He pointed to the main terminal entrance. "Right outside the main doors. Ya can't miss it. I think I see one out there right now. If ya run, ya might catch it."

"Oh… thanks so much, Derek… goodbye," she shouted over her shoulder as she began running toward the exit, the wheels of her carry-on bag rolling along behind her.

As the terminal doors slid open, another blast of steamy air greeted Angela. She looked for the downtown hotel shuttle, and then realized it was only steps away. Instead of the large tour-sized bus she envisioned, she saw an aging mid-sized van with a trailer in tow. The driver was busy loading a stack of luggage into the trailer and people clambered into the cramped vehicle. By the time Angela dropped her bag and got to the door, there was only one seat left at the back of the tiny bus.

If she thought it was hot outdoors, Angela was shocked to find the inside temperature of the shuttle was even worse. The driver had turned the motor and the AC off while he was loading. At least a dozen sweaty bodies were squashed into the small vehicle, with only the main door and a few small windows letting in any air. Angela quickly dropped Derek's card into her purse and grabbed the envelope containing her airline ticket and boarding pass. Feeling faint and slightly nauseated, she started fanning her face in a desperate attempt to cool herself. She wiped perspiration from her face and neck with her free hand.

The last thing you need is to throw up in here!

Just when she thought she might vomit or faint from the heat, the driver climbed into the van and the doors closed. He started the engine, and Angela finally started to feel a breath of cooler relief coming from the vents above her. She kept fanning the dry refreshing air over her face with her envelope full of flight information.

As the shuttle made its way downtown via wide streets, Angela started to feel more like herself and began taking notice of the scenery. They were now travelling along a winding boulevard adorned with many modern homes.

"It's a nice city, isn't it, dear," said a tiny elderly woman in the seat beside her. "Everything has been rebuilt since Tracy. There isn't a building in town much over thirty years old."

"Hello," Angela replied. "It *is* very pretty. I'm impressed with what I've seen so far. My name is Anna. Do you live here?"

"I'm Clara. Pleased to meet you. Yes, I've lived here for thirty years. Came as a nurse after Tracy blew the city down, and didn't see any need to leave."

Clara pointed to a small village of tents in a park to the right of the boulevard. Angela saw the ocean in the background.

"What's that in the park?" Angela asked.

"It's the Mindil Beach Sunset Market," Clara replied. "It's open every Thursday and Sunday afternoon and evening. This is Friday, isn't it? If you're in the city for a couple of days, you should go on Sunday. It will be packed with people. There's lots to see and it's beautiful—everybody stays to watch the sunset from the beach."

"I might just do that, Clara. Thanks for the tip," Angela said. "Are you going to one of the hotels?"

"No, dear. I have a flat downtown. It's right beside a big hotel, so the shuttle is convenient for me."

"Where are you staying, dear?" Clara asked.

"Holiday Inn, on the Esplanade," Angela said. Do you know it?"

"Of course. We're almost there. Do you see that park over there, to the right?" Clara asked.

Angela nodded.

"That's the Esplanade. When the light turns green, we'll be going around that corner. Your hotel is just a few buildings on the left. If you're lucky, you'll have a nice view of the harbour," Clara added. True to her word, the driver's voice crackled over the van's speakers.

"Holiday Inn on the Esplanade," the driver announced. The shuttle pulled up on the street in front of the hotel and the driver opened the sliding door. The hot humid air immediately invaded the cramped space again.

"It was nice speaking to you, Clara."

"You too, dear. I hope you enjoy your stay."

Angela proceeded to climb over people, legs, backpacks, and miscellaneous small bags to work her way to the front of the tiny bus. She never thought she'd be happy to breathe the steamy afternoon air in Darwin, but after being squashed into the back seat of the van, it actually felt like a breath of fresh air to her.

She waited while the driver retrieved her bag from the baggage trailer, then she walked up a set of about ten stairs to the hotel entrance.

I know one thing for sure. As soon as I get checked in, I'm going to take a shower, and then go out to find a couple of long, cool summer dresses and a nice big hat.

But it wasn't just the sun that worried Angela the most. She needed something to hide her face too. The last thing she needed was for Soren to recognize her before she had a chance to find him and call the police.

ANGELA gazed out the window of her hotel room at the broad expanse of park that stretched along the length of the Esplanade. Beyond the park, she watched a freighter cruise cautiously into Darwin Harbour. She had a white hotel towel wrapped around her body.

She sighed and retreated from the window, retrieving the carrying case with her laptop from the floor. She pulled the computer from its case, opened it on a table near the window and powered it on.

While she was waiting for the machine to boot, Angela caught a glimpse of herself in a mirror. She noticed a fine covering of blonde hair starting to grow out from her previously shaved head. She raised one eye, cocked her head to one side, and then shrugged.

I actually like it. I could live with keeping it this short for a while.

The laptop was ready to use. Angela's fingers moved and clicked the machine's track pad and opened her email. Nothing in her *Inbox*, not that she expected anybody to contact her. She pulled up a chair and sat in front of the screen, then she clicked the track pad to begin a new message:

FACES

To: Dan Whitney
Re: Soren and Jonah

Thank you for your last message. I can understand that you and Anika don't trust me. All I can tell you is that I'm in more danger than you and Anika. I discovered things about Soren that I shouldn't have found, and now I am paying for that by having to hide from him.

I think I have good news for Anika. I believe that Soren is hiding in Darwin, Australia, and I've just arrived in that city. I haven't seen Soren or Jonah yet, so I don't have enough information to pass along my suspicions to the police yet. Please tell Anika to fly here as soon as possible, so that she's here when I find them.

For my safety and Anika's, I don't think it's wise to reveal my identity just yet. Tell her to email me when she arrives so that I can bring her up to date on my progress.

Guardian Angel

CHAPTER 21

ANGELA walked slowly along an asphalt path at the Mindil Beach Market, weaving her way through the thick Sunday evening throng of people, between rows of vendors in their trailers and tents. She gazed at the crowd from behind the safety and anonymity of her dark sunglasses. She split her attention between navigating through the teeming crowd, while also trying to get a good look at every small child she could see. She was thankful for the new white linen skirt, white sandals, large straw sunhat, and the colourful shawl she had purchased after her arrival in the city. Her new attire made the city's tropical humidity much more bearable. She passed a booth that sold freshly squeezed, ice-cold lemonade and realized how thirsty she was.

I have to remember to drink more water here. Las Vegas may be hot, but I can't believe how much I sweat here!

She found a small picnic table beside the lemonade stand. It felt good to give her aching feet a rest. She had decided to walk to the market. It didn't look very far from her hotel on her map, but it seemed much further in the reality of Darwin's tropical heat and humidity.

Next time, I'll take the hotel's advice and ride the bus.

The sun sank lower in the western sky, casting an increasingly orange hue. Angela kept her eyes glued on the mobs of people that jostled along the path, comparing every young face with the photo of Jonah Kristiansen that was etched into her mind.

She had walked the streets of downtown Darwin all morning and early afternoon, giving special attention to the Smith Street pedestrian mall and Mitchell Street, with its jungle of backpackers' accommodations, restaurants, and pubs, with no success. She saw surprisingly few families or young children, except in the usual locations such as McDonald's.

Angela downed the last of her lemonade, now ice cold but diluted by an excess of ice in the drink. She felt a throat freeze coming on, rising slowly and painfully from deep in her esophagus. She winced and held her breath for a few seconds until the worst of the pain passed. Finally, she shook her head to get rid of the remaining discomfort, then rose to her aching feet and rejoined the crowd of humanity on the pathway. She saw families sitting on blankets on the grass between vendors and grassy banks.

Angela came upon a path on her right that went through a break in the bank. She followed a number of people who were taking the path. It quickly became very sandy and Angela realized that it led to the beach. She stepped off the path to remove her sandals, and then she got back in line with the people who were heading toward the beach, carrying her sandals in one hand.

Despite the sun sinking lower in the sky, the sand was still hot on the soles of her feet. Angela emerged through the break in the sandbank onto a long expanse of hard, sandy beach at low tide. Within seconds, the hard sand felt moist and cool on her tired soles. She removed her sunglasses to get a better view of people, many of whom were silhouetted against the setting sun. This was where the families were congregating, parents keeping careful watch over their children as they frolicked and played in the sand.

Angela understood why people raved about Darwin's sunsets. The western horizon was ablaze in orange and gold, while the sky above her was turning an increasingly deep shade of blue. The few lingering clouds were taking on a fiery orange-pink hue. Sailboats and dragon-boats adorned the gently rolling sea, which sparkled like it was covered with precious jewels in the setting sun.

She walked into the shallow surf, feeling the cool, refreshing waves splash over her feet and ankles, then she walked slowly southward, gazing intently at the face of every child she encountered. With the sun now partially at her back, faces were now well lit by the sun, rather than appearing as silhouettes. After a few minutes, the crowds of people had thinned so she reversed direction and headed back to the south. She passed the point where she'd entered the beach and continued northwards.

A sudden loud bark startled Angela from her concentration. Angela turned and saw a large German Shepherd immediately behind her. It was chasing a Frisbee thrown by its owner. She jumped at the unexpected blast of sound, and the huge dog almost knocked her over as the Frisbee landed at Angela's feet. The Shepherd scooped up the plastic disk between its teeth, and then it loped and panted its way back towards the teenage boy who had thrown the Frisbee. Suddenly, Angela noticed a slender Asian woman leading a small Caucasian boy away from the water. There was something about the boy that seemed eerily familiar. She could only see his face from the side and slightly behind, but she sensed that she needed to follow this couple to check them out more thoroughly.

Angela wandered slowly behind them, zigging and zagging in wide arcs, biding her time while the boy constantly stopped to examine objects he found on the beach. Eventually, the slight woman managed to guide the boy through another gap between the sandbanks, back toward the market. Angela followed, trying to keep ten or fifteen steps behind the pair. She watched while the woman bought two soft-serve ice cream cones at one of the trailers.

If that's Jonah, who is that woman?

She recalled the news reports that suggested that a blonde Caucasian women had accompanied Soren when he fled into Washington State. Was she no longer with him? Suddenly she remembered the news reports of the suspicious death of the woman in Little Rock. A chill ran through her body as she realized the implications. At the same time, Angela had a flashback of the sick smile on Soren's face the day he'd threatened the safety of her own children, Julia and Nicholas. She felt her heart starting to pound. She turned her body, warily surveying a full three-sixty-degree circle around her—making sure she didn't see Soren's face in the crowd—making sure she wasn't being followed herself.

Their ice cream cones in hand, the woman and boy started walking again. Angela still hadn't got a good look at the boy's face. She kept a safe distance, making sure to keep the boy in her sight while dodging bodies that came at her from the opposite direction. The pounding beat of music reached Angela's ear. She saw the boy point in the direction of the music, taking the woman's hand and dragging her behind him. As they drew closer, the pounding of the music became more intense. An eerie sound lofted above the rhythms of drums and electric guitars.

Angela saw a crowd ahead. The boy wiggled his way in between some people and wormed his way into the crowd, disappearing from sight. The Asian woman tried to follow, getting looks of disgust from onlookers who weren't keen on having somebody butt in ahead of them. Angela came up against the crowd. Rather than follow the boy, she worked her way slowly around the perimeter of the crowd. As she moved, she caught glimpses of an Aboriginal man, his cheeks puffing in and out as he blew into a long, hollow, wooden tube. She realized that she was hearing a didgeridoo for the first time. The combination of the traditional wind instrument, together with drums and modern sounds, was electrifying. The crowd, an equal mix of Aboriginal and non-Aboriginal people, clapped enthusiastically and danced in unison to the pounding rhythm of the music.

Angela worked her way around to a point on the south side of the mob, where she didn't have a very good view of the music, but she could see the faces in the crowd more clearly. Her eyes scanned the fired-up audience. She saw the outline of a small round white face, squeezed into a space between an Aboriginal man and woman in the front row. The bodies swayed back and forth. Suddenly, the small round face popped completely into view.

Angela stopped breathing. There was no doubt in her mind. She was staring at the face of Jonah Kristiansen.

"FRAN, I'm not Philippe!" Dan exclaimed. "I'm not Paolo or your father either. I'm not going to abuse you or abandon you like they did. I want to be an active part in your life—in our child's life. Please give me a chance to prove that to you!"

Dan gazed intently at Fran on the other side of thick glass. Her face was stony and expressionless.

"I felt a connection with you the moment we met," he continued. "I know you did too. I feel myself growing more in love with you every day. What more can I do to prove it to you?"

More silence followed. Fran's head hung low, avoiding eye contact with him. Finally, she raised her head. She met his eyes briefly, looked away, and then met his eyes again. Dan felt her fear, and he desperately wanted to reassure her and hold her safely in his arms.

"I just don't know if I can do it, Dan," she said quietly. She gave a nervous swallow. Dan saw the hint of redness in her eyes. He understood that she was torn in two completely opposite directions—that she was afraid of committing to him. He also knew she had an independent side to her personality that would be able to survive on her own, if she chose to go that route. But he also remembered seeing the look of desperation in her eyes when they were making love—how desperately she wanted to be loved by somebody. He wanted to be that somebody.

"Fran, I know how confused your emotions must be right now, especially when Mulholland seems so intent on keeping you behind bars. All I ask is that you don't rush into any decision yet. Let's focus on getting you out of here. Once you're free, you'll be under so much less pressure. You'll be able to think about this more clearly. What do you say?"

"I suppose," Fran said resignedly. Another silence ensued. Dan realized that those two words were all the commitment he was going to get from Fran today. She finally broke the lengthy silence.

"Have you heard anything about Jonah yet?" she asked.

"Actually, there may be a break," Dan said. "Remember the email I told you about? From the person who claimed to be our 'Guardian Angel'?"

"Yes. Did you get another message?" Fran asked.

"We did, a couple of days ago. He or she claimed that Soren and Jonah may in Darwin—in Australia. The message told Anika to get a flight to Darwin right away," Dan said.

"No idea yet who this person is? Do you think you can trust whoever it is?" Fran said, still no emotion showing in her voice.

"No sign yet," Dan answered. "But Anika is supposed to email them when she gets to Darwin. The person said that he or she found out something about Soren, and he threatened the lives of his or her children. If that's true, then I can see why they're afraid of Soren."

Fran's eyes remained in contact with Dan, but her mind went someplace else for a moment.

"You don't suppose your Guardian Angel could be that woman, Angela Baranyi, do you?" Fran asked.

The question caught Dan off guard. He'd never considered the mysterious woman in Fran's portrait. He let Fran's suggestion sink in for a moment.

"I wonder," he said. "It might be an important piece in this whole puzzle. Let's assume it *is* her. Didn't the NYPD detectives say that Baranyi had children? If she discovered something about Soren while she was working for him, that might explain why she disappeared."

"The detectives claim she's the woman in my portrait," Fran added. "That links her to me."

"And he thinks you might know where she is? If so, maybe it's Soren who's putting pressure on Mulholland to get the information from you," Dan said. "It's funny, but I had the same thought about Soren after I met Secretary of State Rice in New York. She suggested the pressure could be coming from somebody closer to home. And we know Soren had business dealings with Philippe and others in Palm Springs. Do you think we should tell Joanna about this?"

"It's only a guess. We really don't know anything for sure," Fran said.

"You're probably right. It's nothing but a hunch—but a very interesting one. I suppose there's nothing Joanna can do with that," Dan said.

Fran remained silent while she continued to think. Finally, she looked Dan directly in the eyes. He felt a sense of relief. He saw a look of determination on her face.

"You have to go to Darwin with Anika," she said at last. "You have to help her find Soren and Jonah."

"I can't," Dan said. "Everything's different, now that I know you're pregnant. Being with *you* is more important than anything else to me right now."

"But there is nothing you can do for me here," Fran answered. "And if your Guardian Angel is the Baranyi woman, and if Soren is putting pressure on the District Attorney, then you might also be helping my case by going."

This time it was Dan who was silent. He mulled things over in his mind and realized that Fran was right. If Soren's disappearance and the questions around the District Attorney's obsession with Fran were related, then he owed it to both Anika and Fran to go to Australia.

"You're right. I'll phone Anika as soon as I leave here. She's on a flight to Sydney from LAX tonight. I'll see if I can get on the same flight," he said.

For the first time in his last two visits, he thought he sensed a slight look of relief on Fran's face. It didn't last for long, and the side of her that was struggling to be strong and independent soon replaced it. But it gave Dan a glimmer of hope. And it was more hope for their future than he'd had after his last two visits with her.

"I'll be back as soon as I can," Dan said. "I love you." He replaced his telephone receiver on its cradle. Then he put the tips of his fingers to his lips and threw Fran a kiss. He watched for her response, not realizing he was holding his breath. It seemed to take forever for her to respond. In reality, it was probably only a matter of a few seconds. She put her fingers to her lips and reciprocated his gesture.

Dan resumed breathing again. He got to his feet feeling like a weight had been lifted from his shoulders. As he walked from the room, his pace quickened. He walked from the Indio Jail as quickly as possible. Once outside, he reached for his phone and quickly dialed Anika's number.

"Hi, Anika, I just talked with Fran and I'm coming with you. She insisted I go. I'll see about getting on your flight… what?… You already booked me a ticket?… And got me a visa?… Okay, then I'll see you at the airport… Fran had some interesting ideas about Soren… I'll tell you when I get to the airport… okay, see you soon," he said.

Dan rushed from the Indio Jail and into the parking lot. He looked at his watch. He had to get back to Palm Springs to pack a bag. He was going to have to hurry if he was going to make it to LAX in time.

A BLAST of hot, humid air hit Dan as he followed Anika out of the aircraft, down the portable stairs, and onto the tarmac of Darwin International Airport. They followed the long line of passengers toward the shelter of the covered walkway that would take them to the terminal. Dan was exhausted after the fifteen-hour flight from Los Angeles to Brisbane, followed by another three-and-a-half-hour flight to Darwin. He glanced at Anika, who looked haggard and grim as she made her way toward the air-conditioned terminal.

"How are you doing?" Dan asked, as they walked.

"I can't wait to get to the hotel," Anika answered. "I just want a shower and want you to check your email to see if there's any more word from our Angel, whoever he or she is. Do you really think it could be the Baranyi woman?"

"The more I think about it, the more it makes sense," Dan answered. "It could explain why D.A. Mulholland is making such a big deal out of keeping Fran behind bars, if Soren is depending on her to help him find Baranyi. The only question is: what's the connection between Soren and Mulholland? You're sure Soren never introduced her to you or talked about her?"

"I'm positive," Anika said. "Soren didn't talk much about church business, apart from what went on with the Victoria congregation. But I know now that there was probably a lot that he was keeping from me."

They reached the terminal entrance, feeling immediately re-energized by the chilly, dry air. As they arrived at the luggage carousel, Dan put his arm around Anika's shoulder and gave her a reassuring squeeze.

"I suppose we need to stay up, at least until early evening, to deal with the jet lag. What would you like to do for the rest of the day, depending on what we hear from our Angel?"

"I guess we could walk around downtown for a while to get our bearings—who knows, maybe we'll get lucky and see Jonah or Soren while we're out. If nothing else, we can find a place to have dinner. Airplane food didn't do it for me—I'm getting hungry," Anika said.

Ten minutes later, they climbed aboard the cramped hotel shuttle bus and were on their way to downtown Darwin. Dan glanced at Anika again, seeing the look of grim determination on her face as she stared out the window, taking in the sights of the young city. Dan felt nervous anticipation in his stomach—a sense that they were getting closer to their goal. His mind conjured scenarios of what might happen when they finally found and confronted Soren—when Anika finally found Jonah.

SOREN KRISTIANSEN made his way along the shady side of Darwin's Mitchell Street. Young backpackers clogged the sidewalk, their belongings on their backs and plastic bags full of groceries weighing them down. As he passed the bus terminal, he looked over his shoulder for a break in the traffic so he could cross the busy street. He had just finished a short visit with Jonah and Lucy. The weathered white exterior of their apartment complex backed onto Mitchell Street, only a matter of blocks from the hotel where he was staying. It was better that they didn't stay in the same place, and better that he didn't have much contact with the boy. The less they were seen together, the less likely anybody was going to put two and two together and recognize them. He was so close to making it to the safety of Asia, he couldn't take any unnecessary risks now. Helen would be furious if he did anything to jeopardize their plan now.

Seeing a break in the traffic, Soren jogged across Mitchell Street, sweat dripping from his face and soaking his shirt. "Godforsaken place," he muttered. "They keep saying the wet season is almost over, but it can't end soon enough for me!" He hurried along the opposite side of the street, past more pubs, ice cream shops, restaurants and tourist attractions. He was coming up to Briggs Street, where his hotel was located. The patio of one of the more popular pubs extended onto the sidewalk, forcing pedestrians to slow down as their path narrowed. As he approached the pub, one of the patrons lifted an icy mug of beer to his lips, took a large gulp, and took the large mug away from his lips. Something about the man set alarms off in Soren's brain.

Where have I seen that face before?

Soren's legs froze. He lowered his hat over his eyes and pulled off the sidewalk to his right, pretending to look at travel posters in the neighbouring travel office. He lifted his head and snuck a quick glance at the man. He was at a table for two, facing a blonde-haired woman whose back was to him. Soren shuddered. A chill surged down his spine. Even from behind, he recognized that head and figure anywhere. The pieces dropped into place in his mind.

Anika! What the fuck is SHE doing here! And that man… it's that guy from the news… what's his name?… Whitney… what's HE doing with her?

Instinctively, Soren whirled around and hurried back from the direction he had come. He'd have to take the long way around the block to get back to the hotel. His mind raced. He was confused, trying to make sense of the sudden turn of events. He was sweating profusely now, not just from the tropical heat and humidity.

I've been so careful. How could they possibly have tracked me to Australia? How am I going to tell Helen? She's going to be furious!

He rushed along the sidewalk, oblivious to other people around him, often bumping into others along the way.

"Hey, watch where yer goin', mate!" a burly man snarled. Soren had just rudely brushed the man's wife aside. Soren mumbled a sort of apology under his breath and continued bustling along, making left hand turns on Peel and Smith Streets to bring him full circle back to Briggs. He rushed the half block down the street to the hotel entrance, his head down and his hat pulled low over his eyes.

Finally reaching the entrance, he heaved a gigantic sigh of relief as he felt the cool air and the safety of the lobby. Impatiently, he waited for the elevator to open. His heart pounded in his chest. Despite the air-conditioned environment, Soren continued to sweat profusely. The elevator door finally opened and he rushed into the safety of its confines. He pounded on the buttons, first for his floor number and then for the door to close as quickly as possible.

Come on, come on! I don't have all day!

It seemed to take forever, but the door finally closed. Soren felt an almost imperceptible bump as the elevator began its painstakingly slow ascent to his floor. He tapped his right foot rapidly up and down, huffing impatiently at the turtle-like pace of the aging lift. When he thought he couldn't stand it any longer, he felt another distant bump, and the door started creeping open. He squeezed his portly body through the slowly expanding opening and rushed down the hallway to his room, fumbling with the key and dropping it on the floor. He bent down to pick it up and thumped his head on the doorknob.

"Shit," he muttered, picking up the key and finally directing it into the lock properly. He heard a click and pushed the door open, rushing into the room and slamming the door closed behind him. His body sagged and he leaned backwards against the door. His lungs took rapid, short breaths and his heart continued to thump away in his chest. He felt panic starting to take over his body and realized he needed to calm himself.

Soren forced himself to slow his breathing by taking deeper breaths. Within seconds, he felt the panic and urgency in his body starting to reverse itself. He continued taking slower, deeper breaths, gradually wresting control of his body away from its protective fight-or-flight response. He made his way across the room and collapsed in an easy chair.

You need to stay calm. You need to be in control when you tell Helen.

His mind started scrambling for ways to break the bad news to her. No matter how he did it, she was going to be most displeased with him. He knew she would take it out on him the next time they were together. Finally, he took one last deep breath and got up from the chair. He rummaged through the carrying case for his laptop, finally finding the small, disposable mobile phone he had purchased upon his arrival in Australia. He dialed the only number programmed into the phone's memory. After a few clicks and pauses, his call connected and he heard ringing.

"Helen," a curt voice at the other end of the line announced. "Why are you calling me on this line? This better be important!"

Soren swallowed, trying to muster his courage and find his voice.

"I just saw Anika and that psychologist, Whitney. They were in a restaurant having dinner—here in Darwin," he said, trying to appear calm and in control.

"You fool! Did they see you?" Helen bellowed.

"No!" Soren shouted in return. "Whitney didn't get a good look at me, and Anika's back was toward me. I turned around and got out of there as fast as I could."

"You idiot!" Helen screamed. "How could they have found you there? Have you been phoning or emailing anybody?"

"Only you," Soren answered submissively. "I've only used The Agency's secure internal mail, as you ordered. And this is the first time I've used this phone. You know I would never go against your wishes."

"Then how…" Helen's voice trailed off. "Our laptops—somebody's hacked one or both of our laptops. It's the only possible way."

Soren's forehead wrinkled, trying to make sense of Helen's assertion. "Who would want to hack into my computer?"

"Who indeed," Helen said accusingly. "You're an idiot, Soren. Can you think of anybody who might have hacked your computer before?"

Soren's eyes opened wide. His jaw dropped.

"No, it couldn't…"

"It couldn't?" Helen countered. "Your arrogance is your biggest weakness, Soren. You really think that just because your little friend Angela disappeared, that she isn't up to no good again?"

Soren heard nothing but silence over the airwaves. He braced himself for another verbal assault.

"She must be watching everything you do," Helen concluded. "But she doesn't know that we know…"

Her voice trailed off again. She was thinking. Soren understood where her line of thought was going.

"So we plant some misinformation," Soren said. "Then we bring her out of hiding and catch the little bitch!"

"Now that's my Soren," Helen replied. "Finally, you're thinking. And if she's working with Anika and Whitney, we can take care of all three of them at once."

Soren started feeling uneasy. Even though he and Helen agreed that they were both free to have other lovers, he had sensed her jealousy when he had told her about his plan to seduce Angela. And he had always sensed her being envious of Anika's position as Soren's wife.

Is she suggesting killing Anika? I can see killing Angela—that bitch crossed the line when she stole from me and made me look like an idiot. But why Anika and Whitney? They didn't do anything to us.

"All three of them?" Soren asked meekly. "We don't need to harm Anika and Whitney. Can't we just scare them? Anika is Jonah's mother, I can't…"

"*Was* Jonah's mother!" Helen screamed. "Jonah is *our* son now —remember? As long as Anika is alive, she is always going to be a threat to us. If we get a chance to eliminate Angela, then we may as well get rid of Anika too?"

"But…" Soren began.

"Are you questioning me?" Helen shouted. "Are you forgetting who serves who?"

"No," Soren answered passively.

"Pardon me?" Helen demanded. "No *what...*"

"No, my Lady," Soren replied.

"That's more like it," Helen said. "Let's get down to business. How are we going to get rid of our three troublemakers?…"

CHAPTER 22

AS THE swing started soaring upward again, Jonah Kristiansen lifted his hands from the chains and slipped off the seat. His small body flew through the air.

"Wheeeee…" he shouted as his body began descending towards the ground. His feet hit the ground and his momentum caused him to fall forward on his hands and knees. He looked behind him and smiled at Lucy.

"I'm going to the climbing fort!" he shouted. Then he took off running, leaving Lucy far behind. He headed straight for the ladder and ascended to the second level of the play centre.

"I'm the king of the castle!" he shouted to the distant Lucy. Jonah looked out over his domain—the rest of the park and the harbour. As usual, groups of Aboriginal people were gathered, some sitting on blankets, some singing and playing instruments. He saw a lady in a white skirt with a big floppy straw hat walking her small white puppy towards his make-believe fortress. He jumped onto the slide and flew down the plastic tube, landing on his feet and breaking into a run, all in one smooth motion. He ran around the play structure for the ladder and almost ran into the lady with the puppy.

"I'm sorry," Jonah said, and then he noticed the small dog. "A puppy… I love puppies! What's his name?"

The lady looked at Jonah and gave him a friendly smile.

"He's a *her*, young man. Her name is Sally. Would you like to pet her?"

Jonah bent down and ran his hand over the small dog's head. Sally lifted her head and licked his hand. Jonah giggled.

"She licked me!" he squealed. "She likes me."

"Yes, she does," the lady said. She knelt down beside Jonah and smiled once again. Jonah liked her smile—she seemed like a nice lady. Suddenly, the lady's face became more serious and she started whispering.

"Don't be afraid, Jonah. I'm a friend of your mommy's. I don't have much time. Can you keep a secret?"

Jonah was stunned. He looked into the lady's eyes and nodded warily.

"Your mommy told me to tell you that she loves you very much, and she's coming very soon to look for you."

Still shocked, Jonah didn't know what to say.

"Just keep patting Sally," the lady said. "Pretend that I didn't tell you anything. You can't tell anybody—not the lady who is taking care of you—and especially not your daddy. He might not let you see your mommy, so you must promise to keep this a secret. Do you promise?"

Jonah didn't know what to feel or say. Part of him was delirious with joy—his mommy was coming to see him! *But Daddy said that Mommy is one of the bad people. What if she brings the bad people with her*? He didn't know whether to be afraid or happy. He was confused.

"Jonah, do you promise?" the lady repeated.

Instinct took over. Jonah wanted to see his mommy more than anything in the world.

"Okay," he said. "I promise."

"Just smile and keep patting Sally," the lady said.

Lucy walked up to Jonah, eyeing the lady and the puppy.

"Look, Lucy," Jonah said. "The puppy's name is Sally, and she likes me. Look, she licks me!" He smiled at Angela, then looked at Lucy and smiled while Sally licked away at his face. Lucy knelt down and looked suspiciously at Angela.

"He really likes her," Angela said to Lucy. "Hi, my name is Anna."

"Hi, my name is Lucy. I haven't seen you here in the park before."

"You're right," Angela laughed. "I just got Sally. She's a good excuse to start getting out for more walks. You'll probably see me more often. Either me or my son over there." The lady nodded towards a group of teenage boys, huddled in a group at the edge of the park, next to the street.

"Well, I need to get Sally back to my son. He wants to take her to his friend's place so he can show her off. I'd better be going now. It was nice meeting you, young man," the lady said. She extended her hand and shook Jonah's hand. She smiled warmly and winked. Jonah smiled back, letting her know that her secret was safe with him.

The lady and Sally started walking back towards the street.

"She was nice," Jonah said.

"You really shouldn't talk to strangers," Lucy said. "We talked about that. Your daddy wouldn't be happy if he knew you talked to her. But we won't tell him about meeting Sally, will we?"

"Nope. It's our secret," he said. "Can I play on the fort some more?"

"Just a little while longer," Lucy said. "Then we should go home."

Jonah jumped onto the ladder, quickly climbing up to the second level. Once again, he surveyed his kingdom, watching Sally and the lady in white fade into the distance. He smiled to himself, feeling the excitement build inside him. For the first time in weeks, he felt himself smile.

My mommy's coming to see me!

He watched as the lady handed Sally back to one of the teenage boys. She seemed to be giving the boy some money. For a second, Jonah thought that was strange. Then his mind drifted to happier thoughts—thoughts of his mommy. He tried to remember what she looked like and tried to hold the image of her face in his mind, an image that was becoming less clear with each passing day. As he did, a single tear managed to escape from one of his eyes, beginning to make its way down his cheek. He wiped it away quickly so Lucy wouldn't see. He couldn't let any tears betray the secret he shared with the lady in the white skirt.

SOREN SAT in the darkness of his hotel room, his face lit only by the glow of his laptop's screen. It was one-fifteen in the morning, the usual time for going online to send messages to Helen via the security of the secret USDA network. But tonight, he felt different. It was strange, knowing that somebody was following his keystrokes. On the other hand, he felt a sense of omnipotence, knowing that Angela didn't realize that he knew about her—that he could use that to finally catch the little bitch. He would leave his laptop on long enough to make sure she had read both his message and Helen's reply.

Soren re-read his message while he waited for Helen's reply to arrive:

To: Helen
From: Socrates
Subject: Getting Away

Helen:
The waiting here in Darwin is so tedious. Boredom is my biggest challenge. When I saw Jonah and Lucy yesterday, they complained that they were getting restless in their apartment. Lucy says Jonah is whining and complaining more often. She's afraid that he'll say or do something when they are out that will draw attention to them.

I've been thinking that we could take a short trip into Kakadu Park—some place that is off the beaten track, where there aren't many people and the danger of being recognized will be less. I thought maybe we could take a 2-or-3-day tour, where we could blend in with other tourists. Sometimes the best place to hide is in plain sight. The tour leaves tomorrow morning, staying in Jabiru tomorrow night and at Gagudju Lodge on Sunday night, before coming back to Darwin Monday morning. I hope you approve, as I think the risk of being recognized is low.

Since I will only have my disposable phone with me, I will not be communicating with you for three days. I'll be online again after midnight Monday.

Your Servant Forever

Socrates

While he waited for Helen's reply, Soren got up and went to the room's small bar fridge, removing a tall can of Foster's. He popped the tab, hearing the familiar hiss of escaping gas, and then he raised the can quickly to his lips to catch some escaping foam. He smiled with satisfaction as he reflected on how productive the past twelve hours had been. He had been online frequently this morning, when he suspected that Angela would likely be offline and sleeping. First, he attempted to log into Anika's email account. He knew she wasn't very adept with computers and was lax with her passwords. As predicted, getting into her account and reading her email had been child's play. He sneered as he read her emails to and from a family lawyer in Vancouver with interest.

Go ahead. Get a court order for the boy's custody. A lot of good that will be when I've disappeared and have a new life!

He read through her emails quickly, since they weren't the primary focus of attention. He read down the list of headings in her messages until he saw what he was looking for.

Great News! Jonah spotted in Darwin, Australia by our Angel!

He sneered again. *So the little bitch is calling herself an angel, is she? We'll see about that!*

Soren captured Dan Whitney's email address from the message, carefully writing it down. Next, he pulled out his disposable Australian mobile phone. After all, this was an emergency and he could no longer rely on using his laptop to send messages he didn't want Angela to see. He passed on the urgent assignment to his IT man in Hanoi, giving him the email address and ordering him drop everything to hack into Dan's email account. His man was good, phoning Soren back within six hours with the password.

Soren sat back down in the room's easy chair, reaching for his laptop and resting it on his lap. He smiled, seeing a reply from Helen in his *Inbox*:

To: Socrates
From: Helen
Subject: Getting Away

I'm nervous about you taking the boy out in public, and I was concerned when I first read your message. But after I thought about it, I think you're right. Hiding in plain sight as a family is a clever idea. As far as I've heard, nobody suspects that you have an Asian woman as an accomplice. Just make sure the boy keeps referring to her as 'mommy'. Besides, I will have instructions for you soon on your travel arrangements. I am hoping that I will have the details arranged by the time you are back in Darwin on Monday.
Forever Your Mistress
Lady Helen

Soren's face broke into a wide grin. *Excellent! Hopefully this will give Angela a sense of urgency. She'll need to act soon or risk losing track of us! She'll send an email to Whitney or Anika in a matter of minutes. I'll check Whitney's, and Anika's emails in an hour or two to see how they react.*

Soren clicked the button to power down his laptop. He felt a warm feeling of satisfaction settling through his body. It felt good to be back in control again.

ANGELA felt the excitement build inside her as she read the email exchange between Soren and the mysterious Helen. She realized she had a narrow window of opportunity to take advantage of this new information, if she was going to help catch Soren and help get Jonah back to Anika. Her mind shifted into high gear, trying to figure out how to get Anika and Dan out to Kakadu as soon as possible. Suddenly she had an idea. She leapt from her chair and ran across the room to grab her purse. She rifled through its contents until she found what she was looking for.

Derek Hardy—Territory Air Service. Perfect! I'll see if I can charter a plane for Anika and Dan. With any luck, they can be in Jabiru when Soren and Jonah get there. I'll also need to rent them an SUV to get around.

Angela ran back to the laptop, refreshing her screen to see if there were any more exchanges between Soren and Helen. Nothing more. Soren's laptop had shut down and her cloning program had lost contact. Without wasting a second, she opened her email and began typing out a message. It was time to come out of hiding and to make direct contact with Anika and Dan.

To: Dan Whitney
From: Guardian Angel
Subject: Urgent! Phone me immediately!

I've just discovered that Soren and Jonah will be coming out of hiding and will be in Kakadu National Park for the next two or three days. After that, it sounds like they may be on the move again. First thing in the morning, I'll be making arrangements for you to get to Kakadu as quickly as possible. I have a contact at Territory Air Services, and I'll be trying to charter a flight to Jabiru sometime tomorrow. If that's not possible, I'll rent a car for you. It's time for us to talk and meet. Phone me at the Holiday Inn on the Esplanade, Room 404, as soon as possible in the morning.

Your Guardian Angel

Angela closed the lid on her laptop, putting her computer into sleep mode. *Time to get some sleep. Looks like things will be hectic over the next couple of days.*

She turned off the lights, pulled the covers over her, and closed her eyes. But sleep did not come easily. Instead, all she could think about was having Soren safely behind bars, and reuniting with Julia and Nicholas. She remembered what it felt to hold her daughter and son in her arms. Before long, tears streamed from her eyes. Loneliness, sadness, and the longing of a mother for her two children had soon consumed her. She wept until she lost track of time. Only then did she finally drift off into a restless sleep, filled with dreams of Soren standing between her and the children, his eyes filled with hatred, his face sneering, taunting Angela to just try and reach her children.

"ANGELA just sent Anika and Whitney an email," Soren said. "She's planning on chartering a flight on Territory Air Service to get them to Jabiru as soon as possible. You said you have contacts here in Darwin. Do you think you can get in touch with them in time to stop them?"

"Relax, my dear. That won't be a problem. You've done well. Let me take care of the details. You just make sure you get the boy and the woman ready to travel right away. Somebody will pick you up at your hotel at five-thirty and will take you to pick up the others. Understand?" Helen ordered.

"Yes, My Lady," Soren answered. He swallowed and summoned up the courage for one more question. "Do you have any idea when you and I will be able to be together? I don't know how much longer I can wait."

"Patience, Soren," Helen replied. "If we take it one step at a time, things will work out. The only way we'll fail is if we get impatient and stray from our plan. So stay focused and get yourself ready to move. Your contact will have a new mobile phone for you. I'll call you at your next destination. That's all for now. Goodbye, my pet."

Before Soren could answer, Helen hung up and was dialling another number. She listened to the phone ring until there was a click and a man's voice answered.

"Territory Air Service. Watch for a last minute charter to Jabiru for two or three people. Passenger names will be Whitney, Kristiansen, and possibly one other—a woman. Let me know as soon as you hear anything," she ordered, and then she ended the short call.

They had come too far and were too close to success to let anything derail their plans now. She felt thankful for her worldwide network of connections. She had worked long and hard to build that network, and now was the time to start calling in some debts.

Helen looked out into the pre-dawn darkness at the city lights and sighed. The streets below her were almost deserted and silent. She didn't like loose ends. She also didn't need Soren to panic. There was no need for him to know that she was in the city. She paused for a minute to calm herself and get herself focused. Then she reached for her purse, pulled the long strap over her head, and let the purse rest on her opposite hip. She grabbed the handle of her rolling carry-on bag and headed for the door. Her driver would be downstairs in five minutes for the short trip from the hotel to Darwin International Airport.

THE EASTERN sky glowed with an iridescent pink and orange hue. The driver stopped the black Toyota Highlander at the marina gate. Soren swung his door open and jumped out of the vehicle onto the pavement. He reached for the rear passenger door behind him, swinging it open as well.

"Hurry up," he hissed at Lucy. "Go with the driver. He'll take you and Jonah down to the boat. Wait for me there."

"Where are we going, Daddy?" Jonah whimpered. He rubbed his sleepy eyes, managing to wipe away the tears that were forming. "I like it here. I don't want to go anywhere else."

"Shhh," Lucy whispered. "We get to go for a boat ride on the ocean. Who knows, maybe we'll see some whales. Would you like that?"

"I don't want to see any whales. I want to stay here. I want to wait here for my mommy," Jonah whined.

"What's that nonsense?" Soren snapped. "If your mommy's coming, it's the bad people who are bringing her. You don't want the bad people to catch us, do you?"

"What bad people?" Jonah cried. "I don't know any bad people. I just want to see Mommy!"

Jonah started sniffling and tears began streaming from his eyes. His whimpering turned into full scale weeping.

"Get him down to the boat before anybody hears him," Soren snapped at Lucy. "And shut him up, will you? What do you think I'm paying you for?"

Lucy bent down and gathered Jonah in her arms, whispering in his ear to calm the heartbroken five-year-old.

"Follow me," the driver said. He was sharply dressed in a black suit, not the attire of a fisherman. He led Lucy and Jonah to a locked gate and pulled a key from his pocket to unlock it. The gate swung open and the driver motioned Lucy and Jonah through the gate. He followed them and let the metal gate's lock click gently behind them. Lucy let the man take the lead. He descended a wooden gangplank that took them to a large series of floating docks. Small private yachts, sailboats, and some larger fishing boats were docked alongside the maze of docks. The driver led them to one of the larger fishing boats at the end of the outer dock.

"I don't want to go for a boat ride," Jonah whimpered. "I don't like this boat. It's not big like the boat from Victoria."

"Come on, Jonah. It's going to be fun," Lucy said, giving his hand a gentle squeeze. "It's too hard to see whales from the big ferry. If you really want to see whales, you need to go on smaller boats like this one. Let's think of this as a big adventure—a whale-watching adventure! Come on, I'll be with you all the way."

Reluctantly, Jonah followed Lucy aboard the grungy-looking fishing boat. A small man with dark, leathery skin said something to them in an Asian tongue, motioning with his hand to follow him below. He sat them on benches in a cramped galley, and then scampered back up the stairs to the main deck. Jonah resumed his whimpering. The boat shook from the vibrations of its ancient diesel engine. The smell of diesel fuel was nauseatingly strong.

"I don't feel well," he said to Lucy. "I don't like this boat. It doesn't smell good."

"It will be better once we get going," Lucy said, trying to reassure Jonah. "Then we can go up on the deck, get some fresh air, and watch for whales."

The weathered Asian man came scurrying back to the fishing boat with the remainder of their luggage, which was all stowed below deck, away from prying eyes. A moment later, Soren hurried on board and went directly to the galley to join Lucy and Jonah. Almost as soon as he was aboard, the rumbling of the idling diesel engine turned into a roar and the boat started pulling away from the marina.

Jonah watched through a porthole in the galley as they moved slowly past a breakwater of large rocks and out into Darwin's main harbour. As his last hope of being reunited with his mommy disappeared in the distance with the marina, tears continued to stream down his cheeks. Despite Lucy pulling him against her chest, he couldn't be consoled.

It's all my fault... I never should have talked to the lady in the white dress... daddy told me not to talk to anybody or the bad people would come... now the bad people came to take me away... it's all my fault!

CHAPTER 23

DAN AND ANIKA sipped on cups of vending machine coffee while they waited for their pilot to arrive for their flight to Jabiru. There was little else to do in the tiny departure area of Territory Air Services at Darwin International Airport.

"So Francesca was right," Anika said. "Angela Baranyi *is* our Guardian Angel after all. It's kind of ironic, don't you think? Angela… Guardian Angel? It's too bad she doesn't feel safe enough to meet us yet. I can't wait to thank her in person for all she's done."

"Yeah, I can't wait either. But I see where she's coming from. Until Soren is in custody and isn't a threat to her children, I understand why she needs to stay in the shadows," Dan answered.

"So what are we going to do when we get to Jabiru?" Anika asked.

"I managed to check out Kakadu tours on the Internet before we left. The most likely tour Soren booked is with Aussie Venture. We'll have to find out from them where their tour is going. Apparently they've had to change their usual itineraries because there's still too much water left over in some areas from the rainy season," Dan said.

Before Anika could reply, they were interrupted by a trim, athletic-looking man with sandy-colored hair and blue eyes, who had just walked into the departure area.

"You must be Anna's friends, Dan and Anika," he said. "I'm Derek Hardy."

Anika stared blankly at Dan, wondering who Anna was. Dan shrugged his shoulder initially, and then his face lit up as he figured out that Angela must be using a different name while she'd been in hiding.

"Oh yes, Anna," he said. "I'm Dan Whitney and this is my friend Anika. We really appreciate you guys doing this flight on such short notice."

"No worries, mate," Derek replied. "That's our business. We should be ready for you folks in a few minutes. We just have a bit of delay—last minute security check of our plane by the Air Force. Probably some big American brass stopping off at the Air Force Base on their way to Afghanistan. I'm afraid it's one of the hazards of sharing an airstrip with the Air Force. I'll come and get you when we're ready."

"Thanks, Derek," Anika said. "We're ready when you are."

Dan wandered over to a large window, where he saw an RAAF truck parked beside a small single-engine plane. A male driver remained in the vehicle, but Dan saw movement through windows near the rear of the plane. He walked back to Anika and they sat down to wait for the word from Derek, still sipping from their cups of coffee.

Ten minutes went by. Wondering why it was taking so long to do a quick security check on a single-engine plane, Dan walked over to the window in time to see a lone figure emerge from the plane. It walked quickly to the passenger side of the RAAF vehicle, which faced the terminal. As the person opened the door and climbed in, they cast a quick glance over their shoulder. Dan only caught a quick glance of the face because the person's cap was pulled down low. But he saw enough long blonde hair around the edges of the cap to realize that the person doing the security check was a woman.

The vehicle circled around in front of the terminal and stopped. The driver, a male officer, got out of the vehicle, leaving the female passenger in the truck. Her hat was pulled low over her face, and her head was bowed. She looked away from the terminal. The driver walked calmly into the building and talked briefly with a woman at the customer service counter. Both the driver and the woman had a good laugh, then the officer waved goodbye and walked calmly back to his waiting truck. After that, the military vehicle headed back across the tarmac to the Air Force base at the far side of the airfield.

Something about the blonde woman and the security check bothered Dan, but he couldn't put a finger on what it was.

"Dan. Anika. We're ready for ya, mates," Derek called, interrupting Dan's feeling of unease and bringing him back to reality.

Relieved to finally have clearance to take off, they picked up their overnight bags and followed Derek to the small aircraft, climbing up the folding stairs suspended from the side of the plane. Derek climbed in after them and pulled up the stairs, which doubled as the aircraft's rear door.

"Yer welcome to sit in the front row, mates. I can give you a bit of a guided tour of Kakadu on our way to Jabiru. It'll be a short hop so we'll just see the highlights," Derek said, as he seated himself in the pilot's seat and started his pre-flight check.

"What's up?" Anika said to Dan. "You're frowning. You always do that when you're concentrating on something."

"It's nothing," Dan said. "Do you think it's odd that it was woman doing the security check on our plane?"

"Dan!" Anika replied, surprise written on her face. "I can't believe you just said that. There are women in Air Forces all around the world. Why couldn't it be a woman?"

"That's not what I meant," he said. "There was something about her that looked familiar, that's all."

He took a deep breath and gave his head a quick shake. Then he smiled at Anika and chuckled.

"We've been chasing Soren for so long, I think I'm starting to see the boogie man everywhere. I'll be glad when we've found him and Jonah. At least that part of it will be over," he said, taking Anika's hand. "Then you can start dealing with the custody issue."

Anika's face became serious. Her lower jaw was set tight, her brow was creased, and her eyes narrow.

"As long as I have Jonah," she said. "I can handle the rest. Obviously I'll be divorcing Soren and asking for full custody of Jonah. After what he's done, there's no way I could live with him again, even if he didn't kill that woman in Little Rock."

"I know," Dan said, as the plane's engine started rotating and the aircraft began wobbling slightly from side to side. The noise from the engine started growing rapidly from a low-pitched growl into a steady drone. Derek spoke into the microphone on his headset to the control tower, and then the plane started rolling slowly onto the tarmac. They bounced steadily over seams in the airfield, taking a couple of turns before they finally arrived at the end of their runway. They waited, with the plane's engine droning steadily. Suddenly, a 737 swept onto the runway in front of them, just before the roar of its engine drowned out all sounds aboard their little plane.

Within seconds, Derek started the plane moving and swung to the right onto the main runway. He contacted the tower once more and waited. Finally, he pulled back on the throttle and the little plane's engine roared to life. It surged forward, gradually picking up speed. Finally, Dan felt the nose tip upward and felt the last runway seam bump beneath them. There was a sudden feeling of calm as the aircraft lifted into the air and started to gain altitude.

After a couple of minutes, the cabin speakers crackled and they heard Derek's voice.

"Can ya hear me, mates?" Derek asked, looking over his shoulder into the cabin. Dan gave him a thumbs up.

"Right," Derek said over the engine noise, as the plane continued to climb. "That road down there on yer right—that's the Arnhem Highway. It's the main road into Arnhem Land, the sacred land for the Yoingu people. It includes Kakadu Park, and it's the largest, most isolated Aboriginal reserve in Australia."

The small aircraft droned on steadily as Dan gazed over the vast landscape. He tapped Derek on the arm to get his attention. The pilot slid his headphones off his ears.

"You really have to fly over the Northern Territory to appreciate how big and how desolate it is," Dan shouted. "I was blown away by the view when we flew over the outback the other day. It sure makes me appreciate how resourceful the Aboriginal people have been to have survived here for thousands of years. And also how tough the white settlers must have been."

"If ya ever get a chance to get down to Alice, you'll hav'ta see the School of the Air and the Royal Flying Doctor Service museum. They'll both give ya an idea how challenging it is to survive in the Territory," Derek shouted.

"By the way, Anika, Anna told me why this flight is so important. I hope we find your son and you have a much happier return flight." He looked back over his shoulder and gave Anika a warm, genuine smile. Anika nodded to acknowledge, then gave him a thumbs up.

"If you look out your windows now, you'll see a river coming up. It's the South Alligator River."

Dan tapped Derek on the arm again, and once again their pilot removed his headphones.

"I didn't think there were alligators in Australia," Dan shouted. "Aren't they all crocodiles?"

Derek laughed and replaced his headphones so he was speaking over the intercom.

"Good question, mate. The first white man to explore this area —the man who named the river—thought they were alligators. He didn't realize that they were really crocs. So he named this river the South Alligator. There's another river northeast of here that he named the West Alligator."

Suddenly, the aircraft jolted and Dan felt the plane's nose point downward.

"Shit, what's going on?" Derek muttered. "Sorry, mates. No cause for panic. I've got somethin' goin' on with my elevators. Just relax while I figure out what's goin' on. It's probably just a sticky cable."

Dan felt Derek ease off the throttle, and then heard the pitch of the engine increase as Derek gave the engine more fuel.

Dan felt confident that Derek knew what he was doing. He looked at Anika. From the fear in her eyes, he knew she didn't share his confidence in their pilot. He reached for her hand and held it to reassure her.

"Don't worry. He seems to know what he's doing," Dan said.

After a minute or so of gently experimenting with the plane's controls, Derek's voice came over the intercom.

"Okay, mates. Here's the situation. It looks like the cable for my elevators has either snapped or it's loose. It's not an emergency, but I hav'ta fly 'er very easy—no sudden movements—and I hav'ta take 'er down slow and easy. The runway at Jabiru is long enough. Jus'ta make things a bit easier, can I get ya to move one row back, one person at a time, just to shift our centre of gravity a bit. That'll make 'er a tad easier to fly."

Dan and Anika unfastened their seat belts. Dan let Anika get out of her seat first, watching as she carefully guided herself into an aisle seat in the row behind them. Dan began moving toward the other aisle seat in that row when another sudden jolt rocked the plane, sending it lurching to the side. Dan overshot the seat he was aiming for, diving head first into the window seat beside it.

"Shit!" Derek cursed over the intercom. Dan felt the plane slowly and unsteadily rolling back onto its centre of gravity.

"Now we've got a real problem, mates," Derek said calmly. "I can't believe it, but it looks like I've also lost my rudder. So it looks like Jabiru isn't an option anymore. I'm gonna have ta try to take 'er down."

Dan felt Anika's hand reach across the aisle, gripping his hand like a vice. Her hand was now clammy with sweat. Her normally pale white complexion was flushed and the muscles in her jaw were taut. Her teeth were clenched firmly together.

"Where are you going to try to land?" Dan shouted. "The highway?"

Derek shook his head but didn't turn around. His head moved quickly from side to side, looking out of the windows on both sides of the cockpit and straight ahead—desperately looking for a place to land. Dan felt the plane coming around gradually in a slow, wide arc. He and Anika tightened their grips on each other. He saw the worry in Anika's eyes. Then he heard Derek's voice coming from the cockpit.

"Mayday. Mayday. This is Territorial Air Services Victor Hotel Whiskey Alpha Foxtrot. I've lost control of both elevators and rudder. Will be ditching in the South Alligator River, north of Arnhem Highway. Repeat. This is Territorial Air Services Victor Hotel Whiskey Alpha Foxtrot. Have lost control of both elevators and rudder. Will be ditching in the South Alligator River, north of Arnhem Highway." Derek poked his head out of the cockpit and looked at Dan. His voice came over the intercom.

"Can't land on the highway today, mate," Derek said. "Too busy and too dangerous. We've only got one option, so listen closely. I'm gonna haveta bring 'er around an' take 'er down on the river. That may sound soft an' cushy, but it won't be. We don't have floats, just wheels. So when we hit the water, we're gonna stop very fast and very hard. The water's still quite deep 'cuz we're at the end'a the wet season, so we're gonna take on water. We'll haveta exit the aircraft as quickly as possible."

The plane gave another lurch to the right and nosed downwards. Derek brought it back to centre with his ailerons and Dan heard the engine respond to more throttle, bringing the nose up slightly. Then, just as quickly, the plane lurched down and to the left. It was clear that Derek was now struggling to keep the plane from spinning out of control.

"I'm gonna take 'er down as slow as I can, mates. But that means I can't reduce my airspeed as much as I like. There's flotation vests under yer seats—put 'em over yer heads, but don't inflate 'em until we leave the aircraft. I need ya to get into crash position—take off any glasses and get your head down an' rest it on yer arms, against the back o' the seat in front of ya. When we come'ta rest in the water, we'll hav'ta move quickly to exit the aircraft. We're gonna have to swim for shore. Wish us luck, mates —'ere we go."

Dan felt Anika's hand reluctantly let go of his. They both reached under their seats and grabbed for their vests. Once they had them over their heads, they leaned forward, resting their heads on their arms. Dan felt the engine cut back. Almost immediately the plane's nose tilted downward and they started their descent. The aircraft rocked unsteadily from side to side as they descended. Dan felt Derek alternating between cutting the throttle and giving small bursts of fuel in a desperate effort to control the plane's nose and the speed of their descent. He also felt his heart pounding in his chest and caught himself holding his breath. He had to remind himself to keep breathing and to stay calm.

The small plane continued to lurch from side to side. The pitch of the droning engine rose and fell as Derek continued to artfully guide the crippled aircraft back to earth. Dan snuck a peek underneath his arms to see out the window on his left. The wetlands and bush were much closer now. Dan quickly replaced his head so that it rested on his arms again. The pitch of the engine was changing more quickly now as Derek tried to fine-tune their speed and keep the plane's nose from diving straight down into the earth.

"Hang on, mates!" Derek shouted into the intercom. "Almost there—about ten more seconds—good luck!"

Dan braced his head and neck against his arms and the seat in front. The final ten seconds seemed to take an eternity, as the plane continued to rock back and forth, from side to side. Suddenly, Dan felt the power disappear from the engine. There was silence—and then it felt like all of hell was breaking loose. Dan felt the wheels hit the water, coming to an abrupt halt while the rest of the plane seemed to want to keep going. Over the ear-splitting sound of twisting and groaning metal, he heard Anika scream.

Dan's head slammed against his arms and the seat in front. His lap belt dug into his body and he felt pain searing through his hips. Then just as quickly, he felt his head snap back and slam against the back of his own seat. He felt numb and seemed to lose track of everything around him. Then there was darkness.

IN THE distance, Dan heard a woman's voice screaming.

Dan!... Dan!... Wake up!... Please!...

He felt hands shaking his body. Gradually, he became aware of another person—a woman—shaking him and screaming at him. Slowly, out of the fog, he started to recognize Anika.

"Dan! Snap out of it. I think Derek's hurt—he's not moving! Help me! We have to help him and get out of here!"

Dan became more aware of pain in his neck, and he noticed that his hips were burning. Anika's face came into focus and he began to see the devastating effects of their landing on the aircraft's cabin. The row of seats in which they had initially been seated were now crushed against the bulkhead behind the cockpit. The row in which they were seated was now lodged against the front row of seats. He realized that his knees were pinned between his seat and the one in front. The entire row of seats had come loose and was all askew. He felt Anika pushing his seat back and the pressure easing off his knees. He became aware of the sound of water. His shoes and socks were soaked. Water was oozing steadily into the cabin.

"Come on, Dan! Get up, we have to help Derek!"

He felt Anika tugging at his arms, pulling him to his feet. Initially, the world around him was spinning and he wobbled on his feet. He felt Anika's arm around him, trying to steady him. He looked up and saw the cockpit. Derek's head was resting against the dashboard, and Dan saw a small stream of blood trickling down over the top row of gauges. He felt a surge of adrenaline take hold of him, filling him with energy. The scene suddenly became clear, as though somebody had just given him glasses to wear. He forced his aching body into action, stumbling his way into the cockpit. Anika followed closely behind.

Derek's seat had collapsed and had been pushed forward against the dash and the control panel, pinning his knees, which were oozing blood.

"Check his pulse," Dan shouted. "I'll see if I can make some room for his legs to get him out of this cockpit!"

He saw Anika holding her fingers on Derek's neck.

"He's alive!" she shouted. "His pulse is relatively strong—that's a good sign." She started shaking his shoulder and shouting his name.

"Derek!… It's Anika… Can you hear me?… C'mon, wake up!" she shouted. She continued to shake his shoulder, trying to bring him back to consciousness while Dan worked furiously to push rows of seats back in the cabin. That task complete, he had to push the bulkhead behind Derek's seat back into the cabin where it belonged. Finally, he was able to wrench Derek's seat back a couple of inches. Derek groaned weakly and began to stir. Anika kept nudging and rocking him while she shouted to get his attention. Finally, he opened his eyes. This time he emitted a loud painful groan.

The water in the aircraft was now over their ankles and rising quickly. Anika's voice took on a more urgent tone. Dan's mind, now back up to speed, quickly assessed the situation. Once the wheels hit the water, the plane nose-dived into the water. It was now floating, but the cockpit's windshield was badly cracked and leaking water badly.

"Can you hear me, Derek? We've got to get out of here. The plane is starting to fill with water. You've got to help us get out!" The word *water* must have kick-started Derek's brain. He lifted his head and groaned, then slowly moved it from side to side, taking in information. A moment of silence followed while his brain painstakingly processed the overwhelming input from all of his senses. Finally, he spoke.

"Help me out of this seat," he groaned. "We have to get the cabin door open before we take on too much water."

Dan got his hands beneath the other man's armpits and pulled on the heavy torso. Anika's hands felt up and down the length of Derek's legs, searching for fractures while Dan moved his torso, exposing more and more of his legs. Adrenaline poured into Dan's bloodstream, making the weight of Derek's body suddenly seem manageable.

"Stop for a second!" Anika shouted. "Let me finish checking his legs!"

Her hands worked quickly and efficiently, covering both limbs completely in a matter of seconds.

"I don't feel any compound fractures. I think his knees took the brunt of the crash, but I don't know how bad they are. Okay, let's get him out of here!"

As Dan resumed pulling and Derek's body slid off the seat, Anika grabbed his legs, guiding them out of their cramped prison.

"Ahhhhh… " Derek screamed, as Dan and Anika finally began dragging him back into the cabin, supporting him between their two shoulders.

"Do you think you can stand?" Anika asked.

"My knees hurt like hell," Derek moaned. "But I'll try."

Dan and Anika dragged and guided Derek through the cabin, around twisted seats, until they were at the cabin door.

"Time to inflate our vests," Derek said between large breaths. "Once they're inflated, one of you will have to pull on the big lever to release the door. It won't open easily, with all the water pressure on the other side. You'll both have to push it open. When you do, the water's going to start pouring in here, so we'll have to be quick."

Dan looked Anika squarely in the eyes. "You pull the lever while I hold Derek upright, okay?" She nodded and reached for the lever.

"One more thing," Derek said, his voice suddenly stern as he looked out through a cabin window. "Once you open the door, don't shout. Stay calm. No thrashing in the water. Use nice slow strokes of your arms. Let the river carry you downstream. Work your way gradually to the near shore. When you get to the shore, get yourselves out of the water as quickly as you can. Understand?"

Dan saw Anika's forehead wrinkle initially, then he saw the look of understanding in her eyes. They both understood the implicit warning in Derek's words. They both nodded in silent acknowledgement.

"Ready?" Dan said to Anika.

"Okay, let's do this," she replied. She grabbed the lever in both hands and swung the lever in an arc to her left. As she did, the cabin door lifted off its seals and water began gushing through the cracks into the cabin. Dan propped Derek against a seat and joined Anika in pushing the door open. The pressure was surprising, but the adrenaline surging through their bloodstreams gave them the energy they needed to slowly push the door and stairway out into the river. Water now gushed unimpeded into the aircraft.

Dan and Anika reached for Derek together and helped him out the door first. The current grabbed him and pulled him the rest of the way out of the plane. The cabin was filling quickly while Dan helped push Anika through the surging water. He waited until she was clear before he moved into the opening himself. The water was now up to his chest. He summoned the strength to force himself out through the exit against the torrent of water that was surging into the plane. Finally, he felt the river's current grab him, sucking him out the door and into the South Alligator's swirling waters. He was thankful for the life vest that kept his head above water.

Once away from the plane, Dan gave a glance back over his shoulder. The plane was sinking quickly, with only the top of the tail, the wings, and the last few inches of the fuselage still poking out of the water. He had barely made it out alive. Quickly, he turned his head back to the river in front of him, looking for Derek and Anika. It didn't take him long to see two heads resting on bright orange pillows, bobbing along on the current. Anika was nearest to shore. Dan began using long, smooth breaststrokes to start navigating his way towards the shore. Instinctively, his eyes scanned the water, looking for any signs of danger. He breathed slowly, trying not to panic.

Slowly but surely, the shore grew closer. Dense bush grew along the bank. It wouldn't be easy finding a place to get out of the water. Dan scanned the shore as the river carried him downstream, looking for a possible landing site. Finally, about two hundred yards downstream, he saw a break in the bush where a spit of gravel extended a few feet into the river. He saw that Anika was floating towards that spot, with Derek trailing about twenty yards behind her. It was clear that Derek's legs were of little help and he was depending totally on his arms to guide him to shore. Dan was quickly catching up to Anika.

The current was strong and the river swift. Dan gave smooth, mighty thrusts of his legs and strokes with his arms, guiding himself steadily towards the shore. He didn't want to miss this landing area and have to look for another. He continued to gain on Anika and was only a few feet behind her as they neared the shore. Suddenly, he saw Anika stop and her body began to rise out of the water. Dan realized that her feet were now on the river bottom, just as his feet also scraped bottom. He kept stroking with his arms until his feet had a strong foothold, then he began walking steadily and rising out of the water until he joined Anika on the beach. He let out a sigh of relief and smiled at Anika. He looked back over his shoulder to find Derek, happy to see that their pilot was going to make landfall on the same part of the beach. He was about ten yards offshore.

Dan turned to Anika, his face breaking into a huge smile. But instead of a smile on Anika's face, he saw a look of terror. Her mouth opened and a blood-curdling scream emerged from deep in her lungs. Dan whirled around.

Derek's feet were now on the bottom and he was labouring to walk up onto the shore. But right behind him, Dan saw an elongated head with two large, green, beady eyes. A long tail swept from side to side as a huge crocodile closed in on Derek. At the same moment that Derek heard Anika's scream and saw the looks of terror on their faces, the reptile's head disappeared under water. A look of understanding, then of horror, crossed Derek's face. As the croc's powerful jaws latched onto the unfortunate man's unseen legs, he emitted a blood-curdling scream. Within mere seconds, the reptile had dragged Derek underwater and back out into the river. Apart from the sound of rushing water, the air was silent.

Derek Hardy's life was over in a matter of seconds while Dan and Anika looked on from the riverbank, helpless and frozen in shock.

CHAPTER 24

DAN AND ANIKA huddled together on a grassy embankment on the side of the Arnhem Highway. Their clothing was soaked and they were both still shivering from shock, despite the thirty-five-degree Celsius temperature. Behind them, a Northern Territory Police SUV, adorned with heavy metal 'roo bars' over the front grill, was parked on the side of the highway, lights flashing. In the driver's seat, Constable Jillian Brown relayed information back and forth to the station in Jabiru. Dan heard the constable's side of the conversations clearly. But from their vantage point outside the police cruiser, the responses from Jabiru came across as unintelligible squawking.

"Affirmative. Anika Kristiansen. Her husband, Soren Kristiansen, is wanted internationally for parental child abduction. They think he's been living in Darwin, and that he was going to be spending a couple of days in Kakadu," Constable Brown confirmed.

More squawking from Jabiru drifted from the SUV. Finally, Constable Brown stepped out of the cruiser and squatted down beside Anika.

"I've informed my station about your suspicions that your husband is in Australia. They've confirmed that he is definitely wanted by Interpol. They're also taking your information that he might be intending to leave the country very seriously. They're alerting airports and the coast guard to be on the lookout for anybody who looks like your husband or your son. The ATSB will be here shortly to ask you some questions about what happened on the flight. Then we'll get you back to Darwin," Brown said. "Until then, do you mind if I ask you some more questions?"

Anika shrugged her shoulders ambivalently. "Sure," Dan answered. "I'll do anything I can do to help. But I think Anika's still in a state of shock."

"Of course, Doctor Whitney," Brown answered. "You mentioned that there was some kind of special security inspection before your flight departed from Darwin?"

"Yes," Dan replied. "By two Australian Air Force personal. One was an officer, but the other one—the person who went into the plane—I'm not sure—that one was smaller and I caught a glimpse of the face. I think it might have been a woman. She was in the plane for at least five… maybe ten… minutes before she came out. The other man, the officer, just waited in their vehicle until she was done. Then he went in and talked with people at the airline's customer service desk. After that, they drove across the tarmac to the air force base, I think," Dan said.

"Did you notice anything unusual about either the driver or the person who was in the plane?" Brown asked.

"It was hard to tell," Dan said. "She looked like she was trying to hide her face, but I caught a glimpse. And I think I saw blonde hair sticking out from beneath her cap. I had the feeling I'd seen her somewhere else before. You know how it is. You see somebody's face but it's way out of context—someplace where you'd never expect them to show up. She seemed like she didn't belong there, but I just can't remember where I've seen her before."

Dan's mind searched through his recent memory for the faces of any blonde women he'd met recently. An image of Miriam Fox sitting in the Chateau Eden spa popped up, her face looking distant and serious. Even the image of Angela Baranyi, from Fran's candid portrait, flashed into his consciousness. He brushed both thoughts aside as being ridiculous—neither woman's face fit the image of the woman from the airport.

"Did your pilot say anything else about the security inspection?" Constable Brown asked, her voice jerking Dan back to reality.

He thought for a moment. "Derek said it probably had to do with some U.S. Air Force big-wig en route to Afghanistan. He said security was always tighter when something like that happened."

"My station already checked into that," Brown answered, her voice serious and curt. "There were no VIP's at the RAAF base in Darwin today, and no special security checks. They're already investigating into who those two RAAF personnel could have been."

At that moment, a white truck slowed on the other side of the highway, then did a U-turn and parked behind Constable Brown's SUV. Markings on the truck identified it as being from the Australian Transport Safety Bureau, or ATSB.

"Thank you for your cooperation, Dr. Whitney. I'll let the ATSB investigators take it from here. Where are you staying in Darwin?"

"The Holiday Inn, on the Esplanade," Dan replied.

"I'll arrange for transportation back to the hotel for you and Ms. Kristiansen," Brown said. "Will you be in Darwin for a while in case we have more questions?"

Dan looked at Anika, who just shrugged her shoulders again.

"I don't think we know what we're doing next," Dan answered. "Anika's devastated right now—not just about the crash and Derek's death—but because her hopes were so high that she was going to find her son today or tomorrow."

"I understand," Brown said, turning to Anika. "I can't imagine having one of my children abducted. Especially by their father! Good luck to you in your search. I hope you find the bastard." She shook Dan and Anika's hands.

Jillian Brown turned to the two men who had just climbed out of the ATSB truck.

"They're all yours, gentlemen. I'll think you'll find their story very interesting." She walked back to her SUV and climbed in, grabbing the microphone. She resumed talking to Jabiru station. Once again, Dan heard her radio squawking. He heard the voices of the two men from the ATSB introducing themselves to him and Anika. He even heard his voice answering them, somewhere in the distance. But his mind was someplace else. It was focused on the image of the woman's face from Darwin Airport—and he was trying desperately to place where he'd seen that face before.

THE ELEVATOR door opened at the third floor for Dan and Anika. The faint orange-yellow glow of sunset shone through a window at the far end of the hallway. Dan was relieved to be back in the familiar setting of their hotel after the horror of today's tragedy. He knew Anika felt the same; her legs moved faster as they approached her room at the end of the corridor. He felt the warmth of her hand clutching his. She hadn't let go since they witnessed Derek's death, desperately needing to stay connected to somebody who was alive.

Anika pulled out her magnetic card key from her purse, attempting to swipe it in the lock. Her hands shook so badly that she couldn't get the card into the slot to swipe it.

Dan took her hand gently and held it still—helping her to get the card into the groove and to swipe it. The light flashed green and the lock clicked. Together, they pushed the door open and walked inside. As the door swung closed behind them, their bodies both collapsed with their backs against the door. Simultaneously, they let out long, slow sighs of relief. It was like they'd both been holding their breath all afternoon—waiting to breathe until they could finally feel safe. Dan's hand found Anika's again. Their hands locked together, craving closeness and each other's warmth.

Dan looked into Anika's eyes. She burst into tears. All of today's fear, horror, disappointment, and a myriad of emotions burst from her as if the floodgates of a dam had just opened. She wrapped her arms around Dan's neck. He felt her hanging to him as if her life depended on it. He held her as tight and as close as he could, trying to reassure her that she was safe with him.

He felt her respond. She wrapped her arms around his torso and pulled her body as close to him as she could. She sobbed like a small child who needed to be consoled, taking short, jerky breaths between each sob. As she did, Dan felt not only the depths of his own fear from earlier today, but also the depths of Anika's despair. Their eyes met, passing an unsaid message between them.

Anika opened her lips and pressed them firmly against Dan's. He felt her hunger to feel loved and safe. And in that moment, he felt the aching emptiness he'd felt since Chelly died so suddenly, and since Fran had been taken from him and imprisoned.

His lips and his body responded to Anika's desperate longing. His hands started roaming, following every curve on her body, from the delicate softness of her face, to her neck, her shoulders, her back, and the delicious firmness of her buttocks.

Anika's hands reciprocated, searching beneath his t-shirt and running her fingers through the hair on his chest, massaging his nipples, which were now erect and hard. In desperation, they tore their clothes from each other, leaving only their undergarments. Dan put his hands under her buttocks and lifted. She responded by jumping up and wrapping her legs around his waist. He carried her to the bed. Their lips were still locked in passion, desperate to get as close to each other as humanly possible.

Dan lowered Anika onto the bed and removed the last barriers of clothing that kept their bodies apart. Their hands and lips explored each other's arousal, unable to get enough. Finally, Anika rolled Dan onto his side. Their legs became entwined and she guided him inside, taking him as far as she could and gripping him tight. They remained perfectly still, not wanting to spoil the moment—savouring the feelings of safety—feeling as close and intimate as any two people can get.

Then Anika rolled over on top of Dan. She started moving, leaning forward and locking her mouth onto Dan's, her small breasts pressed tightly against his chest. His penis pressed tightly against her G-spot. Her pelvis started moving in ever-widening, ever-faster circles.

Dan was engulfed by their passion and their mutual need for each other. It was a moment he had always longed for—a fantasy that had been finding its way into his dreams for years. He let himself go and rode the wave with Anika. For the moment, all thoughts of Chelly and Fran were forgotten. The only thing that mattered in the moment was him and Anika, and their desperate need to feel safe, to feel close, and to feel loved.

DAN'S EYES fluttered open. Daylight was just beginning to creep into the hotel room. In the dim light, he gazed at Anika's face. He was grateful to see her sleeping peacefully after the horrors of Derek's tragic end and their own brushes with death. As he watched her sleep, he found himself overtaken by a jumbled wave of conflicting emotions. He felt overwhelming sympathy for what Anika was going through—the nightmare of having her only child abducted, along with the unbearable sense of betrayal by her husband. He wanted to wrap his arms around her and hold her again, feeling the need to protect her and keep her safe. Was it love he felt for her?

Part of Dan was aware that, although he had always loved Anika, he might not be *in love* with her. And at the same time, another side of him was slowly, but surely, being consumed by guilt—guilt for having taken advantage of his long-time friend in her moment of greatest vulnerability—and guilt for not telling her that Fran was pregnant with his child. But most of all, he felt guilty for having been unfaithful to Fran, after so recently committing himself to building a future with her and their unborn child.

The part of Dan that needed to protect Anika won for the moment. He moved close and wrapped his arm around her, kissing her gently on her forehead. Her eyelids flickered momentarily, then she opened one eye long enough to orient herself. Her other eye also opened a slit, allowing her eyes to accommodate to the early morning light. She placed a hand on the arm that Dan had wrapped around her body and gently removed it. Instead, she held his hand.

"We can't do this again," she whispered. "I can't do it again. I'm sorry, it's just not right. We needed each other yesterday. Desperately. But we can't let it happen again. I don't want this to ruin our friendship. Do you understand?"

Dan let Anika's words sink in, integrating them with all of the thoughts and emotions that were swirling through his brain at the moment. He nodded to Anika, not saying a word.

Anika kissed him on the forehead. She sat up and wrapped herself modestly with the bed's blanket—as though they had never seen each other vulnerable and naked—as if yesterday had never happened. She pulled the blanket from the bed and stood up, making sure that her private parts were covered, and then she shuffled off to the bathroom.

Soon Dan heard her turn on the shower. His mind drifted to Fran, depressed and still captive in Indio Jail. She was helpless, with nothing to do for the next three weeks but wait for a Grand Jury to decide whether she would stand trial for conspiracy and murder. He resolved that he had to tell Fran about yesterday and last night. What he couldn't decide, was *how* he was ever going to admit his transgression, knowing that it would most likely push her away from him for good.

DAN AND ANIKA took turns getting up and filling their plates and bowls with items from the breakfast buffet, without exchanging any words. Dan opened the morning edition of the

Darwin/Palmerston Sun. His face blushed a light shade of pink as he read the sensational front-page headline: '*CROC CLAIMS PILOT'S LIFE - COUPLE SURVIVES CRASH*'.

He took furtive glances at other restaurant patrons, wondering if any of them had recognized him from the article's photo. Apparently not, he decided, since most of them were more interested in breakfast and few had opened a newspaper yet. He scanned through the article, slowing down suddenly when he got to the section where the article's author hinted at the possibility of foul play. ATSB investigators would neither confirm nor deny the allegation. The partial facial image of the woman who searched their plane yesterday prior to taking off, flashed through his mind again. The image wouldn't leave him alone. He continued to feel frustrated that he couldn't recall where he'd seen her before.

Anika returned to the table with some scrambled eggs, hash browns, and a plate of fruit. Dan was about to bring the headline to her attention when a woman wearing a white skirt, a colourful flowered blouse, and a white straw hat, entered the restaurant. She paused to look around. Dan realized that she'd spotted them and was heading towards their table. It was difficult to see the woman's face beneath her hat, but something told Dan that he'd seen her before.

Suddenly, Dan recognized the face.

The portrait at Fran and Philippe's Palm Desert estate!

It was Angela Baranyi—their so-called guardian angel.

"Looks like we have company," Dan said to Anika, motioning in Angela's direction with his eyes. Anika's mouth dropped open in surprise when she recognized the identity of their unexpected visitor. Together, they rose from their chairs to greet her. They extended their hands, but Angela ignored them. Instead, she took Anika into her arms and embraced her tightly.

"Ms. Kristiansen. I'm so glad to finally meet you," Angela gushed. "I'm Angela Baranyi. And I'm so glad to see you both alive!"

She broke her embrace with Anika and extended her hand to Dan. "Dr. Whitney. It's pleasure to finally meet you. I'm sorry to interrupt your breakfast," she said, lowering her eyes and her voice. Dan was grateful that she didn't want to attract attention to their table. "We need to talk—somewhere private—as soon as possible!" she whispered.

TEN MINUTES later, the trio sat in Dan's room on the fourth floor. He sat on one of the room's twin beds, facing Angela, who sat on the edge of the other bed. Anika sat in the room's only easy chair. Angela and Dan sipped from paper cups of hot coffee. Anika waited for a tea bag to steep in a cup of piping hot water.

"I'm so sorry about what happened yesterday. If I'd had any idea, I never would have arranged that charter for you," Angela said, her voice quivering. "Poor Derek. He was such a nice man. I feel so responsible for his death. He didn't deserve what happened to him."

Angela wiped a tear from her red eyes. Dan felt for the woman, who was obviously ridden with guilt over what happened.

"Don't beat yourself up," Anika said from across the room. "You couldn't have foreseen what happened. It was just a fluke accident."

"What if it wasn't?" Angela replied. "The papers suggest there might have been some foul play—that somebody might have tampered with the plane. I've been doing a lot of reading about parental child abduction. You wouldn't be the first spouse to be killed while looking for an abducted child."

"We don't know that's the case," Dan said, keeping his own questions about the identity of the female who searched their plane to himself.

"But we can't rule it out, either," Angela answered.

Not wanting Anika to feel any more afraid than she already was, Dan decided to change the subject.

"How did you manage to track Soren and Jonah to Darwin, when every police force on the planet couldn't find them? How did you know he was going to Kakadu?"

Angela realized this was the first time she had told anybody, apart from her friend Ricki Marshall in Las Vegas, about what had happened between herself and Soren. It was a giant step to come out of hiding. She tried, with no success, to swallow. She gave a second bigger swallow and finally managed to clear the lump from her throat.

"Ms. Kristiansen. As you probably know, I worked for your husband in the WWCC office in New York. I was working in his IT department on a secret project." Angela started to blush and lowered her eyes so she wouldn't have to meet Anika's gaze. "He started making inappropriate advances towards me. It started in his office. And at the same time he was making those advances, all I could see was the portrait on his desk—a portrait of him with you and Jonah. I kept asking myself: 'why is he doing this? He has such a beautiful wife and child. He has everything'!"

"Please," Anika said. "Call me Anika. I really don't want to be known by that asshole's name anymore."

Angela paused for a sip of coffee to moisten her mouth and clear her throat again.

"Okay… Anika… where was I? Oh, yeah, his portrait of you and Jonah. I didn't believe it at first, but his advances became more persistent, and I couldn't ignore them. I decided to leave New York and the WWCC, but he threatened to harm my children if I did," she said.

Anika sat erect in her chair. Her jaw clenched. The veins and muscles in her neck looked like they were trying to jump out from under her skin.

"That bastard," she hissed. Her eyes narrowed, staring at Angela, silently demanding answers. "What secret projects?"

Angela held her coffee cup in both hands, taking another anxious sip.

"He has other businesses," she answered meekly. "Illegal businesses. He was using the church to launder money from those activities, and I stumbled on it."

"Illegal businesses?" Dan said. "What do you mean?"

Angela blushed again. "He had pornography websites, based in Asia. They were making him a small fortune. Dominance, submission, bondage… and much worse. Some of it was nothing less than sadistic torture. He was also getting into cybercrime. He used the WWCC website to mine information about church members so he could eventually steal money and their identities."

Dan and Anika stared at each other in disbelief. Anika's face was turning red, her anger continuing to build.

"So Pastor Soren and the WWCC were just a big lie?" Anika asked rhetorically. "And my marriage was just a lie too?" She glared at Angela. "Did you find any child porn?"

Angela shook her head. "No, but I'd seen enough. I didn't keep looking. I was afraid of what I might find," she answered.

"You said you decided to leave and he threatened you?" Dan said.

"I told him I was extremely thankful for the opportunity he gave me, but I missed my kids and parents in Cleveland. I tried to pretend I didn't know about his illegal activities, but I must have let it show. I'd make a crappy poker player. He gave me the creepiest smirk, saying that he understood how important my family was to me. Then his eyes narrowed and he said what a shame it would be if anything happened to them. That smile was pure evil. It gave me the shivers. I knew he meant what he said."

"So you made a plan to disappear," Dan said, as the pieces starting falling in place in his mind. "You turned the tables and threatened him—your silence about his business activities in return for your kid's safety. But your threat was only good if he couldn't find you."

Angela bowed her head and nodded her acknowledgment.

"So you were living on the streets of L.A. That's where Fran ran into you and took the candid portrait. Do you remember that?" Dan asked.

"Yes," Angela said. "I was mortified. The last thing I needed was for somebody to identify me, and for Soren to come after me. Is she with a magazine or the newspaper?"

"No. You were lucky. She's just an amateur photographer—a very good one. She was embarrassed to show her work in public, so she just displayed a few portraits in her estate in Palm Desert," Dan explained.

"You still haven't explained how you managed to trace Soren to Darwin," Anika interjected impatiently.

"I saw the news about Jonah's abduction on TV. When I saw what he did to his own wife and child, it must have brought out the anger I'd kept inside when he threatened my kids and me. I felt ashamed to be hiding, and ashamed of what I was doing to my kids. I couldn't just sit back and watch. I had to do something. So I used what I knew about Soren from my work with the WWCC to hack into his computer. It took me a while, but I built a clone of his hard drive. So I have a copy of every file that changes on his computer, and a list of every website he's visited."

"Why didn't you just take control of his computer?" Dan asked.

"Good question," Angela answered. "That way, I would have been able to follow him in real time. But it was too risky to do it that way—too easy for him to notice somebody else using his computer. It wasn't worth the risk."

"So the cloning method isn't in real time and has limitations, but it's safer," Dan reflected.

"Exactly," Angela said. "But I got lucky. I accidentally captured some emails he was exchanging with somebody using the codename *Helen*. They're using internal email on a secret U.S. Government website. They're smart. They're only communicating through the internal email on that website."

Anika jumped to her feet, unable to contain her rising frustration and anger. "So, the bastard's been cheating on me with this Helen too?" she shouted. Unable to bottle up her emotions any longer, Anika burst into tears.

Dan and Angela both rose to their feet to console her. Angela reached her first, wrapping her arms around Anika.

"Shhh," Angela said softly in Anika's ear. "We don't know that for sure."

Dan watched Angela attempting to calm Anika down, but his mind was still working. Before he realized it, he was thinking out loud.

"So, if Soren's involved in these illegal activities, how is he able to log into a secret U.S. Government website? Is he working undercover for the CIA? Or even worse, are he and this Helen working for the other side? Have they compromised a government site?"

Anika's crying had subsided into sniffles and occasional whimpers. Angela helped her back into the easy chair.

"I can't tell," Angela replied. "So far, any emails I've seen have been related to Soren's flight from the police. Helen seems to be helping him from a distance—probably from the States, as far as I can see. What worries me is that she said she was going to contact Soren about new travel plans today—probably later tonight. If we don't find him in Darwin soon, we may lose him again."

"Shit," Dan muttered, looking at Anika and feeling her frustration and pain. "We were so close."

Frustration and silence permeated the room. Finally, Dan broke the silence.

"Do you think they knew we were in Darwin?" he asked. "Do you think they had anything to do with the crash yesterday?"

Angela took a moment to recall the emails she'd intercepted.

"I don't think so. There was nothing in the emails to indicate they were concerned. I think Darwin was just a stopover for him. Nothing more than a place to stay while all of the commotion died down. It seems to me like he was getting ready to move on anyway."

"Asia," Anika said, her voice completely devoid of emotion. "He's going to Asia so he's safe from the Hague Convention. So far, Thailand is the only large Asian country that has signed the convention. He could be going anywhere—Indonesia, Malaysia, Vietnam, or even India. If he gets there, it will take a miracle to get Jonah back, even if we find Soren and apply for extradition."

"It's going to be a lot harder for him to get there now," Dan said. "The airports in Australia will be crawling with extra security now that we've alerted them. And the coast guard will be watching for any boats trying to make it to East Timor or Indonesia. But he might go somewhere else here in Australia and go further underground."

"Then we have to find them as soon as possible," Angela said. She went to Anika and knelt on the floor in front of her, taking her hand in both of her own. "I'm so sorry, Anika. I should have just called the police right away. But I thought you'd want to be here first. I'm so stupid. I hope you can forgive me."

"Don't blame yourself. It's not your fault," Anika said. She went silent—thinking. Then she appeared to perk up, energized by a renewed sense of hope.

"If they come back to Darwin from Kakadu, we might still have chance of seeing them in the park today or tomorrow! And there must be something else we can do today," she blurted.

"Did you bring a copy of that missing person poster of Jonah, and the *Wanted* poster of Soren?" Dan asked.

"Yes, I almost forgot about them," Anika answered.

"Why don't I find someplace to make some copies? Then I'll spend the day downtown, putting up posters, asking questions, and keeping my eyes open. You ladies can spend the day keeping an eye on the park and surrounding area. We can keep in touch with our cell phones. If we make a sighting, we'll call Darwin police first, *then* we phone each other. Agreed?"

"That sounds good," Angela said. "They may not be getting back from Kakadu until late in the afternoon. In that case, we'll have a better chance of seeing Jonah and his nanny in the park tomorrow morning. I'll stay up late tonight on my laptop, since that's when Helen promised to contact Soren next. Do we have a plan?"

Dan looked to Anika, whose face was much more optimistic than it was just minutes earlier.

"I like it," Anika said.

"Okay," Dan said, also feeling a renewed sense of purpose. He directed his next words to Angela. "Anika and I can't tell you how much it means to us that you've been watching over us and helping us. Let's get Jonah back to Anika, get Soren behind bars, and let you get back to your kids."

He reached out for Angela with one hand and to Anika with the other, bringing them together in a group huddle. It was Angela who eventually broke the silent embrace.

"Let's do it," she said.

"And most of all, let's all be careful," Dan added.

SOREN squeezed the last of their bags into the rear hatch of the small SUV that doubled as a taxi. He felt pumped. Even though the seas had been rough, the decrepit old fishing boat had creaked, groaned, and growled its way across the Timor Sea, finally reaching Kupang safely after a thirty-two-hour journey.

Soren jumped into the front seat beside the driver.

"Airport," he shouted. The Indonesia driver didn't seem to understand, so Soren spread his arms the best he could in the confines of the tiny vehicle, pretending to be an airplane. The driver smiled and nodded his head. He put the vehicle in gear, leaving the fishing boat and the dock in the rear view mirror.

Soren looked behind him at Lucy and Jonah in the back seat. He had to admit, the woman was a real trooper. Jonah had been seasick much of the way, beginning as soon as the seas got rough. She had good maternal instincts, comforting the boy and keeping him calm the whole way.

It's too bad that she's nearing the end of her usefulness.

He smiled at Lucy and Jonah. He felt on top of the world. By now, Helen should have taken care of Anika and Whitney. With Anika out of the way, it would be so much easier to disappear.

He didn't look forward to the gruelling overnight flight from Kupang to Surabaya. But, at least he wouldn't have to worry about the Australian and Indonesian coast guards any more. He could finally relax.

Soren removed a pouch from his small carry-on bag, taking a good look at the new passports Helen had delivered to him in Little Rock. John Dailey and John Dailey Junior had met with a tragic end when Soren threw those old identities into the Timor Sea. He smiled at their new names. He was now Magnus Larssen and Jonah was John Larssen. Once again, Lucy was listed as his spouse, Lucy Larssen. Most importantly, with their new Norwegian passports and identities, they were now safe in Indonesia. They were out of reach of the protective umbrella of the Hague Convention.

CHAPTER 25

DAN WAS exhausted and discouraged from walking the streets of Darwin in thirty-five-degree heat and humidity for the past day and a half. He'd spent all day Monday and all Tuesday morning putting up posters and making inquiries at hotels. So far, nothing at all. Anika and Angela hadn't fared any better. Jonah and his nanny hadn't appeared in the park on the Esplanade yesterday. He reached into his pocket for his mobile phone, and then he dialed Angela's number.

"Hi, Angela. Dan here. How are you guys doing?… Nothing yet?… Same here… I'm just about at the Noodle House on Mitchell, are you girls close?… It's just a few blocks up the street… Okay, I've got one more hotel to stop at… I'll meet you at the restaurant in twenty minutes… see you there."

Dan crossed McLaughlan Street, headed for a small three-story motel situated behind the restaurant. As he walked into the dark lobby, a chilly blast of much appreciated air conditioning greeted him. He walked up to the check-in desk, where he was welcomed by young woman with brown skin and black hair, neatly attired with a navy skirt and white blouse.

"G'day, sir. Can I help you?" she inquired with a cheery Australian accent.

"I hope so," Dan answered. He opened his folder with the posters of Jonah and Soren, laying them on the counter for the woman to see. "I'm looking for the missing boy in this picture, or his father on this other poster. You wouldn't happen to have seen either of them, would you?

The clerk looked carefully at Jonah's picture and shook her head.

"Sorry, sir. I haven't seen the boy," she said. Dan was ready to pick up the posters when the young woman put her hand on Soren's photo and stopped him.

"But the man in this picture… it looks a lot like Mr. Dailey. Is this poster what it says it is? Is this a police matter?"

Dan snapped to attention. "Mr. Dailey? He's a guest here?"

"I'm sorry, sir. I hope you understand, but I'm not free to give out that kind of information. If you come back in an hour, you might try talking to my manager."

"Never mind," Dan said, reaching into his pocket for his phone again. He dialed 000 as fast as his fingers would work. "Hello, emergency? I'd like to report a possible sighting of Soren Kristiansen, wanted in America for parental child abduction and suspicion of murder… yes, K-R-I-S-T-I-A-N-S-E-N… Soren… pardon me?… The man on last night's news TV news?… Yes, probably… Northern Territory Police were alerted two days ago… my name?… Dr. Dan Whitney… yes, I'm at the hotel on McLaughlan, just off Mitchell… that's right… I'll be waiting."

Dan pressed the *Hang Up* button, then dialed Angela's number again.

"Angela. I've got a possible sighting of Soren at a hotel, just behind the Noodle House… what!… Jonah and the nanny?… The white apartments?… You're kidding… you've called the police?… Yeah, this might take a while too… Let me know when you're done and I'll meet you at the restaurant… okay, bye."

Dan closed his phone and dropped it back into his pocket with shaky hands. As he waited for the police to arrive at the hotel, he realized that his entire body trembled and his heart pounded with anticipation. This was finally the break he and Anika had been looking for since the day Jonah had disappeared. Despite yesterday's near disaster on the South Alligator River, they were finally closing in on Soren Kristiansen and Jonah.

ONE HOUR later, over a midday lunch of Thai food, Dan listened while Anika barely contained her flood of mixed emotions.

"We were just going into those rundown white apartments that back onto Mitchell Street when you phoned us," she said. "I showed Jonah's picture to the building manager and she recognized him immediately. She said she didn't see them come out of the apartment often, but Jonah was always with an Asian woman. The manager said she'd never seen Soren."

"I'm so stupid," Angela cursed. "The apartment is only a block from the park where I saw them, but it's hidden behind a couple of large hotels. I tried following them from a distance, but they always disappeared so quickly. I was so convinced that they might be living in one of the hotels that I never thought to look any further at the apartments."

Anika placed her hand over Angela's.

"Don't be so hard on yourself. If it wasn't for you, we would never have known they were in Darwin," she said, giving the other woman a smile of thanks. Then she turned to Dan and continued.

"When the manager realized that Jonah had been kidnapped, she took us straight to the apartment, but nobody answered. She let us in, but it doesn't look like anybody's been there for two or three days. All the dishes were washed, the trash has been taken out, and the fridge was cleaned out. The Asian woman knew they weren't coming back."

"Exactly what we found in Soren's room," Dan added. "Housekeeping reported that the room hadn't been disturbed after they made it up on Sunday. And there was no sign of any luggage or personal belongings. He was paid up until the end of the week, so nobody at the hotel paid any attention."

"We were so close!" Anika cried out in frustration.

"They can't be that far away," Dan replied, trying in vain to help Anika remain hopeful.

"They didn't have to go far!" she wailed. "Indonesia is just a stone's throw away. Don't you see, Dan? Soren's won! He made it to a country that doesn't recognize the Hague convention! Even if I get my court order for custody of Jonah, no court in Indonesia, or most other Asian countries for that matter, will recognize it!"

"That may be true," Angela replied. "But don't forget - Soren is also wanted on suspicion of that murder in Little Rock, so he's still on Interpol's *Wanted* list."

"That's right," Dan agreed. "And now that they know he's using an alias, they'll be watching more closely for them. It's going to be a lot harder for Soren to keep a low profile if he keeps running."

"I agree," Angela said, this time taking Anika's hand in hers, trying to keep her new friend's hopes up.

"So what do we do now?" Dan asked, his eyes looking towards Anika and Angela for suggestions. Anika's face was blank —her mind was somewhere else. He looked to Angela for help.

"I think I'll keep a low profile here in Darwin for a few days. Don't forget, I'm still hiding from both Soren and the police too. I'll stay glued to my computer because I don't want to miss it when he comes back online. He'll probably be checking in with that woman, Helen, as soon as he gets where he's going. What about you guys?"

Anika's eyes blinked. Her face came back to life.

"I'm going to go back to Calgary to be with my family," she said. "And I may need to go back to British Columbia to deal with the court order for Jonah's custody."

"I'll be going back to Palm Springs," Dan said. "I'm worried about Fran. Being in prison is taking a toll on her. She's becoming more withdrawn and pessimistic, and that's not like the Fran I met. But she doesn't go before the Grand Jury for another three weeks, so I might be available to help if you if something comes up. Will you let us know the minute you find something?"

"Of course," Angela answered. "Now that I have Anika's information, I'll contact her first. I don't want to drag you away from Fran if she needs you."

"I appreciate that," Dan answered. His eyes made contact with Anika's. She looked away quickly, and Dan felt the awkward distance that had developed since their unexpected lovemaking.

"I'll do whatever I can for Anika," he continued.

"So, it's decided," Angela said, reaching for Anika's hand again. "You two go home and do what you need to do. I'll keep searching for Soren, and I'll contact you as soon as I know anything."

They rose from their table and wrapped their arms around each other in another silent group embrace. Dan felt a contradiction of positive and negative emotions. On one hand, he felt more hopeful that they were finally closing in on Soren and were much closer to returning Jonah to Anika. But on the other, the shock of their airplane crash and Derek's death, and the disappointment of knowing that Soren may have slipped through their fingers to a non-Hague Convention country, was disheartening.

And then there was also the awkward distance that had grown between himself and Anika after their unexpected sexual encounter, along with his growing guilt. He hadn't yet told Anika about Fran's pregnancy, and now he had to tell Fran that he and Anika had made love.

Now you've really done it, Dan. How could you have done that to Fran? How are you ever going to tell her? Maybe you're no better than all the other guys who've treated her like shit. Maybe she's right about not wanting to commit to you!

THE JUMBO Boeing 747 finally levelled off at cruising altitude. Dan and Anika had settled into another uncomfortable silence.

"I'm sorry about what happened between us the other night," Dan finally said. "I took advantage of you, and that wasn't right. I hope you'll forgive me."

Anika took Dan's hand in hers and managed to look him in the eyes.

"Don't blame yourself," she said. "I'm just as much to blame as you. I shouldn't have led you on. It wasn't fair to you or Fran. I love you as a friend, Dan. And I don't ever want to lose that. But I just can't do it again. We're two people who almost died together. We're thousands of miles from our friends and families. In the heat of the moment, we both needed the comfort of someone else's arms. It wasn't anything more than that, as far as I'm concerned."

Dan swallowed, trying to clear his voice, and trying to find the courage to say the words that were lodged in his throat.

"There's something else," Dan blurted, giving another large swallow. He found himself having difficulty looking at Anika.

"Fran's pregnant. The baby is mine."

A look of shock flashed across Anika's face. Then, slowly, a knowing smile replaced the shock. Dan almost thought he saw a look of relief.

"I see," she said, allowing herself to digest this new bit of information. "No wonder you're beating yourself up so much. It also explains why you've seemed more distant over the past couple of days. You're feeling guilty, aren't you?"

"No kidding," Dan answered. "I've been trying my hardest to let Fran know that I want to be there for her and the baby—that I want to make a life for us. And then I go and do something like this to her—and to you."

"I wish I could help," Anika answered. "I'd like to be able to tell Fran that what we did was just an accident—two close friends who desperately needed each other at that moment. But I'm *the other woman* now. I'm just as guilty as you are. I'm sorry. Maybe it would have made a difference if I'd known she was pregnant…

maybe it wouldn't. Maybe we just needed each other too much after the crash and Derek's death."

"It's not up to you to help me," Dan said. "I'm going to have man up as soon as I get home. I can't blame her if she decides to give up on me. But it's better that she does it now, rather than later."

"You said you'd been trying to convince her that you're committed to her and the baby. Doesn't Fran want you to be involved?"

"That's what it's starting to look like. The more I try to convince her that I'm committing myself to her, the more she seems to be pushing me away. It's like she's lost all of her self-confidence and all of her trust in everybody," Dan answered.

"Didn't you say she has a history of not being able to trust people?" Anika asked.

"Yeah. Her mother, father, and older sister all neglected her. And her brother in law sexually and physically abused her while she was growing up. So I understand how hard it is for her."

"Is there anybody in her life she does trust?" Anika asked.

Dan paused, trying to think of the people he knew in her life.

"She doesn't really have anybody close. She did most of her socializing with Philippe and his circle of friends and associates when he was alive. The only two people I can think of are Shelley and Tim. But she hasn't even known them for very long," he said.

"Was there *anybody* who might have had a positive influence on her while she was growing up? A girlfriend, or maybe a teacher?"

Dan let his mind float back to the few conversations that he and Fran had about her past. She'd been guarded about saying too much about it.

"She did mention something about a teacher who encouraged her to start swimming. Now that I think about it, it might have been the same teacher who sparked her interest in photography. But I don't recall her mentioning a name."

"That's too bad," Anika answered. "Everybody needs at least one close friend they can confide in while they're growing up. I was lucky—I had you."

Dan felt Anika's warm hand squeezing his.

"I just remembered," Dan blurted. "There *was* somebody else. An American woman she worked with in Manarola. But I can't remember her name. I think they must have been quite close. She gave Fran her first camera—an old-school SLR—but Fran still uses it. In fact, she took the portrait of Angela in Los Angeles with that old camera. Fran said she doesn't want one of the new digital SLR's—she won't let go of her old Pentax. I wish I could remember that woman's name."

"Does Fran still have any contact with her?" Anika asked.

"I have no idea," Dan answered. "I'll try to find out more about her when I visit Fran next. But it might be too late. When I tell her about us, it might not make any difference. I wouldn't blame her if she kicks me to the curb."

Dan felt another squeeze from Anika's hand.

"Well, if nothing else, we still have each other for support," Anika said. "If you need to talk, you know I'll always be there."

"Thanks," he said, leaning forward and giving her a chaste kiss on the forehead.

"So, what do you think of Angela?" Anika asked.

"I have to admire her for taking a stand against Soren," Dan answered. "It must have been excruciating for her to disappear in order to protect her children. She seems like a genuinely warm person. You two seem to have a lot in common. What do you think of her?"

"The same. I wish I'd had the guts to stand up to Soren like she did. And we both know what it's like to be without our children," Anika answered. Her eyes were getting red and starting to water. "I feel like I need to find Soren even more now—not just to get Jonah back for myself. But I feel like I need to do it for Angela too, so she doesn't have to fear Soren anymore; so she can be together with Julia and Nicholas again."

"I was afraid you two were going to hate each other," Dan said. "After all, she was allegedly having an affair with your husband."

"We had a long talk yesterday morning when we were showing the photographs of Jonah and Soren to people in the hotels. She told me what it was like to work for him. It gave me a better picture of the *real* Soren—the side he never showed to me when he was at home. She even told me all about that last night in New York. Did you know she staged the sexual encounter in Soren's car that night so she could plant evidence before she went missing?"

"You're kidding?" Dan said. "She went to that much trouble to make it look like he might have killed her? That must have taken some nerve."

"Yeah," Anika answered. "And even though Soren knew he didn't kill her, it put him on the defensive. Nobody believed him and the police still suspected him."

"She's one smart lady," Dan concluded. "We're lucky to have her on our side."

"I just hope we hear something from her soon," Anika replied.

"Me too," Dan said. He squeezed Anika's hand this time. The smell of hot food wafted through the cabin, teasing his olfactory senses. "Looks like we're getting breakfast. After that, I'm going to see if I can catch some sleep. I don't know about you, but I'm still not sleeping well. I keep dreaming about being chased by a mystery woman who keeps her face hidden. Every time I'm about to see her face, something happens so I never find out who she is. Weird, eh?"

"Not so weird," Anika replied. "I wish I knew who this mystery Helen is. She's a complete wild card. We have no idea who she is, but she seems to be able to help Soren whenever he needs her."

"I agree," Dan said.

But Dan didn't reveal an even deeper concern to Anika. He still had the gnawing feeling that he should already know Helen's identity, and it was driving him crazy.

PART SIX: LOST AND FOUND

CHAPTER 26

DAN WATCHED through the thick plate glass as a guard ushered Fran into the small booth opposite him. He flashed a smile at her, but she managed only a weak one in return. She had clearly gained weight under her orange prison jump suit. Her complexion was pale, and her dark hair was stringy and unkempt. Overall, she looked tired and haggard. Dan felt an overpowering feeling of alarm and concern for her.

"Hi," he said. "I missed you. How are you doing?"

Fran shrugged her shoulders. Her eyes made brief contact with Dan's, but then darted downward. Every few seconds he saw her eyes make brief contact, only to look away when he tried to see into them. Unlike the time they had spent together at the Palm Desert estate and at Chateau Eden, when he'd been able to read the emotions in her eyes, it felt like she was slamming the pages shut every time he tried to read her now.

"I'm okay, I guess," Fran answered. "How are you? Did you and Anika find Jonah?"

Dan felt self-conscious. His ears and face began to feel hot, and he was afraid he'd started blushing. He tried to push the memory of his night of passion with Anika to the back of his mind, focusing instead on the timeline of events after their arrival in Darwin.

"No, we didn't," he answered. "But that doesn't mean the trip was uneventful."

Fran's eyes made contact and Dan read concern in them. "What happened?" she asked.

"Well, you were right about the identity of our Guardian Angel," Dan said. "It is Angela Baranyi, the street person in your portrait. She found out that Soren was taking the boy for a vacation into Kakadu National Park."

Dan told her the story of their fateful flight to Kakadu, of Derek Hardy's death, and of their harrowing escape. He thought he saw more flashes of worry and empathy in Fran's eyes. But as quickly as they came, they disappeared, leaving her face virtually emotionless. When it came to getting back safely to their hotel, Dan tried to muster the courage to tell Fran about making love to Anika. But the more his responsible side insisted that he admit his indiscretion, the more another part of him—a wary, fearful part—kept telling him not to do it.

Not now, Dan. She's too fragile. She's in no state of mind to deal with that right now.

He bailed out on his admission.

"Angela stayed in Darwin for now. She's managed to hack Soren's laptop so she can read any new files that are created. She can even take snapshots of his computer's desktop. That's how she found out that Soren was in Darwin. We're hoping he'll go online again and reveal where he is now. But, more than anything, we're hoping he didn't make it to Indonesia, since it will be a lot harder for Anika to return Jonah from most of the Asian countries."

"How is Anika doing?" Fran asked. "She must be very disappointed that you didn't find Jonah."

Once again, Dan felt his ears and face getting hot. He had to push the memory of his encounter with Anika to the recesses of his mind.

"She was devastated," he answered. It was his turn to avoid eye contact. "But it helped for her to meet Angela. They had a lot in common, since Soren mistreated both of them, and both of them can't be with their children until Soren is safely behind bars."

Feeling self-conscious talking about Anika, Dan changed the subject. "Any new progress in your case? What's Joanna saying about your chances now?"

"Nothing new," Fran said, her voice still flat and lacking emotion. "She says we have all we need right now. She will start preparing me in another week or two, so I will know the kinds of questions the prosecution will be asking."

"Did she say anything about the protesters outside the jail?" Dan said.

"No, why?" Fran asked, frowning.

"Remember the protesters we saw outside the courthouse on the day of your arraignment?" Dan said. "They've come back. They started off with one or two of them outside the jail twenty-four hours a day. I noticed them when I came to visit you the last time. But now there are half a dozen of them all the time. And they've got good contacts with the local media. They were all over the news last night, calling you a harlot and a murderer. They really seem to be trying to sway public opinion against you."

"Do you think Pastor Soren is influencing them?" Fran asked. As she did, she let her guard drop and Dan saw the worry in her eyes.

"It's a good bet," Dan said. "Now that we know for sure that Angela's alive. If Soren knows it too, then he's going to do everything he can to find her. Apparently she found out some pretty damning things about him and the WWCC while she was working there—illegal things that he wants to keep quiet. That's why she's gone back into hiding. She's not safe until Soren is caught and criminal charges are brought against him."

Dan suddenly remembered something he needed to ask Fran.

"Speaking of Angela," Dan said. "I was talking with her and Anika about Angela's candid portrait. I was telling them how you still like using your old 35mm camera, but I couldn't remember the name of the lady who gave it to you. Who was that, anyway?"

Fran cocked her head sideways, seemingly caught off guard by Dan's question.

"Why do you ask?" Fran answered.

"I was just telling them that we can thank that lady for bringing out your natural talent as a photographer," Dan said. "But I couldn't remember her name."

"Susan," Fran said. "Susan Keaner. She ran the art gallery outside the train station in Manarola, but she also had a portrait studio. I worked in both of them."

Dan saw a brief glimpse of pride on Fran's face and in her eyes, and then he saw her eyes beginning to water. When she realized that Dan was watching her, she quickly shifted her eyes back down toward the floor.

"Susan Keaner," Dan repeated. "Of course. I don't know why I couldn't remember. Do you ever think of her?"

Fran's head remained bowed, her eyes gazing down at the floor. She shook her head from side to side. "Those days are gone now," she said.

"Have you ever wondered if she still has the gallery, or if she's still alive?" Dan asked. "Have you ever thought of going back and visiting Manarola?"

Once again Fran just moved her head slowly from side to side. "Too many bad memories," was all she said.

"It was just a thought," Dan said. "Don't you think you'd like to take our child back to Italy someday, to show him or her where you came from? I know I'd like to do that."

Fran's head snapped instantly to attention and her eyes narrowed and homed in on Dan's eyes. He instantly saw her anger.

"No child of mine is going to go there! I will never let the things that happened to me, happen to my child. Why would you want to go there? Why would you want to do that to me?" she demanded, her eyes burning into him like lasers.

"It's okay, Fran. I'm sorry I asked. If you don't want to go there, we don't have to do it," he said, trying to pacify an angry side of her identity that hadn't seen since that night at Palm Desert, when she had first begged him to punish her.

"I'm tired," Fran declared. Just as quickly as her eyes had zeroed in on Dan's, her head bowed and she resumed gazing down at the floor. "I think you should go now."

Dan understood that he'd inadvertently pressed one of Fran's powerful emotional triggers. Now was not the time to keep pressing it. Slowly, he nodded in agreement.

"You're right. You're tired," Dan said. "Are Shelley and Tim going to visit you on Monday again?"

Fran nodded affirmatively, her head still hanging down and resting on her chest.

"They're good friends, Fran," he said. "They believe in you, like I do. Just don't give up on yourself. I love you. I'll see you next week, okay?"

Another nonverbal nod of the head from Fran. It was all Dan could do to stay positive for another moment. He was alarmed at the deterioration in Fran's moods since he'd gone to Australia. She had all but given up on herself.

Dan stood up as Fran's guard guided her away from her chair, and out of the visiting area. He felt more determined than ever to find a way to help Fran. On the other hand, he was terrified about how she would react when he told her about making love with Anika.

You may be giving up on yourself, Fran, but I'm not going to give up on you. Even if I don't deserve you!

He turned and walked quickly from the visitors' area, already planning what he had to do next.

DAN'S FINGERS slid over his laptop's track pad, clicking on results from his Google search. A surprising number of galleries came up from his search of Cinque Terre, the collection of five small coastal towns that included Fran's home, Manarola. The first two attempts yielded nothing. The third seemed to be more promising. *Arte Dell 'Aquila* appeared to be the most serious looking art gallery in Manarola. It advertised original art by local painters, potters, and photographers. Dan clicked on the *Contact* page. It listed the gallery's manager as Gianni Cesarelli.

Dan's heart dropped. Either Dan had the wrong gallery or Susan Keaner no longer owned it. He went back to his search results and clicked his way through the other top choices. All of the other possible galleries were in the neighbouring villages of Monterosso, Corniglia, or Vernazza. None of them mentioned Susan Keaner's name either.

Despondent and ready to give up, Dan had one last thought. It was so obvious, he wondered why he hadn't thought of it before.

His fingers typed in Susan Keaner's name in Google's search box. He waited for a few seconds while a page loaded. Then, suddenly, he was back at the *Contact* page for *Arte Dell 'Aquila*. He was confused, since the contact page clearly listed Signor Cesarelli as the manager of the gallery. Dan was just about ready to click on the back arrow to return to his search, when he caught a glimpse of some fine print at the bottom of the web page: *Gallery Owner—Susan Keaner.*

He heaved a long sigh of relief, and then he clicked on the box to begin typing a short message to Signor Cesarelli.

Dear Signor Cesarelli,
I am the friend of a friend of Susan Keaner, and I would very much like to contact her. Please tell her that our mutual friend, Francesca Capellini, is in trouble and needs our help.

Dan completed the entry by supplying his email address, and then clicked the *Submit* button. He leaned back in his chair, stretching and emitting a long sigh.

If this doesn't work, I don't know what I'll do.

He allowed himself to see a distant glimmer of daylight, his only hope at the end of the long tunnel of Fran's hopelessness and his frustration. All he could do now was wait.

"I THOUGHT you were going to take care of all three of them!" Soren shouted, a mobile phone pressed against his ear. "Angela, Anika, and Whitney are all still alive. Now we have a dead pilot and the ATSB is involved. What happens if they find out you were involved?"

"Calm down!" Helen ordered. Her voice crackled and broke up often over their long distance mobile connection, but the authority in her voice was still unmistakable. "Get a grip on yourself. How could we have known if Baranyi was going to be on the plane or not? It was a long shot. We were unlucky that their pilot was so skilled. That's all. And don't worry about them linking the crash to me. There was no trace of me even entering Australia."

"So what do we do now?" Soren asked, waving his free arm in frustration. The line went quiet on Helen's end for a few seconds before she answered.

"We need to create a diversion and draw them out into the open," she said, her voice still calm and confident.

"A diversion? What kind of diversion? Where?" Soren squawked.

"Calm down and think, my love," Helen said. "Where do you think they expect you to go with the boy?"

The question confused Soren momentarily. His mind raced to figure out where Helen's question was leading him. Suddenly his eyebrows raised, the furrows in his forehead disappeared, and his eyes opened wide. The corners of his mouth started to turn upwards, revealing a hint of a smile.

"Of course. Somewhere in Asia, where the Hague convention isn't an issue," Soren answered. He emitted a sigh and his body began to release the tension that he'd been storing in his muscles since fleeing Darwin.

"That's right," Helen replied. "What about Vietnam? Surely our business contacts in Hanoi will be able to help us. They've shown themselves to be up to the task before. They were quite good at convincing our police friends to turn a blind eye to our operations."

"That's true," Soren answered. A broad smile was spreading across his face and his confidence was returning. "What do you want me to do?"

"Log onto your computer tonight. Stay online for a long time to make sure Baranyi notices you. Do some online searches for travel—let's say from Bangkok to Hanoi—and make sure you put in departure and arrival dates. Do lots of searching, then log into the secure email account and take your time composing a message to me. Make it sound confident that you've escaped to Asia, and that you think you're in the clear now. Tell me your proposed travel dates."

"I can do that," Soren replied. "But how can we be sure she'll see me online?"

"Don't underestimate that little bitch!" Helen muttered. "She's screwed you twice now! She's devious, but she has a weakness. She's overconfident because she thinks we can't find her. She probably hasn't figured out yet that we know she's hacked your computer. I'll reply to your email and confirm that I'll meet you in Hanoi. In the meantime, plan an outing in a public park in Surabaja for tomorrow afternoon. Phone me with the location and time, and I'll make sure somebody's there with a camera. Just make sure it's just you and Jonah sitting on the bench together. Send the girl for ice cream or something."

"I thought you told me never to be alone with Jonah in public —just the two of us together," Soren answered. His forehead was creased, his face frowning with confusion.

"Just this once," Helen answered. "It will only be for a few minutes. And remember, you're in a non-Hague country. Just make sure you're well away from public buildings where there might be security cameras. Phone me when you're in Surabaja. I'll make sure there's somebody there to take photos. Just make sure you and Jonah look like you're having a good time. Stay there for five or ten minutes—that should be good enough—then phone me. I'll let you know if we've got what we need."

"Photos? You want pictures of us in Surabaja? What if somebody sees them and recognizes the park?" Soren whined.

"Relax, my love. I have friends who are wizards with Photoshop. By the time they're finished, Baranyi will never know you're in Indonesia."

Once he realized what Helen was planning, Soren's face broke into a grin.

"So we're going to convince Angela, Anika, and Whitney that we're in Hanoi!" Soren exclaimed. "You're so good at everything you do."

"Of course I am," Helen replied, matter-of-factly. "That's why I'm in such high demand. Just do your part, and I'll take care of the rest. Make sure you're online tonight. I'll watch for your email."

The phone went dead in Soren's ear before he could answer. He slid the disposable phone into his pocket and smiled, feeling a renewed sense of confidence that he and Helen would soon have everything under control.

ANGELA'S EYES were getting heavy. She got up from the small desk in her Darwin hotel room, making her way to the coffee maker on the other side of the suite. The room was lit only by the single incandescent lamp Angela had left on. She knew the hotel coffee wouldn't be good, but caffeine was more important than taste at this hour. After placing the pod of coffee and some water in the small machine, she pressed the start button and wandered to the window. She gazed out over the Esplanade, illuminated only by a few streetlights, and the harbour, which was enveloped in darkness. Distant lights on the other side of the harbour twinkled as Angela's mind wandered aimlessly and the coffee maker gurgled in the background.

Where are you, Soren? And why haven't you logged into your computer yet? Did I blow my cover by bringing Dan and Anika to Darwin? Do you know that I've hacked you?

The gurgling sound had ceased, so Angela went back and poured the weak brew into a small cup. She took a small slurp of the steaming liquid. It tasted like dishwater, but at least it was hot.

Suddenly, the silence was broken by the harsh sound of a klaxon—the alarm on Angela's disk cloning software. Soren had logged into his computer and some files had changed. She jumped to attention, almost spilling the burning coffee as she hurried to her computer. She pressed the shortcut keys to refresh the view of Soren's desktop.

You're on the Internet. What are you up to now?

The screen shot of Soren's computer showed that he had accessed the web site of a Hanoi travel agency.

"Going somewhere, Soren?" she said aloud. She refreshed the desktop image every few seconds, following the trail of Soren's search. Slowly, a pattern started to emerge.

"So you're in Bangkok, or you're going to be there soon," Angela mumbled. "But where are you going?"

As she watched, he searched for tickets to a number of different cities: Phnom Penh, Vientiane, Ho Chi Minh City, Can Tho, and then Hanoi. His search narrowed, searching for fares to Hanoi on different airlines on different dates. She refreshed the view of Soren's desktop repeatedly. Finally, she struck gold.

The snapshot showed Soren logging into the phoney USDA website.

"Hello!" Angela said excitedly. "Getting in touch with your friend Helen again?"

Angela felt her heart starting to pound in her chest. Her anticipation grew each time she refreshed her screen. Suddenly, her eyes went wide and she held her breath.

"You're taking Jonah to Hanoi!" she said aloud. She refreshed the screen again. "Holy shit. You're going to be there on June fifteenth—that's the day after tomorrow!"

Angela kept refreshing her screen, watching as Soren continued composing his email to Helen. Then his screen froze. Angela sipped nervously at her coffee, continuously refreshing her screen every ten to fifteen seconds, waiting for something to happen. Ten minutes passed. She began to feel restless.

"C'mon, c'mon," she muttered. She became aware of another bodily sensation. She needed to pee. "Damn, not now!"

She refreshed her screen two more times and nothing happened. The urge to pee kept growing. Finally, she bolted from her chair and hurried to the washroom to relieve herself.

Finally finished, she dressed quickly and ran back to the computer. Her fingers trembled with anticipation as she refreshed the screen.

"Okay, we're back in business!" Angela whispered to herself. "Hello, Helen."

Her eyes grew wider as they raced through Helen's reply to Soren.

"Yes!" she said emphatically, as she realized what she was reading. "You're going to meet Soren and Jonah in Hanoi on the fifteenth!"

Angela felt the excitement surging through her body. If she acted immediately to warn Anika, they might be able to get to Hanoi in time. Not only might they have a chance to find Jonah and catch Soren, but they might also have a chance to apprehend his mysterious accomplice, Helen!

Nervously, Angela kept refreshing her screen. Finally, she saw the entire email. On the next refresh, she saw Soren's short acknowledgment of Helen's message. Over the next few minutes,

Soren's screen showed him checking out prices of flights from Bangkok to Hanoi for June fifteenth. Then the screen froze and went inactive. She refreshed the screen again. This time her heart sank as she read the message from her cloning program.

'Contact with host computer lost.'

Angela was overwhelmed with a wave of emotions—dejection that Soren had logged off—excitement that she knew where and when Soren was going to surface next—and fear about what might happen when they finally confronted Soren and Helen.

Her fingers flew into action, opening the email app on her own laptop. Hurriedly, she typed out a new message:

To: Anika Kristiansen
From: Angela
Cc: Dan Whitney
Subject: Soren Found Again!

Great news, Anika! I've intercepted an email message between Soren and Helen. They're going to be meeting in Hanoi, Vietnam, in two days on June 15! That's tomorrow for us in Australia and Asia. Let me know ASAP if you can get on a flight and meet me there. I'm excited to see you again. I know that we'll successfully rescue Jonah soon and return him to you for good!

Angela clicked on the send button, hearing the familiar *swoosh* as her message was sent. As she did, an unsettling fear began to dampen her excitement. She opened her web browser and Googled *Hague Convention*. She clicked once again to bring up the page with all of the countries that are signees to the agreement. She scanned the list once, then another time for good measure. Her shoulders slumped and her hopes sank. Vietnam had not yet signed the Hague Convention. Even if she managed to help Anika find Jonah, getting him out of Vietnam and back into Anika's custody, was likely going to be a long and costly battle. Before long, her thoughts of Anika and Jonah turned to thoughts of her own children, Julia and Nicholas. Tears began filling her eyes, knowing that neither she nor her children would ever be completely safe again until Soren Kristiansen was securely behind bars.

CHAPTER 27

THE CONSTANT roar of jet engines was beginning to feel routine for Dan. Once again, he and Anika were high above the Pacific, this time en route to Hanoi.

But this flight was different than their previous flights. Dan felt a palpable tension between himself and his old friend this time around. After their recent hook-up in Darwin, Dan knew that their long-time friendship would never be the same. But there was more than that to the tension he felt. After their near-death experience in Australia, he and Anika were both acutely aware that their quest to find Soren and Jonah was no longer a game. They had to be vigilant. Any careless mistake could cost them their lives.

After he returned from Australia, Dan was more agitated and paranoid, constantly looking over his shoulder to see if he was being followed. He knew that his PTSD symptoms had returned, worsened by their close brush with death on the South Alligator River.

Anika's voice jolted him from his daydream.

"There's something I need to tell you," she said. "I probably should have told you before, but I never got an opportunity because we were in such a rush."

"What's up?" Dan asked. "Is it serious?"

"I don't know… it could be, I suppose. I got a threatening email from Soren a few days ago—before Angela found out about him taking Jonah to Hanoi. He was angry with all three of us for interfering in 'their' happiness. He warned me that he couldn't be responsible for anything that happens if I don't stop chasing him. I should have told you and Angela, but I was afraid you guys might stop helping me. I'm sorry, I should have told you earlier. It wasn't fair to drag you away from Fran again…"

"Shhhh…," Dan whispered, interrupting her. "You're not telling me anything we didn't know already. They've already tried to kill us once. I promised you that I would be by your side until you find Jonah. And nothing—not what happened between us, or a threat from Soren, is going to change that."

"But there's more," Anika added. Her eyes were bloodshot, and worry was etched into her forehead. "Angela told me something about Soren that has me scared to death. She told me that she found out that he's operating pornography sites in Asia. What if he's into child porn, Dan? What if he's molesting Jonah? Of even worse, what if it's not just Soren?"

She burst into tears as the last words left her mouth, burying her head in Dan's chest and sobbing so hard that she gasped for breath. All Dan could do was hold her and stroke her hair in a futile attempt to console her. Eventually, her frustration, fear, and her tears were totally spent. She lifted her head and gazed at him through tear-stained, bloodshot eyes, still clutching his arm. She furrowed her eyebrows and wrinkled her forehead, still deep in worry.

"What do you think he meant by 'their' happiness?" she asked. "Was he just talking about himself and Jonah? Do you think that Helen is in on this too? I mean, not just helping him evade police —but is she going to be living with him and Jonah?"

"I can't say for sure," Dan answered. "But it's looking more and more like she's a big part of the picture. I don't think we should underestimate her involvement, do you?"

"Not at all," Anika answered. "She's probably the one who's responsible for what happened in Australia. I'm really scared this time, Dan."

"Me too," he replied, taking her hand. He looked up to see flight attendants arriving at their row. "Looks like breakfast time."

He and Anika pulled down their trays from the seats in front of them.

Minutes later, with no elbow room to spare, he and Anika silently juggled the assorted components of their breakfast, trying to spread frozen butter on cold rolls while trying not to spill their miniature cups of so-called coffee on each other.

Anika finally broke the silence.

"Did you tell Fran about us?" she asked.

Dan shook his head slowly from side to side.

"She didn't give me a chance," he said. "She was so avoidant and defensive—so much more fragile than when I last visited her. I was ready to tell her… honestly… I was going to admit everything. But I knew the timing was wrong. There's no way she can handle it right now. I'm more concerned than ever that she's sinking into a deeper depression. I have to find a way to get her out of that prison cell before it gets any worse."

"Still feeling guilty?" Anika asked.

Dan thought for a moment. He realized that his guilt had taken a back seat to the fear and paranoia he'd been feeling for the past nine days since their return from Australia. "Surprisingly, not as much," he said. "Too many other things on my mind, I guess. What about you?"

"About the same. At some level, I think sleeping together was something that had to happen for us eventually. Otherwise, we'd always wonder about what might have been," she said.

"So what did you decide about what might have been?" Dan asked.

"That you're the best friend a girl could ever have, and that's how I want to keep it. Nothing against you, Dan. You're the best. But I just don't feel that kind of attraction to you. I think I needed to find that out so I wouldn't keep wondering if I should have married you. So I don't feel as guilty now. I'm glad it happened the way it did. I think everything happens for a reason, don't you?"

Dan felt a sense of relief at finally having the subject out into the open. At the same time, he found himself blushing. "I'm a bit ashamed to admit that I've always had a recurring dream about making love to you."

Anika managed a smile, and then she chuckled. "So how did reality compare to your dreams?"

"I hope you don't take it personally, but it wasn't the fireworks I'd envisioned as a young man. Maybe my guilt got in the way," he admitted.

Anika smiled and Dan felt the warmth of her hand in his. "No offence taken. Your relationship with Fran is important to you. I understand that. As rough as things are for her right now, she's still the mother of your future child, and I know you have strong feelings for her. Those things aren't fantasy, Dan. They're real and they're worth fighting for."

"That's the conclusion I came to when I saw how she's struggling," Dan said. "So I did some searching. I found out the name of Fran's mentor in Manarola—a lady named Susan Keaner. I looked her up on the Internet and I've tried to contact her."

"What a great idea," Anika said. "Any luck?"

"Not yet," Dan answered. "I had to relay a message through another person who works for her, so I hope she gets it. Right now, I feel like it's more important to help Fran survive her ordeal, than it is to tell her about us making love. I'll tell her when she's stronger, and I'll face the consequences then."

"Just remember, she's lucky to have you," Anika said, squeezing Dan's hand again. "And if she kicks you to the curb, I'll be the first one to tell her she's crazy to let you go."

Dan cracked a weak smile as he imagined such an encounter. "Thanks anyway," he said. "But somehow I think you might not be the right person for the job."

Anika laughed again, then she squeezed Dan's hand one last time before releasing it. "You're probably right."

Once Anika's laughter subsided, an uneasy stillness descended on them. Dan finally broke the silence, his face now serious and businesslike.

"Are you scared about Hanoi?" he asked.

Anika nodded slowly.

"But I'm not as scared of Soren as I am about not finding Jonah—or about what could happen to him if we don't find him. I got my hopes up so high in Seattle, Atlanta, and Darwin… and I've been devastated every time we came up short. Part of me is terrified that I can't stand that happening again."

Dan saw tears forming in her eyes yet again. He knew he truly couldn't imagine the disappointment and frustration she must have felt each time, and the fear she must still have for Jonah's safety. His heart ached for his friend. Anika sniffled and sat up straight, seeming to gather her strength once more.

"But now that I know what kind of person Soren really is, there's another part of me that is far more angry than afraid," she continued. "It's hard to believe that he'd sink as low as killing people to have possession of our son. My lawyer, Rashad, hasn't candy-coated the situation. Even if I find Jonah, it could cost me a small fortune in legal fees to take Soren to court, and he knows it."

"Are you ready for that?" Dan asked.

"Hell, yes! If he thinks he can intimidate me—physically or financially—he's underestimating me. I'll die or go broke fighting to get my son back. Apart from my family in Calgary, he's the most important thing in my life. I'm pissed off now, and Soren better not underestimate the determination, desperation and tenacity of a mother whose child has been taken away. Any fear I have right now is nothing compared to the anger and loathing I feel towards him."

This time it was Dan who reached for Anika's hand to comfort her. "That's the spirit. I can't let you do that alone, so I'll be right beside you. And don't forget, we still have Angela helping us. It will be good to see her again in Hanoi."

Dan thought he saw Anika's eyes break contact with him for a split second at the mention of Angela's name. But before he could think anything of it, her eyes were looking at him again. He felt the warmth of her hand in his.

"I'm looking forward to seeing her again too," she said. "Soren better not underestimate all three of us. Together, I'm sure we're going to find Jonah. After that, it's up to me, Rashad, and the legal system, whenever and wherever we end up going to court."

"Then we'd better get some sleep if we're going to hit the ground running in Hanoi," Dan said. He reached up and turned out his reading light. Anika did the same. She leaned towards him and rested her head on his shoulder, her arm resting across his chest. The jet engines droned on. Dan felt relieved that they'd cleared the air between them. It felt good to feel her head on his shoulder. They had always been a team when they were young, and they were a team again—a team with a common mission and a shared strength that helped to calm Dan's fear for the moment. He closed his eyes, feeling temporary relief from the confusing mix of emotions that had been plaguing him for the past nine days. Within moments he drifted off to sleep.

JONAH SAT quietly in the backseat of the taxi beside Lucy, gripping her hand and huddling against her warm body. His eyes gaped as a gigantic mass of steel framework, gleaming like gold in the late afternoon sunlight, and adorned with enormous white triangular arches, floated past like giant sails in the distance.

"Where are we?" Jonah asked, his tired young eyes looking for answers in Lucy's eyes.

"We're near the airport in Bangkok, Thailand," she answered.

"How come we're not stopping?" Jonah asked.

"We're not quite there yet. That's the brand new airport. It's not quite finished yet, so we still have to go to the old one."

The cab took an exit to their left and made its way slowly along another busy highway. Jonah felt overwhelmed by the sheer size of the city and the seemingly endless masses of humanity. Apart from their brief time in Seattle and Atlanta a few short weeks ago, this was easily the biggest metropolis that he had ever seen. He sat quietly, spellbound by the ever-changing scenery in front of him.

Before long, the taxi slowed as they approached the stately, weathered, box of a building known as Don Mueang. Compared to the sparkling new terminal they had just passed, Don Mueang looked to Jonah like a tired, spooky old building. The cab came to a rest in front of the terminal.

"Time to get out now," Lucy said. "Make sure everything is in your backpack. Don't leave anything behind."

"I don't wanna go anywhere," Jonah whined. "I'm tired. I just wanna go home. I wanna see my mommy!"

"Shhhh!" Lucy whispered. Jonah saw her sneak a quick glance out the window at his father, who was now out of the cab, retrieving their bags from the rear hatch. "You mustn't say that. I'm your mommy, remember? If your daddy heard you say that, he would be very angry!"

"I don't care," Jonah whined. "I'm tired. I just wanna go home."

"It's okay," Lucy said softly. He felt her warm hands holding his. Almost instantly, her soft voice and warmth made him feel safe. "Your daddy says we're almost at our new home. Be patient. You've been such a good boy. Things will be better when we get there and settle down."

"Where are we going?" Jonah asked wearily.

"I don't know," Lucy whispered. "It's still a secret—a big surprise. We don't want to say it too soon, or the bad people might hear us talking. Then they might follow us to our new home. You wouldn't want that, would you?"

"No, I guess not," Jonah whimpered.

"Don't worry, your daddy will tell us soon," Lucy said, her voice hushed. "Just be quiet and try not to make him angry."

Jonah knew that Lucy was trying to make him feel better, but he knew she was scared too. He often saw it in her eyes. He didn't like it when she sometimes left him alone and went to see his father at night. He couldn't sleep when that happened. He felt too lonely and sad and scared. When she came back, he pretended to be asleep, but he took quick peeks. Sometimes she had bruises and red marks on her face, and he knew from the redness around her eyes that she had been crying. He felt sorry for Lucy and wished he could do something to protect her.

"Don't worry. I'll be quiet," he said, squeezing Lucy's warm hands to try to make her feel better.

Suddenly, his father wrenched the cab door open.

"Hurry up, you two! What are you waiting for? We haven't got all day!" Jonah watched as Soren reached into the cab and hauled Lucy out. He slid across the seat, getting ready to climb from the cab's back seat when Soren's hand snaked into the cab and yanked him unceremoniously out of the cab and onto the concrete sidewalk. His shoulder hurt, but he dared not cry out or complain.

Lucy helped him pull out the handle of his backpack so that it was ready for him to pull. Father walked away from him and Lucy, toward the decaying terminal building, soon leaving them far behind him. Jonah saw the angry look on father's face as he looked back over his shoulder. Jonah started running, but somehow managed to tip his little backpack onto its side. Lucy stopped to right it for him and took him by the hand, walking quickly alongside him. Father was waiting for them just inside the terminal doors.

"Hurry up," he snarled. "Get in this check-in line."

Jonah saw his father open the leather folder he was carrying, pulling out three sheets of paper and their passports. Father gave two sheets to Lucy and kept one for himself.

"Here's your tickets and passports," his father hissed quietly. Lucy looked at the piece of paper in her hand.

"Amsterdam?" Lucy said. "I thought you said we were going to Vietnam?"

"I'm going to Hanoi. I have some business there for a couple of days. I'll meet you and the boy in Amsterdam in a few days. Here's a hotel reservation in your name."

"What are we supposed to do in Amsterdam until you meet us?" Lucy asked.

"I don't give a damn what you do," Soren said. "Just keep the kid out of sight and out of trouble. I'll leave a message for you at the hotel to tell you when to have him ready to travel again. And don't get any ideas about running to the police about the kid. I'll have people watching and listening in on you, from the moment you arrive in Amsterdam until the time I get there. One wrong move and they'll be all over you like flies on flypaper. Understood?"

Lucy nodded affirmatively, not saying a word.

Jonah was scared and confused.

Again? When are we going to stop travelling? I'm tired. I just wanna go home! I don't like it when Father curses. It scares me. He and Mommy always told me not to curse, so why does he do it so much? And why does he always just call me 'boy' or 'kid'? Why won't he call me Jonah? It's my name. I really miss Mommy.

A single tear dripped from one eye onto his cheek. He wiped it off with his hand before Father could see it. Father stuffed his own airline ticket back into his folder and hurried off to another airline's check-in counter. Jonah looked up at Lucy, recognizing the same fear and helplessness he was feeling. As they waited silently in line, he took her warm hand in his, hoping it would help her to feel just a little bit better.

COMPLETELY exhausted after almost twenty-four hours of travelling, Dan and Anika finally cleared immigration in Hanoi. Dan observed that it was after eleven o'clock at night, local time. The terminal was almost deserted, apart from the long queue of weary travellers in front of them, which had slowed to a crawl.

"What's going on?" Dan asked impatiently. "Can you see what's happening?"

"I'm not sure," Anika said, craning her neck. "It almost looks like they're checking everybody's baggage tags. We'd better get ours out again."

The queue crept along slowly until it was finally their turn at the front of the line. A bored-looking woman held out her hand, saying something to them in Vietnamese. Dan and Anika looked at each other briefly, then Anika grabbed Dan's luggage tag from his hand and turned their tags over to the stone-faced inspector. Satisfied that their receipts matched their bags, the woman waved them forward impatiently.

"You go," she muttered. They were finally in the clear.

Dan looked up and saw a familiar face about twenty paces ahead. He managed a weak smile as he recognized Angela's blonde hair and beaming face waiting for them. Anika noticed her at almost the same instant. A look of relief, followed by a broad grin, flashed across her face.

"You're here!" Anika squealed, her voice elevating to a high pitch that reminded Dan for a moment of Chelly when she was talking to her girlfriends. The moment of déjà vu passed quickly. Dan's mind jumped back into reality to see Anika and Angela embracing excitedly. Suddenly, he realized how exhausted he was and how relieved he was to see their enigmatic new friend and ally in the race to find Soren and Jonah.

"You couldn't keep me away," Angela said to Anika, before turning to Dan. "Great to see you too, Dan. How were your flights?"

"Too long," Dan answered. "We're just glad to be here."

"I've got a cab waiting outside to take us downtown. I've got a couple of rooms for us at a hotel on Church Street. It's quiet and just a couple of blocks from Hoan Kiem Lake and the heart of the old city."

"I'm sure that will be perfect," Anika answered.

"Follow me," Angela said, motioning for Dan and Anika to follow her. "I'll bring you up to speed on Soren's activities while we drive into town. It's about a twenty-five minute ride from the airport."

THE YOUNG Vietnamese man, dressed in sneakers, t-shirt, and blue jeans loitered in the airport terminal. His motorcycle helmet lay on the floor at his feet while he spoke on his mobile phone. He still wore his sunglasses indoors, even though it was approaching midnight. Seemingly uninterested in the line-up of arriving passengers, he kept them in his peripheral vision, keeping a close eye on the stone-faced woman who was checking the arriving passenger's baggage tags. Anybody who saw him wouldn't have guessed that his phone was idle and he wasn't talking to anybody real.

About half of the passengers had passed the woman when she stood up straight, seeming to stretch her back muscles for a few seconds. She made eye contact with the young man, then nodded towards the Caucasian man with sandy brown hair and the blonde, Caucasian woman who had just passed her checkpoint.

The young man nodded back, then watched while an attractive, blonde, middle-aged Caucasian woman greeted the couple. The threesome appeared to be good friends. The young man pushed memory dial on his phone. After a few seconds, there was a click on the other end of the line as the call was answered.

"They've arrived. All three of them are together."

"Good," said the voice at the other end of the line. "Follow them and let me know where they're staying. And don't let them out of your sight. Is that clear?"

"Yes, sir," the young man said. He hurried outside in time to see the trio get into a white Toyota Camry taxi. He made a mental note of the make, model, and color of the car, as well as the cab's license. Then he ran to where his motorcycle was parked, quickly unlocking the sleek racing machine and donning his helmet. He started the engine and revved it a few times, the high-pitched cackle of the speedy bike reverberating through the night. Finally, his target moved away from the taxi stand and started the twenty-five minute drive into Hanoi. He eased his motorcycle onto the road and fell in behind the white Camry at a discreet distance, making sure there was at least one vehicle between his bike and the cab until they entered the city proper. He was thankful for the darkness, which made it difficult for them to recognize him.

DAN SAT in the front seat of the small cab, with Anika and Angela beside each other in the cramped rear seat. Other cars and a multitude of motorcycles buzzed by their cab on the left side, even at the late hour.

"I don't think I've ever seen so many motorcycles," Dan said.

"Wait until you see the city in daylight," Angela said. "They're everywhere. The noise they make during rush hour can be deafening. And the exhaust fumes are horrible. It's no wonder so many Asians wear those masks over their faces."

Dan shielded his eye from a single bright light that kept reflecting into his eyes from the passenger side mirror.

Damn, that's annoying. Why doesn't that guy pass us like all the others?

Before he could say anything, the piercingly bright halogen light disappeared into the darkness.

"So, here's what I got last night," Angela said, barely able to contain the excitement in her voice. "Soren contacted Helen by email, and this time he attached a photo of both of them—Soren and Jonah—sitting on a park bench right here in Hanoi. I checked it out. The background is unmistakable. They were sitting beside the pedestrian bridge at Hoan Kiem Lake!"

Dan twisted his body and looked at Angela through the gap between the front seats.

"How do we know they're still here?" he asked, not wanting to see Anika's hopes needlessly inflated again.

"That's the best part," Angela continued. "He told Helen that he was seeing a real estate agent in Hanoi today. He's looking for a place to rent, either in Ha Long or further south near Da Nang and China Beach."

"Did he tell her the name of the real estate agent?" Anika asked.

"Not exactly, but there was a second photo of him with the boy. They were having ice cream, and Soren told Helen that it was only a two minute walk from the real estate office. There's a very distinct building in the background, so we might be able to get the location from the picture. I captured the photo on my screen and got it printed when I arrived here today."

She handed the photo to Anika, who looked at it and shrugged her shoulders. She passed it to Dan, who turned on his reading light and studied the print intently, his eyes squinting and his forehead furrowed.

"I'm not sure if the building looks familiar or not. But it's a place to start," Dan said, trying not to be overly enthusiastic.

The taxi slowed as it entered the city and made its way towards the dense central core of Hanoi's old city. After a few moments, it stopped at a red light. A bright red glow shone in the passenger side mirror, attracting Dan's attention. He saw the face and eyes of a motorcyclist, his face and eyes clearly displayed in the soft red illumination from the taxi's taillights. Dan's eyes locked with those of the rider for a split second, before the man looked away quickly.

Is that the same guy whose lights have been shining in my mirror? Is he following us?

Another voice in Dan's head joined in his internal conversation.

Don't be so paranoid! You've been extra jumpy ever since Darwin. You're seeing bad guys in every shadow. Stop it! You'll drive yourself crazy.

"So, what's our plan for tomorrow?" Anika asked.

"Sorry?" Dan answered, not hearing her because he was lost in his delusional self-talk. "I must be starting to doze off."

"I think we need to find the real estate office first," Angela said. "Maybe we can find out where he's looking in Ha Long and China Beach. Maybe even when he's planning on going there. What do you guys think?"

"We could also start going from hotel to hotel, showing Soren and Jonah's pictures like we did in Darwin," Anika suggested.

"That sounds like looking for a needle in a haystack," Angela said. "Do you have any idea how many hotels and hostels are in the old city? And who knows, maybe he's not even staying in the old city?"

"We could do both," Dan suggested. "You and Anika could try to find the real estate office. I don't mind going door to door to hotels and shops in the old city. If we don't find the office, then all three of us will have to start pounding the pavement on foot. We won't have any other choice."

Dan saw Anika and Angela exchange glances with each other. As he looked back at them, the cab stopped at another red light. There, illuminated by the soft red glow of taillights, Dan saw the motorcycle and rider stopped behind them. It was the same rider. Dan was almost sure of it. He was a young man, and he looked away again as soon as their eyes met. Dan made a mental note that he was riding a performance motorcycle with bright red markings.

The light changed and their cab made its way through the intersection. As they did, the motorcycle made a right hand turn behind them and disappeared.

Dan, you're just being hypervigilant. Stop looking for ghosts around every corner.

Angela broke the silence this time.

"That sounds like a plan," she said. "Are you still awake up there, Dan?"

"Yeah, just barely," he replied, looking back between the two seats at the two women again. "But I sure need some sleep. It's going to be a long day tomorrow with the jet lag. It looks like we have our work cut out for us. But I'm up for it, no matter how tired I'm going to be. How about you, Anika?"

"You know me. Nothing's going to stop me from finding Jonah."

Dan smiled. Angela was holding Anika's hand. He was glad the two women were bonding. Each of them with their own horror stories to tell about Soren Kristiansen. He was lucky to have both of them as friends, and happy to be helping them get their children back.

AS THE white Camry taxi reached Hanoi, Thuán narrowed the gap between it and his bike to ensure he didn't get cut off or lose them, sometimes getting as close as being immediately behind the cab, then dropping back for a while. He was sure the man in the passenger seat had spotted him a couple of times at red lights when he was right behind them. But he was sure his right turn at the last light would allay any suspicion. He had sped into the night for two blocks, then raced through side streets and cut back towards the cab's route, managing to slide into traffic behind the cab once again. This time, he stayed well back in traffic, knowing the cab couldn't outrace him through the narrow streets of the old city.

Finally, the taxi came to a roundabout. On the left, the lights of old Hanoi twinkled and reflected off the calm waters of Hoan Kiem Lake. The cab took the first exit from the roundabout, followed by a quick right turn, then another. He followed the Camry into a short street that ended only a block away at a T-intersection. Behind the T-intersection loomed Church Street's namesake, Hanoi Cathedral, a lavish relic left over from the days of Catholic French colonization of Vietnam. Thuán stopped his bike and dragged it off the street into the shadows. He watched from a safe distance as the cab dropped off his fares at a modest looking hotel about half a block from the church. Once they were safely inside their hotel, he removed his helmet and dialed the same number as before.

"They've arrived at a hotel on Church Street," he said in a flat, emotionless voice.

"Thank you, Thuán. You've done well. Get some sleep. We have a big couple of days ahead of us."

"Yes, sir. My relief will be here in the morning. There will be two sets of eyes on them tomorrow morning, just in case they go different ways, and so they don't recognize me."

"Just make sure you don't lose them. I want to know everything they do, no matter how inconsequential. Good night, Thuán."

"Yes, sir," he said, as the phone went dead in his hand. Despite being May, there was a slight chill in the air tonight. Thuán zipped up his jacket and curled his body up on the seat of his bike. He pulled the jacket's collar up around his neck, watching the hotel from the shadows. It was going to be a long chilly night until help arrived at five-thirty in the morning.

CHAPTER 28

CHURCH BELLS tolled ominously in the background. The skies over Detroit were heavy and grey. A cold wind blew hard from the northeast off Lake Huron and Lake St. Clair. Dan and Francesca were running for their lives. Chelly's funeral was due to start any minute now, and Dan knew he was supposed to be there to read the eulogy for his deceased wife. But they were being chased, first by Chelly's family and friends and then by a black-clad figure on a motorcycle. Dan was frantic.

"I know… I parked… the car… around… here… somewhere," he panted, gasping for breath.

"Keep running, Dan!" Francesca shouted. "He's coming!"

Dan was confused. "Who's coming?" he shouted.

"The guy in black on the red motorbike! Come on!"

Dan heard the telltale roar of a performance motorcycle in the distance.

"Forget the car!" he shouted to Fran. "Let's run for it. Across the cemetery!"

He grabbed her hand and they took off on foot over the manicured lawns, dodging and crouching low behind ornate hundred-year-old headstones. The clanging of the church bells grew louder, but so did the sound of the motorcycle behind them.

"Over there!" Francesca shouted. She pointed to a line of black funeral vehicles and a crowd of people about two hundred yards away, near the top of a lush green hill. They sprinted towards the relative safety of Chelly's family and friends. The ominous sound of the motorcycle was rapidly closing in on them. Dan looked over his shoulder and he saw the sleek white cycle with red markings racing around the cemetery, as if it was on a racetrack. Its driver leaned into the corners like he was closing in on a finish line.

Dan and Francesca gasped for every breath of air. Dan's legs felt like rubber, each step feeling like his legs would collapse and fold beneath him. They kept running towards the safety of the crowd, managing to reach the fringes just before the motorcycle arrived.

As the mourners heard their desperate gasps for air, they turned in unison towards Dan and Fran. Dan was stunned to see Chelly amongst the crowd. Then, to add to his horror, Derek Hardy emerged from the mourners, still dressed in his Territory Air Services uniform. The mourners, now led by an angry Soren Kristiansen, sneered at Dan. They pressed forward towards Dan and Francesca while the motorcyclist, having dismounted from his bike, closed in from behind. The church bells kept tolling, growing louder with each ear-splitting gong…

Dan's eyes popped open. The hotel room was filled by the clanging of the enormous bell atop Hanoi Cathedral's steeple. Dan rubbed his eyes, trying to get his bearings. The clock beside the bed read 6:00. Daylight was just beginning to creep around the edges of the room's curtains. After what seemed like minutes, the seemingly endless gonging of the church bell finally relented.

Dan was dripping in sweat. His heart pounded in his chest and he was panted rapidly. He finally realized where he was… a hotel room in Hanoi. He lay in bed for a few moments, allowing his breathing and heart rate to slow, and then he reluctantly pulled back the covers and sat on the edge of the bed. There was a knock on his door. Seconds later, another.

"Yeah, just a minute," he said, looking to see if he had any clothes nearby.

"Just checking to see if you're awake," Anika said, her voice muted by the room's wooden door. "We'll wait for you down in the breakfast room."

"Okay, I'll meet you there in twenty minutes," he called.

Dan sat for a moment, trying to collect his thoughts. But all he could think of was the random collection of characters and the frightening nature of his nightmare.

That's what happens when you get paranoid, Dan. After a while, everybody starts to look like the bogeyman.

He got up and walked slowly to the bathroom. He turned on the shower, cranking it up so it was good and hot.

Looks like there won't be any sleeping-in with that church nearby, Danny boy. Oh well, a quick shower should clear your thinking, then downstairs to meet the girls and have some coffee. Forget about the dream, Dan. Something big is going to happen today. I can feel it.

DAN SIPPED on his strong black Vietnamese-style dripped coffee. It was taking a little getting used to, but it was strong and it tasted good. He looked up and saw Anika and Angela running excitedly down the stairs and into the crowded breakfast room.

"Dan! We think we know where the real estate office is!" Anika shouted, unable to conceal her enthusiasm as she ran to his table. Angela followed close behind.

"The woman at the desk recognized the building in the photo. It's Ho Chi Minh's tomb!" Anika announced.

"That means that Soren's realtor is within a few minutes' walk of Ho's mausoleum," Angela said, her face beaming. "Our ride is going to pick us up at seven-thirty."

"You phoned for a cab already?"

"No. The woman on the front desk is getting us a private driver. It's somebody they use a lot, and it's much cheaper," Anika said enthusiastically. "We'll pay a flat rate for the day and the driver will wait for us whenever we need to stop."

"Sounds ideal," Dan said. "Angela, do you have those photos of Soren and Jonah? I'll need to make some photocopies to hand out at hotels and restaurants."

"Sure, but they're upstairs. I'll run up and get them now," she said. She got up from the table and jogged up the half dozen stairs into the lobby. Dan turned to Anika. The corners of his mouth turned down and his smile disappeared.

"You girls be careful out there today," he said. "We don't need a repeat of what happened in Australia."

"Don't worry about us. We can take care of ourselves," Anika answered.

"Remember, we're not playing with amateurs anymore," Dan warned. He told Anika about his dream.

"Relax, Dan. It's just a dream. Don't let it spook you, it doesn't mean anything. You've got a lot on your plate with Chelly's death, then with Fran being in jail and the close call in Kakadu."

"Yeah, I know. I usually don't read anything into dreams. But I wouldn't be able to live with myself if anything bad happened. Especially to you and Angela, okay?" Dan said, pleading with his eyes.

"I promise," Anika replied.

"I hope you ladies had a better sleep than I did," Dan said.

"Not too bad, considering," Anika said. "Angela's a great roommate. Nothing against your company, Dan, but it's nice to be with another woman, and to talk about Soren. Especially since Angela knows him, and we understand each other. We're getting to be good friends."

"I see that. And because I'm very fond of both of you, I don't want anything to happen to either one of you."

Anika leaned down and kissed Dan on the side of his head. "We'll be careful. Make sure you text Angela as soon as you get a Vietnamese phone. We'll text you as soon as we find out anything positive."

"I will," Dan answered, just as Angela returned with the photos of Soren and Jonah.

"C'mon, Anika. We should get ourselves ready. Our ride will be here in about twenty minutes. Good luck with the photos, Dan."

"Same to you girls," he said. "I'll text you later."

Dan sipped his coffee and tried to relax as he watched Anika and Angela rush from the breakfast room together. He knew that being paranoid and having a sense of foreboding was part of dealing with the trauma of both Chelly's and Derek's deaths. He tried to convince himself that they weren't in any real danger. But the feeling was hard to shake when so many terrible things had happened around him recently.

"THE ICE CREAM stand!" Anika shouted. "Stop the car, Dinh!"

No sooner had their driver pulled the SUV to the side of the road than Anika and Angela had their doors open and jumped from the vehicle. Angela held the photo from Soren's email. They walked around, changing positions, until they'd almost recreated the view in the photo.

"This is the place," Angela said, a note of satisfaction in her voice. "Now for the hard part: where is the real estate office?"

"It can't be north," Anika said. "That's where the mausoleum and park are. It looks like there might be more businesses to the west and south of here. What do you say?"

"Makes no difference to me," Angela said. "Let's ask Dinh what he thinks." They walked over to the SUV and Angela tapped on Dinh's window, motioning for him to lower it.

"Do you know where there might be a real estate office west or south of here?" she asked, pointing first one, then the other, direction as she talked. Dinh shrugged his shoulders.

"We're going for a short walk," Anika said. "Please wait here. We'll be back in a few minutes." She stood beside Angela, resting her hand on the other woman's shoulder as they gazed first south, then west, then looked at their map.

"Let's try this street first—Doi Canh—to the west," Angela said. "It looks like there might be more businesses this way."

"Okay, let's go," Anika said, leading the way.

Angela paused for a moment, watching from behind as Anika walked ahead. Her mind drifted back to the first time she ever saw Anika, in the family portrait on Soren Kristiansen's desk in New York. She didn't even know the striking blonde woman in that photo. But as Soren started propositioning her, Angela remembered feeling an almost instantaneous empathy for the other woman.

"Hey, wait for me," Angela called. She jogged to catch up with Anika, this time placing her hand on Anika's shoulder for an instant. They began walking west along Doi Canh. The first shop they passed was a florist shop.

"My God," Anika said. "Those are the most beautiful arrangements I've ever seen! The Vietnamese sure know how to do it right, don't they?"

"I know," Angela said, "But we don't have time right now, girl. Maybe after we find Jonah."

Anika grinned briefly at her new friend, and then became more sullen. "You're right, but I'm going to hold you to your promise once we find him!"

Angela flashed a warm smile in return. "You're on. Let's keep walking."

They surveyed both sides of the street as they walked west on Doi Canh, finding a butcher, a bakery, a shoe store, and three mobile phone shops, but no realty office.

"I think we've been walking for almost five minutes," Anika said. "No real estate office in this direction."

"You're right. Let's head back to the car and go down the other street."

"I wish I could come here for a vacation someday," Anika sighed. "It's so different from home. I can't believe the number of cell phone shops. And you were so right about the motorcycles. Look! See those two guys carrying a door frame on a motorbike!"

"And look at this," Angela said, pointing up the street. "There's a family of four riding on the family motorbike."

Angela noticed that Anika was silent as she watched the family pass by. She put her arm around Anika's shoulder and pulled her close to her side.

"Don't worry, girl. We're going to find Jonah, and we're going to send Soren to prison. We're going to be together with our kids soon. And when we are, we're going to get together for the best family celebration anybody ever saw."

Tears started flowing from Anika's eyes, causing Angela to start tearing as well. The two women embraced, feeling each other's pain and giving each other comfort.

"You've got yourself a deal," Anika sniffled. "I'll even host the party in Victoria—you'll love it there. We can take the kids whale watching, kayaking, and to the beach. Would you like that?"

"I'd love it," Angela said, sniffling back her own tears. "But first, we have some work to do. Feeling okay?"

Anika reached into her purse and retrieved tissues for both women, who wiped away their tears and purged their sinuses. They covered the remaining block quickly, finding Dinh dozing behind the wheel of the SUV. They opened the door and Angela shook his shoulder as she climbed in the back seat.

"Wake up, Dinh. We'll drive south on Thanh Bao whenever you're ready."

"Yes, madam," he said in fluent English. He pulled out into the light traffic, heading south. Angela felt her heart drop. The buildings were mostly apartment buildings on the right, and a large government building on the left, with few businesses in sight. She looked at Anika and saw disappointment written on her face. As they approached the next intersection, things didn't look any more promising. There was only a lone business sign standing on the corner. Then she heard Anika gasp.

"There!" she shouted. "This could be it!"

THE REALTOR, a short, thin man with wire-rimmed bifocals, glanced nervously at the photo of Soren that Anika showed him. He looked up at her, and then looked back at the picture, clearly not wanting to make eye contact with her.

"You've seen him, haven't you?" Anika declared. "He was here, wasn't he?"

Anika watched as the small man deliberately removed his glasses and reached for a cloth to clean them. His eyes finally looked up and met Anika's.

"I not remember," he said, his English rusty, but adequate. "Even if I see, you know I not tell names of customers."

Angela reached into her purse, pulling out a billfold bulging with U.S. dollars, Vietnam's second unofficial currency.

"Maybe this will help you remember," she said, slowly peeling two crisp hundred-dollar bills from the billfold. She placed them on the counter within his reach. "The man in this photo is wanted for kidnapping his own child and possibly for murdering an innocent woman." She took one of the man's business cards from a ceramic card holder on the counter.

"Do you have children, Mr… Tránh?" she asked.

Mr. Tránh nodded his head up and down slowly.

"They all grow up now," he answered. "Not small now."

"What would you have done if somebody had taken them from you when they were children?" Anika asked, her eyes zeroing in on the nervous little man's face, trying to force him to look her in the eye again. "Would you have wanted somebody to tell you where you could find them?"

Mr. Tránh's hand reached tentatively for the money on the counter, then stopped momentarily. He seemed to be checking in with his conscience. Finally, he collected the two bills. His eyes finally lifted. She thought she saw fear in them.

"If I tell, you not tell anybody?" he asked,

"You have our word," Anika answered. "What can you tell us?"

Mr. Tránh's eyes darted from side to side, seemingly wanting to make sure nobody was watching or listening. He lowered his voice.

"This man want to rent flat in Vietnam… somewhere nice… not Hanoi or Ho Chi Minh City. I take him to Ha Long tomorrow to look at flats. If he not happy, he go look in Da Nang next week."

"Ha Long," Anika repeated. "How far away is that from here?"

"One hundred sixty kilometre… three, maybe four hour," he replied.

"Do you have some apart… er, flats, that you'll be showing him?" Angela pressed. "Can you tell us where you'll be taking him?" She watched Tránh finger the bills in his hand. He looked at the bills, then over at Angela.

"Two hundred dollar more. Then I tell you," he said.

"One hundred," Angela countered. Tránh shook his head from side to side, and then carefully began folding the bills to put them in his pocket.

"He scary man. Too dangerous. One hundred no good. Only two hundred, or you go now."

Panic flashed through Anika's eyes. She pulled out her purse, desperate not to lose Tránh's help.

"Anika, I've got it," Angela said, putting her hand on Anika's hand to stop her from using her own money. Angela saw tears of relief start to well up in Anika's eyes. She peeled two more crisp hundreds from her billfold, and then she laid them on the counter.

This time, Tránh wasted no time swiping the two bills from the counter, folding them, and hiding them in his pocket. "You wait," he said.

Anika's foot vibrated up and down nervously, while the little man sat down at his computer, clicked away with his mouse, and opened and closed windows on his monitor. Finally, an old dot matrix printer, yellow-grey from years of use and smudged printer ribbons, rattled to life. It buzzed back and forth a few times, then the printer paper crinkled as the cogs on either side of machine advanced to the start of the next blank page. Tránh stood up, ripped the page from the printer, and then walked back to the counter. He held the page out and Anika almost tore it out of his hand.

"We start with number one flat on that paper," he said. "If I see you, we not know each other, okay?"

"We've never met," Angela replied, nodding their acceptance of his conditions.

"Thank you so much," Anika said. "You've done the right thing, Mr. Tránh. I don't think I can ever thank you enough."

Angela saw her new friend's eyes watering again. As she did, she felt her own heart longing to see Nicholas and Julia. It was all she could do to hold back her own tears.

TRÁNH WATCHED the door close behind the two women, then he waited patiently while they jumped into their waiting SUV and it sped away. He pulled the four new U.S. bills from his pocket and smiled, proud of his performance. He pocketed the money, and then climbed a set of stairs behind the counter until he reached the second floor. He punched in a code on the door's electronic lock and waited for it to click. When it did, he swung the door open and walked into a room housing his second business. A row of computer servers lined the wall to his left. Along the opposite wall, a row of young men and women sat before large video monitors. They were editing video clips of well-endowed men and big-busted women of every race and color, engaged in various stages of almost every kind of sex act imaginable. He nodded to his workers, and then he went to his own desk at the back of the room.

The workers resumed editing, occasionally uploading finished product to the servers behind them, making the brand new pornographic videos available to paying audiences around the world, all of them eager to feed their sexual addictions.

Tránh reached for his telephone and put the receiver to his ear with one hand, while he dialed with his other. After two double rings, the line clicked and a man's voice answered in fluent English.

"Yes."

"This is Tránh. They just leave. I give them addresses of flats in Ha Long, just like you say."

"You've done well, old friend. If all goes well, we won't have to worry about our American and Canadian friends anymore. I'm sure we'll be doing business together for many more years. You have my thanks, Tránh."

"No problem. Good day, Mr. Kristiansen."

CHAPTER 29

"SO, CAN WE go over this one last time before we leave for Ha Long?" Dan asked, his voice hushed. He sat across the table from Anika and Angela in the hotel's breakfast room.

"Okay, Dan," Anika said. "We get Dinh to drop you and me off at the first flat on Mr. Tránh's list, where we wait for Tránh and Soren to show up. Angela waits in the car with Dinh to let us know when Soren arrives. That way, she and Dinh can follow Soren if he bolts and we don't make contact with him."

"As soon as I can positively identify Soren, I call the police," Angela added. "I'll report that I've sighted a fugitive on Interpol's most wanted list. This time we don't wait until we ID Jonah before we confront Soren. We can't afford to make the same mistake I made in Australia."

"I assume everybody's cell phones are fully charged?" Dan asked.

"Locked and loaded," Angela said, forcing a weak smile, attempting to inject some levity into the situation. It didn't work. Dan saw the tension etched on both women's faces, especially Anika's. Her foot vibrated up and down rapidly, giving away the anxiety that continued to surge through her body.

"All joking aside," Dan said. "Even though we don't know for sure that somebody tried to kill us in Australia, we need to keep our eyes and ears open every minute. We can't let our guards down."

"Don't worry, Dan," Angela said. "I've got your backs. I'll text *X* if you're in danger and we need to abort. Dinh and I will be waiting outside the building to pick you up if that happens."

Dan looked up and saw Dinh waving to them from the lobby. He looked at his watch. It was seven a.m.

"Dinh's right on time," he said. I'll take our overnight bags to the car. I'll see you out there in a few minutes, okay?"

"We just have to run up to the room for a few minutes, right, Angela?" Anika said.

Angela nodded her agreement. "We'll be right down," she added.

Dan picked up the three light bags, which they'd packed in case they needed to stay overnight in Ha Long, and headed for the lobby. He let Dinh take one of the bags. The two men walked the short distance through the lobby, and then out to the street where Dinh's SUV sat waiting with its flashers on.

As Dan exited the hotel, he was greeted by an unusual spectacle. The sidewalks on both sides of the street were packed with a migration of uniformed school children and their parents, walking up the street in the direction of the Cathedral. To add to the noise, loudspeakers mounted on light standards spouted a daily dose of government propaganda to the passing throng.

"Their parents are all walking them to school?" Dan asked. Dinh nodded affirmatively. "So early in the morning?" Dan added in amazement.

"School start at seven in morning in Vietnam," Dinh announced. "They all come back this way in afternoon."

Dan had to wait for a gap in the cavalcade to carry his bags across the sidewalk to the SUV. When he finally saw an opening, he made a quick dash across the sidewalk to the rear of Dinh's vehicle. "I've never seen such a mass of school kids all at once," Dan said. "Especially so early in the morning. Is that why the church bell rings every morning at six?"

"Yes," Dinh replied, as he hoisted the remaining bags into vehicle's rear. "Hanoi wake up at six. You go down Hoan Kiem Lake you see many people walk, meditate, and do Tai Chi exercise."

"I had no idea. I'll have to get up early tomorrow to go for a walk, if we're back in Hanoi by then," Dan answered. He thought he caught a shift in Dinh's eyes—a fleeting moment of anxiety. But when he looked again, he saw a smile on their guide's face.

"You enjoy that, I think," Dinh replied. "Ah, I see the ladies come now."

Anika and Angela exited the hotel onto the sidewalk, where the mass of children and parents had now thinned dramatically.

"Thanks for waiting, Dinh," Anika said. "Dan, go ahead and sit up front. Angela and I can sit in the back. We'd better get moving if we want to catch Soren at that first flat." She opened the rear door for Angela, who slid into the back seat behind the driver's seat. Dan closed their door before he and Dinh took their places in the front.

Dinh wasted no time moving the SUV into the slow moving traffic on Church Street. It was the morning rush hour, not that it made much difference. The narrow winding streets of Hanoi's old city were almost always congested. Dan noticed Dinh's fingers tapping impatiently on the steering wheel. He was mumbling curses under his breath at the traffic, even laying on the horn on a few occasions.

"I wonder what's eating him?" Dan said to himself. "Swearing and hitting the horn isn't going to make the traffic move any faster."

They turned left at the bottom of Church Street, then took a right to take them the one block, where Dinh was finally able to make a left turn at Hoan Kiem Lake. Dan flipped down the makeup mirror on the passenger side for a look at Anika, who hadn't spoken a word. Her facial muscles were taut, and Dan caught her chewing on a fingernail. He could only imagine what was going through her mind this morning, with a potential confrontation looming with Soren in the next three or four hours.

"How are you doing back there?" Dan asked.

"Not good," Anika answered. "No matter how many times I rehearse it in my mind, I can't prepare for seeing Soren. I know I need to keep my cool. Rashad keeps telling me to stay calm—to let Soren know I'm willing to sit down and discuss options. I know he's right, but every time I think of what Soren's done, all I can think is how badly I just want to scratch his eyes out. It's not fair! He's the one who's stolen my son. Why should I have to negotiate?"

"She's right," Angela added from the back seat. "Anika's the parent who's being abused. The onus shouldn't be on her to negotiate something for herself and Jonah. What about her rights?"

Dan nodded visibly as he watched the two women in the back. "You're right," he said. "But we have to remember that Anika doesn't have any Hague Convention rights here in Vietnam—so we have to be careful. Your lawyer is right. We don't want to piss Soren off or scare him so he goes on the run again. Or even worse, we don't want him angry. As we all know from what happened to us in Australia, it's far too common for spouses like Anika to have attempts made on their lives to scare them off—some have even been killed. So let's all do our best to be patient with Soren if we run into him. And most importantly, be careful!"

Dan noticed Angela place her hand on Anika's shoulder, trying to calm her. He flipped the mirror up and watched the hustle and bustle of early morning Hanoi around the lake. Their vehicle crept through the roundabout at the end of the lake and was just coming up to where the Water Puppet Theatre was located on their left. On his right, Dan saw local residents meditating, exercising, and walking the pathways around the perimeter of the lake. Parked vehicles lined the curb around the lake. As they passed a black SUV Dan glanced casually into the vehicle's open windows, seeing a Caucasian man and a blonde-haired woman seated in the front seat, both wearing ball caps and sunglasses. An uneasy feeling crept into Dan's stomach as they passed the black SUV. The ball caps, especially the blonde hair protruding from beneath the woman's cap, were giving him a sense of déjà vu. Dinh continued to guide their vehicle through the heavy traffic for another hundred yards, and then traffic came to a complete halt.

"What's happening? Why are we stopped, Dinh?" Anika asked from the back seat.

"Traffic jam," Dinh answered. "I not sure why. This is bad, even for Hanoi."

Dan saw beads of sweat breaking out on Dinh's forehead. His movements were jerky. Alarms were going off in Dan's head, but he didn't know why.

"I go see what problem is," Dinh said. "Back in a minute." He swung his door open and almost jumped out of his seat, and then began walking quickly away from their SUV. Dan saw fear in Dinh's eyes. At the same moment, looking out through Dinh's open window, Dan saw a man sitting on a red and white performance motorcycle. The face was strangely familiar, and the eyes were staring directly at Dan. He felt a chill rush down his spine. At that moment his mind flashed back to images of the woman in the SUV, with her blonde hair and ball cap. He finally made the connection. It was the same woman who searched their plane in Darwin! The man on the motorcycle pulled a mobile phone from his pocket. As he did, the man directed an evil stare in Dan's direction. The alarms in Dan's brain went berserk.

"Get out of the car!" he screamed. "Now!"

Dan flung his door open and leapt out of the car, reaching for the handle to Anika's door all in one continuous motion. Angela had already thrown her door open, her feet hitting the ground and running towards the other side of the street. Dan grabbed Anika's hand and dragged her away from the vehicle, towards the lake. They hadn't run twenty feet when Dan felt something slam violently into his back, picking him up and lifting him into the air. By the time the sound of the explosion reached his ears, the catastrophic force had already stunned his brain. He was unconscious by the time he and Anika hit the ground, a full fifty feet from the blazing wreckage.

"SHIT!" Helen shouted. "How could we be so unlucky! Whitney and that fucking wife of yours both have nine lives. How did they know there was a bomb?"

Soren and Helen slouched in the front seat of the black SUV, both wearing dark glasses and ball caps pulled down low over their faces.

"He looked our way as they drove past. You don't think he recognized us, do you?" Soren asked.

"From that angle? With our faces virtually covered? How could he?" Helen snapped. "If I'd known your friends were so incompetent, I would have brought in professionals to do the job right!"

"It wasn't their fault," Soren countered. "It was that bitch Angela again. Every time she shows up, she manages to throw a fucking wrench into things. And when she does, she disappears underground again. We need to get rid of her—once and for all."

"Shut up, Soren. Are you daring to disagree with me?" she snapped. Her cold eyes, full of anger and hatred, stared at Soren.

"No, Hel… my Lady," he mumbled.

"That's better. Don't you ever forget your place! Understand?" she hissed.

"Yes, my Lady," Soren answered contritely.

"Now, as for getting rid of Angela. All in good time." Helen said. "She's not our biggest problem right now. It's your wife I'm more concerned about. She's the biggest threat that's getting in the way of us finally being a family."

"The explosion hit them hard," Soren answered. "We don't even know that Anika and Whitney survived."

"But we certainly know they weren't blown to bits either," Helen cursed, bitterness oozing from her voice.

"Do you want me to get out and have a closer look?" Soren asked.

"Not now, idiot! We need to get out of here before somebody *does* recognize you."

"But what if any of them survived?" Soren whined. "What if they already recognized us?"

"Listen to me!" Helen muttered. "Even if they did survive, they'd better be getting the message that we're trying to kill them. All isn't lost if we managed to scare the shit out of Anika and Whitney. Maybe they'll finally give up."

"But we can't go anywhere in this traffic," Soren replied. "Especially after the explosion."

"Then leave the fucking car!" Helen snapped. She took a deep breath to regain her composure. "We'll walk. Get out of the car slowly and follow me. Don't run or draw any attention. We'll go by foot until we're clear of this traffic, then we'll take a taxi to the airport, just as we planned. Understand? You need to catch up to Jonah and Lucy in Amsterdam, and I need to get back to the States. I've been away too long and people will start asking questions."

"As you wish. You're right, as usual," Soren answered. His tone of voice was now contrite and submissive.

"That's better," Helen said. "We'll be fine. You know I'm right. I always am."

SOREN PLOPPED himself down in an empty seat in the departure lounge at Hanoi airport. Relieved to be through security, he was anxious to be on his way to meet Jonah and Lucy in Amsterdam. He could finally see the end of their long journey now. They would settle in the small Norwegian city of Moss, where it would be easy for himself and Jonah to blend in—his Scandinavian ancestry was responsible for both his own, and Jonah's, blond hair and Nordic appearance. Once they were settled, Helen… she'd always preferred that he call her that… would quietly retire, walk away from her career, and join them. They would finally be together and have the family they had always dreamed of having.

He loved Helen. But he also felt relieved to be alone. She could be so intense and domineering when things weren't going right. Those were the times when the angry side of her surfaced. It was the side of her that he both feared and craved at the same time. It turned him on instantly, but it could be emotionally exhausting too. She was an expert at not letting her anger show outwardly to others. He knew her too well. He saw the emotional and sexual tension building inside her when Angela and Anika survived the bombing today. But there was no time this afternoon for them to be together to release her anger and their pent up sexual tension. Soren finally felt some relief when they separated and headed to their different departure gates.

His mind flashed back to when they first met at Lackland Air Force Base. Together, they discovered firsthand the secret culture of sexual harassment and abuse of power that existed at the base. A bond developed between them. It began with helping each other endure the officers' abuse. Eventually, he began to trust her enough to tell her about his past. He knew Helen's childhood wasn't good either. She refused to talk about it—as if it had never happened. But he knew what that was like. He usually didn't like to talk about his past either, but somehow he knew he could trust Helen with his story. She listened as he told her about his childhood. She helped him endure the humiliation and degradation they continued to experience during their training.

But Helen refused to let him feel sorry for himself. Instead, she taught him how to be strong by teaching him how to endure pain and humiliation. *'What doesn't kill us just makes us stronger,'* she would say. He knew she was much stronger than him, and he accepted that. In return, he learned to trust her and to love her. They were meant to be together, and their destiny was close to being fulfilled.

CHAPTER 30

THE MEDIA frenzy outside the LAX baggage claim took Dan and Anika by complete surprise. They both looked around them, expecting to see a celebrity like Brad Pitt, Angelina Jolie, George Clooney, or Scarlett Johansson. After all, this was Tinseltown.

It took a moment for reality to sink in for Dan. Anika was the celebrity today. Before she had taken five steps, the media mob blocked her path and an array of microphones had been thrust into her face, completely bewildering and overwhelming her.

"Do you think your husband was responsible for the Hanoi bombing?"

"Any idea where Pastor Soren and your son are now?"

"Do you think what happened in Hanoi is connected to the plane crash in Australia?"

"Ms. Kristiansen, do you ever think you're going to see your son again?"

Dan pushed himself between Anika and the teeming mob.

"No comment! Ladies and gentlemen, please let Anika through. It's been a long flight and she's still in shock over the events of the past few days. Please… no comment… Let us through please!"

Dan took Anika's free hand and started pushing his way through the frenzy. A handful of LAX security finally arrived to salvage some order out of the chaos, creating a protective circle around Dan and Anika.

"Where to, sir?" shouted a young woman on the security crew.

"Parking 4," Dan shouted back. The woman put a microphone to her mouth, shouting something to her dispatcher as the small security circle moved Dan and Anika slowly through the crowded terminal. Within seconds Dan saw a flashing yellow light and heard a high-pitched beeping sound. An electric cart inched through the crowd until it met the security ring with Dan and Anika inside. Two security guards took their baggage and loaded it into the rear of the cart.

"Jump in," the driver shouted. "I'm your ride. Parking 4?"

Dan helped Anika onto the cart and nodded affirmatively to the driver. Within seconds, the cart was leaving the media posse behind, its yellow light reflecting a circular pattern around them while it chirped merrily to warn pedestrians it was coming.

"That was all for me?" Anika asked, finally gathering her wits and finding her tongue. She still wore a look of dismay on her face.

"It's one thing to have an Amber Alert for an abducted child," Dan said. "It disappears from the front pages pretty fast if the child isn't found. And it's been almost two months since the abduction. But a second murder attempt on the mother of an abducted child? I guess that's more newsworthy."

"I suppose," Anika answered. "But it isn't right. The longer a child is missing, the more urgent it should be to find him or her. It should be in the news *more* often over time."

"I agree," Dan said. "But you know that's not how the media works. By tomorrow, you're yesterday's news."

"That's why I'm meeting with Rashad in Vancouver, hopefully within two or three days," Anika continued. "Even before the bombing, he thought I needed to start doing more regular press conferences and videos—some of them appealing to Soren and offering to negotiate with him—others appealing to people all over the world to keep an eye out for Soren and Jonah. I'm going to call another press conference to take advantage of all of this renewed attention. The RCMP will make the videos available to the media in all Hague Convention countries, and as many non-Hague countries as possible. We want to keep their faces in the news as much as we can, until somebody recognizes them."

"You're still staying at the Chateau tonight?" Dan asked.

"Absolutely, I need a day to calm down and get some sleep. The peace and quiet of the Chateau are exactly what I need right now."

Anika managed a weak smile.

"Who knew I'd ever be looking forward to spending time at a nudist resort! I'll see if I can get on a flight to Vancouver in a couple of days."

"That's great," Dan said. "Tim, Shelley, Pam, and Richard are probably going to be there this weekend. In fact, Shelley's coming tomorrow afternoon to visit with Fran at the jail. I'll probably be visiting tomorrow morning, if Fran's up for the visit."

"You're going to tell her about us in Darwin, right?" Anika said.

"Yeah. Unless she's really fragile. I know I have to come clean," Dan said. "But with the Grand Jury hearing starting in just five days, I don't want anything to have a negative impact on Fran or the case. It could take weeks before the jury reaches a verdict on whether to take the case to trial or not. I just want her to stay as positive and strong as possible during that time."

"But you know it's just going to get harder, the longer you wait," Anika said.

"Yeah, I know," Dan admitted.

Their cart arrived at the terminal exit. "Parking 4 is just across the street, sir," their driver said. Dan reached for his wallet and passed the driver a tip.

"Thanks for saving us from that mob," Dan said.

"Yes, thank you," Anika said, smiling. "I'm afraid I was like a deer in the headlights back there. I'd probably still be standing there without your help."

"No worries, ma'am," the driver said. He retrieved their baggage from the rear of the cart. "It happens all the time in this city." He climbed back aboard his cart and waved to Dan and Anika as he pulled away, the yellow light spinning and the chirping alarm announcing the electric vehicle's departure.

Dan and Anika pulled up the handles on their bags and started pulling them behind them as they entered the parking garage.

"I'm worried about Angela," Anika said. "She didn't tell us she was leaving. She just slipped away in the middle of the night. Did she tell you where she was going?"

Dan shook his head. "She didn't say a word to me. You spent more time with her in Darwin and Hanoi. Did she ever say much about what she's been doing since she disappeared from New York?"

"No, she's always been vague and doesn't talk much about that. She mostly talked about her kids and her life back in Cleveland, before she moved to New York to work for Soren and the WWCC," Anika said. "She mentioned something once about living a few minutes away from the strip, but she didn't say anything more. That would mean Las Vegas, right?"

"Maybe," Dan said. "Or it could be Sunset Strip in L.A. I think there's even a district in Pittsburgh with the same name, if I'm not mistaken. I guess she's gone back underground while she tries to figure out what to do next. It's going to be a lot harder to track Soren down now that he knows she's hacked into his computer. It's almost certain that he planted the information that took us to Kakadu and then to Hanoi. She has to be worried that Soren is still looking for her too."

"It's ironic, isn't it?" Anika said. "We let ourselves think that Angela was our guardian angel—looking out for us and protecting us from Soren. In the end, we were pretty naive to think that. It almost got us all killed."

They reached the parking garage and pressed the button for an elevator, just as a door opened for them. As the door closed, Anika turned to Dan. He saw fear etched on her face—her forehead looked like it had now become permanently creased. Her jaw muscles twitched with tension. For the first time, he saw small crow's feet appearing at the corner of her weary eyes.

"What about us, Dan? How do we know he isn't going to come after us too? I'm terrified to go back to Calgary to visit my family again. What if he comes after me there and somebody in my family is hurt or killed? I couldn't live with myself if that happened!"

The elevator beeped and the door opened on their floor. As they exited the elevator, Dan stopped and turned to Anika. He let go of his bag and wrapped her in his arms to calm and reassure her.

"Maybe I'm still being naive," he said. "But I don't think he'll come after us here in the States or in Canada. He's just trying to put the fear of death into you so you'll stay away and stop looking for Jonah. You can't let him do that, Anika. If you give up, he wins! You have to keep on doing everything you can to search for Jonah, including reaching out to Soren from home."

"That's why I'll be doing the press conference in Vancouver in a couple of days," Anika answered. "Rashad wants to get my face, and pictures of Soren and Jonah, out there as soon as possible, while the Hanoi bombing is still fresh in people's minds."

"Then what?" Dan asked.

"Then I'm going back to Calgary to be with Dad while he fights his cancer. My practice in Victoria is in good hands for now. Besides, I can't stay in the house. All I feel is emptiness there while Jonah's still missing."

Dan released Anika from his arms. "Then that's where you should be—with your family," he said. They grabbed their bags and resumed walking, the rumble of the tiny wheels sounding like rolling thunder, amplified by the concrete all around them.

"Wherever she is, I hope Angela's safe," Anika shouted over the rumbling wheels.

"You two bonded pretty quickly," Dan said. "I was worried you wouldn't get along, given all of the innuendo about her night on the town in New York with Soren."

"It was Soren who was unfaithful," Anika answered. "Angela just did what she had to do to get away from him. We're good."

"Well, I'm glad you're both getting along," Dan replied.

"Yeah," Anika said. "I like her a lot."

What Dan didn't see, because Anika was trailing couple of steps behind him, was the flush of pink that had just crossed her face.

ANGELA stared into the darkened aircraft cabin. She felt bad about leaving Anika and Dan without saying goodbye, but her mind was overwhelmed by too many emotions. At the moment, she felt paralyzed by confusion.

Like Anika, she was devastated that they hadn't been able to confront Soren and find Jonah. With every passing day, her longing to be with her own children, Nicholas and Julia, grew stronger. She knew Anika felt just as frustrated, lonely, and guilty for not being there for Jonah, as she felt for having to disappear as a way to keep her children safe. And like Anika, her anger was eating away at her too—anger at Soren for not only taking Jonah away from Anika, but for stooping so low that he'd try to kill his own wife, just to keep her from having custody of their son. It was the same anger she felt towards Soren when he made his sexual advances on her in New York.

Angela also felt angry towards herself for allowing Soren to fool her. She'd made the near fatal mistake of feeling cocky and indestructible, never thinking for a moment that he might find out he was being hacked. He had to have been playing her ever since Darwin. How else would he have known that Dan and Anika would be on that flight to Kakadu National Park? She should have realized then that he was onto her. She felt terrible that her overconfidence had almost caused Dan and Anika to lose their lives—not just once, but on two different occasions.

But something else—something much deeper in her psyche—was compounding her confusion. She first noticed the strange feeling back in Las Vegas, after that reporter, Ricki Marshall, had coaxed her out of her solitary existence in the Las Vegas floodways. Every time she went out with Ricki and her friends, she felt an eerie sense of belonging like she'd never felt before. The feeling was even more noticeable in Darwin. She'd assumed that she was just feeling more like herself because she'd come out of hiding. She finally felt useful because she was doing something to help Anika. But by the time she arrived in Hanoi, she could no longer ignore the feeling.

Of course you feel empathy for Anika. You're a mother and you miss your kids desperately, just like her. But is it more than empathy? Are you physically attracted to her? Did you really want to kiss her and touch her breast, or was I dreaming that?

Angela's mind drifted back in time, jumping from memory to memory. She recalled that first time she was in Soren's office, when he started coming onto her and she saw the family portrait showing him with Anika and Jonah. She felt angry towards him for cheating on his beautiful wife and young son.

Beautiful wife! Admit it, Angela, you found her attractive before you ever met her in person!

Her mind jumped back even further in time, to her marriage to David.

Now that I think about it, you never really enjoyed sex with him, did you? You thought it was because of being molested when you were young, but maybe that wasn't the only reason. What about the sleepovers at Dori's house when you were a teenager? You giggled and laughed, and talked about lesbians—the giggling and laughing of young girls. You experimented with kissing each other and touching your small breasts? You talked about doing it with boys too. Isn't that what all young girls do?

But the more memories Angela recalled from her past, the more she realized something she'd never admitted before.

You enjoyed doing it with Dori. And you never daydreamed about kissing or doing it with boys. You had a crush on Dori, didn't you?

Angela's mind did a fast-forward to that night in Las Vegas when she and Ricki went to see the *Showgirls of Illusion*, the topless burlesque and magic show. And the other nights she went out with Ricki and her friends—all female friends.

Being on stage with those bare-breasted women turned you on, didn't it, Angela?

Another disturbing thought drifted into her consciousness.

You felt like you totally belonged with Ricki and her gay friends! You really felt like you belonged for the first time in your life. Face it, Angela. You like women more than men!

There it was.

Out of the deep, dark recesses of her subconscious and into the wide open spaces of her consciousness, for all the other parts of her identity to see and feel. Angela allowed herself to remember the last two days in Hanoi—the times that she and Anika touched each other on their arms or shoulders, or briefly held each other's hand while supporting each other. She felt an electric sensation flowing through her body—a tingling in her nipples and a warm sensation in her vaginal region.

You didn't dream it, girl. You're getting turned on just thinking about touching her. You're attracted to Anika, and you can't deny it! You're ga— or at the very least, bisexual!

Angela allowed herself some time to process this new piece of information—seeing whether it was compatible—whether it fit— with the rest of her identity. She waited for the feelings of guilt and revulsion that she felt sure would follow. But nothing came. Instead, she felt her confusion beginning to ebb.

Angela found herself chuckling aloud in the quiet darkness of the aircraft cabin.

It feels like you just came out of the closet to yourself. And you know what? It feels okay. It feels like when you finally find the right dress or pair of shoes when you're shopping. You just know it's right when you put it on. It's just a feeling, but you know when it's right.

Angela's sense of peace lasted for about thirty seconds. Then her mind started racing ahead into the future.

You can't tell Anika! She'll laugh at you. Or even worse, she'll hate you. Do you really think it's going to be as easy to come out to the whole world, as it was to admit this to yourself? What is everybody going to think? What about Mamma and Papa? Or Julia and Nicholas?

Angela's feeling of disquiet was replaced by a much more palpable sensation. Fear. A tear formed in one eye, soon followed by a stream of tears running from both eyes. She realized that she had just added another layer of complication to her already complicated life. She sniffled and cried softly for another ten minutes, until she finally recognized how exhausted her body and her mind really were. Then, finally, she slipped into a much needed sleep.

CHAPTER 31

DAN swallowed, feeling like he'd just unloaded a giant weight from his shoulders. But now he had to live with his guilt. His eyes studied Fran for her reaction. Her head dropped onto her chest, her eyes staring downward, away from him. She said nothing. Silence started to build like black storm clouds in the distance.

"Say something," Dan said, the ominous calm causing his anxiety to start building again. "Anything. I understand if you're angry. I understand if you feel you can't ever trust me again. But just say something."

Dan felt his legs vibrating up and down, trying to discharge the growing tension in his body. He couldn't bear the silence. It felt worse than any anger, or any other emotional outburst he had imagined.

Finally, Fran looked up, and then looked away almost immediately.

"I knew this would happen eventually," she muttered. "You've always loved her, starting years before you married Chelly. Why should I be surprised?

Fran paused, then she lifted her head. Her eyes finally met Dan's.

"Now that Chelly is gone, you are finally free to be with the woman you've always loved. I don't want to get in the way of your happiness. I don't want to be a burden."

"A burden?" Dan exclaimed. "You're not a burden to me. I'm falling in love with you, Fran. I told you, Anika and I aren't in love. It just happened, before either one of us knew what was happening. We were both so scared… so lonely… I guess we both just needed to feel safe and loved after what happened that day. As soon as it was over, we both knew instinctively that it was wrong… that we didn't love each other romantically… that it would never happen again!"

Dan swallowed again, trying to find some saliva to get rid of the parched sensation that was causing him to trip over his tongue.

"It's *you* I'm falling in love with, Fran! It's *you* I want make a new life with—you and our child. You have to believe me. Please give me a chance!"

Fran's head sagged against her chest again. Dan saw the weariness in her body and felt her pain—pain that he had inflicted upon her. Silence once again filled the gulf between them. The suspense was agonizing for him. Finally, when he didn't think he could stand it any longer, she lifted her head. She was looking away from him.

"I don't know if I can do that, Dan. Maybe it is best for both of us if we go our separate ways."

The words hit Dan like a body blow. He felt the air being sucked out of his lungs. Then he saw a tear drip from Fran's right eye, trickling its way slowly down her cheek.

THE WALK back and forth from the visitor's area was becoming routine for Fran after almost two months in custody. She knew that her guards no longer saw her as the dangerous murderer they perceived when she first arrived, since they no longer assigned two guards to escort her to and from the visitor's area. Today, it was the mousey-looking redhead who ushered Fran into the room.

Shelley was already waiting for her in one of the booths. She greeted Fran with her trademark warm smile.

"Hi, Fran," she began. "How are you this week? Did you see Dan this morning?"

Fran swallowed and nodded timidly.

"So he told you about everything that happened to him and Anika?" Shelley asked.

Once again, Fran nodded. "He told me everything. I just knew it would happen. It was only a matter of time. I knew he would eventually choose Anika over me."

Shelley's eyes narrowed. She frowned and cocked her head to one side. "You're talking about the bombing in Hanoi, aren't you?" she asked.

"No," Fran answered. "I'm talking about him sleeping with his old girlfriend. I knew it would happen eventually."

"Whaaaat?" Shelley gasped. "You're sure?"

Fran nodded again. She swallowed, then managed to push away the emotions and tears that threatened to escape from behind the walls in her mind.

"After the plane crash in Australia. He said it just happened one time, out of the blue. He thinks it happened because they were both scared and lonely. They had nobody else, so they comforted each other."

Fran saw Shelley's shoulders slump. Her eyes looked downward towards the floor while she let out a long breath.

"I don't know what to say," Shelley said, lifting her head. "I'm so sorry that happened to you."

"Don't feel sorry," Fran answered. "It is better this way. I think they were always meant for each other. They just needed the right time and circumstances to finally bring them together. It is better I should find out now, before we live together. Before Dan bonds with the baby."

"You're breaking up with him?" Shelley asked. "Don't you want him to be part of the baby's life, even if you're apart?"

This time it was Fran's turn to cast her eyes down at the floor. She shook her head slowly from side to side.

"I have always managed to find my way. I can survive by myself with the baby too," Fran said. Her voice was flat, devoid of emotion.

"Are you sure?" Shelley asked. "I'm obviously no expert, but I know it's a lot harder to manage as a single parent. Are you sure about this? The last time I talked with Dan, he seemed excited about making a life with you and the baby."

"After this, how can I trust him? Every man I have ever known has either abandoned me, abused me, or betrayed me. Dan is no exception. I would spend every day wondering when he is going to leave me for Anika. I cannot live that way. I'm not meant to live with any man. I'm probably going to spend the rest of my life in prison. I may not even have to worry about taking care of myself or a baby," Fran said.

"What do you mean," Shelley asked in surprise. "Doesn't Joanna think she can win your case?"

"Joanna is still confident, but I'm not," Fran answered. "Who is going to believe me? I helped Philippe kill those people. I put drugs in their wine. I helped bury them in the desert. I lied to the police. And then I drowned my husband. I'm a terrible person. I don't deserve to be a mother."

"You'd give up your child?" Shelley said. Genuine concern was written on her face.

Fran shrugged. She felt numb. All of her emotions were now pushed safely behind her internal mental walls.

"The Grand Jury hearing starts in just five days. You've got to stay positive, Fran. Don't rush into a decision about Dan or the baby yet. Just focus on the hearing for now and take things one day at a time. Trust Joanna. She's an expert in spousal abuse cases. If anybody can get you off, she can."

Shelley's words sounded like a distant echo to Fran. She felt like she was looking down at Shelley and herself from above. The whole scene felt surreal. She felt almost as if she was floating in a big bubble, shielded from any kind of physical or emotional pain.

She became vaguely aware of somebody taking her by the arm and pulling her to her feet. She saw tears in Shelley's eyes, then saw her blowing a kiss through the glass in her direction, just before a door closed behind her. She felt nothing. She shuffled slowly down the corridor, on autopilot, back to the safety and isolation of her cell. Strangely, although she had initially felt only panic and fear in her prison cage when she first arrived, she had gradually given in to a growing sense of helplessness. It was better this way—better than letting herself feel that she had any hope for the future.

AN EERIE feeling of déjà vu descended on Dan. He sat in the cozy surroundings of the Mexican restaurant on Palm Canyon Drive, with its closely spaced tables and red checkered table cloths. It seemed like years since he had brought Chelly here, when she had so quickly become friends with Tim, Shelley, Pam, and Richard. And yet, it was only three months since that night. And just one week later, he would be a widower when Chelly suffered the fatal gunshot wound at Fran and Philippe's Palm Desert estate.

The mood three months ago had been one of laughter and relaxation. Tonight, the mood was much more sombre. Not only were Chelly and Philippe dead, but Fran remained behind bars in Indio Jail without bail. If that wasn't enough, the recent attempts on Dan and Anika's lives, and the failure of their mission to find Jonah, was foremost on everybody's minds.

For Dan, admitting his infidelity to Fran this morning had gone worse than he ever expected. She had closed herself off emotionally and pushed him away. He had failed her. He had lived up to her pessimistic expectation that she couldn't trust any man to treat her well.

Dan felt a hand patting his right leg under the table. He glanced at Anika, who was sitting to his right. He gave her a weak smile, acknowledging her presence and silently thanking her for bringing him back from his daydream. Anika knew how hard it had been for him to tell Fran about their liaison, and he knew she felt just as guilty as he did.

Pam Holloway, sitting across the table from Dan and Anika, brought Dan's mind back into the conversation.

"Shelley says that Fran isn't doing so well," she said.

To Pam's right, her husband Richard drained the last drop of red wine from his glass and set it on the table.

"Sounds t'me like she's givin' up," he added, with his pronounced Texan drawl. "I kin see why. Ain't natural t'be caged like an animal when y'all ain't done nothin' wrong. Especially with her bein' pregnant an' all. Ah still don' understand how the D.A.'s been able to keep 'er there without bail."

"I think Fran's totally overwhelmed right now," Shelley added from her seat across the table on Pam's left. She stared directly at Dan. Normally warm and friendly, her dark eyes were cold and accusing. "She's got a lot on her plate right now."

From the look in Shelley's eyes, Dan had no doubt that Fran had told her about his indiscretion in Australia. If Shelley was trying to make him feel guilty, she had succeeded. He was thankful that their waiter, a young man with jet-black hair and a Hispanic accent, interrupted the awkward silence to take their orders. He began with Shelley and her partner Tim, who was sitting on Dan's left.

Dan shifted his gaze to the far end of the table, where Richard's two friends and associates, Miriam Fox and Gwen Perkins sat. The first time he had met Miriam and Gwen at the Orange County rally for victims of military sexual abuse, he and Anika hadn't yet met Angela Baranyi in person. But for a moment, he almost thought it was Angela beside the red-haired Gwen, instead of Miriam. He was shocked by Miriam's resemblance to Angela. He touched Anika's hand to get her attention.

"Have you noticed how much Miriam looks like Angela?" Dan asked.

"I know," Anika exclaimed. "They could almost pass as twins!"

"You know what they say," Dan added. "Everybody's got a look-alike somewhere."

"Yeah," Anika said, allowing herself a rare smile. "There's only one way I'd be able to tell them apart."

"How's that?" Dan asked.

Anika rolled her eyes at Dan.

"Duh! We just spent the afternoon sunbathing in the nude with all of these people. How do you think I know? Didn't you see that big cobra tattoo on Miriam's right boob?"

"And Angela doesn't—how do you know that?" Dan chuckled, raising a playful eyebrow.

For a second, he thought he saw Anika's face taking on a shade of pink. But if he did, she managed to recover quickly. When he looked more closely, it was gone.

"Of course I do. We shared a hotel room for three days in Hanoi. Remember? Even with towels wrapped around us, we would have seen if either one of us had a tattoo that big on our boobs."

"Silly me," Dan said, chuckling. "I should have known."

The waiter came around the table to take their orders.

"I don't eat Mexican much," Anika said to Dan. "What do you recommend?"

"Last time we were here, I had the *Chicken Molé*," he said. He turned to Tim on his left, who had ordered the same thing that night. "It was excellent, wasn't it, Tim?"

"Absolutely. It's their specialty!"

"Okay. I'll try it. What are you going to have?" Anika asked.

Dan's mind drifted back to March again—connecting to images of himself and Chelly, trading tastes of each other's meals. Suddenly, as he remembered what Chelly had ordered, he felt choked up.

"I think I'm going to have the *Shrimp in Pipian,*" he said quietly. "I've been told it's very good."

"More wine, everybody? These first two bottles are about done," Pam shouted, helping to startle Dan back into reality. Everybody at the table nodded their agreement with Pam.

"One more each of the red and the white," she shouted to the waiter.

In the brief moment of silence that followed, Dan decided to change the subject and to break some good news to the gathering of friends. He looked across the table at Shelley, making eye contact with her.

"I think we all agree that Fran's having a tough time staying positive. But I think I've got something that will help to lift her spirits," he announced.

"What's that?" Shelley asked, a puzzled look appearing in her eyes and creases of curiosity etched in her forehead.

"Most of you know that Fran came from a small village in Italy. She had a pretty rough childhood. But she did have one positive influence—a lady who believed in her and was very much a mentor to her."

Dan raised his glass and took a sip of red wine to moisten his dry throat.

"Her name is Susan Keaner," he said, licking the wine off his lips. "She ran the gallery and the portrait studio in Manarola where Fran worked as a teenager. She's semi-retired now, but I managed to track her down through the gallery. I told her about Fran's situation, and she dropped everything to come and support Fran through the Grand Jury deliberations."

Dan saw the cold, accusing look in Shelley's eyes begin to soften.

"You did that for her?" Shelley asked.

"Yeah. Fran only gives me bits and pieces of what happened in her childhood. But she mentioned Susan a couple of times, and I recognized how much she must have meant to her. I thought it was worth a try."

"Thanks… for Fran," Shelley said. "When is she coming?"

"She'll be arriving Monday afternoon on the shuttle from LAX, in time for the start of Grand Jury on Tuesday," Dan answered. "Are you guys going to be able to be there?"

"At least for the first day," Tim interrupted. "We wouldn't miss it for the world."

"It depends how long it goes on," Shelley added. "We can't take much time off work. But between the two of us, we'll go as much as we can."

"Thanks… both of you," Dan said. "It's going to mean a lot to her. She's never had much of a support network."

"We're all goin' t'be there too," Richard boomed with his Texas drawl. "Me'n the girls hav'ta do a quick trip to Kuwait on Wednesday, but we shouldn't be more'n a week or ten days. Right, girls?"

"It's the least we can do for her," Gwen replied. "We can't stand seein' anybody gettin' screwed over by the system, right, Miriam?"

"For sure," Miriam agreed. "Anything we can do to help. We'll be right beside Pam and Richard."

Dan felt Anika's hand on his shoulder. "I have to use the girls' room," she whispered. "Back in a minute."

As Anika rose and walked away from the table, Dan heard Tim clear his throat.

"How's Anika doing?" he said to Dan, once Anika was gone.

"As well as can be expected," Dan answered. "It's been a real rollercoaster ride for her. Every time she gets a bit of good news, it just leads to more bad. She's going to be doing another press conference on Sunday, after she gets back to British Columbia. This time, they're going to try to distribute it worldwide to the media."

Dan's eyes met with Shelley's while he was talking. He felt the elephant in the room getting bigger, especially since Anika left the room.

"So, what about you?" Shelley asked quietly, trying to keep the conversation low key at their end of the table. "You've been spending a lot of time with her. It must be a rollercoaster for you too. Has it brought you two together after all this time?"

For the first time, Dan realized he didn't have to think about his response.

"Quite the opposite," Dan replied. "I think I had to answer her call for help and spend all this time with her to find that out. Otherwise I always would have wondered if we were meant to be together."

He reached for his glass of wine, feeling relaxed and confident in his answer.

"The minute we hooked up in Darwin, we both knew it was a mistake. It happened out of fear and loneliness—we both desperately needed somebody to hold in that moment. It wasn't because we love each other romantically. We're always going to be best friends. But apart from that one night in Darwin, there's no real physical chemistry. It just didn't feel right to either one of us. I don't know if Fran will ever believe me, but I swear it's true. I know now, more than ever, that it's Fran and our child that I'm committed to."

Dan saw Shelley and Tim reading each other's eyes.

"We believe you," Tim said. "But I guess it's not up to us. We'll put in a good word for you, but it's up to Fran in the end."

Dan caught Shelley raising her eyes and looking towards the washrooms, signalling him that Anika was returning. She arrived back at the table at the same time as their meals.

Dan realized he'd been holding his breath for much of the time that he had been talking with Shelley and Tim. He let the air out of his lungs, and then filled them again slowly. He was glad to have Shelley back on his side. But he knew he needed all of the help he could possibly get over the next few days and weeks, *if* he had any hope at all of getting past the walls Fran had erected between them. He'd need a favourable Grand Jury ruling, as well as support from the people who were closest to Fran—Shelley, Tim, and Susan Keaner. It was a lot of *ifs*, and Dan knew he was fighting an uphill battle.

"IS THIS IT? Are we *finally* in Moss?" Jonah whined.

The train gradually decelerated as it pulled into the station after its fifty-minute journey from Oslo. The late June sun was still relatively high in the western sky, even though it was nine o'clock in the evening. Their flight from Amsterdam to Oslo had been short, but Jonah was still tired of travelling. He felt excited to finally be in Norway. Father had said they would live here, so Jonah hoped that all of the travelling was finally over.

"Shhhh… Not so loud," Lucy whispered. "The whole train doesn't want to know you've arrived! Remember what your father said. You mustn't make a scene or the bad people will find you!"

Jonah looked around at the people in their rail car. It was a mixture of men with their noses in newspapers, old people, and young couples with children like himself. Teenagers with headphones and earplugs moved silently to the beat of music from their generation's new electronic version of the *Walkman*—the *iPod*. None of the people looked very dangerous to him. He was glad to finally be in Norway, and he felt more like his playful five-year-old self.

"But I don't *see* any bad people," Jonah whispered.

"That's just it," Lucy said. "They're like spies. They look and dress like good people, but they're pretending. You never know who the bad people are because they're disguised to look like normal people, just like you and me. We should stop whispering too. The bad people will notice you if you whisper too much too."

The train finally came to a stop.

"Okay, make sure you've put your books, your crayons, and your colouring book in your backpack. You don't want to leave anything behind," Lucy warned.

Jonah quickly scanned their seats, and then he dropped to his knees to search on the floor under their seats.

"Ah hah," he said with a satisfied little grunt. He got on his stomach and reached way under the seat, barely managing to grasp a runaway crayon between two of his fingers.

"The red one almost got away, but I found it!" he announced proudly as he popped to his feet. He quickly opened the lid to his crayon container and dropped it in.

"Hurry," Lucy urged. "The train only stops for a few minutes. We have to hurry or it will take us to the next town. Your father will be furious if he can't find us."

Lucy reached up to lower their two suitcases from the overhead rack. A young man across the aisle jumped to his feet.

"Let me help you," he said to Lucy. "I'll carry this one off the train for you."

"You speak English," Jonah shouted impulsively. "Don't you speak Norwegian?"

"Jonah! Don't be so rude," Lucy said. He noticed that she was blushing.

"That's okay," the man said. He turned and bent down to speak to Jonah. "Most people in Norway learn to speak English in school, so we know how to speak both languages."

"I'm going to be learning Norwegian," Jonah announced. "Then I'll know two languages too!" He noticed Lucy's face turning bright red.

"Quickly, Jonah, we must get off the train." Jonah felt her nudging him along, while she bumped and dragged his suitcase down the aisle behind her. The young man trailed behind with Lucy's larger bag.

When they had descended the stairs from the train onto the platform, Jonah watched as Lucy turned to the young man and retrieved her suitcase.

"Thank you, sir. We're meeting somebody, so we have to run," she said nervously. "Come, Jonah. Let's go."

Jonah felt Lucy grab his arm with a yank, dragging him away behind her. When they were safely away from the man, Lucy bent down. She waved her finger and scolded him.

"Remember what your father said? You *must* not talk to strangers. What if that man was one of the bad people?" she said.

Jonah was about to tell her that the young man was nice. He didn't think he was one of the bad people, when he noticed Lucy looking behind him. She seemed afraid. He turned around and realized that Father had been following them. He was staring at them from the other end of the platform, and he looked angry. Jonah forgot about the kind man. In the blink of an eye, his playfulness vanished. He shut himself down, turning into the frightened, meek, submissive little boy he had been since Father had picked him up from kindergarten in Victoria.

"Come on, follow me," Lucy whispered sternly. She rolled their two larger suitcases awkwardly through the station, with Jonah trailing behind with his small backpack on wheels. They emerged from the station and Lucy waved for a cab. When the driver had managed to squeeze their luggage into the small taxi's trunk, Jonah watched Lucy hand the man a slip of paper with an address.

"Where are we going now?" Jonah whined, as Lucy fastened his seat belt for him.

"We're going to meet your father at the new apartment," she answered. "He'll be meeting us there later."

"I need my booster seat," Jonah said. "Mommy says it's dangerous not to use it."

"Don't worry, Jonah. Our new apartment is only a few minutes away. And I'm sure your father will get you one once he gets a car in Norway."

The cab pulled away from the station. Jonah looked out the window at the country that was to be his new home. He saw water and a big dock with ferries, much like the one they had taken from Victoria to Washington. Lucy rummaged through her purse, finally pulling out a set of keys, just as the cab pulled up in front of a modern, three-story apartment building on Fjellveien. Lucy was right. The ride from the train station had taken only a few minutes.

The driver hoisted their luggage from the trunk and set the bags on an asphalt pathway that lay between the road and the apartment building. Jonah stood and surveyed the building while Lucy paid their driver. The outside of the building was covered in cream-coloured siding. It looked to Jonah as if every apartment had its own large balcony.

"Which one is ours?" Jonah asked. "Which floor will we be living on? Will we have a balcony too?"

Lucy smiled and laughed. "Patience, Jonah. We'll be there in a minute. I think we're on the third floor." She pulled up the handle on the two larger bags, and then pulled the handle out on Jonah's rolling back pack. "Let's go and find out."

Lucy used her keys to let them in through the main entrance, and then they took the elevator to the third floor. Jonah followed Lucy down the hallway until she stopped in front of a door. "Here we are. We're finally here."

Jonah waited impatiently while Lucy fumbled with her keys. Finally finding the right one, she inserted it into the lock and the door finally swung open. Jonah ran into the apartment. It faced south and was bright, airy, and spacious, even with the sun being so low in the sky. It was a big relief after living in the dark, dingy, rundown apartment in Darwin. He spotted a sliding door to the balcony and ran to it, trying in vain to pull it open.

Lucy laughed again as she closed the apartment's main door behind them. "Jonah, slow down! You have to be careful if you go out there. Just wait a second and I'll go out there with you." She flipped the lock on the door and unfastened a metal safety bar, allowing Jonah out onto the balcony. The evening was starting to cool down, but it was still a mild summer evening. He found himself looking out over a quiet neighbourhood, composed mostly of small wooden houses and tree-lined streets. To Jonah, Moss wasn't too different from his old home near the ocean in Victoria. He decided it would be okay to live here until it was safe for Mommy to finally be with them.

"When do you think Mommy will be able to come?" Jonah asked. "When will she be able to get away from the bad people?" Suddenly, he remembered his father from the railway station platform. "Where's Daddy?" he asked.

Lucy's face took on a pinkish tone. Jonah saw her swallow. His short-lived optimism gave way to an ominous feeling of foreboding.

"The bad people are still looking for us," she said. "It's still not safe for you and your daddy to be seen together too much. He's going to live in a hotel for a little while, like he did in Darwin. But only for a little while, until he finds a safe place for us to live in Norway."

Jonah's heart sank. He felt his dream—that they were finally free from the bad people, and that it was finally safe for Mommy to join them—slipping away. And as his dream slowly vanished, his familiar companions from the past two months—loneliness and hopelessness—returned to replace it.

Jonah had seen enough. He turned his back on Moss and walked dejectedly back into the apartment, throwing himself on the large sofa in the living room. He struggled to keep his tears from escaping, but managed to succeed. Hiding his disappointment was something he had gradually mastered over the past two months, since the day he last saw his mommy.

CHAPTER 32

DAN SAT quietly in the Italian-themed room at Chateau Eden. The TV in front of him was tuned to CNN, but his mind was preoccupied. On one hand, Dan felt relieved to finally admit his sexual encounter with Anika. But now he had to deal with the fallout. Fran was even more distant than ever, seemingly determined to end whatever relationship they had forged so far. He couldn't stop thinking about her. Everywhere his eyes focused in this room, he saw her influence—the light, airy atmosphere, with the pastel watercolors of Italian villages perched on cliffs overlooking the ocean, the modern furniture, the fluffy white duvet on the bed, and the subtle bursts of color in the decorations she had carefully handpicked for the room.

He felt a rumbling in his stomach and realized it must be close to dinnertime. He glanced at his watch, surprised to see that it was almost seven o'clock Sunday evening.

The press conference, he thought to himself. Anika's press conference had probably ended by now. He wished he could have watched it live, but he had no way of watching the Vancouver CTV station in Palm Springs. He reached for his laptop on the coffee table and Googled the Vancouver station's news department. Because Anika's press conference was the most recent event, it appeared at the top of a column of top news stories.

Dan clicked on the thumbnail photo, which showed Anika standing behind the podium and microphone. The press conference had taken place in the RCMP's British Columbia headquarters in Surrey. Anika's lawyer, Rashad Ramsey, stood behind her. A group of dignitaries stood beside him, including a man and a woman who both wore their crimson RCMP dress uniforms. Ramsay and the police were sending a clear message to Soren and the rest of the world that Jonah's abduction was considered to be an international crime, with RCMP involvement.

The video finally downloaded sufficient content into the laptop's memory cache and began playing.

'Soren, I'm reaching out to you, offering to meet with you, wherever you are. We can discuss our differences as mature adults, in a spirit of give and take, to come up with a solution that is in Jonah's best interests. If you like, I'm prepared to meet with you in a country where the Hague Convention is not in effect—where having Jonah with you is not considered a crime—as a show of good faith.'

"Very clever," Dan said to himself. "Don't mention that Interpol still wants to interview him about Elizabeth Anderson's murder in Little Rock."

'I'm sure we can negotiate a joint custody agreement where everybody—you, Jonah, and me—can move forward and have a happy future. Jonah, if you can see and hear me, I hope you know how much Mommy loves you and wants to be with you again. Even though your mommy and daddy aren't getting along right now, I want you to know that it's not your fault. It's up to Mommy and Daddy to work things out so that you'll be able to see both of us as much as you want in the future. I love you.'

Dan heard the quiver in Anika's voice and saw her hands tremble. He felt the despair that he knew his friend felt deep inside. She looked down at her notes, not wanting to look directly at the TV cameras. He knew she wouldn't want Soren to see any tears or any sign of weakness.

Ramsay must have sensed the same thing. He stepped forward and rested his hand gently on Anika's shoulder. Her part in the press conference was now over. The female RCMP officer stepped forward to the podium, adjusting the microphone as Ramsey guided Anika into the background.

"Mr. Kristiansen, if you wish to reach out to your wife, please phone the local number displayed at the bottom of your TV screen to arrange a meeting. The phone number is for the local Surrey women's shelter. We urge you to reach out on your own accord. Your call will be passed along confidentially to Ms. Kristiansen."

A split screen replaced the image of the RCMP officer. It had a photo of Jonah on the left and one of Soren on the right side of the screen. A yellow banner appeared at the bottom of the video with another local phone number superimposed.

"If members of the public think they might have seen either Jonah or Soren Kristiansen, whose photos you now see, you are urged to phone the number at the bottom of your screen."

Dan saw that the second phone number was different from the first. It was a subtle message to Soren that he could either turn himself in voluntarily, or somebody else would eventually report him and he would be apprehended.

The press conference wrapped up with a woman who represented a Vancouver women's shelter, who reminded the audience that International Child Abduction is a form of domestic abuse, and is also a criminal offence in countries who have signed the Hague Convention on International Child Abduction. Dan watched for a few seconds, and then his mind began to drift again. He found himself staring at the TV, with the image of his life-long friend standing in the background. Before long, he found himself reliving their recent brushes with death in Australia and Vietnam.

Moments later, Dan came back into the present to find himself staring at one of the watercolour paintings of Italy on the wall in front of him. Fran had told him it was her home village, Manarola —one of the five villages in Cinque Terre that are perched precariously atop coastal cliffs, overlooking the Mediterranean. Then his mind drifted to nights that he and Fran had spent in this room, after the nightmare of Chelly and Philippe's deaths was over —nights when he and Fran had made love in this very room.

I'd give anything to live that night in Darwin with Anika over again... I should have known Anika and I weren't meant to be together... if we were, it would have happened when we were young...

Dan felt a warm feeling flow gently through his body as he remembered his nights with Fran. He felt the empathic connection he had with her—knowing instinctively what she was feeling inside. And he felt the love that had been growing for this enigmatic woman. She might appear rigid and mysterious to others, but he had started getting to know her from the minute he first lay on her massage table—when he first felt her hands kneading away the tension in his neck and back.

Dan, you should have known it in Darwin. Fran's the one you've always been looking for. Don't make the same mistake you made with Chelly—don't neglect that side of Fran that so desperately craves romance and love. Just remember, there's also a part of her that's terrified of letting herself go there. If you really want her, you're going to have to win back her trust, but you're going to have to do it carefully.

Dan continued to stare at the watercolour painting of Manarola. Suddenly he remembered the only other person he knew from the little village.

Susan Keaner. You finally get to meet her at the airport tomorrow!

His fingers moved to the trackpad on his laptop. The CTV Vancouver video had ended, so he closed his web browser. His fingers moved the cursor to open his email. He searched for the recent message from Susan Keaner.

Dear Dr. Whitney,
I will be arriving at LAX about noon on Monday, June 26. I will be taking a connector that arrives in Palm Springs at 2:10 PM. I look forward to meeting you then. More than anything, I

look forward to seeing Francesca again. I hope there is something,
no matter how small, that I can do to help my young friend.
    Ciao,
    Susan Keaner

Dan re-read the email. A warm feeling began to spread across his face and into his eyes. The pastel colors in the painting became blurred as his eyes became moist with tears. He realized how desperate he felt about the possibility of losing Fran, and losing the chance to start a family with her. He was certain now that he needed her in his life. He prayed that Susan Keaner was right—that her presence might give Fran a sense of hope, as it had done many years before.

KELLY MULHOLLAND rushed into her office, having successfully avoided the crush of reporters waiting outside the building's front entrance. She was a bundle of nerves, with the Capellini Grand Jury due to begin tomorrow. She felt anxious about their chances. Kevin Vasquez was bright, no doubt about it. He had a solid case against Capellini for conspiring with her former husband to kill Diego and Juanita Alvarez. But it was the case against Capellini for killing her husband, Philippe Morel, that had Mulholland worried. She and Vasquez were up against Joanna Sullivan, whose record for defending battered spouses was stellar. If the Grand Jury rejected laying charges on that count, it was highly likely they'd reject the conspiracy charges too. And if they rejected the charges against Capellini, and the woman walked out of Indio Jail, Kelly would have to face serious consequences with Helen.

The sudden ringing of the phone on Mulholland's desk startled her back to reality. She was so lost in thought about the repercussions of a bad outcome in the Capellini case, that the call almost caused her to fall out of her chair. She regained her balance and grabbed the receiver.

"What is it, Shannon?" Mulholland snapped at her secretary. "I thought I told you I didn't want to be disturbed today!"

"I have a reporter on the line, ma'am. She says she'd like to have a few moments to ask you some questions. She assured me it's not about the Capellini case. What should I tell her?"

"Tell her this isn't a good week. She can try me again after the Capellini Grand Jury is over," the D.A. replied.

"She said it was important. She said something I didn't understand. I can't remember exactly what it was… Skyhook… Tailhook… something like that. She said it would only take a couple of minutes of your time."

Kelly Mulholland almost dropped the phone. She thought she'd put *Tailhook* far behind her.

What's her name? What does she want? she thought to herself frantically.

"Ummh… Shannon… tell her I'll be with her in a minute. It sounds like it's about an old case from a few years ago, so I'll take the call," she said, trying to keep the panic from showing in her voice.

"Yes, ma'am. She's on line two when you're ready."

"Thank you, Shannon. That will be all," Mulholland answered.

Images of faces and places began flooding back at Kelly Mulholland from the past. The images blurred together into a river of debauchery—orgies of sex, drugs, and gambling—many of them with herself as a victim, but many as an instigator too—images and events she thought she'd buried long ago. Kelly felt like her heart was going to explode inside her chest. Her breathing was rapid and shallow. She realized that she was sweating rivers of perspiration. One of the expensive new silk blouses she'd bought for the Grand Jury hearing was drenched. She scrambled to bring her mind back into the present, focusing on the family photo of her husband and kids on the desk. She struggled to slow her breathing,

and to regain some control over her panicked mind and body.
When she finally felt that she'd got herself back under some
semblance of control, she picked up the phone.

"District Attorney Mulholland. To whom am I speaking?"

*"My name is Ricki Marshall. I'm a freelance reporter from Las
Vegas, and I'm writing a book about sexual abuse in the military.
I've been doing some research on one of the scandals—the
Tailhook scandal in Las Vegas—and your name came up as one of
the victims. I'm looking for people who might want to talk about
their experiences. I would naturally protect your confidentiality, as
I do with all of my sources. Do you mind if I take a few moments of
your time to ask a few questions?"*

Mulholland's heart threatened to race out of control again. She
took one long, slow deep breath, struggling to gain the upper hand
over her body and mind.

"I'm sorry, Ms. Marshall. I really would like to help you, but
I'm sure you understand that the memories are very painful for
me."

*"Of course. I understand perfectly. Just one question, if you
don't mind. In my research, your name came up as one of the
female officers who was a victim. But I've also found a couple of
conflicting statements where you were named as one of the
abusers. Could you help me to resolve the discrepancy by telling
me exactly how you were involved?"*

Mulholland felt panic building from deep within her body
again. She tried taking another deep breath. This time it was
ragged. She struggled to feel fresh air flowing into her lungs.

"Once again, I'm sorry Ms. Marshall. I'm sure you've seen that
I was exonerated from having any involvement with the other
officers. I suffered terribly and I received an honourable
discharge."

"I understand, but..."

"This interview is over, Ms. Marshall. Have a good day."

Kelly Mulholland slammed the phone back in its cradle. Her breathing was short and erratic. She was in a state of near panic. Like her heart and her breathing, her thoughts threatened to race completely out of control.

Helen... need to warn... need help...

Frantically, Mulholland reached for her purse, first tossing its contents around in the bag, then dumping them onto her desk, until she found what she was looking for. She grabbed the disposable cell phone, flipped it open, and dialed frantically. The phone seemed to ring forever. Kelly Mulholland was on the verge of a full-blown panic attack. Finally, there was a click on the other end of the line.

"What do you want! You know you're never to call me during the day! This had better be important."

"I've got... we've got a problem... Tailhook... Helen... I need your help..."

DAN GAZED out through the terminal windows as a twin-engine turboprop aircraft taxied towards Palm Springs International Airport. A young woman wearing an orange vest and hearing protection, and wielding red-tipped flashlights in each hand, guided the connector flight from LAX into place on the tarmac. The aircraft stopped and the propellers gradually came to a rest. Workers scurried to get service vehicles and carts into position. The rear door finally opened, its built-in set of stairs lowering itself into place. After a few seconds, passengers began descending the stairs onto the tarmac. Many of them retrieved carry-on bags from a cart at the bottom of the stairs.

Dan stood patiently as the plane emptied and the stream of passengers began to thin. He checked his watch, wondering if he had the right flight. Just then, an elderly woman with short, silver hair, emerged through the aircraft's doorway with a flight attendant by her side, holding onto an elbow with one hand and the woman's carry-on bag with the other. The woman shook off the flight attendant's arm and grabbed the handrail. She guided herself down the stairs on shaky legs, pausing to straighten herself and to take a breath at the bottom.

The woman took the carry-on bag from the flight attendant and began walking towards the terminal, her legs appearing to gain strength with each step. She entered the terminal through an arrivals gate and paused, looking bewildered and lost. Dan hurried forward to meet her.

"Ms. Keaner?" Dan asked.

The woman's head turned toward the sound of Dan's voice. The bewildered look transformed into a friendly smile when she saw him.

"Dr. Whitney, I presume," she replied. "I'm so glad to finally meet you. Thank you for picking me up. You didn't have to trouble yourself, you know. I could have taken a taxi to the hotel."

"It's no trouble at all, Ms. Keaner," Dan said. "It was the least I could do after you flew all the way from Italy to be here for the hearings."

"Nonsense. I'd do anything for Fran. She was the closest I've ever had to a daughter. It's you I should thank for telling me about her troubles and inviting me here. By the way, you can stop with the 'Ms. Keaner' crap. My name is Susan," she said. Her smile was genuine and warm.

"Okay… Susan. And you can just call me Dan. The baggage carousels are this way," he said, pointing to the central core of the terminal. "Let me help you with your bag." Dan took the small bag and they began walking at a leisurely pace through the terminal.

"I'm sorry we can't put you up in the Chateau, but with all of our friends coming down from L.A. for the hearings, we were already fully booked," Dan said.

"No need to apologize," Susan replied, laughing. "It sounds like Chateau Eden might have been my kind of place forty years ago. But I don't think it's a place for a seventy-year-old woman anymore."

Dan smiled. He was already beginning to like Susan's down-to-earth, casual nature.

"I don't know about that," he answered. "We've got plenty of 'old hippies' who come to relax. Everybody who visits the Chateau regularly is comfortable with their bodies, so age just doesn't seem to matter."

"All the same, I think my days of skinny-dipping are long past," she said, chuckling.

They reached the luggage conveyor at the same time that a loud buzzer sounded and the machine came to life with a loud clunk.

"You'll like the Riviera," Dan said. "I had to spend a couple of nights there after… after what happened at Fran's estate," he said, choking back a wave of emotion as a flashback of Chelly took him by surprise.

"I'm sorry for your loss, Dan," Susan said. "From what I saw on CNN and the Internet, it must have been terrible for both you and Fran."

Dan swallowed hard and nodded in acknowledgment.

"I'll take you right to the Riviera so you can get some rest," he said. "Would you like to join some of Fran's friends for dinner tonight? It might be later in the evening, since they're all having to drive in from the city."

"If it's all the same to you," Susan added. "I think I'll just eat in the hotel tonight so I can get to bed at a decent time. I'll need my beauty sleep if I'm going to be up early tomorrow." She smiled at Dan.

"I like you," Susan said abruptly. "You seem like a genuinely caring person, unlike that Philippe fellow she married. I only met him once, that night in Manarola, but I didn't like him from the moment I set eyes on him. He had all the charm of a used car salesman. But he was Fran's ticket out of Manarola, and I knew I couldn't stand in her way. I understood. I felt the same way when I was young and couldn't wait to leave the States."

"Thanks, Susan," Dan said quietly. "I'll pick you up at eight o'clock tomorrow morning. That will get us to the courtroom in plenty of time. I can bring you up to date about Fran's case on the drive over to Indio."

"You're sure about picking me up?" Susan asked. "I can just arrange for a taxi. I'm sure you have others from the Chateau who could use the ride."

"I don't mind at all," Dan replied. "They all have their own cars. Besides, it will give us a chance to get to know each other, and to talk about Fran some more."

Once again, a warm smile radiated from Susan's face. "I look forward to it… oh, there's my bag, the big red one…"

"WHAT MORE could I have done for you?" Kelly Mulholland screamed.

She sat alone in her black BMW Z3 in the parking lot behind the District Attorney's office in Riverside. It was nine-thirty at night. The lot had long since emptied as other workers headed home to their families for the evening. The air was still hot on this late June evening, but Kelly's anger had her feeling superheated. The BMW idled with the air conditioning blowing directly in her face.

"Apparently you have a short memory, Madame District Attorney," Helen bristled. "Have you forgotten everything we've done for you in the past? Who took you under their wings to protect you from the others during your basic training? And who covered up for you and kept your name out of the Tailhook scandal? Do you think you ever would have got that honourable discharge, and had a political career, if people knew you were involved in that debauchery?"

"Are you kidding?" Kelly shouted into her cell phone. "I was a more a *victim* of Tailhook than one of the abusers! Anything I did was because you commanded me to do it. How dare you imply that I did anything wrong! And somebody must have found out. Why else would that nosey reporter—what's her name?—Marshall?—why would she be asking me about Tailhook all of a sudden? Are you responsible for that?"

"Hey, Kelly. The Pastor and I can vouch for your innocence," Helen said, her voice perfectly calm. "But I'm not so sure your husband or your constituents would believe you. You were an officer at that event, remember? And the careers of a great many officers—mostly men—went down the tubes afterwards. But not you, Kelly. You would have been one of them if I hadn't intervened on your behalf."

"I should have blown the whistle on *both* of you years ago," Kelly shouted. "Then whose careers would have ended?"

Kelly heard Helen howling with laughter on the other end of the line. She felt her face growing hot with rage at the other woman's lack of respect.

"And who would have listened to you, my dear?" Helen said, still chuckling. "A well-respected *female* officer *and* a chaplain sexually abusing you? Come on, Kelly. You and I both know they would have laughed you out of the military. And as for some snoopy reporter, don't flatter yourself. Don't think I'd waste my time passing information along to a small time reporter like her if I wanted to destroy you."

Silence filled the car. District Attorney Kelly Mulholland knew that Helen was right. She held Kelly's fate in her hands, and Kelly felt powerless to defend herself against the other woman. And the more powerless she felt, the more she hated Helen and that phoney, arrogant pastor.

"Are you still there, counsellor?" Helen asked. "Have you forgotten who helped cover up your drinking and your old cocaine habit, and who got you into rehab? And don't forget about your affair and those gambling debts. Bad things just seem to happen whenever you go to Las Vegas, don't they, Kelly?"

Mulholland fell silent again.

"Do I have your attention now, counsellor?" Helen hissed. It was a demand, not a question. Any sign of humour had left her voice.

There was more silence while Kelly Mulholland pondered her options. She felt numb and defeated.

"What do you want me to do?" she asked, her voice now totally emotionless.

"That's better. I don't care what you have to do during that hearing, but I don't want to see Capellini leave that jail until she tells you where Angela Baranyi is hiding!"

"But we've been through that," Kelly whined. "The woman doesn't know anything. Once the Grand Jury sees there's no connection between them, our case is going to look awfully weak. There's nothing more Vasquez and I can do! I beg you, just let it go!"

More silence on the other end. Kelly felt a faint glimmer of hope that she had finally got through to Helen. Her hope was short-lived.

"Maybe Capellini doesn't know. But her boyfriend, Whitney, and that fucking Anika Kristiansen—they know where she is! So find a way for Capellini to find out from them!" Helen screamed. "Listen, you ungrateful bitch. You dare talk back to me like this after all I've done for you? Do you know how easy it would be for me to destroy your career? One phone call to a reporter at the local paper or TV station and your career is over! So what's it going to be, Kelly? Are you and Vasquez going to do your job, or can I assume that you are no longer of any use to me?"

Kelly Mulholland couldn't stop her racing mind, but she gradually managed to salvage a semblance of order out of her internal chaos. There *was* one option—one dim light at the end of the tunnel. She made up her mind. Almost immediately, she felt a sense of relief wash over her, like the weight of the universe had just been lifted from her shoulders.

"So, Kelly. What's it going to be?" Helen's voice at the other end of the line jolted Mulholland out of the chaos within her head, and back into reality inside her car.

"Okay. I think there's a way out of this," she said calmly. "Leave it to me. I won't disappoint you again. I'll need tonight to work out the details with Kevin. Just keep an eye on tomorrow's proceedings at the hearing. I guarantee it will be anything but dull."

"That's my girl," Helen said. It occurred to Kelly that it was like somebody had just flicked a switch—as if Helen had become another person. Her mood had gone from sweet and patronizing to psychopathic rage, then back to sweet and patronizing in a matter of only a couple of minutes.

"Thank you, Kelly. I knew you'd understand," Helen said. "I'll be watching, so just make sure you don't disappoint me. Watch for a call from me tomorrow night."

"I wouldn't miss it for the world," Kelly said, a smile finally lifting the corners of her mouth upward and smoothing out the creases in her forehead for the first time in weeks. "Goodnight."

She pressed the *Hangup* button on her mobile phone, and then sat in silence while she collected her thoughts. Finally, she pressed the speed-dial number for her husband's mobile phone and listened while it rang continuously.

"Come on!" she muttered. "Pick up, will you!" Her call went to voicemail. "Hi, babe. Kelly here. Gotta stay late to get ready for the big case tomorrow. Don't wait up, I'll see ya later."

Kelly Mulholland reached under the driver's seat and pulled out the full bottle of vodka she had bought over the lunch hour. She screwed off the top and tipped the bottle back, letting the burning liquid go straight to the back of her throat without lingering in her mouth. She felt its heat shooting down her esophagus and into her stomach. But the liquor didn't feel like it was burning. Instead, she felt a numbness, at first localized in those tissues, but then spreading slowly outward. She sat in the darkness, letting her plan crystallize in her mind. She sat up and threw her head back for a second shot, adding to the numbness that was spreading through her body. At the same time, she began to feel more relaxed. She could almost visualize light at the end of a long tunnel. She stashed the bottle of vodka between her legs.

"Fuck you, Helen!" she screamed.

Kelly Mulholland turned up the radio until it was blaring. She selected some CD's, scrolling through Norah Jones, Ne-Yo, and Shakira until she came to something that fit her mood. The dark wailing sounds of Nirvana filled the car. She turned up the volume, put the Z3 in gear, and the sound of squealing rubber echoed through downtown Riverside. Before long, she had the sleek car on Highway 60, racing east towards Interstate 10. She reached between her legs and took another swig of vodka.

Like the Z3, Kelly Mulholland's mind raced. Her adrenaline pumped. Her vision became blurred. She failed to notice that she was blazing along the Interstate at a hundred and ten mph. She drifted across the centre line, but a blast from a transport truck's horn startled her. She jerked the wheel back to the right. Over-steering slightly, she momentarily lost control of the car and the results were almost disastrous. Kelly finally managed to wrest the vehicle back under her control.

The faster the car went, the faster Kelly's thoughts raced, and the clearer her plan became. A few minutes before the turnoff to Palm Springs, she geared down and the powerful engine roared. She slowed for the right turn into San Jacinto State Park. She drove up the road for about two hundred yards before gearing down again, then finally bringing the Z3 to a stop on the side of the road. She let the engine idle. Reaching between her legs again, she raised the vodka to her lips and took a long, satisfying shot.

Kelly now had a serious buzz from the crystal clear liquor. She felt lighter and more carefree than she had felt for years. She leaned to her right, opened the glove box and reached inside. The shiny, dark steel of the new revolver was still warm from the intense afternoon heat. She reached back into the glove box for the new box of shells. It had been years since she'd used a gun in the military, but tonight the weapon felt totally at home in her right hand.

"Just like riding a bike," she said to herself, laughing out loud as she loaded the shells into the firearm. She laid the gun down on the seat beside her and tipped the bottle back with both hands.

Mulholland let another blast of the fiery liquid shoot deep into her throat. The numbness had now invaded her entire body. This last shot made her feel both more relaxed and more powerful at the same time. She put the bottle between her legs, turned the key, and shut down the Z3 so that she was now enveloped in darkness. The sleek black vehicle was invisible from the highway. District Attorney Kelly Mulholland now had all the confidence she needed that her plan would succeed. Still holding the vodka in her left hand, she reached for the revolver with her right. Without any further thought or hesitation, she thrust the barrel into her mouth and pulled the trigger. The sound of the explosion and the smell of gunpowder filled the vehicle. Kelly Mulholland was finally free from Helen, the bane of her existence, forever.

CHAPTER 33

DAN'S STOMACH gurgled. His hands were moist with nervous anticipation as he surveyed the courtroom. A muted rumble of conversation from onlookers, reporters, and Fran's small group of supporters drifted through the room. Unlike Fran's arraignment, when the room was filled to capacity, there were still plenty of empty seats today. A mere three months after Chelly and Philippe had died so tragically, Fran's Grand Jury hearing was already becoming old news. Dan recalled the crowds of protesters and reporters that had previously turned the arraignment into a media circus, forcing their entourage to use the rear entrance to the Courthouse. Today was a different story. Dan, Joanna Sullivan, Susan Keaner, and the small band of Fran's loyal friends from Chateau Eden were able to enter the courthouse by the front door. They barely attracted any attention from the few reporters who were assigned to cover the proceedings, which were expected to take up to two weeks.

Fran and Joanna were already seated at the Defense table, engaged in conversation. Fran wasn't yet aware that Dan and Susan had arrived. Dan turned his gaze to the Prosecution table, where Kevin Vasquez reviewed a thick sheaf of notes in front of him. He looked down at his watch to check the time. As usual, Vasquez was impeccably dressed and his jet-black hair was neatly groomed. He shuffled and rearranged the notes in front of him, then checked his watch again.

"Probably waiting for Mulholland to make another one of her grand last minute appearances," Dan said to himself. Vasquez shifted in his seat and checked his watch again.

Dan looked down the row at their friends, feeling thankful that Fran had such a close group of faithful supporters. He smiled at Susan, who was sitting beside him on his right. Dan had told her all about Jonah Kristiansen's abduction, his long friendship with Anika, and their night together in Darwin, as they drove from Palm Springs to Indio this morning. He summarized, as best he could, his conflicting feelings for Fran and Anika in the weeks following Chelly's death, and his realization that he loved Fran and wanted to make a life with her and their future child. Susan responded to Dan's smile with a nervous one of her own. She took Dan's hand in hers. She had listened to him without judgment and she had believed him.

He looked down the row and made eye contact with Pam Holloway, who nodded and smiled in return. Richard was engaged in conversation with Gwen Perkins and Miriam Fox. Shelley and Tim sat at the end of the row. Tim acknowledged Dan with a smile, raising his hand to show that his fingers were crossed for good luck. Shelley made brief eye contact. She was still more distant since learning about his indiscretion with Anika.

"All rise," the bailiff called. The gallery rose to their feet as a door at the front of the courtroom opened and a familiar silver-haired man in black robes entered. "Riverside County Grand Jury is now in session, His Honor Ernest Hartley presiding."

"Please be seated," Hartley announced as he took his seat at the front of the courtroom. The sounds of people settling into their seats slowly dissipated, leaving a few seconds of expectant silence. Dan saw Joanna Sullivan look at the Defense table, then look at her watch. She said something to Fran. At that moment, Fran shifted in her seat and turned her body slightly, looking over her shoulder at the gallery, searching for her friends and supporters. Her eyes met Dan's, then just as quickly broke eye contact and moved slowly to his right as she recognized her friends. Suddenly, her eyes jumped back in Dan's direction. She stared at Susan Keaner. A look of initial shock, followed by one of recognition, spread across her face. Dan watched as she wiped a tear from one eye, and then turned her attention back to Joanna.

The door at the front of the courtroom opened. A female police officer rushed up to the bailiff and whispered into his ear. A look of surprise and shock replaced his usual stony demeanour. He thanked the officer and rushed, almost breaking into a jog, up to the bench and Judge Hartley. He whispered something into Hartley's ear. Almost immediately, Hartley's face went white. He placed his hand on the bailiff's shoulder, seemingly thanking him for the message. After a brief pause, he picked up his gavel and gave it one abrupt bang.

"Mr. Vasquez, will you please approach the bench." Joanna Sullivan started to rise from her seat. "Ms. Sullivan. Just a moment. You'll have your chance after I talk with Mr. Vasquez."

Dan saw Kevin Vasquez exchange puzzled looks with Joanna as he approached the bench. Judge Hartley leaned forward and whispered quietly in Vasquez's ear. A look of shock replaced the young prosecutor's normally calm appearance and his face went pale. Hartley waited while Vasquez digested whatever the judge had told him. Finally, Vasquez leaned forward and engaged Hartley in a short conversation. When Kevin Vasquez was finished, another look of surprise crossed Judge Hartley's face. Dan read his lips as he responded to Vasquez.

Are you sure? Kevin Vasquez bobbed his head up and down to confirm. Hartley turned his attention to Joanna.

"Ms. Sullivan, would you please approach the bench." Joanna leapt to her feet and rushed to the bench to join the conversation. Whatever it was they were discussing, the looks of shock were contagious, soon spreading to Joanna Sullivan's face. She stared at Kevin Vasquez and said something to him. He nodded affirmatively, then both lawyers stood still in front of the judge. Hartley cleared his voice, and then gave another abrupt bang of his gavel.

"The court has just been informed of the sudden, unexpected death of District Attorney Mulholland." A collective gasp rose from the gallery, followed by a crescendo of conversation. Hartley brought the gavel down again. "Order… Order, please!"

Fran turned in her seat and her eyes met Dan's. He saw both shock and fear in her eyes, uncertain about what the sudden news might mean for her. Her eyes drifted to Dan's right again, staring at Susan Keaner as if she'd just seen a ghost and wanted to make sure it was real. Hartley slammed the gavel one last time.

"After consulting with Mr. Vasquez of the District Attorney's office, he has informed me that Riverside County wishes to drop all charges against Francesca Capellini in regards to the deaths of Philippe Morel, Diego Alvarez, and Juanita Alvarez."

The gallery erupted and Judge Hartley's voice was lost in the uproar. Dan saw the gavel come down again and saw that Hartley's lips were still moving.

These Grand Jury proceedings are hereby dismissed. Ms. Capellini, you are free to go.

Dan sat in shock. He felt Susan Keaner's hands gripping and shaking his right arm. He saw Fran's head go down on the table and rest on her arms, presumably from a mixture of shock and relief. To Dan's right, Pam, Richard, Miriam, Gwen, Tim, and Shelley were on their feet, clapping or throwing their hands in the air, shouting with joy. Shelley managed to give Dan a slight smile.

Dan took Susan by the hand and helped her to her feet. She let go of his hand and placed hers on his back, nodding and pushing him forward. The reality of what had just occurred finally hit Dan. He made his way to the aisle and ran up to the Defense table, where Fran and Joanna were locked in an embrace. When it was over, Fran turned her head and found Dan standing expectantly beside them.

Dan's eyes met Fran's. She paused, unsure what to do. Dan raised his arms and held them open. It was all the invitation she needed. Fran collapsed into his arms and tears began streaming from her eyes. Dan held her, allowing her to weep and vent all of the emotions and frustration that she'd stored inside for over two months. Dan turned to Joanna.

"What happened?" he asked.

"To Kelly? I don't know yet," Joanna replied. "But Vasquez admitted this case was her baby. He conceded that he didn't think he could win. He couldn't understand why she wouldn't let it go. I guess we'll never know why now."

Dan extended his right hand.

"Thank you for everything you've done for Fran," he said.

"It was my privilege," Joanna replied. "Now you two can look forward to your baby and moving ahead with your lives. Anyway, I'll leave you two alone now. All the best to both of you."

Fran lifted her head from Dan's chest and wiped the tears from her eyes. She and Dan exchanged final handshakes with Joanna, who gathered up her briefcase and hurried from the courtroom, surrounded by a cluster of reporters.

Dan and Fran stood alone, facing each other in awkward silence. She hesitated, and then she fell back into Dan's arms, her head resting on his shoulder. She resumed sobbing. Her tears of exhaustion and relief refused to stop, causing her body to tremble. Finally, when her tears were depleted, she lifted her head and whispered in his ear.

"Susan? Susan came?"

Dan squeezed Fran even more tightly.

"I asked her to come. I didn't know what else I could do for you," he admitted. She gazed into Dan's eyes.

"Thank you," Fran whispered. She pressed her lips onto Dan's, kissing him once, then a second time—this time full of longing. She wrapped her arms around him and pressed her body close to his. It was then that Dan felt the warmth of her round belly, and their child, pressing against him for the first time.

FRAN FELT the tears streaming from her eyes, her body vibrating with the rhythm of her sobs. She clung her long lost mentor, as if she was afraid she'd never see her again. She saw Dan from the corner of her eye and barely heard his voice.

"I'll leave you two to reconnect while I talk with the others," Dan said, placing his hands briefly on their shoulders before he stepped back, He walked towards their friends, who were waiting patiently a few yards away.

Finally, Fran released her grip on her old friend. She placed her hands gently on each side of Susan's face and gazed into the older woman's friendly eyes.

"When?… Why?… How did you find out?"

Susan turned her head and looked towards Dan, who was now hugging and shaking hands with the crowd from Chateau Eden.

"I think you have a very special man over there. He went to a great deal of trouble to track me down. He cares a great deal for you, Fran."

Fran nodded her head slowly and silently. She had trouble finding the right words.

"I'm so afraid, Susan," she whispered. "After Philippe…"

The older woman took Fran into her arms and held her against her chest.

"I know, dear. I know you're afraid. But he's not at all like Philippe, is he?" Fran shook her head against Susan's chest. "I had the worst feeling when you left with Philippe."

Fran lifted her head from Susan's chest. "Then why didn't you say something?"

"Would you have listened?" Susan asked. "I knew how badly you wanted to get away from Manarola—to see the world—and I know you thought he loved you."

Fran nodded. "You're right, as you always were. I was so vulnerable and naive. I know now that I mistook his interest in me for love. But now I know he was only interested in money and control."

"I think Dan is genuinely sorry for what he did with his old girlfriend," Susan said. "Don't you think he needed to find out if he had any feelings left for her?"

Fran nodded silently again. "I don't know if I will ever be able to fully trust a man. What if it doesn't work out with Dan?"

"I can't answer that, Fran. But I do know that you'll never know unless you give him a chance. And more than anything, I know you. I've always known that the strong, independent side of you will manage to survive, no matter what happens to you," Susan said, holding Fran firmly by the shoulders. "I believe in you."

Fran felt more tears welling in her eyes as she looked into the kindly eyes of her former mentor.

"That's the part of me that you named Fran. With your help, it's the part of me that managed to rise above a frightened little girl named Francesca. I think I lost touch with that part of me over the past few weeks. I think I became that little girl again—the little girl who trusted nobody."

Fran embraced Susan again, holding her tightly.

"Thank you for coming, Susan. Thank you for reminding me of who I am."

Fran released Susan and took her by the hand.

"Have you met my friends yet?" she asked.

"Just Dan," Susan said. "I only arrived yesterday afternoon, and he took me straight to my hotel."

"How long are you going to be able to stay?" Fran inquired.

"At least three weeks. I haven't been back to the States in a while, and I can change my return flight without a penalty. Some of my old friends from the gay community in Seattle are living in Laguna Beach and San Diego now. They've invited me to stay as long as I want."

"Then you will have lots of time to meet my friends," Fran said. "Let me introduce you to them."

"I'd love that," Susan said.

Fran took Susan by the arm and walked her towards Dan and the rest of the group. As she made introductions, she gradually moved closer to Dan, as if she was attracted by a magnet. He turned his eyes towards her. She was hesitant, like a shy young girl. A weak smile formed on her face. She felt traces of the strong, independent Fran trying to struggle their way to the surface. Her hand searched until it found the warmth of Dan's hand. It felt awkward, but she also felt a sense of reassurance from his touch.

Susan is right. I have to give him a chance. I'll never know unless I try.

THE FRENCH door closed behind Fran as she and Dan stepped into Chateau Eden's Italian-themed room together for the first time in over two months. Predominantly white, with touches of pastel colours from the room's watercolour paintings and accessories, the room was immediately soothing. Dinner with their friends had been a celebration that nobody had expected. Dan had sat in the background for most of the meal, allowing Fran to take centre stage and to reconnect with their friends. Now, they were finally alone together.

Dan felt an awkward silence fill the room. He almost felt like they were strangers on a first date, just starting to get to know each other. He didn't quite know where to start.

"I can't tell you how wonderful it was to see you with everybody tonight—smiling and laughing—everybody celebrating and drinking wine—almost as if none of this had ever happened. What's it like to be home again, and to be free?" Dan asked.

Fran, looking tired and pale, kicked off her sandals and sat on the edge of the bed. Dan sat down beside her.

"It feels so surreal," she answered. "Almost like a dream—like I don't belong here. I can't really explain it. It is like I'm lost and I don't know where I belong anymore. Does that make any sense?"

"I think so," Dan replied. "I know I can't ever truly understand what it must have been like for you in that jail. But I felt something similar while I was on the road helping Anika. For the longest time, I felt totally disconnected and anxious about my future. I was struggling with the fact that Chelly is gone—and about whether or not you and I had a future. And I admit it—I also wondered whether it was fate for Anika and me to get together. I'm pretty sure I was feeling lost too."

"And now?" Fran asked.

"I remember waking up that morning after Anika and I made love. I watched her sleep, and I had the overpowering feeling that it was all wrong. For some strange reason, I just knew that Anika and I weren't right for each other. And I found myself longing for the connection that we'd made, right from the day you gave Chelly and me our massages after we arrived at the Chateau. I knew I belonged with you and wanted to spend my life with you—even before I knew you were pregnant. Watching Anika that morning is the moment I stopped feeling lost.

"I've had lots of time to think about this—especially after coming so close to dying in Australia and Vietnam. I can't tell you how sorry I am for what happened between Anika and me. I'm sorry if I hurt you and betrayed your trust. But I promise you that I'm totally committed to you and our baby now. I'll do whatever I can to show that you can trust me. I have something worth living for now. You and our child are my future, wherever we go, or whatever we decide to do, starting today."

Dan felt his emotions welling up inside him and his eyes getting teary. He moved closer to Fran and kissed her gently on the forehead.

"You know I had a lot of time to think too," Fran said. "Too much time. After all the things that happened to me during my childhood in Manarola, and with the way Philippe treated me, you know it is hard for me to trust anybody. Part of me secretly hoped that you would choose Anika over me. I thought that it would make it so much easier. It would just prove to me again that I can never trust anybody—that I should keep pushing people away for the rest of my life. But another part of me knew that I didn't want to lose you. So I needed to find out, once and for all, if you had any feelings left for her. If making love to Anika that night helped you to figure that out, then I suppose it is something that was meant to happen. Thank you for telling me. It must have been very difficult."

Fran leaned forward and kissed Dan gently on his lips.

"One more thing," Fran continued. "I don't know if I can ever thank you enough for finding and inviting Susan to come here. She is the only person in this world I have ever been able to trust. She thinks that you're a very special man, so I have to trust her instincts and give you a chance. Can you forgive me for being so distant and for pushing you away while I was in prison? Can you give me time to learn to trust you and to love you?"

Dan took Fran in his arms and held her close. He gazed into her eyes and touched his lips gently to hers.

"Fran, I know it's not going to be easy for you. But I'll do whatever it takes to prove that you can learn to trust me," Dan said. He placed a hand on Fran's dress, on top of her abdomen, feeling the bump that was their child. "Can I touch it?"

Fran nodded. She stood up and reached behind her neck to unfasten the zipper on her loose white summer dress. Dan stood and moved around behind her, grasping the zipper himself and pulling it down. He slid the dress from her shoulders, leaving her standing in front of him in just her bra and panties. Fran took his hand and placed it on her bump, then rested her own hand beside his. They stood together, silently, waiting for something to happen.

"Did you feel that?" Fran said. "That tiny little flutter?"

"I did!" Dan answered, his voice full of wonder. "I can't believe you can feel it already."

"It only just started this week," Fran said.

"When are you due?" Dan asked.

"Around Christmas time."

"Wow. I can't think of a better Christmas present. Can you?" Dan exclaimed. "What do you think about having a pregnancy portrait taken when you get bigger? Seeing you pregnant is the most beautiful thing I've ever seen."

"Thank you," she answered, laughing. "We'll see how beautiful you think I am when I'm nine months pregnant."

Fran looked into Dan's eyes and moved her lips to his, barely touching them with a series of small butterfly kisses. She began undoing the buttons on his shirt. When she finished, she loosened his belt and his pants, and began removing his clothing. Dan felt himself growing long and hard as her fingers brushed against his manhood. Finally, when she removed his underclothing, his erection sprung free.

Dan undid Fran's bra. His fingers, then his lips, gently brushed the skin on her breasts, and then teased her nipples until they stood erect. He slid her panties off slowly, carefully caressing the skin on her legs in the process, until she finally stepped out of the undergarment. He let his lips and tongue leave a trail of light kisses up the inside of her legs and thighs, working his way carefully towards the centre of her arousal, until his tongue lingered and teased her outer lips, now sweet and moist.

Dan stood and faced Fran, taking her in his arms and pressing himself against her, skin on skin, his erection pressing against her genitals. Their lips pressed together, this time kissing with more passion and desperation. Their breathing quickened.

"Punish me, Dan." Fran whispered. "Spank me or use the crop. I deserve to be punished for all I've put you through."

Dan was stunned. He stepped back and held Fran by the shoulders. He looked into her eyes, then down at her abdomen, his mouth hanging open in surprise.

"But you're pregnant! I can't do that. I'll hurt the baby," Dan answered.

"You don't have to do it hard," Fran said. "Just enough to make my skin come alive."

"No. I can't do it," Dan replied. "If anybody should be punished, it's me. I'm the one who was unfaithful to you and slept with Anika. Please… you know that a part of you has been angry and wanted to punish me, ever since I told you."

Fran pressed her lips and body against Dan again, her desire continuing to grow. Then, without warning, she stopped.

"Kneel on the bed," she ordered. She walked around the bed to a bedside table. Opening the table's lower cabinet, she removed a riding crop. Now kneeling on the bed, Dan saw Fran snap the crop sharply against her other hand. He felt his erection growing harder, pulsing as she moved around behind him at the foot of the bed. He waited breathlessly for a sharp snap against his skin. Instead, he felt Fran slowly tracing patterns on the bottom of his feet with the crop, tickling them and teasing him. Then, without warning, she gave it a quick snap on his buttocks. It stung at first, and then he felt the skin getting hot and his nerve endings coming alive. Next, the crop was teasing the inside of his thighs, even sneaking beneath his scrotum and teasing his balls. Then another sudden sting on his rear end. She picked up the pace, snapping the crop on his buttocks until it was covered in red welts, like a collection of bee stings.

Dan felt her drop the crop beside his knee. Before he had time to think he felt a sharp smack on one butt cheek as Fran spanked him hard. The pain quickly turned to heat, the energy from the stimulation channeling directly into his already straining erection. Then she stopped.

"Stand up on your knees," she ordered. Dan complied, rising onto his knees on the bed. He felt Fran climb onto the bed, then felt the heat of her body pressing against his back, her arms wrapping around him, and her fingers running through the hair on his chest. She covered the side of his face and his neck with kisses. One of her hands worked its way slowly downward, first teasing his balls, and then stroking his hard shaft with light, purposeful stimulation. Then, without warning she grabbed his throbbing member and squeezed. The intensity of the sensation, somewhere between pain and ecstasy, caused Dan to moan.

"I need you inside, Dan. On your back, now."

As soon as he was on his back, Fran climbed on top of him. She wasted no time lowering herself and guiding him into her. She leaned forward, pressing his hard shaft against her G-spot, while locking her lips against his. Then he felt her dig her fingernails into his back. And she started to ride him—desperately—like he'd never been ridden before.

FRAN LAY with her head on Dan's chest, enjoying the peaceful afterglow of their lovemaking. Eventually, Dan had dozed off. She ran her fingers through the hair on his chest, gently twirling and playing with it. His body twitched and his eyes opened, reorienting himself to where he was. She felt his lips kiss her gently on the top of her head.

"You're still awake?" Dan asked. "Trouble sleeping?"

"No trouble," she answered. "Just enjoying the moment— touching you and smelling you—realizing how much I missed you and need you. Sorry if I woke you up."

"No worries. Sorry I fell asleep."

They lay in silence, their fingers wandering, stroking, and enjoying every small touch of each other's bodies.

"What are you thinking?" Dan asked, breaking the silence.

"About Susan… and about home… Cinque Terre. There's a special place there—the Via del Amore—*The Way of Love*. It's the walking path between Manarola and Riomaggiore, the town next to mine where I went to school. At night, you can walk along the coast between the two towns. When the full moon is reflecting off the waters of the Mediterranean, I think it is the most beautiful place on earth."

"Sounds idyllic," Dan whispered.

"Young lovers go there at night," Fran continued. "They fasten locks to the fences along the pathway, with their names inscribed on the locks. Custom says that it seals their love forever. I would like to take you there sometime."

Dan sat up. She felt his fingers running through her short, dark hair, massaging her scalp. She loved the relaxing sensation.

"I thought you never wanted to go back there again," Dan said. "Too many painful memories."

"I did," she replied. "But seeing Susan again, and realizing how much I need to learn to trust myself to love you, I realize I need to go home—for closure, if for nothing else. I want you to see where I come from—to see Susan's gallery. I want to swim naked in the Mediterranean at sunrise again. And I want you swimming by my side to see how magical and beautiful it is."

"I'd love to do that with you," Dan said. Fran fell back into his arms again.

"There's something else I want to do with you," Fran said softly.

"Make love again?" Dan said, chuckling.

"That too!" Fran replied, smiling. "But something else."

"What is it?" Dan asked.

"It's a secret. I can show you tomorrow if you like. Can you come with me?" she said.

"Sure, I don't have any plans. So it's a secret, eh? Can you give me a hint?"

"No, I don't want to give it away. You'll have to wait until tomorrow," Fran whispered, teasing.

Dan's hand moved from Fran's breast onto her stomach and then over her baby bump. She felt him rub it gently, affectionately.

"I'm not very sleepy anymore," he said. "What are we going to do until tomorrow morning?"

Fran gazed into his eyes, seeing the love in her man's eyes. She let her fingers do the talking. Her hand started circling Dan's chest, her fingers playing with his chest hair, gradually working their way downward. She felt him stirring. By the time her fingers arrived at his manhood, he was well on his way to another erection. Her lips found his. This time, her kisses were gentle, exploring, less desperate and demanding. She decided she was going to make this night last as long as she could. It was going to be a night to celebrate and remember.

CHAPTER 34

JONAH KRISTIANSEN sat on the carpet, Lego blocks scattered around him, crying. It had been two whole days since Lucy had gone to the store for groceries, but she never came back. This morning, Father introduced him to his new tutor, Agnetha, who would be teaching him to speak Norwegian. He missed Lucy terribly, and he felt sick to his stomach with fear. His young mind drifted back to the last time he saw her.

"Why don't you go to the store for groceries while Jonah has his Norwegian lesson?" Father said.

"Why hasn't Lucy come home yet?" Jonah asked later.

"She decided to go back home to America," Father said.

Jonah had a bad feeling that Father lied to him.

"Is Mommy going to be coming to live with us in Norway?" he asked.

"Not yet, Jonah. The bad people are still following her. It's still not safe for her to come. Daddy has a friend who wants to come and help take care of you, just like Lucy did. But she might not be able to come for a few weeks. Do you think you can wait that long?" Father answered.

"No, I'm lonely. I miss Mommy," he said. *"I don't want your friend."*

Jonah resumed his crying as he remembered his mother. He got up off the floor and went to the sliding door onto the balcony. Lucy and father had told him not to go out there on his own. But Father went out for a few hours and Lucy was gone. Nobody would know. He released the door lock and flipped open the safety bar. The door was heavy and he had to throw all of his weight on the handle to overcome inertia.

The warm air and sunshine felt wonderful after the chilly, air-conditioned atmosphere of the apartment. He heard the wind rustling through leaves on the trees in yards across the street. He wanted to go for a walk. He missed his walks with Lucy. He remembered his days with Lucy in Australia—when she took him to the park, and when he played on the climbing fort and pretended he was the king of his castle. He remembered the lady with the hat who told him that Mommy was going to come and find him in Australia. Then he remembered Father waking him early in the morning, while it was still dark. And then the scary boat ride on the ocean. Mommy would never find him in Australia now. He started to cry again and went back inside the apartment. He was lonely and bored.

Jonah took the TV remote in his hand, pushed the big orange button and waited for the picture to turn on. The TV was still tuned to an English language station that he and Lucy watched together. It was noon hour and the news was on. He wished there were some cartoons to watch.

Weary and hungry, he wandered into the kitchen and opened the fridge. Father had bought him fruit, yogurt, and granola bars to eat, so he reached for a container of strawberry yogurt and then he got a spoon from a drawer. He wandered back into the living room, but immediately stopped in his tracks.

'Police are still trying to identify the body of an Asian woman that was discovered last night in the harbour in Moss. The woman, who was about a hundred and fifty centimetres in height, was not carrying any identification. Anybody who is missing a loved one, or who has any information, is encouraged to contact the Moss Police Department at the number shown on your screen.'

Jonah shivered. A chill went down the length of his spine.

Why did Lucy go out for groceries if she knew she was going back to America?

He spooned yogurt slowly into his mouth. Tears began welling in his eyes again. Shivering, he put the yogurt and spoon down on the coffee table and went to the sliding door again, pushing it wide open. He retrieved the yogurt and spoon and took them out onto the balcony so he could sit in the summer sun. Its warmth helped to make him feel safer. He spooned the yogurt slowly into his mouth. He watched two young children playing under the shade of a tree across the street. Watching them only made him feel lonelier.

Finished eating his yogurt, Jonah rose from his chair to get something else to eat. As he closed the patio door behind him, he froze. The voice on the TV was unmistakable.

"... *we can negotiate a joint custody agreement where everybody—you, Jonah, and me—can move forward and have a happy future. Jonah, if you can see and hear me. I hope you know how much I love you and want to be with you again. Even though your mommy and daddy aren't getting along right now, I want you to know that it's not your fault. It's up to Mommy and Daddy to work things out so that you'll be able to see both of as much as you want in the future. I love you...*"

Tears filled Jonah's eyes as he gazed at his mother on TV. "She *is* looking for me," he said aloud. He felt excitement exploding in his small body. A split screen, with a picture of himself on the left, and one of Father on the right, replaced the image of his mother. A yellow banner appeared at the bottom of the video with a local Norwegian phone number superimposed. Jonah listened to the voiceover in the background. Suddenly, he jumped up and ran to the coffee table, grabbing his colouring book and a red crayon. He scribbled the phone number, finishing just as the banner with the phone number disappeared.

Jonah stared at the phone number, his small body trembling with excitement. He ran into the bedroom and dropped to his knees, and then to his stomach, on the floor. Spying what he was looking for, just beneath the edge of his bed, he reached for Lucy's mobile phone.

Thank you, God, for making Lucy forget her phone when she went for groceries.

He ran back to the living room and his colouring book. He carefully pressed the buttons corresponding to the numbers scrawled in red crayon. When he finished, he held the phone to his ear, but nothing happened. He stared at the phone again, then he noticed two other buttons - one with a green image of a phone off hook, and another red image showing the phone hung up. He pressed the green button and held the phone to his ear. He felt his heart pounding in his chest as he heard the phone start ringing. Suddenly the line clicked and a voice answered. At first, Jonah couldn't find his voice. Then, suddenly, words started spewing from his mouth.

"Hello? My name is Jonah Kristiansen. I'm five years old and I just saw pictures of me and my mommy on TV…"

"OW! I can't believe I let you talk me into this!" Dan squawked. "You didn't tell me it was going to hurt!"

"Stop being such a big baby," Fran replied. "Millions of people get tattoos, and they have all survived. Besides, we're both trying to get better at living in the moment. Remember? Think of it as living up to your part of the bargain."

"Ow!… How long is this going to take?" Dan muttered, craning his neck to talk to the young lady who was injecting dyes into the design on his lower back.

"Only about two or three more hours. Can you please lie still?" she said impatiently.

"If I'd known that, maybe I would have picked a simpler design," he answered, chuckling.

"I never told you this before, Dan," Fran said. "But this is something Chelly and I were going to do… before she died. She wanted to see you…"

"Take a walk on the wild side," Dan said quietly, finishing her sentence. Apart from the buzz of the tattoo machine, the room suddenly became quiet. "That's why you suggested the eagle too—you're doing this for Chelly, aren't you?"

Fran nodded silently.

"Are you sure you're okay with this? Having my ex-wife's tattoo on my back?" Dan asked.

"If not for Chelly, we would not be together right now—having a child together." Fran leaned forward and kissed Dan on the side of his head. He reached out his hand and Fran clasped it with hers, their fingers intertwined.

"Then I guess I can put up with a little bit of pain. Are you excited about the new house—and moving here to Las Vegas?" he asked.

"Yes. I'm glad we decided to get away from Palm Springs and the valley. I love the new house. Like Chateau Eden, it is private and quiet. And the pool is private too—perfect for both of us to swim nude, and to feel the water flow freely over our skin."

"Speaking of the Chateau," Dan said. "It's a wonderful thing you did for Carmen and Rodrigo—offering to let them buy the hotel over time. They're good people and it means a lot to them."

"I'm looking forward to a new beginning for all of us," Fran answered. "What about you? Are you excited about your new office?"

"You bet... ow!..."

"Keep still," the tattoo artist said. "You want this to look like it was done by some kid in kindergarten?"

"Sorry," Dan answered. "Oh yeah... the office. I've always wanted to start my own practice, but I never really had the guts to do it. Besides, I needed to be in a bigger city if I'm going to specialize in treating trauma and PTSD. The valley just wasn't the right place for that. I think we made the right decision, don't you?"

"Yes," she replied. "It will be a good place to move the art agency too. Just as many high profile clients visit Las Vegas as Los Angeles."

"And don't forget your photography," Dan added. "What better place for doing professional portraits of celebrities?"

"Perhaps… after the child…"

"Don't be so shy, Fran. Listen to what Susan told you. She knows how talented you are. She believes in you. And so do I. Even Philippe knew you could have sold your portraits for a good price - and you have to admit he knew the art business."

"I know you're right," she admitted. "I suppose I also need to learn to take a walk…"

"… on the wild side," Dan added. They laughed together. "Ow!…,"

"Will you two stop horsing around," the young woman scolded. "If you don't, this is going to look more like a vulture than an eagle."

"Yes, ma'am," Dan said sarcastically. He smiled at Fran and tried not to laugh again. It felt good for them to finally be on the same page. They both still had a lot of demons to exorcise, but he felt more confident each day that they were going to be able to make it together.

"So your ex had this same design?" the artist asked. Dan looked at Fran.

"Yes," Fran answered for him. "She was special to both of us, and the design was very meaningful for her. She'd been through some bad times. For her, it meant that she was free of her past. Now I know what she must have felt…"

Fran fell silent. Dan knew her mind was drifting. He squeezed her hand. "You don't have to talk about it now," he said.

"I need to," she answered. "Do you know what it's like to be in jail—to feel like there is nothing you can do about it? Like you are just a puppet, with somebody else controlling the strings?"

Dan felt a lump forming in his throat, and tears of empathy starting to form in his eyes. He was well aware of the classic psychological research, now considered unethical, where animals simply gave up when they learned they were helpless to escape pain. He knew how helpless Fran must have felt, and how it must have affected her.

"I felt that way when I was young, in Manarola… also with Philippe… and again when I was in prison. It's easy to give up, and to feel nothing. I never want to feel that way again," Fran said, as she squeezed Dan's hand.

"Like Chelly, I know now what it feels like to be free. And I think I learned a lesson when my charges were dropped so unexpectedly. When things are completely out of control—even if I cannot control anything—I can always control myself and how I react. I think I knew that once. It's probably why I chose to leave Manarola with Philippe. But after many years with him, I forgot. And while I was in that prison cell, I forgot again. It's a lesson I can never allow myself to forget again."

Dan swallowed. He was proud of her inner strength and her resilience. He squeezed her hand again.

"We should have a house-warming party for our friends after we move," Fran said. "To celebrate our new beginning."

"Great idea," Dan answered. "It's a good thing we have immediate possession. Do you think we could do it while Susan is still here in the States?"

"We could try for two weeks from now, just before she goes back to Italy. That would give Pam and Richard, Tim and Shelley, and the others lots of notice," Fran replied.

Dan was happy to hear the excitement in Fran's voice. Despite the pain in his lower back from the tattoo machine, he felt a warm feeling of contentment spreading through his body.

"Do you think Angela and Anika would be able to come?" Fran asked. Dan was caught off guard by the question, unsure how to answer. His eyes looked up at Fran, questioning her silently.

"Are you sure? After what happened?" he said, after the awkward pause.

"They're your friends, and you went through a lot together. I'm okay," Fran added.

"Well… Angela has dropped out of sight, now that she knows Soren is after her. I think she's very worried about her kids and parents. Anika feels pretty helpless right now. There's been no word about Jonah since her latest press conference. And her dad is going through a rough time with his chemotherapy."

"I understand," Fran said. "But I would like to meet her sometime."

"Well, if you're okay with it, I'll invite them both," Dan answered. "Thank you. I'm a lucky man to have found you." Fran squatted down to kiss him on the lips. He strained his neck and twisted his body so his lips could meet hers.

"Okay, you two love birds," the tattoo artist said. She wiped away some blood from the surface of the tattoo. "Get a room!"

Dan and Fran joined in laughter with her. The artist handed Dan a mirror.

"Here, have a look. How's it looking so far?"

Dan strained to see the design in the mirror.

"I like it," he said, feeling himself getting emotional. "I like it a lot…" He reached for Fran's hand, but jumped as the sound of his cell phone, ringing on a table beside them, startled him.

"Do you mind getting that?" he said to Fran.

She retrieved his phone and flipped it open.

"Who is it?" Dan asked.

"It's Anika."

A look of concern spread across Dan's face.

"I wonder what's up. Maybe she's heard something about Soren. I hope it's not more bad news. I don't think she can take any more of that…"

SOREN tipped back his new Tilly hat, mopping perspiration from his forehead as he walked briskly along Fritjof Nansens Gate. He was enjoying the sunshine and comfortable warmth of this late June day. He had a good feeling about this smaller, quiet Norwegian city. The day was calm, with only a light breeze—the sound of a distant siren the only sound intruding on the peaceful residential neighbourhood. "What a relief this temperature is, compared to that heat and humidity in Darwin," he said quietly to himself.

It was an easy ten block walk from his small flat, and the parking garage where he parked the small second-hand Fiat he had just purchased, to the flat on Fjellveien where Jonah and Lucy were living. He was in a particularly good mood today. Helen told him that she was going to retire from her job in the States in a month, so she could join him and Jonah in Moss. It wouldn't be long before they could finally become the family that he and Helen had long desired.

Soren felt good that Lucy was out of the picture now. Whoever it was that Helen had hired, they had done a professional job. The police investigation into her death was going nowhere, and there was virtually no chance that they would be able to link her disappearance to him. The distant siren grew louder, but Soren was lost in thought. He was fortunate that Agnetha, the young Norwegian woman, had agreed to move in with Jonah this weekend, to teach him Norwegian and care for him until Helen arrived. Things were falling nicely into place. The siren, now nearby, stopped abruptly.

Soren turned the corner onto Fjellveien, still deep in thought. Had it not been for the urgent shouts ahead, he may not have raised his head and noticed the commotion. He resisted the urge to stop dead in his tracks. Instead, he casually crossed the street and stopped, joining a small crowd that was now gawking at the two police cars blocking Fjellveien.

One of the officers manning the blockade, a woman, looked in Soren's direction, staring at the gathering crowd. Soren felt like she was staring directly at him. He had to resist the urge to start running away. Suddenly, the officer's attention was distracted by something her partner said. Soren paused for another thirty seconds to observe the unfolding drama, and then he casually turned around and walked back across the street. Once out of sight of the police, he made his way briskly up Fritjof Nansens Gate towards his tiny flat and the parking garage.

When he reached the parking garage, Soren opened the trunk and removed a gym bag full of supplies that he'd stored for just such an emergency. He slung the bag over his shoulder, and walked quickly back to his secret flat.

Thirty minutes later, he looked approvingly at himself in the mirror. His hair and beard were neatly trimmed. His appearance was now a perfect match to the photo on yet another new Norwegian passport, belonging to Sean Anderson. With his hair and beard freshly died, his new look would easily pass for someone of Scandinavian descent. He walked from the bathroom and sat down on the flat's small bed. He pulled the map from his gym bag and began plotting his escape route. Satisfied that he had the route stored in his memory, he replaced the map in the gym bag. He sat in silence and let a long, slow breath escape.

Soren braced himself for what came next. He pulled his mobile phone from his pocket. From memory, he began dialing the numbers that he dared not store in the phone. He looked at his watch while he listened to the phone ringing in his ear. It was six o'clock a.m. in Washington. The ringing stopped and a woman's voice answered.

"What's so important that you had to call me at this hour of the morning? Don't you know I'm getting ready for work?"

Soren felt a lump in the back of his throat that kept him from being able to swallow. "I couldn't help it," Soren said quietly. "I need to see you as soon as possible. We've got a problem—a big one."

SOREN SAT in the Kaffeebar across the highway from the Stena Line ferry terminal in Frederikshavn, Denmark. He looked anxiously at his watch—eight o'clock p.m.—nineteen hours since his near encounter with the police in Moss. The seven-hour drive from Moss, then across the Swedish border to Gothenburg, had gone without a hitch. He didn't like having to check into a hotel, but he couldn't risk attracting attention by sleeping in the Fiat. He purchased his ferry ticket online to minimize the time he would spend in the queue for the ferry. He knew that once his car was in the line-up, his options for making a quick escape would be limited.

After checking out of the hotel in Gothenburg, Soren made his way to the Stena Line terminal and waited impatiently at a nearby coffee shop for his four p.m. departure. He'd been on edge for the entire three-and-a-half-hour crossing from Gothenburg to Denmark. Every time he saw a uniformed crewmember, his body stiffened and he had to remind himself to stay calm. It was only when he was off the ferry, leaving the Frederikshavn terminal, that he finally let out a gigantic sigh of relief.

Soren looked at his watch again. Even with her connections for getting a flight, it took more than a day for Helen to get to Frederikshavn. After the tongue-lashings he took for calling her to Australia and Vietnam, he knew he'd be punished severely. That realization made him both anxious and aroused at the same time. Since he had taken Jonah from Victoria, he and Helen had not been able to be together so that he could submit to her every whim.

A taxi pulled up outside the Kaffeebar. A medium height woman with short brown hair, dark brown eyes, and pale skin emerged. Although not imposing in stature, the woman's face conveyed an inner confidence and sense of control. Helen still wore her military-issue skirt and shoes, but she had replaced the military-issue blouse with a more casual light blue top with a more civilian look.

Soren quickly left a tip at his table and rushed from the shop to greet her. The angry look in her eyes confirmed his predictions.

"We need to talk. Where's your car?" she demanded. Soren nodded to the parking lot, in the direction of the Fiat. He led her to the vehicle and opened the door for her. She plopped herself down abruptly in the passenger seat and emitted an angry huff. Soren hurried around to the driver's side and let himself in.

"Do you have any idea how hard it was to come up with another story so I could come to your rescue! I can't have people becoming suspicious of me when I only have a few weeks before I retire. What the fuck happened, Soren! How did the police find the boy?"

Soren shook his head slowly.

"I'm not sure. But I saw Anika on TV in Moss the other night. She was making a plea for information, and there were photos of both Jonah and me. They had a phone number to call. Who knows —maybe somebody remembered seeing Jonah or me—I don't know what happened. What difference does it make now?"

"You're an idiot! Everything we've worked for is ruined!" Helen screamed. The confident, controlled face she had worn moments earlier had disappeared entirely. The face Soren saw now was one of a woman filled with fear, who was struggling to bring that fear under control. Tension filled the vehicle. Gradually, as Soren watched, the look of terror in Helen's eyes transformed into a hard glare. She slowly gathered her composure.

"We need to find a hotel room," she said sternly. "You know you need to be punished, don't you?"

Soren nodded his head slowly. "Yes, my Lady. You know I'll always serve you faithfully. I'm yours to use as you see fit."

"First we take care of business. Then we'll think of a plan. Even when things seem hopeless, there's always hope. If we're patient, we'll find a way to overcome this obstacle. Let's go," Helen said, her voice now calm, but in total control.

Soren turned the key in the ignition. He swung the Fiat out of the parking lot and onto the highway. His body filled with an intoxicating elixir of anxiety and sexual arousal. The growing sensation in his genitals signalled his elation at finally being reunited with his Lady Helen, and to have her dominate and punish him once again—even if their reunion arrived four weeks early. But the fear rising in the rest of his body signalled his uncertainty about how Helen would punish him this time—and about how intense and painful that punishment would be.

CHAPTER 35

ANGELA followed on Anika's heels as she opened the door to the interview room. The first thing she saw was Jonah, sitting on a couch beside a red-haired Norwegian woman from Social Services. The young boy's eyes moved quickly to the door. In a flash, he was off the couch and on his feet, racing towards the door.

"Mommy!" Jonah wailed. As she saw tears of joy streaming down his cheeks, Angela felt her own tears welling up. In front of her, Anika knelt down, her arms spread wide, to receive her son.

"Jonah… my big boy!…"

Mother and son wrapped their arms around each other, unable to find anything more to say in the moment. Jonah, finally safe in Anika's arms, clutched his mother and wouldn't let go. Anika, after three months of fearing that she'd never hold her son again, enfolded Jonah protectively within her arms.

The last twenty-four hours had been a blur for Angela. Sitting in her lonely office in Las Vegas, pondering her future, she heard her cell phone vibrating on the computer desk. She saw Anika's name on the call display and felt her heart race. It had been over a week since the two women had talked.

"Anika, it's good to…"

"They've found him!' Anika shouted. *"They've found him in Norway. He's safe! I have to catch the first possible flight—can you come with me?"*

"What about Dan? Or your family?" Angela had replied.

"Dan and Fran are in the middle of buying a house in Las Vegas, and Mom can't leave Dad right now. The chemo's been hard

on him. You're my closest friend... please?... I need you," Anika answered.

There was no hesitation for Angela.

"Of course, I'll go," she had answered. *"Where should I meet you?"*

"I'll be flying from Calgary to Frankfurt, then connecting to Oslo. I arrive in Frankfurt tomorrow morning around nine-thirty."

"I'll start looking for flights as soon as we hang up, and I'll get back to you as soon as I know my itinerary," Angela said. She remembered the awkward silence that followed, then the words she had blurted.

"I've missed you... I'm so excited... for you and Jonah!"

"Me too. I'm so excited right now, I can't stop shaking! Thank you... it means a lot that you'll be here with me."

A small voice wakened Angela from her daydream.

"Who's that lady with you?" Jonah's tiny voice asked Anika. His forehead wrinkled and he studied Angela closely. "Hey!... You're the lady from Australia... the lady with the big hat! You promised me that Mommy was coming to find me!"

Jonah finally left Anika's arms and ran to Angela, wrapping his arms around her legs. Angela knelt down to give him a big hug.

"I'm sorry I didn't keep my promise, Jonah. If I'd known your daddy was going to take you away, I would have called your mommy or the police sooner," she said, trying to hold back the tears that threatened to trickle from her eyes. She sniffed and lifted her head to face Jonah.

"But look at you, Jonah. You did what all of us grownups couldn't do. You called the police by yourself. You're the one who got back together with your mommy. What a big boy you are! We're all so proud of you!" Angela looked up at Anika, who gazed at her with tears in her eyes.

"You did that? You promised him that I was coming to find him?" Anika asked.

Angela felt a lump in her throat. The joy she felt for her friend and for Jonah was overwhelming her with a flood of conflicting emotions—joy and empathy for her good friend, but also overwhelming sadness and fear. She couldn't help but think of Julia and Nicholas back in Cleveland. But, more importantly, seeing Anika and Jonah together reminded her that Soren was still on the loose and unaccounted for—that her own life was still in danger.

Anika approached Angela and Jonah, and then knelt down to join them in a group hug. Angela felt one of Anika's arms wrap around her, while the other was wrapped around Jonah. They held each other tightly. Angela didn't want the moment to end. Anika kissed Jonah all over his head and face. Then she looked at Angela and their eyes locked together.

"Thank you," Anika said.

Angela saw the gratitude in Anika's eyes. But, in that instant, she knew for certain that there was more than just gratitude in her friend's eyes. All thought was suspended. Angela felt herself being carried away by emotions, helpless to stop herself. The next thing she knew, her lips felt the warm, fleeting touch of Anika's kiss. They gazed into each other's eyes—mutual looks of understanding and caring reflected in them.

Angela gathered herself together and rose to her feet, smiling at Anika and then at Jonah. Anika looked to the Social Services worker, who smiled and nodded that her business with Anika was complete.

Angela and Anika each wiped the remaining tears from their eyes with their hands and gathered themselves together.

"What do you say, Jonah?" Anika said. "Would you like to go home now?"

Without a word, Jonah placed one of his small hands in his mother's hand. Then he reached up and took one of Angela's hands in his other. He began walking them towards the door, the start of their long journey home.

ANGELA watched nervously from the doorway of Julia's bedroom as her mother nudged and whispered to the young girl, trying to rouse her from her sleep without frightening her.

"Julia… Julia, dear… wake up, darling. Somebody is here to see you."

Julia's eyes flickered open, momentarily disoriented. She looked first into her grandmother's face, and then she let her eyes scan her bedroom to get her bearings. Her eyes froze in place when she saw Angela, dressed entirely in black, standing in the doorway, tears streaming down her face.

"Mommy!" she blurted.

"Shhhh," Angela's mother whispered. "We must be very quiet. We don't want anybody to know that your mother is here." She stepped back and Angela ran to her daughter's bedside, taking Julia and wrapping her in her arms.

"Julia," she sobbed. "I'm so sorry… I never should have left you and Nicholas… I'm so sorry… please forgive me…"

Julia, now ten years old, wiped the tears from her eyes and looked up into Angela's face. "It's okay. Momma and Papa told us. You had to go away to keep us safe."

Angela gazed into Julia's eyes, seeing how much she had matured in the two years they'd been separated. She heard a rustling sound from the hallway and looked up in time to see Papa and Nicholas. At the sight of his mother, the eight-year-old boy ran into the bedroom and into Angela's arms.

"Mama," he whispered. His young body trembled as tears surged from both mother's and son's eyes. Angela's father tiptoed softly into the room.

"You should be going now," he whispered. "You will have plenty of time for your reunion."

"Why do we have to go?" Nicholas whispered.

"Because some bad men have been watching Momma and Papa's house… watching for me. They're outside in a car right now," Angela whispered. "We're going to Canada to stay with some of Mama's friends, where we'll be safe."

"Momma and Papa too?" Julia asked. Julia's mother knelt down beside Julia, Nicholas, and Angela, taking the two children in her arms.

"Momma and Papa have to stay here," Angela explained. "We must make it look to the men outside like you are still living here —to give us time to reach safety."

"Enough!" Papa said, his voice rising above a whisper. "Time to go!"

Papa, Angela, and Nicholas crept from the bedroom while Momma helped Julia dress in dark clothing and pack a small backpack. Moments later, they joined the others in the kitchen, where everybody crouched below window level.

"We're going to go out the back door, one at a time, then we'll climb over the fence into the neighbour's yard. Mama's got a car on the next street. I'll go first and Papa will help you over the fence. Okay?" Nicholas and Julia nodded silently, the gravity of the situation now etched on their young faces.

Moments later, the back door opened slowly. Angela's black figure crept out the door, across the lawn, and then disappeared into trees and shrubbery at the back of the yard. The night was moonless and black. A slight scuffling sound and a couple of small bumps were all that could be heard as her clothing brushed the fence and the toes of her rubber sneakers bumped against the fence. Once over the fence, she gave two quick knocks on the fence.

Papa crept into the darkness, then Nicholas, and finally Julia. All three scurried quickly into the dark shrubbery. When both children were safely over the fence, Angela whispered through a small knothole.

"I love you, Papa. I'll phone to let you know when we've arrived safely. You remember the signal?"

"Three rings, wait one minute, then three more rings," he whispered. "We love you, Angela."

Papa's dark figure crept out of the darkness and back into the house, the door closing soundlessly behind him. Moments later, in the distance, an automobile engine started, then the soft rush of rubber tires on asphalt could be heard. Gradually, the sounds faded and blended into the constant sound of background traffic on a summer Cleveland night.

CHAPTER 36

"IT'S a beautiful portrait," Anika said above the constant buzz of background conversation.

Anika's voice interrupted Angela's daydream. She felt Anika's warm hand come to rest on her shoulder. She turned and looked into her friend's deep blue eyes.

"The moment I saw the shutter opening in Francesca's camera, I knew those pictures were going to be trouble," Angela said. Just then, Dan walked towards them and joined them.

"It's captivating, isn't it?" Dan said. "It grabbed my attention the instant I first saw it hanging in Fran's old place."

"I'm just grateful that it helped to bring us all together," Anika answered, smiling in Angela's direction.

"Me too," Angela added. "Dan, I'm glad we were both able to make it to the party so I could finally meet Francesca, and all of your friends too." She gazed across the room, where Francesca talked to a group of friends. From the side, Fran's noticeable baby bump protruded from her normally slender frame. With her short black hair and dark Mediterranean complexion, she radiated natural beauty. Her face glowed and she was animated, both from her pregnancy, but also from the joy of being surrounded by friends.

"I'm glad you and Anika could make it too," Dan said. "I'm glad you two have kept in touch. I know you went to Norway with Anika to bring Jonah home. But what else have you been doing since we got back from Vietnam?"

Angela took a furtive look at Anika, and then turned back to Dan, lowering her voice to a whisper.

"Please, not a word this to anyone else," Angela whispered, her eyes pleading silently with Dan. "I've reunited with Nicholas and Julia again. With Soren still on the loose, I was pretty sure he had my parents' house in Cleveland under surveillance. So I had to sneak them out of the house, just a few nights ago. They're with Anika's family in Canada right now. You're the only person who knows, apart from Anika. Please… don't tell a soul… not even Francesca. After what happened in Australia and Hanoi, I can't trust anybody except you and Anika."

A look of surprise, then one of relief, crossed Dan's face. He collected himself, looked around the room, and then lowered his voice.

"I understand," he said. "We all have to be looking over our shoulder until Soren is found. I won't say a word."

Anika took Angela's hand, gave it a gentle squeeze, and gazed into Angela's eyes. Angela saw empathy—and also love—on her Anika's face. She was still getting used to the strange new connection she had developed with Anika over the past few weeks. They both knew instinctively how each other felt. But until Soren was found, they also had a cloud of uncertainty hanging over their heads.

"You still have that look of fear in your eyes," Anika said. "I hope they find him soon, for both of our sakes." Anika kissed Angela softly on the lips… for the first time in public. Feeling awkward, Angela took a furtive glance around the room. Nobody else in the room seemed to notice, apart from Dan. She hugged Anika and gave her a quick kiss on the cheek in return.

Dan paused for a moment, and then a look of understanding crossed his face. He didn't say a word, but smiled knowingly at his two close friends.

"Maybe we can get Fran to take a new portrait of Angela, after Soren is safely behind bars," Dan said, smiling. "One where you're smiling and everything is back to normal this time. What do you say?"

"I'd like that," Angela answered. "And a family portrait with Julia and Nicholas would be nice too."

Angela gazed at herself in Fran's photo again, and her mind couldn't help drifting back in time to the day it was taken. Before she knew it, she was talking to herself, unaware that she was speaking out loud to nobody in particular.

"I've come a long way since then…"

A BURST of laughter from Tim and Shelley's group echoed through the great room. Dan noticed the startled look in Angela's eyes, and he realized her mind had been someplace else. The laughter in the room had brought her back to reality with a start. He saw Anika place her hand on Angela's shoulder to calm the other woman. It was now obvious to Dan that Anika and Angela had become much more than just close friends during their time together in Australia and Vietnam.

"Is everything alright? Are you okay?" Anika asked Angela.

"Yes… I'm sorry. I must have been distracted," Angela answered. "You know, apart from you two and Fran, I really don't know a single face in this room yet."

"I know how you feel," Anika said, laughing. "I didn't know anybody when I first went with Dan to Palm Springs. But you're getting off easy. I met most of them for the first time at Chateau Eden, when they were all parading around in the nude!"

"Now that *would* be awkward," Angela said, laughing. "Thanks for not making me do that!"

"As you can imagine, their faces weren't exactly the first thing I noticed," Anika added. "We're going to have to initiate you and take you to the Chateau sometime."

"Fat chance of that!" Angela exclaimed. "I prefer to be introduced to them with their clothes on, if you don't mind. So who are all these people, Dan?"

"Well, let's see. Do you see the attractive darker-skinned lady, standing beside the older guy?"

"Yeah," Angela said.

"That's Shelley and Tim. They've been regulars at Chateau Eden for years, and they're close friends with Fran. They're talking to Carmen Herrera and her husband, Rodrigo. They're going to be taking over Chateau Eden from Fran. The other older lady is Susan Keaner, Fran's friend from Italy."

"And that other group outside by the pool?" Angela asked.

"The black couple are Richard and Pam Holloway. They're incredibly friendly people. They've also been going to the Chateau for years. The other two women both work with Richard overseas. They're all with the same private security firm. The redhead is Gwen Perkins and the blonde is Miriam Fox."

"Does Miriam remind you of anybody you know?" Anika said to Angela. Angela looked at the blonde woman but her face was blank.

"Who do you see in the mirror every day?" Anika hinted. "She looks just like you. She could be your twin!"

Angela stared at Miriam, then shrugged and smiled. "Yeah, you're right, except for that scorpion tattoo she has on the back of her neck."

Dan's eyes moved quickly toward the front door. He noticed Fran, wearing a stylish maternity dress with multi-colored vertical stripes, walking towards them. A solid-looking blonde woman with short, spiked hair accompanied her.

"Somebody else just arrived," Dan interrupted. "Is this the friend you invited, Angela?"

Angela's face lit up instantly as she spotted Fran and a blonde woman walking towards them. She raced to greet the other woman.

"Ricki!" Angela squealed.

"Angela!" the woman shouted. They embraced in a long bear hug, then kissed each other on the both cheeks. When they finally released each other, Angela turned to the group.

"Everybody, this is my friend Ricki. She's a freelance journalist here in Las Vegas."

Everybody shook hands with Ricki. Dan noticed Anika looking Angela's way, her forehead wrinkled in curiosity.

"So how did you two meet?" Fran asked. Angela looked at Ricki and they both started laughing.

"I met her while I was writing an article about people who were living in the Vegas floodway system," Ricki said.

"Then she took me to an all-girl burlesque magic show that night," Angela added, laughing. Anika looked even more puzzled now. Angela smiled at her and wrapped one arm around her shoulder while everybody else broke into laughter.

"I didn't know there was such a thing!" Dan exclaimed.

"One of the best kept secrets on the Strip," Ricki said, still laughing.

"There's still a lot you don't know about me, girl," Angela said to Anika, smiling warmly.

"Apparently," Anika replied.

"Since Anika's here in Las Vegas, maybe we'll have to take this pretty lady to see the *Showgirls of Illusion* for herself," Ricki said, chuckling. "What do you say, Angela?"

"I'm game to see them again," Angela answered, smiling at Anika. "I think you'd enjoy them. They're surprisingly good magicians—and it doesn't hurt that they're hot looking too."

Anika shrugged and smiled back at Angela. "What the hell— what goes on in Vegas stays in Vegas. Right?" Once again, laughter erupted. As the group laughed, Susan Keaner walked from the far side of the room and joined them.

"Anika, Angela and Ricki," Fran said. "I would like you to meet my friend Susan. She came all the way from Italy to support me in my recent court case. I'm so lucky she could stay for our house warming party."

"I wouldn't have missed it for the world," Susan replied. "It's nice to meet you, ladies."

"I hope you will all excuse me," Fran said, as Angela, Anika, Ricki, and Susan shook hands all around. "I just remembered I have to take something out of the oven." She walked swiftly out of the room and into the kitchen.

"Dan has told me so much about you two ladies," Susan said to Angela and Anika. "You've had quite the adventure over the past three months."

"More like a nightmare," Anika said.

"I'm not a parent," Susan replied, putting her hand gently on Anika's shoulder. "But I can't imagine anything worse for a parent than having your child abducted."

"And especially by your spouse," Angela added.

"Did I hear that there were also attempts on your lives?" Susan asked.

"That's right," Anika answered. "The Australian ATSB has confirmed that somebody sabotaged our plane in Darwin. Crashing into the river in Kakadu Park was no accident. Our poor pilot, Derek, was killed by a crocodile before we could all get out of the water." Tears began to form in Anika's eyes. Dan rested his hand on her shoulder, his face solemn.

"That's awful," Susan said, a look of shock written on her face. "Do they have any idea who was responsible?"

"We can't be sure," Dan said. "We have to assume that Anika's husband, Soren, had something to do with it. But he probably had one or more accomplices."

"We know Soren is responsible for bombing our car in Hanoi," Angela added. "Dan saw him at the scene. We were all lucky to get away before the bomb exploded."

"You're right, my dear," Susan said to Anika. "It has been a nightmare, but I'm glad it's finally over for you."

"We wish," Anika said solemnly. "But my husband is still at large. I'm still worried he'll try to abduct Jonah again, and Angela is worried about the safety of her kids too."

At the mention of her children, Dan noticed Angela's eyes grow distant again.

"… he can't run forever," Anika said. Dan noticed that Anika's voice brought Angela back to reality. "He's wanted by Interpol for child abduction and possibly for murder."

The sound of the doorbell chimed over the conversation.

"Somebody's at the door!" a male voice boomed. It was Tim. "Want me to answer it?"

"I'll get it," Fran shouted, running from the kitchen.

FRAN OPENED the door. Few of the guests could see her from where they were standing in the vast great room.

"Flowers for Angela… Baranyi? Is that how you say it?" the delivery person said.

Fran realized that the delivery person was a woman, not too tall, wearing a ball cap with a florist's logo. The cap didn't completely hide the woman's shoulder-length blonde hair. Her head was low and the brim of her cap hid the parts of her face that weren't already partially hidden by the large bouquet of flowers she held. Her delivery jacket, and the white blouse she wore, were open at the neck.

Fran stepped back into the house.

"Flowers for Angela!" she shouted. Tim, who stood nearby, realized Fran's voice wouldn't carry into the great room. He relayed Fran's message.

"Angela!" Tim shouted. "There's a flower delivery for you!" The message reverberated through the great room.

"Flowers?" Angela said, looking at Anika. Then her face broke into a smile. "From you?"

A puzzled look crossed Anika's face. She shrugged her shoulders and shook her head.

"Coming!" Angela shouted, making her way toward the front door. "I'll be there in a second."

"Angela Baranyi?" the delivery woman said as Angela approached the doorway.

"That's me," Angela replied.

Fran stared at the delivery woman's blonde hair. There was something strangely familiar about it. Then she saw the spider tattoo on the woman's neck.

Fran felt the hairs on the back of her neck stand up. A chill went down her spine. Then she saw the woman's hand slipping down towards the pocket of her pants. When it emerged, Fran saw a dark blue metallic reflection. Without thinking, Fran screamed,

"She's got a gun!"

Even as she screamed, Fran lowered her head and rammed the shorter woman in the chest, forcing her backwards and out of the doorway.

THE CRACK of a single gunshot echoed through the house. The first shot was followed by others, coming from outside. Pandemonium broke loose inside the house. The guests all dived for cover. Tim, who stood nearest to Angela, grabbed her arm and dragged her to the floor, slamming the front door shut at the same time. Everybody was screaming.

Richard Holloway and his colleagues, Miriam and Gwen, raced into the house from the pool area. All three carried handguns that were previously concealed beneath their clothing.

"Everybody, stay down!" Richard shouted, taking control of the situation. He and his two colleagues took cover beside the house's front-facing windows.

"Gwen! Miriam! Upstairs!" he shouted. As Miriam raced up the stairs, a blast of automatic gunfire shattered the glass beside the front door, chasing her up the stairs. Gwen dived for cover downstairs.

"Miriam, what'cha got!" Richard screamed. Another blast of gunfire shattered more glass upstairs.

"Miriam!" Richard screamed. Seconds passed before Miriam's voice shouted from upstairs.

"I see one automatic… could be two… weapons firing from two directions… third person… smaller, probably female… is dragging somebody… looks like Fran… back to a delivery van… third perp's got a handgun."

Before Richard could answer, the sound of screeching rubber came from the front of the house. The delivery van's engine roared, then the sound receded rapidly as the vehicle raced away from the chaos. Just as quickly as pandemonium had erupted, the house became eerily silent. It probably only lasted about five seconds, but the silence seemed like an eternity as the party guests waited to hear if there was any more gunfire.

Gwen came bounding back down the stairs. "They're gone!" she shouted. When she reached the bottom, she threw open the door, then ducked quickly back into the house. When nothing happened, she leapt out the front door, taking cover behind a pillar. "All clear!" she shouted. This time, Richard poked his head out the door, and then dashed through the doorway to take cover behind another pillar. Finally, Miriam took up position by the front door, covering Gwen and Richard.

"It's all over," Richard called, lowering his weapon. "Is anybody hurt?"

"Hey, Richard. Look at this!" Miriam shouted, pointing to the front porch.

ONE BY ONE, people inside the house got to their feet. Anika raced to Angela's side, tears pouring from her eyes.

"You're alright?" she sobbed. "Oh, my God. You're alright!"

Angela and Anika held each other tightly, their two hearts still pounding from the terror. Their lips pressed together—urgently.

Tim jumped to his feet, looking anxiously around the area near the front door. Then he looked back into the great room, searching for Dan. Their eyes met. Dan instantly read fear on Tim's face.

Richard, Gwen, and Miriam hurried back into the house to assess the situation.

"Fran!" Dan screamed. "Where's Fran? I can't find her!"

His eyes raced around the room. She was nowhere to be seen. His eyes met Miriam's. She shook her head. Dan recognized the anger that was etched onto her face. Not wasting any words, she spoke to Dan.

"They've got Fran. And we found blood on the patio and the driveway."

Dan's mind flashed instantaneously to images from the past three months—Chelly lying in a pool of blood—Fran in the pool, desperately holding Philippe's head under water—Fran in prison, telling him she was pregnant.

A feeling of doom descended on him. Just when he thought the Palm Desert nightmare was finally over, another was just beginning.

EPILOGUE

THE ENGINE roared and tires screeched as the delivery van careened around corners and raced from the scene of the shooting. Helen slammed against the side of the van as it took another corner. "Fuck, fuck, fuck!" she screamed.

Lying on the floor of the van, Fran felt the woman's hatred burning into her like lasers. She had finally recognized the woman. It was her mysterious cellmate, Helen, who had questioned her in Indio Jail and then disappeared.

"Capellini, you bitch! Don't you ever get tired of fucking me over? Well, you're going to pay this time. Nobody fucks with Lady Helen and gets away with it!"

Fran realized that Helen's anger was so intense that she was only vaguely aware of the van's progress. Helen's field of vision had narrowed, almost as though she was looking at the world through a high-powered telescope. Darkness filled her peripheral vision. She ripped the cap from her head and stared at Fran. It was only then that she saw blood on the floor of the van beside her captive.

Fran looked down at her right arm. It burned with pain and was oozing blood. At almost the same time, Fran saw Helen's eyes shift from her wound to her swollen belly.

Suddenly, Helen's mood started to soften. "How far are we from the garage?" she shouted to the driver.

"Almost there. Just a couple of blocks," the driver replied.

"We're going to have to improvise," Helen shouted. "We need a doctor. This woman's been shot."

Helen's demeanour continued to mellow. Fran almost sensed compassion—a complete hundred and eighty-degree shift in emotions.

"Don't worry, we'll take care of your baby," she said to Fran.

Helen went silent. Fran sensed the wheels turning in her captor's mind.

"This might just work out after all," Helen mused.

Fran stared at Helen's face.

Do I know you from somewhere else?

There was something familiar about Helen's face. It wasn't just the Indio Jail visit. It looked vaguely like a face from Fran's distant past. Similar, but different. Fran's mind worked furiously, floating back through time, and seeing images of countless faces from the past, desperately trying to match it to the one that was gazing down at her. But her mind was racing so frantically that she couldn't think clearly.

Fran drew a blank. The feeling continued to nag at her.

"Yes, indeed," Helen said. "You may just turn out to be very valuable after all. I think you'll make a first class hostage."

Fran felt like she was going to be sick as she heard those words and stared at the enigmatic Helen's face. She felt as if she was dreaming. She hadn't yet enjoyed a month of freedom since the charges against her were dropped and she had been freed from the Indio Jail.

But this was no mere dream.

It was a nightmare—Francesca Capellini was a prisoner once again.

To Be Continued ...

ACKNOWLEDGEMENTS

Once again, I would like to thank my loving wife and best friend, Peggy, for her continued love and infinite patience with my exploration into the world of writing.

A very big thanks goes to Lianne Viau for your vision and collaboration in creating the truly unique cover photography for both *Walls* and *Faces*.

I would like to extend a special thanks to Julia Gibbs for proofreading this manuscript and for spotting and correcting all of the little irregularities and typos that an author inevitably fails to see. For more information about Julia, go to https://juliaproofreader.wordpress.com/.

Finally, thanks once again to all my friends, family, coworkers, and the other writers I've met through the social media. I thank you all for your support and positive feedback about *Walls*, and also for your encouragement while waiting so patiently for its sequel, *Faces*. I truly hope that it was worth the long wait, and that you enjoy this novel as much as I enjoyed writing it.

David Alex Jones

December 2022

OTHER BOOKS BY DAVID ALEX JONES

THE NIGHT CLASS
An Alternative Tale of Reconciliation

***

Originally written as Alex Jones:

WALLS:
The Survivor Trilogy, Book One

ANGELA'S EYES:
The Survivor Trilogy, Prequel

SPIRITS:
The Survivor Trilogy, Book Three

Find out where to purchase David Alex Jones' books
by visiting his website:
http://www.davidalexjones.com

ABOUT THE AUTHOR

David Alex Jones is a retired Clinical Psychologist who lives in Ontario, Canada. In his writing, he combines his understanding of human identity and personality, his passion for helping victims of trauma, abuse, and Post-traumatic Stress Disorder, and his love of reading fiction, to create a unique brand of psychological suspense and political commentary. His writing is rich with complex characters and controversial social issues, resulting in an abundance of internal and interpersonal conflict, dysfunction, and tension. Dave also enjoys spending time with his grandchildren, travelling with his wife, photography, and home brewing craft beer.

EXCERPT: SPIRITS

The Survivor Trilogy (Book Three)
by David Alex Jones
(Originally as Alex Jones)

DARKNESS SETTLED over the streets of Las Vegas as the sun disappeared behind the Spring Mountain Range. Lights twinkled peacefully and a surreal spectacle of flashing neon and glowing hotel towers emerged from the desert landscape. Suddenly, the squealing of tires shattered the silence. A white delivery van careened around a corner onto West Cheyenne Avenue. Its engine roared as the vehicle accelerated away from the intersection on the six-lane road, weaving and swerving around vehicles that impeded its progress.

The driver, clad in black, leaned hard as his vehicle careened around another corner. Another black-clad man sitting in the passenger seat gripped an automatic weapon on his lap with one hand, while tightly gripping the handhold above him on his right. A brown-haired woman, clad in the brown uniform of a UPS delivery person, tried in vain to sit on the floor of the vehicle's cargo compartment, but her body slammed hard against the side of the van as it took another corner.

"Fuck!" Helen screamed.

She glared down at Fran, lying on the cargo floor beside her, with blood oozing from a wound in her right shoulder. The hatred in her eyes burned into the other woman like lasers.

"Capellini, you bitch! Don't you ever get tired of fucking me over? This time you're going to pay. Nobody fucks with Lady Helen and gets away with it!"

Francesca Capellini wrinkled her forehead and stared back at her captor. *We've met before?*

Francesca quickly averted her eyes from Helen, turning her gaze to the blood oozing from her wound. She winced from pain, then she looked up at her captor again.

Helen's eyes shifted from Francesca's wound to her swollen belly. At the same time, the look in Helen's eyes suddenly softened, signaling a one-hundred-eighty-degree shift in her mood. For an instant, Fran almost thought she saw compassion in the other woman. Then, just as quickly, Helen's eyes became distant while she was deep in thought.

"How far are we from the garage?" she shouted abruptly to the driver.

"Almost there! Just a few minutes."

"Well, hurry it up! We're going to need to improvise. We need a doctor. This woman's been shot and the bleeding won't stop."

Time felt like it was standing still for Fran. An uneasy feeling spread through her as she stared back into Helen's eyes. Hazy images from long ago flashed through her mind, trying to intrude into her consciousness … a rear view of a nude woman, passionately kissing an unidentified man in a hot tub.

Fran's mind felt cloudy … confused.

Is it the same woman? Was I in that tub too?

She couldn't be sure. She almost felt as if she was floating over the hot tub scene, looking downward. She saw another woman with short black hair, also nude, sitting beside an older, grey-haired man. His hands wandered over the woman's body. A shiver surged through Fran's body and jolted her back into reality.

The seconds ticked as Fran strained to make a conscious connection to the distant memories. Nothing came. Suddenly, she became aware that Helen was still staring at her. A grin spread slowly across Helen's face and she started to laugh.

"You know what, Capellini? This could just work out alright after all."

Helen's smile turned wicked. "You may turn out to be a blessing in disguise as a hostage."

Helen's words brought Fran crashing back to reality: only a few short weeks after she had been freed from Indio Prison, she was a prisoner yet again! The realization swept over her like a tsunami. Hopeless and dejected, she looked down at her wound, then at the blood on the cargo bay floor. She curled up in fetal position, clutching at her stomach. She felt like she was going to vomit. All Fran heard was the roar of the van's engine.

"Slow down!" Helen screamed to the driver, above the roar. "Last thing we need is an effin' speeding ticket!"

The van's engine instantly lost its urgency as the driver backed off the accelerator. The ride in the cargo department stabilized, allowing Helen to reach into her pocket. She pulled out a cell phone and quickly dialed a number. She waited impatiently while the number rang: … once … twice … three times … and then a fourth … finally there was a click on the line.

INSIDE the gates of the lavish Las Vegas estate, Las Vegas PD squad cars littered the driveway and long strands of yellow tape marked the area as an active crime scene. CSI technicians in protective clothing combed the area like a colony of ants. A black SUV passed through the gates and crept slowly up the driveway, receiving directions for where to park from a uniformed police officer.

An overweight middle-aged man, wearing a poorly-fitting black suit, climbed awkwardly from the driver's side of the vehicle. He removed his sunglasses to survey the scene. FBI Agent Gabe Martinelli's eyes were as keen and sharp as his wardrobe clearly was not. A younger woman who was shorter, muscular and fit from competitive running, slipped easily from the passenger side of the vehicle. Unlike her male counterpart, Agent Lindell Simpson was stylishly dressed in expensive navy slacks and a jacket. They walked up to the officer who had directed them to their parking spot.

"You in charge here?" Simpson asked.

"No, ma'am. Over there," the officer said, pointing to another young man in a suit who was interviewing a group of people. The younger man looked up, saw the two new arrivals, and began walking towards them.

"Hi. Detective Ryan Lewis, LVPD. I'm in charge here." He exchanged handshakes with the two newcomers. "My partner and I were nearby, so we were first to arrive when the call came in."

Lewis nodded towards his partner, another male officer, who was now taking statements from the same group of people whom Lewis had been interviewing.

"They sure didn't waste any time calling you guys in when we told them about the abduction."

Simpson's skilled eyes quickly took in the scene: she glanced at the group gathered outside the front door of the estate, and then brought her gaze back to two other men, one Caucasian and the other African-American, standing a few feet in front of her. The Caucasian man was clearly distressed and agitated. While she scanned the scene, Martinelli took control of the situation.

"Hi, Detective. I'm FBI Agent Martinelli. This is Agent Simpson."

"Good to meet you," Lewis said.

"Who are those two men in front of us?" Simpson said.

"The white guy is the homeowner. The black guy is a friend … appears to have a background in the military and private security."

Simpson glanced at Martinelli, then back at Detective Lewis. "Guess we may as well start with them, if it's okay with you."

"Go ahead. It's your case now," Lewis replied.

Simpson and Martinelli wandered over to where the homeowner and his friend were standing.

"I'm FBI Agent Martinelli; this is Agent Simpson. And you are?"

"Whitney … Dr. Dan Whitney … my girlfriend … the woman who was abducted … this is our new home.

Martinelli and Simpson glanced at each other and raised their eyebrows after hearing Dan's name. Simpson pulled a note pad from a pocket in her suit and scribbled a note to herself.

"And you sir?" Martinelli asked, turning to the African-American man.

"Holloway … Richard. I'm a friend of Dr. Whitney an' Fran. My wife an' I were here fer th'party," he drawled. His voice had a distinct Texas accent.

"Party?" Simpson replied. "What were you celebrating, Dr. Whitney?"

"Our housewarming. We'd just moved here from Palm Springs, so we invited some friends to celebrate with us," Dan answered.

"So, what happened?" Martinelli asked.

"I'm not exactly sure," Dan answered. "My girlfriend … Fran … Francesca Capellini … She went to answer the doorbell. Somebody said there was a delivery for Angela, one of our guests. They were shouting for her to go to the front door. The next thing I knew, we heard shots and screams."

"Shots? How many?" Martinelli interjected.

"I don't know … a lot," Dan replied. He looked to Richard for help with the question. "What do you think, Richard? How many?"

"One, initially," Richard answered. "Then I ran t'the front door with two o' my colleagues. We're all former military an' we do security work. Once th'intruders saw we were armed, they gave a barrage of coverin' fire - lots of it - t'allow the delivery person t'pull back'n escape. One o' my colleagues caught a glimpse from th'upstairs window. Looks like there were three o'them - two with automatic weapons. The smaller o'the three - th'one that took Fran - looked t'have a handgun.

Simpson looked to Detective Lewis for help.

"Did anybody get a good look at the delivery person?" She looked at her notes. "Have you talked to this … Angela … yet?"

"Yeah, we talked to her. Her name is Angela Baranyi. She only caught a quick glimpse. Apparently, Capellini pushed her out of harm's way … Must have seen the gun or something … Angela thinks the perp was a woman … Only about five feet tall, short brown hair … Looked like she was a UPS delivery agent … Brown ball cap pulled down over her eyes … That's about it," Lewis reported.

Martinelli turned to Richard Holloway. "What about your colleague upstairs? Did she see anything?"

"Not much more'n Angela. She only got quick peeks cuz she was under fire. But it pretty much confirms what Angela said … Short female, shoulder-length brown hair, brown UPS uniform, ball cap, an'a handgun," he answered.

"Any idea why they took your girlfriend, Dr. Whitney? Simpson interjected.

"Not a clue. Fran would never hurt anybody … For some crazy reason, everybody seems to be out to get her … I don't get it," Dan replied.

Martinelli and Simpson exchanged glances and raised their eyebrows again. Simpson paused for a moment, thinking.

"You said Palm Springs, Dr. Whitney? And your girlfriend's name is …?"

Simpson took a quick look at her notes.

"… Capellini? Have I heard your names recently?"

Dan hung his head and sighed, suddenly feeling extremely weary.

"Is this necessary?" Richard asked. "Dan an' Francesca have been through a lot lately. They both lost their spouses …"

Martinelli's eyes suddenly went wide as he made the mental connection. He turned to Dan.

"I remember now. Weren't you the two who were involved in that kinky shooting a few months ago in Palm Desert?" he asked.

Dan managed to raise his head enough to flash Martinelli a look of resentment. Seeing Dan's response, Simpson shot Martinelli a glance that said, "*Lay off.*"

"We're sorry for your recent losses, Dr. Whitney," Simpson interjected. "You stated earlier that everybody seems to be out to get your girlfriend. Do either of you have any enemies we should know about?"

"I already told you," Dan huffed, his frustration surfacing again. "I don't know. If they were after me, I'd understand."

"Why you?" Simpson retorted.

"If you'd really been watching the news closely, maybe you'd already know about the recent attempts on my life by Soren Kristiansen and a woman who calls herself Helen. And you'd know they're still at large," Dan replied sarcastically.

Simpson and Martinelli exchanged glances and raised their eyebrows again. Simpson turned to Richard.

"Anything else you'd like to add, Mr. Holloway?" Simpson asked.

"Not right now," Richard answered. "It all happened so damned fast."

Simpson scribbled a few more lines in her notepad and then looked at Martinelli to see if he had anything else to ask. He shook his head from side to side. Simpson turned to Dan.

"Thanks for your patience, Dr. Whitney. I'm sorry to bother you with all these questions, since you've obviously been through a lot. I think that's all we have for now, but I'm sure we'll have more questions once CSI finishes with the scene."

She pulled a business card from the pocket of her suit jacket and handed it to Dan.

"If either of you think of anything else, you can reach me at that number … Any time of day," she added.

Richard put his arm protectively around Dan's shoulder to help calm him.

"Thanks, ma'am. We'll be sure t'do just that if we think of anythin' else," Richard replied.

Dan and Richard shook hands with the two agents. Simpson and Martinelli turned their backs and began walking back towards their SUV. Martinelli paused to light a cigarette. Simpson stopped and shook her head disapprovingly.

"I thought you'd given those things up," she said.

"Yeah, me too," Martinelli answered. He took a drag, then exhaled slowly while he gathered his thoughts.

"So, if what they say is true, and Whitney's girlfriend was kidnapped, do you think it has anything to do with Kristiansen? Or maybe his mysterious lady friend?" he asked.

"Who knows," Simpson replied. "There's gotta be more to this than meets the eye, but it gives us a place to start. People don't just dress up in UPS uniforms or black camo, arm themselves with automatic weapons, and take innocent people in broad daylight for no apparent reason."

"No, they surely do not," Martinelli replied. He exhaled one last cloud of smoke, then threw the cigarette to the driveway and ground the butt into the pavement with his foot.

COLONEL Bryce Williamson smiled salaciously while two of his subordinate male officers, both partially dressed, struggled to subdue a young female officer.

"Stop! … Please stop!" the woman cried. "I beg you!"

Her pleas were met by a sharp slap to the face from one of male officers.

"Shut up," he ordered. He turned to his male counterpart and grinned. "She's a real fighter, isn't she? Makes it even sweeter when she finally gets tired and gives up."

"Never, you pricks!" the young woman screamed.

"Shut her up!" Williamson snapped. "You want somebody calling the cops?"

The two men joined forces to lift their victim off the floor and slam her onto the bed. One of the men ripped off one of his socks and stuffed it into the woman's mouth when she opened it to scream.

"There, that'll fix you. That's just a taste of what's comin', bitch!"

Suddenly, Williamson's cell phone buzzed in his pocket. Clearly annoyed, he retrieved it and looked at his call display.

"What do you want?" he said gruffly.

"It's Helen. Listen up. There's been some trouble and I need your help, right now!"

"What do you want me to do about it? I'm busy," he replied impatiently. The sound of muffled screams and breaking glass filled the room as the thrashing woman sent a bedside lamp crashing to the floor.

"I hear what's keeping you busy. I'm not *asking* for help, this is an order! Is that clear?" Helen shouted.

Williamson snapped instinctively to attention. "Yes ma'am. Perfectly clear. What do you need me to do?"

"That's better," Helen answered. "I'm going to need someplace very safe and very remote … far off the beaten track. And I need a medic and medical supplies to treat a gunshot wound … right now!"

"Are you crazy?" Williamson replied. "I can't make that happen right away. What happened? Are you hurt?"

He watched and grinned as the two men in the background climbed on top of the female officer. One of them tore off her blouse and bra, then he leaned over her and took one of her nipples into his mouth. The other man pushed up her skirt and ripped off her pantyhose and panties. His penis had tented under his boxer shorts. Still struggling, the woman fought hard as the man with the tent tried to spread her legs for his partner. Helen's voice jerked Williamson's concentration away from the assault and back to the conversation.

"I'm fine!" Helen barked. "I was taking care of some unfinished business. I just had some unforeseen complications, so I need your help, right fuckin' now!"

"I'll need a day or two …" Williamson began.

"Do I need to remind you what happens to *all* of us, if my cover is broken, Colonel?" Helen shouted.

"Yes, ma'am. I understand completely, but …"

"I'll call you at eighteen hundred hours with the address," Helen ordered. "You'd better have a medic and a place for us to stay by then! No excuses, Colonel, or I'll be most displeased with you. And you know what that means, don't you?"

"Yes, ma'am. I understand. I'll find a medic, supplies, and some temporary shelter," Williamson replied meekly.

"Good, you'll hear from me at eighteen hundred," Helen barked, ending the call.

Williamson shoved his phone back into his pocket, annoyed by the conversation.

"Let her go!" Williamson shouted to the two male officers. "We'll finish this with her another time."

The two officers stopped and stared blankly at their commanding officer.

"Let her go?" asked the man who was grasping the woman's struggling legs. "What do you mean? We ain't finished with her yet."

"I said let her go!" Williamson bellowed. "That's an order. That was Helen on the phone. Something urgent's just come up."

At the mention of Helen's name, the two officers immediately stopped what they were doing.

"We shoulda just drugged her an' fucked her brains out. It woulda saved us a lotta trouble," the first man grumbled, letting go of the woman's breast.

"You know Helen won't let us do things that way," Williamson continued. "The lieutenant here has to learn that everything will go a lot better for her when she learns to submit willingly to us … and to Helen's will. Now, let her go and let's get out of here," he ordered.

As Williamson watched, the men released the woman, dressed themselves, straightened out their uniforms, then saluted their commanding officer and left the room. Williamson walked casually over to the bed and sat beside the weeping, gagging woman, who had yanked the sock from her mouth once her hands were free. He picked up her clothing and threw it at her.

"Cover yourself up," Williamson ordered. "I'm sure I don't need to tell you that it would be most unwise of you to mention this event to anybody. This is part of your initiation, as it has been for many excellent officers before you. It's intended to make you strong."

He got up and walked towards the motel room's exit, then he stopped and turned to the woman.

"You wouldn't want anybody to think you were a weakling, would you? Besides, any complaints will inevitably come across my desk. Understand?"

The woman's tears stopped. Her eyes grew wide with a mixture of anger, fear, and helplessness as she fully understood her situation and her predicament. Slowly and silently, her head nodded up and down.

"Very well," Williamson said. "Get yourself dressed and report back to base. I'll expect to see your usual, professional demeanor. That will be all."

Colonel Williamson continued to the door, let himself out, and left the nearly naked woman alone in the empty motel room. Stunned and numbed by what had just happened to her, she froze.

Finally, after a few moments, she began the process of putting on her panties and smoothing out her skirt with robot-like movements. She examined her pantyhose and dropped the ripped garment to the floor. As if on autopilot, she picked up her bra, fastened it around her waist, then rotated it and slid the cups up over her breasts. After adjusting her straps, she picked up her blouse, put her arms through the sleeves, and began fastening the buttons. She paused briefly, noticing that one was missing. She buttoned up the rest as though nothing had happened and tucked the blouse into her skirt.

Now as fully dressed as she could manage, she picked up her purse from the desk and went into the bathroom. She reapplied her makeup and did her best to cover the redness on her face and straighten her hair. Finally, she found a place, somewhere in her mind, where she stuffed the memory and all the emotions attached to it. She imagined herself slamming the door and throwing away the key. Reassuring herself that she was strong, she marched through the motel room's door and closed it firmly behind her.

* * *